BY HEATHER WALTER

Malice
Misrule
The Crimson Crown

The
CRIMSON
CROWN

The CRIMSON CROWN

Book One of the Crimson Crown Duology

HEATHER WALTER

NEW YORK

For Laura Crockett and Tricia Narwani,
Wayward witches both,
who believed in the magic of this book even when I did not.

And for Lindsey, who believes in the magic in me.

The CRIMSON CROWN

PROLOGUE

AGE OF THE LIGHT 36

O N THE NIGHT BEFORE MY SISTER WILL BIND HERSELF TO THE coven fire, the moon is the color of blood.

"It's turned early," the Diviner witches murmured as they watched the blood moon rise like a welling puncture wound behind the scudding clouds. "A good omen—the Spirits must be eager to call her forth."

If they were speaking of any other witch, I might have agreed. An Ascension is a celebration—the night every young witch waits for. When she makes her offering to the Spirits, my sister, Rhea, will receive her gift and take her place in the coven. She'll be transformed.

But as I sneak down the deserted halls of the Sanctum in the dark, apprehension knotting my insides like a patch of fireroot, I can't help but worry—what will Rhea be *transformed* into? What if the flames of the coven fire *consume* her, leaving nothing behind of the witch I love?

A crow calls in the night.

I pick up my pace, bare feet whispering against the stone floor. The door to Rhea's room is slightly ajar. She should be in bed—so should I—but she's sitting at the window. Moonlight glows red against her nightdress, as if she's already wearing her crimson cloak. Already another person. What is she thinking about? Is she afraid? Probably not. Rhea is only ten years older than me, but she might as well be a hundred years wiser. She's not afraid of anything.

My sister turns and spots me. We share the same white skin, black hair, and brown eyes, but that's where the similarity ends. Where I'm all awkward angles and skinny limbs, Rhea is soft and elegant. Beautiful.

"Ayleth. What are you doing here?"

I grin, sheepish, and thrust out the two slices of pie I stole from the kitchen. "I thought you might be hungry. You didn't eat much at dinner."

She'd been preoccupied with entertaining our guests, witches who had risked the journey to Stonehaven for Rhea's Ascension. A dangerous undertaking, with the Covens' War still waging. Personally, I never would have attempted it. But Rhea is about to be named a Second, next in line to lead the coven after Mother. Not only that, but she's a descendant of Millicent, one of the Five Ancients. I am, too, I suppose, though it's often difficult to believe that I share the same lineage as my sister. Rhea is immensely talented. A natural witch.

I'm just . . . me.

"Come on, then." Rhea motions to the bed. "You must be freezing. Watch that you don't get crumbs on the linens like last time."

Before she can change her mind, I clamber onto her mattress and settle myself among the pillows, passing Rhea her slice of pie. "It's apple. Your favorite."

She smiles at me and I breathe in her faint, comforting scent of honeysuckle. I can't count the number of times I've wound up in Rhea's bed instead of my own, sleeping long past the sunrise after we'd stayed up trading secrets or gossiping about other witches. But if Rhea has secrets now, she's not sharing them. She keeps glancing toward the window, her pie untouched.

"Are you nervous?" I venture.

Rhea shifts on the bed. "A little. But I shouldn't be. Hundreds of witches have faced the flames before, Mother included. It will be fine. And soon enough, it will be your turn."

Ascensions normally occur on the first blood moon during a witch's twenty-third year. I still have a decade to go, but even that feels too soon. "Will it hurt?"

"Mother warned me that it might," Rhea admits. "After that, though, I've heard it feels like coming alive. That the gift of the Spirits makes everything . . . more visceral. Nyssandra said it's like color seeping into the world after living in darkness."

Nyssandra also claims her rabbit stew is edible, which it most certainly isn't. In any case, I don't care about color. And I don't care about the Spirits either—not the way I should. All I care about is Rhea. What is this Spirits-given *gift* going to do to my sister? Will her new, colorful world be better without me in it?

"What's wrong?" Rhea asks, guessing my thoughts.

"Nothing."

She nudges her elbow against mine. "You can tell me."

"It's just . . ." I pluck at the coverlet. "After tomorrow, everything will be different. I don't want anything to change between us."

Rhea tucks a piece of my hair behind my ear, her long fingers cool against my skin. "Nothing could ever be different between us. You know that."

I used to. "But with the Ascension and you becoming Second, I'll just be . . ."

Nothing, a voice inside me whispers. My shoulders hunch against it.

"You'll be Mother's favorite," Rhea says. "Like always."

She pinches me, teasing, and I fend her off. "I'm not her favorite!"

"Oh, please." Rhea laughs, gesturing at my pie. "How else do you continually get away with clandestine excursions to the kitchen? And how many lessons have you skipped?"

A guilty smirk tugs at my lips. I can't deny it. *Rhea is my Heir, but you are my heart,* Mother whispers to me when she thinks I'm asleep. But I'm not next in line. And if I'm being honest, I'm glad I'll never be a Second.

My attention returns to the glaring red eye of the moon. "I just . . . I'm worried. I can't explain it, but I feel like something's coming."

Rhea cups my chin with her hand. "Being worried means you're smart."

"Not as smart as you are."

"Stop skipping lessons and you'll catch up."

I smack her with a pillow. "I wouldn't skip them if they weren't boring."

Rhea laughs. "Fine, then. Here—I have another idea."

She climbs out of bed and pulls something from a drawer on the other side of the room. Silver glints in the moonlight—a knife.

"What's that for?"

"I'm going to carve you up and bake you into a pie." She winks and I scowl back at her. "Here. Give me your hand."

I'm still suspicious of the knife, but I do as Rhea says. She turns my palm up, her graceful fingers traveling briefly over the creases of my skin—my Life and Fate lines, as some of the Diviners taught me. Rhea touches the tip of the knife to an area below my ring finger.

"Don't!" I jerk back, but she holds my wrist.

"Do you trust me?"

It's the knife I don't trust. But Rhea's dark eyes are serious in a way that makes my stomach flutter. I relax my hand and let her drag the blade over my skin, wincing as blood wells up in three lines, each crossing the others. A triangle.

"Is that a rune?"

In the lessons I *do* attend, I've memorized a fair amount of such magical symbols, but I've never encountered one so simple. And I've never heard of witches drawing runes on *themselves*. Then again, Rhea knows more than I would. She's to be a Caster, after all. Just like Mother and even Millicent herself.

"Sort of." Rhea cleans the knife on a cloth. "Think of it as our rune."

"Ours?" My brow furrows. "You can't just make them up."

"So, you *have* been paying attention." She arches an eyebrow. I flush. "You're right. We can't. But this one is special. It works because of the shared power in our line. Because we're sisters. Here—we'll connect them."

She passes me the knife and extends her own palm.

But I hesitate, unwilling to hurt her. "Are you sure?"

Rhea nods and gestures for me to continue. As gently as possible, I carve the same triangle into the flesh just below her ring finger. Rhea doesn't even flinch.

"See how the lines of the triangle drift apart but come back together?" she asks when I've finished, holding her palm next to mine, the blood shining like a line of liquid rubies on her skin. "That's like us. No matter how distant we may become, we'll always find our way back to each other. We're sisters. Nothing will change that."

Rhea interlocks our fingers, our hearts beating together through our shared runes.

"Sisters," I echo, like the word itself is a spell.

And even though I believe what Rhea says, trust her more than anyone else, a deep part of me still whispers that my sister is wrong.

Something *is* coming. And no amount of magic will be able to hold it back.

PART I

Witchcraft is hereby abolished in the Kingdom of Riven. All Sanctums and property are forfeit to the Crown. Any persons found practicing witchcraft, or abetting witches, shall be burned, their souls returned to the forces of Malum.

—*Edict of King Reginald,*
Age of the Light 1

CHAPTER ONE

TEN YEARS LATER

A SHADOW SKIMS ACROSS THE COURTYARD.
I glance up just in time to watch a crow land on the statue in front of the Sanctum.

"Portent," I hear someone murmur nearby, probably one of the Diviners. "Ill luck."

"Malum."

The word carries a bite colder than the autumn wind. Mother heard it too. I can tell from the way she pretends she hasn't, her jaw set as she watches the portcullis. The crow ruffles its inky feathers. If I didn't know better, I'd say its beady, obsidian eyes were fixed on me.

One crow for sorrow.

An old rhyme dredges up from my memory. As if in reply, the crow calls, short and staccato. Like laughter.

"They're coming!" a witch in the sentry tower calls, startling the bird so that it squawks and flaps away.

Excitement catches like dry kindling amongst the rest of the witches.

"At last!" someone exclaims.

"I was worried they wouldn't make it."

And I was *hoping* that they wouldn't, today—or ever. On instinct, I touch the place below my left ring finger, where three crossed lines form a triangle on my skin. Rhea's mark. *Our* mark. Three faintly pink scars drifting apart and then coming back together. I press down on the triangle so hard that I feel the thrum of my pulse beneath my skin.

There's no need to worry, I imagine my sister saying to me. *Hundreds of witches have done this before.*

Maybe. But I was never supposed to be one of them—not like this.

A familiar meow interrupts my thoughts, coupled with the pressure of a lithe body rubbing against my ankles.

"Hello, you." I bend to scratch between Nettle's ears, grateful to have at least one friend this morning. Autumn sunlight shines against her dark calico fur.

"I told you to keep that cat away today." Mother throws Nettle a sharp glance. "I won't have her causing any trouble. And fix your cloak."

I'm not a witchling anymore, I almost snap back. But an argument will only worsen my headache. Nettle grumbles as I shoo her away, her tail twitching as she trots back toward the Sanctum. Maybe she'll hunt down a mouse and leave the carcass in Mother's rooms, a habit of hers that I've been encouraging of late.

"I shouldn't even be wearing this." I pull on the clasp of my cloak, which keeps riding up next to my throat like it's trying to strangle me. It probably is. Everything about this garment is uncomfortable, especially its crimson color, one reserved for witches only *after* they Ascend.

"I want them to see you in it," Mother replies smoothly. "You're my Second."

"Not yet," I mutter under my breath. Not for three more days anyway. I can feel the time slipping away from me, only hours now. Would that it could be years—forever.

The portcullis jolts, my nerves clattering along with the rising of the huge metal gate. The other witches press closer, nudging one another. The last time Stonehaven received visitors as important as these—the other Heirs and their Seconds—was at Rhea's Ascension. The mood was different then, though. Even with the war waging around us, it had been a joyous occasion, like one of the large coven gatherings that the older witches describe. Now there is only the rustle of dry leaves and an air of desperation. Because it's not Rhea this time. Rhea is gone.

I clench my left hand again, my sister's words floating on the breeze.

No matter how distant we may become, we'll always find our way back to each other.

But there are some places, I've learned, that no one can come back from. The clasp of my cloak digs into my throat.

"After this, I'll expect you to see to the Seconds," Mother says. "You remember where they'll be housed?"

No, I've forgotten after the first hundred times she's reminded me. "Living quarters—third door on the left."

I thought I'd kept my tone neutral, but Mother detects my exasperation. Her face turns to mine. She's beautiful, in a cold, imposing sort of way. Gray streaks her auburn hair and fine lines crease her white skin, bracketing her eyes and mouth. Some of those lines came from laughter, if that can be believed. These days, it seems impossible that Mother even knows *how* to laugh.

"This is important, Ayleth," she says, her hazel gaze pinning me in place. "The most important time of your life. Do not disappoint the coven."

Again.

Her implication hangs between us, resurrecting the memory of my mistake: A pair of cobalt-blue eyes and the smell of juniper. Promises made . . . and then *broken*. Much as I try to beat it back, a name extracts itself from the bramble and thorn of my past.

Jacquetta.

I hate myself for the way my next breath hitches.

Let her go, a voice in my mind urges. *She means nothing.*

How many more times do I have to say that until it's true?

The portcullis shudders to a halt and hooves clop on the flagstones as the party lumbers through the open gate and into the courtyard. Mother exhales, pulling herself up straighter. The black and green embroidered runes on her own crimson cloak, along with the symbol that marks her as High Witch, glimmer in the late-morning sunlight.

"Selene." Mother greets the witch—another Heir—who steps down from her seat on a small wagon.

Descendant of Aphelia, my years of training provide. *The first Diviner.*

Selene resembles her ancestress as well, at least from the illustrations I've studied in our books. Though it's difficult to determine the exact age of a witch—our latent magic helps us heal and keeps us youthful until it weakens—Selene appears to be about as old as Mother. Middle-aged by human standards, but likely well past her hundredth year. She pulls down her hood, freeing her cloud of dark hair. Her green eyes, stark against the rich black of her skin, travel over the courtyard. Like all Diviners, there's something ethereal about her. The last time she visited, I got the unsettling impression that she could glimpse inside my mind. Given her gift, she probably can.

"Was it a difficult journey?" Mother releases Selene from a noticeably stiff embrace.

"No more than we expected, considering current circumstances." Selene pulls off her green leather gloves.

The other witches, another Heir and the two Seconds, dismount or step down from their own wagon. The younger pair, the Seconds, I recognize—Della and Sindony.

I tug at the clasp of my cloak again. At Rhea's Ascension, Della, Sindony, and I had run wild around the Sanctum together, slipping toads in other witches' boots and sneaking treats from the kitchens. Now it's as if those days—those witchlings—never existed. Even with the strain of the journey, the two Seconds stand tall and poised. They're my age, but they seem so much older—so much more important. Their attention falls on me and the brief shot of recognition in their expressions softens to . . . disappointment, perhaps. Like I've failed to live up to a test.

They see right through you, that voice whispers.

"Where are the rest?" Mother asks, gesturing toward the open portcullis. I don't hear anyone else coming. "Elain, Lettice, and their Seconds?"

Five witches formed the first coven, becoming the Ancients who uphold the pillars of our craft. As such, there should be five Heirs here, descendant of each of those great witches, with their next-in-line in tow.

"Delayed," Selene explains. "The Hunt has been spotted, I'm afraid. Precautions were necessary. I'm sure they'll arrive in time."

The Hunt. A tremble of uneasiness ripples through the courtyard, witches probably fighting down the same memories that I am—the smell of burning flesh and the echo of piercing screams. It was seven years ago that the Hunt found Stonehaven. Thanks to Mother's cunning, we did not lose our home, as most witches do when the Hunt raids their coven. But I would gladly trade Stonehaven, or anything else, for what I lost that horrible night—my sister.

I clench my fist against our rune, wishing I could pull Rhea back.

"Ah—here she is." Selene's steady footsteps approach, her keen Diviner gaze sizing me up. "And she's already wearing her cloak? Isn't that a bit presumptuous, Cassandra?"

I'd told Mother the cloak was a bad idea.

"Not at all," Mother replies coolly. "Ayleth is a true daughter of Millicent. She's shown immense potential."

That is a lie. I clench my back teeth against the urge to correct her just for the pleasure of spoiling the morning.

"Even so, our traditions exist for a reason, do they not? Then again . . ."

Selene's attention drifts to the statue. Years ago, during Rhea's Ascension celebration, it depicted Millicent, one of the Five, to whom this Sanctum was dedicated. Now splotches of plaster riddle the statue's body, where our sacred runes were pried out and replaced with the false goddess's Eyes—one on her forehead and another on each of her outturned palms. Her natural eyes are painted to appear sewn shut, but it was sloppily done. Soot-gray rivulets run like tears down her cheeks. As if Millicent herself weeps to see what's become of us.

"Tradition doesn't seem to be much of a priority here," Selene finishes.

Several witches mutter.

Mother straightens her cloak. "You knew what to expect before you arrived."

Selene smiles, but it reminds me of Nettle's expression when she corners a mouse. "You're right, of course. Forgive me. I'm forgetting my manners."

She motions to her daughter, Sindony, who carries a cloth-wrapped object over from their wagon. "Ayleth, I present this gift in honor of your Ascension. The naming of a Second is a momentous occasion indeed."

Not for me. Reluctantly, I lift the folds of fabric wrapped around the gift to reveal the gleam of silvery glass. A mirror. Revulsion twists in my stomach. I *hate* mirrors.

"Thank you," I say, hastily re-covering the thing. "I—"

"But you must let the others see it." Selene takes the mirror from my hands and displays it. The gathered witches murmur their appreciation. "It's a witch's mirror. It will need to be woken, of course. But I assume a *true* daughter of Millicent can handle so simple a task."

Her green eyes bore into mine and, again, a crawling sensation tingles down my spine—like the Heir is sifting through my thoughts.

"Of course she can," Mother supplies before I can respond. "And I thank you for the generous gift. Witch's mirrors are so rare now. Isn't it wonderful, Ayleth?"

No. Witch's mirrors are even worse than mortal ones. They can talk—and *observe*. I have no intention of waking the unpleasant thing. But I don't miss the command in Mother's tone and plaster what I hope passes for a gracious smile onto my face.

"It's beautiful. Thank you."

Selene turns the mirror in my direction. I flinch. How long has it been since I glimpsed my own reflection? Years, probably. I almost don't recognize myself now. My dark hair falls almost to my waist, the braid pulled over one shoulder. My nose is longer. My chin is softer. More like . . .

"You know," Selene says, tilting her head as she studies me, "I didn't think they looked alike at our last visit. But now Ayleth could be her twin."

Her. Rhea's.

Needle-like pain digs between my ribs at the comparison, one I've heard too many times to count. One that sends me running from mirrors like they carry plague. Because it's true. The years have shaped and re-formed me into my sister's image so much so that it could be Rhea herself looking out from the glass. Mother sees the resemblance as well. Her carefully bottled-up emotion brims behind her eyes. Some aching part of me wants her to say that it doesn't matter who I look like. I'm *Ayleth*—just Ayleth, and that's enough. She would have said it before that harrowing night when the Hunt broke through our wards. She would have combed her fingers through my hair and whispered:

Rhea is my Heir, but you are my heart.

Now Mother doesn't say anything to me. And in her silence, I hear the terrible truth.

It should have been you that night. Not her.

In the deepest chamber of my own heart, I wish the same.

CHAPTER TWO

NOT LONG AFTER THAT, THE OFFICIAL GREETING MERCIFULLY ends. The Heirs accompany Mother to her chambers, and I escort Della and Sindony to where they'll be staying in the living quarters. Eden, another witch from our coven, helps me carry their trunks, which are heavy enough that I suspect the two Seconds have packed rocks instead of clothes or other belongings. Nettle emerges from wherever she'd been hiding and trots along beside me.

Stonehaven isn't the largest Sanctum in the realm of Riven, but it once housed more than a hundred witches. There are two floors in the east wing filled with modest bedchambers, along with a dining hall, a large kitchen, and an equally massive workroom, which houses the Potioners' supplies.

"It's strange to be in a Sanctum again," Della comments as we pass the cloister, where other witches are hanging laundry or tending the small garden.

Given our circumstances, it's easy to forget that most witches aren't fortunate enough to reside in the homes where they were born. If I look closely, I can spot evidence of my years as a witchling. A wobbling banister that was never fully repaired after Eden and I took turns sliding down it. A charred spot on the high ceiling, roughly the shape of a mushroom, left behind after we'd been experimenting with ingredients we filched from the workroom.

By all accounts, those memories should be nothing but ash. Sanctums were originally built to honor the covens, but that was before the White King's edict. In one fell swoop, witchcraft was abolished. All our property reverted to the Crown and the Order. As the Hunt seized our lands, our sacred runes and relics were replaced with effigies of the false goddess, like the statue in the courtyard. Those witches who weren't killed in the raids fled to neighboring realms or scattered throughout Riven. Were it not for Mother's plan, we'd be among them.

"If you can call this a Sanctum," Sindony remarks, her attention lingering on a string of words engraved into a stone archway.

TO BURN A WITCH IS TO FREE A SOUL

One of the Order's abhorrent Illuminations. Nettle lays her ears flat as we pass underneath it, as if even she knows what it means.

"I assumed Mother was exaggerating when she described Cassandra's so-called *strategy*," Sindony goes on. "Evidently, she wasn't. How can any of you endure such indignity?"

Della slides me a sideways look, likely posing the same question. My grip on the trunk's handles tightens. Even before the Hunt's raid, Mother had considered adopting our current disguise. But it was their attack that sealed her decision. We might have survived one battle, but we couldn't afford to risk another. Pretending to be Order Sisters was the surest way—in Mother's mind—to divert the Hunt's attention. The loss of our runes and shrines might be an indignity, but it's kept us alive.

We cross under another archway, this one bearing the false goddess's motto: *Fairest of them all.*

"You get used to it," I tell Sindony, which is accurate enough.

At first, Meira's repulsive Eye seemed to follow my every step. Now I hardly ever notice the Illuminations or the remade statues. Then again, the days of my racing down banisters are long over. Most of my time is now spent trapped in lessons with Mother.

"But the uniforms," Della chimes in, glancing at the front of my dress, which bears an embroidered Eye. "And is there really no magic allowed?"

"Just in training," Eden explains, her white-gold curls bobbing as she walks. "And when necessary, of course. Like with the wards buried in the forest."

"The wards that broke?" Sindony pointedly raises an eyebrow.

I flinch at the reference to the night of the raid, yet again reminded of how much these witches have changed since our last encounter. Not Della—with her, I can still glimpse the young witch who giggled at our harmless pranks. But Sindony is colder, more calculating. More like her mother.

A crow swoops past us in the cloister, its cry resonating against the stone walls.

"The wards have been mended," I explain tightly. "There's no need to worry."

"I'm sure that's true." Della offers a smile. "We wouldn't have made the journey if there were any doubt of that. Besides, after your Ascension, your power will be enough to forge the strongest wards yet."

That's what she thinks, anyway. A bitter taste cuts between my teeth.

"Your room is here," I say, reaching the third door and shouldering it open. But I freeze as soon as I cross the threshold.

The third room on the left, Mother had instructed.

Why hadn't I realized which one she meant? This is *Rhea's* room. I haven't set foot in it since . . .

An image of my sister surges up in my mind, the veins beneath her skin raised and rust-colored as iron poisoning webbed through her blood.

It's up to you now, she'd said, voice fading and raspy. *You must be strong.*

But I'm not. Not like she was.

"Is something wrong?" Della asks as she removes her cloak and drapes it on a bed.

Yes—everything. This room has been unoccupied for years, and that's the way it should stay. Why has Mother put them in here? When had she cleaned everything out? Was Rhea, her own daughter, so easily swept away? Forgotten?

How quickly would she forget you? that voice whispers.

Eden throws me a worried look.

"No," I say, pulling myself together. "Is there anything I can fetch for you?"

Sindony takes stock of the state of her dress and frowns. "A bath, perhaps?"

I set down the trunk. "I'll have one of the Elementals bring up a tub and heat the water."

"You know." Sindony pauses, her dark-blue gaze studying me. *Analyzing* me. "Mother was right. You really do look like her. It's uncanny."

Almost without thinking, I clench my left hand against the scar of Rhea's mark. Sometimes I wonder if our runes are the root of the similarities in our appearances. After all, Selene was correct—Rhea and I never used to look alike. Before I started avoiding mirrors, I used to sit in front of them and try to call to my sister. Maybe the change in my features was the way Rhea answered through the Veil.

"What happened to her?" Della asks gently.

Her. Neither of them have uttered Rhea's name. Perhaps they worry death is catching. "The Hunt. They—"

"We know about the raid." Sindony waves me off. "But what *happened*? I heard she was involved with the wards breaking. That's why the Hunt got in."

I bristle. Is she suggesting that Rhea's magic failed before its time?

"The pack had been waiting outside our wards for days," I answer, barely keeping my anger in check. "They laid a trap. It could have happened to any of us."

It *had* happened to countless covens. Ours was one of the few who actually won their battle against the White King's murderous Huntsmen, not that Sindony seems interested in discussing that particular detail. All she cares about is our *indignities.*

"We're all very sorry for your loss," Della adds. "Your sister was a gifted witch."

And kind and loyal and everything you're not, that voice supplies.

"She was gifted. And do you consider yourself ready to take her place?" There's a glint in Sindony's eyes that sets alarm bells ringing in my mind. "I heard you ran away—something about chasing after another witch? One who broke with the coven?"

Ice flashes in my veins. Who had told her that? Selene? Had Mother informed the other Heirs? I find that difficult to believe, given Mother's efforts to cover up my disloyalty. Everyone knew, though. When the coven split after the raid and I disappeared into the forest, it was painfully obvious which side I'd chosen. Even Eden's cheeks pinken slightly, embarrassed on my behalf. I'm the one who should be embarrassed. An Heir's daughter, a would-be Second, run off with . . .

Jacquetta.

That name again. Would that I could pry it from my mind forever.

It was a mistake, that voice supplies, sharp and vehement. *SHE was a mistake.*

Even so, a breeze filters through the open window, carrying the faint scent of juniper, and a deep part of me *aches*. I stand up taller, steeling myself. I don't feel anything for her—not anymore. Feelings are dangerous.

"I don't know—"

Nettle yowls, interrupting me, and leaps onto Sindony's bed. Keeping her golden eyes fixed on the other witch, she hisses and begins clawing at the pillows and blankets. Feathers and scraps of fabric go flying in every direction.

"By the Spirits, what is that animal doing?" Sindony shrieks.

She flails at Nettle, but my cat just growls at her and continues flaying the bed. Glorious creature. Eden clamps a hand over her mouth, her shoulders shaking with stifled laughter.

"Is this your idea of a welcome?" Sindony wheels on me. "Keep your familiar under control, or I'll—"

A bell begins to toll outside, fast and urgent. Eden and I rush to the window.

"The Elementals went out at sunrise," she says. "I'm sure it's just them. Or the other Heirs finally arriving."

"No." Della shakes her head. "They're at least a day behind."

Metal grinds as the portcullis rises. A few witches stride into the courtyard, a slaughtered boar strung between them. Perhaps it was just the hunting party. But the sentries never ring the bells to announce such a return. What could they—

Someone else crosses through the gate, a woman guided by two Elementals. Not a woman, though, not if our witches are assisting her.

"A survivor," I say.

At the start of the war, as many as a dozen witches would find their way to our gates in the span of a month, drawn by the magic of the wards. Now we're lucky to see two or three in as many years.

Those who do reach us often don't remain once they realize the price of life at our Sanctum. Mother's rules apply to everyone.

Eden clicks her tongue, sympathetic. "She's alone, poor witch."

We can all guess what happened to the rest of her coven. The wind picks up, whistling through the cracks in the Sanctum. Again, the screams from the night of the raid haunt me. I can almost see the Hunt's arrows soaring over our walls, iron tips bright with flame.

But if this witch endured a similar ordeal, it doesn't show. She walks straight-backed and seemingly unharmed. She's older, her deep-brown skin wrinkled. Her white hair is coiled in a tight bun. As she nears the Sanctum, her face tilts up. Her eyes are a rheumy, solid white—sightless. And yet I swear they're pinned directly on me.

Another crow calls, so close that I feel its resonance in my bones.

"That went well," Eden comments dryly as soon as the door closes behind us. "I don't remember them being so . . ."

"Insufferable?" I finish for her, rubbing my temples where my headache from the morning is throbbing. Nettle trills her agreement.

"Della wasn't too bad. But that Sindony." Eden huffs. "If she hates it here so much, I'm sure we can find alternative accommodations for her."

"The stables?" I suggest.

"Perfect." She nods. "Straw might be her best option, given the state of her mattress."

Nettle meows proudly and I reach down to scratch between her ears. "Let's get you some cream, shall we?"

"Oh, and some contortion potion for dear Sindony," Eden chimes in.

I can't help but smile at the idea of Sindony's face transformed into that of a lizard or some other creature. "Yes, Mother will appreciate that."

Eden shrugs. "We just won't get caught."

Such has been her motto since we were witchlings, and it always ends in disaster. Eden is a couple of years older than me, having Ascended two summers ago. Her white skin is smattered with freckles, and her eyes are a unique shade of lavender. Like her mother, Eden is about a head shorter than me, and her figure is all soft curves beneath her uniform.

She winks at me, and I follow her through the halls, which are buzzing with talk of the arrival of both the Heirs and the newcomer. I catch snippets of conversation centered on *me* as well, and I'm grateful when Eden and I retreat into the kitchen, where there is only the smell of food and the sound of Willa's humming.

"Here you are," Willa calls to Eden as we enter.

Willa's sleeves are rolled up, forearms dusted with flour as she works dough on the table, kneading in fragrant herbs for health and protection. To my immense delight, several pies are cooling near the window, their sugared crusts an enticing golden brown.

"All these visitors and you think to slip away?" Willa scolds her daughter. "I've had to enlist poor Nesta's help. Keep stirring that pot. I can smell it burning."

The younger witch stands at the hearth, minding a huge kettle of what I suspect is fireroot, given the faintly charred scent lingering in the air. Nesta's light-brown cheeks are flushed. The fine black hairs at her forehead curl with sweat from the steam.

"I was helping Ayleth." Eden veers over to the rows of potted plants near the windows.

The kitchen is by far my favorite place in the Sanctum. I hardly remember a time when I wasn't perched on a stool beside Eden, entranced by Willa's fantastical stories about trolls and fairies and other magical creatures that once dwelled in Riven. Drying herbs hang from the low-beamed ceiling. Pots line the walls and are stacked on shelves, which are stuffed with various jars of ingredients, bags of flour, and everything else that's needed to feed the sixty or so witches living in the Sanctum.

"And how are our visitors?" Willa asks. "I wasn't able to attend the reception."

Would that I could say the same.

"You didn't miss much," I tell her, shoving a handful of walnuts into my mouth.

"Selene gave Ayleth a mirror," Eden says, waggling her eyebrows.

I shudder at the reminder, making a note to stuff the unsettling thing inside a closet at the earliest opportunity.

"A witch's mirror," Willa repeats, impressed. "They must think highly of you."

Somehow, I doubt that. Nettle leaps up onto the counter and meows at Willa, expectant.

"Nettle," I scold, "get down from there."

But my cat doesn't possess an obedient bone in her body. Willa laughs.

"Stubborn creature. I know what you want."

She pauses long enough to pour out a dish of cream. Nettle descends upon it immediately. I can't scold her for that—she's earned it.

"And what about you, Ayleth?" Willa asks. "How are you faring with all this fuss?"

Like a nest of hornets has taken residence beneath my skin. "Fine."

Willa tilts her head, scenting the lie as always. Like Eden, she's a Blessed, which heightens her awareness of others' emotions. "Nerves are expected before a witch makes her vow. And when it comes to Seconds, I imagine it's tenfold."

Not for Rhea. My sister faced the coven fire with the determination of an Ancient. I can still picture the firelight illuminating her expression as she stood before the coven and offered her blood. Her voice had been firm as stone as she made her vow to Millicent and accepted her place as Mother's successor. It had been *meant* to be. Her destiny. And mine . . .

"Oh, that's lovely." Nesta points, interrupting my thoughts.

At the window, Eden coaxes a small pot of roses to life, their petals a brilliant shade of lavender, the same color as her eyes. White light limns her hands as she works, teasing the blossoms. A thorny, unwelcome feeling twists in my gut, the same one I always experience when I watch the others work. Like they're real witches and I'm . . .

"*Eden.* Stop that." Willa swats at her with a towel. "You know better."

The light dissipates from Eden's fingers. "It was for our guests."

"Yes, and I'm sure they'll thank you if you summon the Hunt with a pot of roses. No more dallying. I need you to—"

A telltale *pop* sounds from the hearth.

"Oh no!" Nesta yelps.

A cloud of smoke erupts from the hearth as the contents of the kettle explode, rattling the windows. Nettle yowls and bounds out the door, abandoning what remains of her cream. Several jars tumble from their shelves and shatter, various oils and powders leaking over the stones.

"By the Spirits." Willa covers her nose with her apron as the rancid smell sets in. "How many times did I tell you to keep stirring?"

"I got distracted," Nesta whimpers, wringing her apron. She's covered with soot, and her eyebrows are all but singed off.

"See what you've done?" Willa brandishes an empty jar at Eden. "And that was the last of it. Go and fetch more. And don't go alone. Take Ayleth with you."

"To the forest?" I balk. I don't go there—not anymore.

But I don't get the chance to argue. Before Willa can catch her,

Eden snatches a whole pie and slides it into a basket, then pulls me along through the side door and out into the front courtyard.

"I should really stay," I attempt, gesturing at the other witches, who are tending the larger front gardens, feeding chickens, or brushing the horses in the small stable. "There's too much to do around here and Mother—"

"Won't notice you're gone until dinner." Eden loops her arm through mine. "When else are we going to get the chance to have a little fun? It will be just like old times."

Old times. If only it were so simple to return to those days. I can practically feel the walls of my life narrowing—the looming flames of my Ascension edging perilously close. Perhaps Eden is right. I should take this opportunity while I have it.

I glance back at the Sanctum. Its arched windows gleam gold in the autumn sunlight. Trails of ivy track along the façade, reaching from the ground all the way up to the highest point of the south tower. At this time of the year, the leaves have transformed from verdant green to a deep garnet. The color causes the snaking vines to appear more like wounds—like the walls of the Sanctum have opened and are dripping with blood.

CHAPTER THREE

THE FOREST FLOOR BLURS BENEATH MY FEET. AHEAD, THE STREAM glimmers like a silver vein cutting through the forest. Eden is a hand's breadth in front of me, her white-gold curls springing with every step. I hitch my skirts up higher and urge myself faster, refusing to let her win. My muscles burn, every worry and doubt melting away in the pounding of my heart and the sawing of my breath through my lungs. After the strain of the morning, the distraction is *glorious*. I give one last push, bounding over a fallen log, and skid to a halt near the water's edge. Eden pulls up beside me an instant later.

"You used a spell," she says, panting, hands on her knees. "I don't know how, but you did. No one can run that fast without magic."

I laugh, breathless. "And here I thought you'd be accustomed to losing by now."

Her mouth flops open and she bends down to cup some water in her hand, tossing it in my direction. I yelp, dodging, then splash her back, soaking the front of her dress.

"All right!" Eden holds up her hands in surrender. "I give up!"

I grin, wiping at my face with the hem of my skirt. Why had I put up such a fuss about coming? I forgot how much I love the forest, with its trees dressed in climbing vines so thick I can hardly see their trunks. A familiar, cedar-sweet tang hangs in the air and I drink it in like a tonic, reveling in the utter freedom of this place.

Wind rattles the branches, pushing in from the direction of trees beyond the stream. *The Other Forest,* I'd dubbed it as a witchling, an area as mysterious as it was forbidden. This stream marks the border of our western wards and the boundary of our land. A small pile of stones nearby indicates the spot where a leaden tablet is buried, engraved with runes for protection and concealment. Only the Elementals are permitted to cross this barrier on their hunts, or the witches who Mother sends for supplies—but even they wear Casters' glamours to further disguise themselves. The shadows shift, the clacking of the branches hollow and ominous. Two spots of light appear in the distance, like eyes.

"Do you see that?" I ask Eden, pointing.

"What?" She steps closer. "Is it a boar? Or a wolf?"

The spots of light glimmer, the color deepening from yellow to *red.* My pulse drums. If it is a wolf, it's not one that belongs on this side of the Veil.

"It might be a Nevenwolf," I whisper, hardly daring to move.

Eden inhales sharply. Before the Age of the Covens, such creatures ran rampant in the realm—supernatural beasts that are twice the size of normal wolves and a hundred times deadlier. And not just them. Willa's stories warn of other monsters—demons and ghouls and banshees—all spun from the inky tendrils of Malum, the dark and sinister force opposite that of our own magic.

As it's been so long—over three thousand years—since Malum was contained, not even the oldest witches have directly witnessed its horrors. But there are plenty of tales relaying the time before the Veil was forged, when Malum gave rise to shadow creatures—like

Nevenwolves—as well as blights and plagues. There are legends of entire towns being swallowed by darkness, or worse. I vividly recall a story about a village whose citizens simply walked into the sea and drowned because Malum compelled them to do so.

Malum could poison a witch's power, as well—sink its hooks into her soul and feed off of her abilities until there was nothing left of her but a hollow shell. It was the threat of this malignant force that brought the Five Ancients together. They were not Ancients then, of course. They were simply five witches, brave enough to devise a spell that would craft the Veil—the barrier between our worlds that holds Malum back.

But those witches understood that a single ritual would not be sufficient to sustain such a barrier. They needed a way to preserve the spell so that the Veil held long after they were gone. And so the Five created the Bloodstones. Like their name suggests, the stones were forged from blood itself, rendering them living vessels capable of holding magic. The witches funneled their spell into the Bloodstones, whose power fueled the enchantment, and thus the Veil itself. But such an act—the strongest spell any witch has ever cast, before or since—required every drop of the witches' latent magic. It should have killed them.

However, as the legend goes, when the final dregs of the witches' power drained into the Bloodstones, the Spirits themselves—the souls of those witches who have perished—intervened. Touched by the selflessness of the Five, the Spirits defied all laws of nature and returned those witches to the Realm of the Living, granting each of them a single, exceedingly powerful gift.

With their amplified abilities, the once ordinary witches ascended into the Ancients, forming the pillars of the covens. From that day forward, each of the Five carried her Bloodstone, a symbol of her sacrifice and the beating heart of the Veil itself, passing it down to her Heir, so that we may always be protected from Malum.

Or at least, that's how it was supposed to happen.

Every year, the Heirs are meant to bring the Bloodstones together and repeat a version of the Ancients' ritual, adding more power to the stones in order to maintain the Veil. But the Bloodstones are gone—stolen in the massacre that ignited the Covens' War. And now the enchantment housed inside the stones is fading. The Veil is thinning. We've all noticed the signs—blackened egg yolks and blighted crops and an unshakeable feeling of *wrongness*. Malum is seeping into our world again. Crows and shadows are just the beginning. If something doesn't change . . .

The brush rustles behind me and I whirl, bracing for the Neven-wolf or some other shadow-spun creature of Malum. Instead, a dark calico shape emerges from a bush, tail swishing.

"Nettle," I gasp, pressing a hand to my chest. "You nearly scared me to death."

The stubborn cat sits in a patch of sunlight and licks her paw, utterly unperturbed by the prospect of my demise. When I look back into the trees, the spots of red have vanished.

"I don't see it anymore."

"Good." Eden exhales. "It was probably nothing anyway. With your mother and the other Heirs here, we couldn't be safer."

She's right. But why don't I *feel* safer?

"Come on." Eden nudges me. "Let's find that fireroot. It's getting late."

I throw one last look over my shoulder, into the shadow-steeped depths of the Other Forest. Wind rattles the branches, like finger bones knocking together.

Ayleth, I think I hear amid the clacking wood. *Ayleth*.

I've been spending too much time indoors. I give myself a shake and follow after Eden. Nettle lopes along beside us, swatting at insects and investigating giant ferns. Eden pulls out the filched pie, scoops out a healthy slice, then passes it to me. Blackberry—my favorite. Willa mixes lavender into the filling, and the taste is magic in and of itself.

"So," Eden starts around a mouthful, "have you made up your mind about your vows? Will you swear to Millicent or another Ancient?"

I pause, mid-bite. When joining with a coven, a witch offers her blood to the fire at her Ascension, just as the Ancients did to forge the Bloodstones. We don't drain ourselves, of course. Instead, our offering is meant as a demonstration—to prove to the Spirits that we are as selfless and dedicated as the Five. To seal our intention, we then swear to one of the Ancients, binding our lives to the covens and the Spirits, and even the Veil itself. In return, the Spirits grant us a gift—an affiliation. It's not as large a blessing as the Five received, as our sacrifice is nowhere near as great as theirs was, but it amplifies our abilities in a specific area of our craft and protects our magic against the forces of Malum. In normal circumstances, a witch can follow the path of any of the Five—Caster, Diviner, Potioner, Blessed, or Elemental.

But my circumstances are anything but normal.

Eden winks, and I realize she's joking. "Could you imagine your mother's face if you swore to Isolde?"

The first Elemental. I can't help but laugh, picturing actual steam coming from Mother's ears. "Don't tempt me."

Nettle trills in what I interpret as amusement.

"Really, though," Eden says, gesturing with what's left of her piece of pie. "Nothing says you *have* to swear to Millicent. Perhaps you're not supposed to be a Caster. It could be why you're having . . . trouble."

The blackberry filling of the pie loses its sweetness. Eden is the only witch privy to even a sliver of truth about my gift—or lack thereof—and that's only because she caught me crying in the workroom after a particularly disastrous lesson. Even then, I only admitted that I felt I wasn't as talented as Rhea.

The real truth is that, though I've memorized every spell and rune Mother throws at me, I haven't demonstrated so much as a hint of natural ability. That's why Mother started "training" me in private, to hide my faults until my Ascension, which is when she's convinced my gift will finally manifest. Even to me, her certainty is starting to feel more like desperation.

"Maybe," I hedge. "But I'm the last of the line."

A line I'd nearly broken once before. Somewhere in the forest, a crow calls.

"There's the fireroot." Eden gestures ahead.

The patch of scarlet stems is easy to spot where it crawls along the base of an ancient oak. But as we approach, I notice something odd about the tree itself. Where the surrounding foliage is practically glowing in the golds and reds of autumn, this oak is bare. The wide, gray trunk twists into the forest canopy, its branches like skeletal hands grasping for life. They clack together in the breeze, ominous.

"Poor thing." Eden clicks her tongue, her Blessed magic strengthening her connection to the forest. "What could have happened?"

"Can't trees just die?"

She presses her hand against the rough bark of the trunk. "This feels different. It's like something inside of it . . . broke. If I didn't know better, I'd say sadness killed it."

Sadness? What could a tree be—

A faint marking on the trunk catches my attention. Two letters are engraved into the bark. They're worn down by years of storms and frosts, but I would recognize them anywhere. And I should. *I'm* the one who carved them.

A + J

Ayleth and . . . *Jacquetta.*

Every nerve in my body hums, and I suddenly know exactly where we are. This is the clearing—*our* clearing. I pull back from the tree as if bitten, but not quickly enough.

"What's that?" Eden asks. Her lips slacken as she registers the carving. "Oh, Ayleth."

The pity in her voice only serves to spark my anger. Not at Eden, though—at myself.

"Sindony had no business mentioning"—she shifts, uncomfortable—"the *incident.*"

Incident. A kind word for what it was. *Disgrace,* Mother called it when the Elementals dragged me home. *Betrayal.*

And she was right. Jacquetta wasn't one of us. I knew that. She'd come to Stonehaven with her mother when we were both sixteen, fleeing the raid on her first coven. That was before our disguise, but even so, it became increasingly obvious that the two witches didn't share our views. They were flippant regarding the Ancients. Jacquetta's mother often experimented with the craft, straying from her affiliation. Mother warned me constantly to stay away from them. I didn't listen. Jacquetta was the only witch who didn't care that I was an Heir's daughter, or that I showed no interest in the craft. All she cared about was me—or so I thought.

"It's nothing," I say, as much to myself as to Eden.

Because it *was* nothing, at least to Jacquetta. The cold light of morning, which found me *alone* in this clearing after Rhea died, proved that fact clearly enough.

"Do you . . . still think of her?" Eden asks quietly.

I shouldn't. The seven years of her absence should have destroyed the rotting roots of any meaningless sentiment. And yet memories still burrow into my dreams. Another breeze winds through the clearing and I catch the hint of juniper.

It smells like winter.

Would that I could rip it all up, my own wretched heart with it.

"I was young," I tell Eden. "I made a mistake."

"It's all right." Eden squeezes my arm. "No one doubts your loyalty."

Anymore, she doesn't say. There had been plenty of sidelong looks and hissing whispers after I returned from my failed venture. It was so humiliating that I almost left the Sanctum again. But where would I have gone? And I didn't possess the will. Much as I try to deny it, after Rhea's death, the blow of Jacquetta's rejection had crushed me. It had killed my soul the same way this tree died, leaving me nothing but an empty, broken husk.

Enough, that voice whispers.

It's right. I stuff the feelings back into their tomb where they belong.

"Let's just—"

Nettle yowls a warning. I whirl around, but there's nothing behind us. Until . . .

A high, tinny ringing followed by a glasslike shatter carries beneath the wind. Anxiety knots in my chest, painfully swift. I *know* that sound.

"The wards," I say to Eden, hardly feeling the words leave my lips. "The wards broke."

Color drains from her face. "Are you certain?"

I wish I wasn't—for it to be something, *anything* else, even a Nevenwolf. But as the noise rises and crests, there's no denying the truth. The wards have broken. A single thought loops through my mind—

The last time this happened, Rhea died. And it was my fault.

Run, run, RUN, my mind screams as my feet fumble through the forest.

Memories crash together, transporting me back to the night of the Hunt's raid on Stonehaven. I was supposed to be on patrol with

Rhea, assigned lookout duty while she maintained the wards with
the other Casters. But I'd skipped it, preferring to spend the hours in
the forest with Jacquetta. Flashes of the night whirl in my mind—an
empty bottle of stolen wine. Leaves tossed in the air. Stars spinning
into a blur above us.

Do you hear them? The stars are singing.

You smell like juniper.

You taste like roses.

I hate myself for how happy I'd been. How I'd been laughing and
dancing and *kissing* while the Hunt had been prowling beyond our
borders, just waiting for the chance to strike. I should have seen
them. I should have warned the others and protected my sister. Instead, I'd made it back just in time to watch the clouds of charcoal
smoke billow above the Sanctum. To witness the arrows soaring over
our walls. To choke on the stench of burning flesh. I didn't know it
then, but Rhea had already been struck. She was always already
dying, while I . . .

Eden and I nearly topple over each other as we come careening to
a halt at the edge of the forest. Farther down the tree line, a party
emerges from the woods. My blood turns to rivers of ice. They're
wearing the green of the Hunt.

They're *here*. Again.

Breathe, I tell myself. *Just breathe.*

Nettle trills beside me.

"They're not armed." Eden squeezes my hand, her pulse thudding
through her skin. "And there's only a few of them."

Not like before, when it seemed like there were a hundred swarming us. Now less than a dozen Huntsmen are clustered outside the
Sanctum's walls. The man I assume to be their leader dismounts.
He's tall and broad-shouldered, striding up to the gate with an air of
arrogance that has me gritting my back teeth.

The portcullis rattles open, and I brace myself for the sight of this *monster* stepping though it, desecrating our home with his murderous footsteps. He doesn't get the chance. Mother intercepts him. She's replaced her crimson cloak with her dull gray Sanctress robes. The Eye of Meira glimmers where it's embroidered on her bodice, and I pray to every Spirit listening that the disguise is enough. That he doesn't suspect.

Mother and the Huntsman engage in a brief conversation. He passes something to her, salutes, and returns to his horse. An instant later, the party steers their mounts down the eastern path—*away* from Stonehaven.

"They're leaving," Eden whispers, leaning into me. "They're gone."

My entire body sags in relief. Nettle nudges herself against my legs. "What did they want?"

Eden shakes her head. As soon as the horses disappear, we race back to the Sanctum and through the open gate. Witches hurry from one end of the courtyard to the other, the bitter-spice scent of panic and fear thick enough to chew.

"Ayleth!" Mother peels herself away from the crowd.

For an instant, she's the witch—the mother—I remember from the years before Rhea died. She reaches for me, her hazel eyes shining with concern, and I half expect her to pull me into an embrace. I'll hardly know what to do if she does. It's been so long since I felt her arms around me. But her hands grip my shoulders instead, fingers like talons digging into my flesh.

"What were you thinking?" She gives me a shake. "The *forest?*"

I wrangle myself out of her grasp. "It was only for a while."

"My mother sent us," Eden supplies, her freckles stark on her white cheeks. "We needed more fireroot. I'm sorry to have worried you, Cassandra."

Mother inhales a visible breath. A nearby witch starts to sob.

"Go to Willa," Mother directs Eden.

Eden casts me a worried look, but I nod and she hurries off to help dole out calming tinctures and other remedies. The smell of lavender wafts on the breeze. At this point, I could use some myself. A whole vat of it, in fact.

"I thought we were *finished* with behavior like this," Mother says, keeping her voice low. "You should have been here."

How she does love to twist that blade. Rage crackles in my wrists, coupled with a healthy shot of guilt. Does she not understand how foolish I feel for what happened? Am I to spend my whole life making up for it?

"We were fetching fireroot," I say tightly. "I would have returned by dinner."

"And I told you to see to the Seconds."

"They were fine," I snap back. "Am I not allowed a few hours to myself? You're about to take my whole life."

Mother huffs. "I'll never understand this flair for dramatics. Your position is one of honor, Ayleth. Plenty of witches would give anything to boast your lineage."

Then let them have it, I want to say. *I relinquish it freely.* But I only stand there, as I've always done, hating the blood that beats in my veins.

"Find something useful to do here." Mother indicates the courtyard. "The others will look to you. I'm meeting with the Heirs and their Seconds to discuss what happened."

That pulls me up short. I would expect the Heirs to attend such a meeting, but the Seconds? Why the others and not me?

You know why, that voice in my mind whispers.

Fresh anger kindles in my belly. How convenient for Mother— naming me Second one minute and witchling the next.

"So I'm important enough to stand beside you and wear a cloak,"

I call at her back, loud enough for everyone to hear. "But not to sit at your council table?"

My pulse hums at my boldness. Several witches slide us surreptitious glances.

"You will join my table," Mother says over her shoulder, not even bothering to turn around, "when you have taken your vow. Until then, I suggest you prove yourself worthy of the flame."

With that, she strides off, leaving me smoldering in my own rage and humiliation. Hot tears sting in my eyes and I furiously blink them away. I hate that she has this control over me. She never treated Rhea like this. Why me?

You know, that voice repeats. *Because you're not Rhea. You never will be.*

Maybe not. But this time, I won't bow to Mother's orders. If I can't be part of the meeting, I can at least listen to it. I stalk toward the Sanctum. There's one place not even Mother's talons reach:

The south tower.

CHAPTER FOUR

EVEN BEFORE THE HUNT'S RAID, THE ROOM IN THE SOUTH TOWER, on the third floor of the Sanctum, was deemed uninhabitable, always damp after a rain or drafty in winter. Abandoned as it was, the place became a playground for us witchlings. Whenever I preferred reading novels to completing my lessons—which was every day—I'd sneak up the thirteen steps to the secluded chamber and hide for hours. It wasn't until I was older that I understood the significance of the room's location, directly above Mother's study. Then, and arguably now, her inner-council meetings were more nuisance than informative, and I ignored them. Such is not the case today.

The hinges are mercifully silent as I ease open the ancient door to the tower room and tiptoe across the floor, careful to avoid any creaking planks as I navigate to a familiar gap in the boards, one just wide enough to allow me to glimpse into the lower chamber. I settle myself on my stomach and slip one of the Potioners' mugwort pellets under my tongue, grimacing as the earthy taste coats my teeth.

The effect is instantaneous. Mother's voice floats up from below, as clear as if I were sitting at the table.

"It seems your disguise isn't as effective as you hoped," Selene comments.

"The Hunt left, did they not?" Mother asks archly. "They weren't searching for witches. It was just some ridiculous invitation for Longest Night. Something about Order Sisters receiving the High Priest's blessing."

Longest Night—the Order's bastardization of our Spirit's Eve. For witches, this season, lasting through autumn and winter, is a time when we commemorate the forging of the Veil and the sacrifice of the Ancients. The Order has twisted it, claiming that this so-called Longest Night is the period during which their false goddess was held captive by the covens.

"Will you answer this invitation?" Selene asks.

"You expect me to send witches to the White City?"

Home of the mad king. The back of my neck prickles.

"Why not? You seem eager to comply with every other command the Order throws at you. What with your uniforms and other paraphernalia."

When Mother first adopted our disguise, she invited the other Heirs to bring their covens to Stonehaven and share in our relative safety. Selene and the others refused, citing the excuse that it wouldn't be wise to house all the Heirs together. After all, the Covens' War began when a gathering of the Heirs was captured by the Hunt. My own grandmother was among those witches hauled to the White Palace and forced to dance in a pair of hot iron shoes. As such, no one could fault the surviving Heirs for being cautious. But despite Selene's alleged concerns regarding safety, plenty of rumors floated around, suggesting that the other Heirs disapproved of Mother's actions. That they believed it disrespectful to even pretend to be part of the Order that hunts us. Judging from Selene's tone, those rumors hold merit.

"I did what was necessary to protect my own," Mother says, clipped. "The same as any of you would have done. All the Hunt saw today was a Sanctum filled with the Order's Sisters. Could you do better?"

"But the wards *did* break," another Heir says. It's Della's mother, Mildred. "Again."

"Is there a point to this interrogation? The last time I checked, you came to Stonehaven for my daughter's Ascension. Not an inquest into the way in which I manage my coven."

Wood creaks as someone shifts in their chair.

"No one is blaming you for the Hunt, Cassandra," Mildred says gently.

"Perhaps not," Selene agrees, unconvincingly. "But there *is* a point. The wards failed today—they failed with Rhea as well. If your power is as strong as you would have us believe, they should not have done so."

"I will not listen to—" Mother starts.

"It's not only your abilities in question," Mildred interrupts. "We're all experiencing similar . . . difficulties. Elain can hardly control the winds anymore. And Lettice's healing powers have significantly diminished."

That pulls me up short. Why would the *Heirs* be losing their power? Given their lineage, their link to the Spirits is strongest.

"She's correct," Selene confirms. "It's been too long since the last Bloodstone ritual. The spell our ancestresses cast is failing. The Veil is thinning. We can all sense the change."

Malum.

I recall the shadows in the forest—the crimson eyes.

"And what do you propose we do about it?" Mother asks. "The Bloodstones are gone."

Not just *gone*.

When the Five forged the Veil and banished Malum from Riven, it heralded a new age for witches and mortals alike. And it was *such* an age—mortals, who once feared us, came to respect and honor the covens. In return, we witches healed their sick and blessed their lands. But, as the centuries progressed, so did the White Kings' greed. They insisted that witches submit to the Crown as subjects. They listened when the Order priests began whispering that the covens needed to be controlled.

During a Spirit's Eve forty years ago, the king dispatched his Hunt to the Heirs' meeting place on the night they were to complete their ritual. With the Heirs distracted, the Hunt attacked. They captured the descendants of the Five and cut the Bloodstones from their fingers. As those witches—my own grandmother among them—danced to their death in hot iron shoes, the Order claimed to have freed its false goddess from her imaginary prison, releasing her so-called Light back into the realm. The Bloodstones—the very backbone of the Veil—haven't been seen since.

"The stones may be gone," Selene says, bringing me back into the conversation, "but there could be a way to change that."

"How?" Mother demands. "Nothing has worked before."

When the war started, the covens assumed they would declare a swift victory over the mortals. While we might have won our share of battles early on, every attack against the White City or the palace itself has ended in ruin. It's like there's some kind of shield around the White King's domain. With each passing year, each coven and witch lost, we get weaker while the mortals' forces only appear to strengthen.

"We have to shift our focus," Mildred says.

"Shift?" Mother repeats. "What else—"

"We reforge the Bloodstones," Selene supplies. "Create new vessels to hold the enchantment—and the Veil."

Silence thrums. *Reforging?* That's . . . impossible. Isn't it?

For once, Mother seems to share my opinion. "That spell *killed* the Ancients."

"And the Spirits brought them back," Selene points out. "Not only that, but they gifted the Five with immeasurable power for their efforts."

Mother huffs. "Is that what this is about? Securing a gift for yourself?"

"It's about our survival," Selene snaps. "We *need* that power. Don't pretend otherwise."

"Be that as it may," Mother says, "there's no guarantee that the Spirits would grant us the same blessing that they bestowed upon the Ancients. Criticize me all you like for my uniforms and effigies of the false goddess, but *this* is a risk we can't afford to take."

"Or is it a risk *you* can't afford?" Selene counters. Even from here, I can feel the rage rolling off Mother's body. "The Ancients came together once before. *We* can do it again. All of us—including our Seconds."

Her meaning begins to take shape in my mind, ringing with a horrible clarity. The Heirs *and* the Seconds. That will mean *me*. Panic lights in my chest. I haven't demonstrated any measurable talent for magic, and they want me to help them forge a *Bloodstone*? Even if it worked—which it wouldn't—I have no reason to believe the Spirits would bring me back to life, much less gift me with anything.

They'll see right through you. That menacing voice again.

"When was all this decided?" Mother asks tightly.

"There have been," Mildred starts, hesitant, "meetings."

"Meetings of the Heirs? Without *me*?"

"We didn't want to overwhelm you, what with Ayleth's Ascension."

Mother laughs. "So you dictate to me instead?"

"It's not an order," Mildred attempts. "It's just—"

"It *is* an order," Selene cuts in, earning a sharp intake of breath. "Risk or not, this is our only chance to turn the tide in this war. We need the Spirits' gift. We need new Bloodstones. We've tried everything else. Rycinthia isn't an option. Even the Dwarves have left us to rot."

Bodies shift at the mention of our failed alliances. Rycinthia, our neighbor to the north, has remained uninvolved in the current conflict. Even the idea that they've accepted fleeing witches into their realm is little more than rumor. But they *do* hold distant ties to the White King's throne. There were a few instances in Mother's council meetings where witches thought to use that connection to spur the Rycinthian rulers into acting on our behalf. But in the end, another mortal-and-witch alliance was judged too risky to pursue.

The Guilds, however, are another matter. Like us, the Dwarves were highly respected in Riven. Their magic is rooted in crafting—they forge enchanted objects and weapons in their mines. But following the White King's edict, the Dwarves vanished without so much as a farewell to the covens. Some witches believe the Dwarves were killed off. But most assume the Guilds simply decided to abandon us to our fate. It was a quiet, personal betrayal that sticks like a thorn in our side.

"And if I refuse this ludicrous plan?" Mother asks.

Wood creaks again.

"It should be said," Selene goes on. "There are rumors—"

"Now is not the time," Mildred warns.

"This is a meeting of the Heirs. What other time is there?"

Tension hums. I press myself closer to the floor.

"Some have suggested that your *experiment* at this Sanctum is more than merely strategy," Selene says. "Questions have been raised as to whether you are still fit to call yourself Heir. Or perhaps . . . Millicent's line is truly dying out. After all, given what I've witnessed thus far, your power does seem to be waning faster than the rest of ours."

Every muscle in my body stills. Does she know about me? She can't. No one knows. Then again, Sindony goaded me about the night I tried to run.

Diviners make the best spies, Mother always said.

Is that what they've been doing? Peering into our lives with their bones and cards and mirrors? I make a note to smash their "gift" this very night.

"How dare you?" Mother seethes. "I am descended of an Ancient— the same as you are. Millicent's blood runs in my veins, as well as in Ayleth's."

"Then prove it," Selene says simply. "After Ayleth's Ascension, we'll conduct the spell. If your line is as strong as you claim, then you have nothing to fear. And everything to gain."

My pulse thuds against my ears. What can Mother say? The truth will ruin us. But it will come out sooner or later. And when I fail at this, it won't just be my own coven that suffers. I'll be letting down every witch in the realm. And I'll probably be dead.

"You know what will happen if we don't try," Mildred presses. "If the Veil breaks, our tie to the Spirits breaks with it. It's not just Malum that's a threat. We'll lose our power."

Those that have it, the voice whispers.

"Very well," Mother allows at last, her voice thin. "After Ayleth's Ascension."

"Then it's settled," Selene returns smoothly.

The room below feels anything but *settled.* More like a hornets' nest—like the one raging behind my sternum.

"Wonderful," Mildred chimes in, forcing cheerfulness. "And I think that's enough for now. We can all use some time to rest before dinner."

Murmurs of agreement. Chairs scrape against the floor as the other witches push back from the table and file out of the chamber.

Mother, however, doesn't move—not even when the door snicks closed behind them. I can't make out the details of her face, but the lines of her body are rigid—angry. There's something else too. Fear? It seems impossible, as I doubt Mother has been afraid of anything in her whole life. Part of me wants to go to her, comfort her. But I'm not even sure I know how anymore.

At last, Mother rises. She passes directly under me and crosses to the other side of the room, toward . . . my stomach knots.

Her mirror.

Through the slit in the floor, I can just make out its ebony frame and the unnatural silver sheen to its glass. As witchlings, Eden and I snuck in to see the thing one night, each of us daring the other to touch the ethereal surface. When Eden finally mustered the nerve, nothing happened. But when it was my turn—

Ayleth, I swear I can hear as the wind sighs against the Sanctum. *Ayleth.*

I shove the memory down, watching Mother as she picks up a knife, slices the skin of her palm, and presses it to the glass.

"*Mirror, mirror on the wall.*" The words of the spell roll through the room. "*Wake now and heed my call.*"

The surface ripples like water and a ghostly face emerges, one that has visited my nightmares more times than I care to admit.

"Mistress," its eerie voice rasps.

Witch's mirrors are living beings, Mother said, years ago. *And living beings require hearts.*

Inside Mother's mirror is a raven's heart. Still beating, I assume, for the bird comes to the Sanctum, tapping on windows until Mother lets it in. Its eyes are silvery and vacant, like extensions of the mirror itself. Mother had been the one to cut out its heart, she'd explained. It was then—with the image of her hands stained with blood—that she changed from being my mother, the woman who combed her fingers through my hair until I drifted off to sleep, into someone *else*. Things were never the same between us after that. Sometimes, I even believe Mother would lock my heart behind glass if she could.

"I assume you heard everything," Mother says to the mirror, confirming my long-held suspicions that the horrible thing is listening in at every moment.

"Yes, Mistress."

"And?" Mother demands. "Can she do it?"

She means *me*. I hold my breath as the mirror contemplates.

"Your daughter's worth is yet unseen," it says at last.

"Don't speak to me in riddles," Mother snaps.

"Her path remains uncertain," the mirror continues. "I sense a greatness in her future. But she must reach for it."

My heart beats harder. Does that mean that I *am* gifted? What am I supposed to reach for? But I don't hear the rest of what the mirror says. A crow calls, close enough that I startle. Talons click on the window casement. I look up to find it watching me—and not just one. A second joins it, then another, then even more—until there are seven perched on the window.

That old rhyme dredges up.

> *Six crows bring ill luck,*
> *But seven worse,*
> *For they carry a secret, mystery or curse.*

CHAPTER FIVE

"WE HAVE TO LEAVE. IT'S NOT SAFE HERE ANYMORE."

Dishes rattle as Enid, another witch in our coven, jolts up from her place at the table. To say that the last hours have been *tense* would be a vast understatement. Usually, I enjoy our dinners, the long dining hall filled with comfortable chatter and laughter. As the night wanes, some of my sisters play instruments, or sing and dance. There will be no dancing tonight—or even eating, by the looks of it. The trestle tables are laden with food, but no one is touching it. Instead of laughter, whispers run in an unceasing current through the chamber, the witches processing Mother's announcement. She'd told the coven about the High Priest's invitation to the White City for Longest Night, but not about her meeting with the Heirs—or the proposed spell to reforge the Blood-stones.

Because she knows you cannot achieve it, that voice whispers.

I stab at the pieces of carrot floating in my stew.

"And where would we go?" another witch asks. "The Rycinthian border is weeks away and they're sure to have the Hunt patrolling it."

"The Hunt is patrolling *here*," Enid retorts. "They'll burn us all. Just like . . ?"

She breaks off in a sob. Torchlight washes over her face, illuminating three raised scars on Enid's left cheek, dark brown against her tawny skin. Too many of my sisters wear such marks—iron-carved vestiges of the Hunt's sword blades or arrows.

You don't boast any scars, that voice needles again.

No. And their absence is yet another reason I avoid mirrors. Because I *should* be scarred. I should be covered in them, ripped apart by the Hunt's weapons. I should have died trying to save Rhea, and instead I was . . .

You taste like roses.

"I understand your fear." Selene rises from her seat at the High Table, mercifully extracting me from my tangle of memories.

Unsurprisingly, the Diviner witch refused to wear the uniform of the Sisters during her stay. Torchlight glistens against the runes sewn into the fabric of her crimson cloak—as if *she* is High Witch and not Mother.

"Following the Ascension, any witch who wishes to leave Stonehaven is welcome to accompany me back to Ravenwood."

Murmurs ripple through the room. I stare at Selene. A witch's bond to her coven is one she holds for life, only broken in the event of dire circumstances, like the Hunt's raids. That, and the few cautionary tales I've heard of a witch being cast out after committing grave offense against her sisters. For Selene to invite our witches to abandon Stonehaven in favor of her own coven implies that there is something irrevocably wrong here. I glance at where Mother stands at the front of the room, her dull Sanctress robes a sharp contrast to Selene's blood-red cloak.

"If any witch feels compelled to leave Stonehaven, I cannot stop them," she admits. "But I would remind everyone here that King Callen *wants* the covens to fracture. That's the point of this interminable war. He expects us to falter under the pressure of his father's edict."

Several witches nod their agreement.

"The mad king wishes us to forget who we were—who we still are. *Witches.*" Fire smolders in Mother's gaze. "Our bloodlines run deeper than the roots of the oldest trees in this realm. We will not break. Not now. Not ever."

Her words ring in the hall, inciting a storm of cheers. Mother stands taller, the witch who led the charge against the Hunt and won. She's a warrior—Millicent herself resurrected.

And I have never been more certain that I am nothing like her.

A single note cuts through the chamber as several witches begin humming the song of coven gatherings. Another joins in, then another, each choosing a slightly different pitch, so that the sound rolls around us, ethereal and haunting. It's not a spell like a Caster might attempt, but the intertwined voices summon the magic around us. A metallic charge crackles in the hall. Even the other Heirs begin to hum, along with their Seconds, the song rising and cresting until I can feel it in my very blood.

"It seems you'll be returning to Ravenwood alone," Mother says to Selene as the hall at last quiets. The Diviner witch dips her chin in the slightest degree possible before resuming her seat. "We will discuss this matter again after I've had time to seek further guidance from the Spirits. Rest assured that, together, we will develop a plan."

Mother's attention twitches to me, and my stomach knots. I already know that plan—and there's no way I'm capable of achieving it.

"Until then, we have a welcome to impart." Mother gestures toward the back of the hall. "There's a newcomer in our midst. Mathilde."

A smattering of applause greets the elder witch as she stands. She looks as though she's had an opportunity to rest. Her deep-brown skin shines with the glow of Willa's lavender soap, and her white hair is freshly braided. Her uniform doesn't quite fit, though. It's slightly too short in the sleeves and the hem. Due to our remote location, fabric is difficult to obtain. Most of our dresses are remade several times over.

"You have my thanks for your hospitality," Mathilde says, her voice low and a touch raspy, like she doesn't use it very often. How long had she been wandering the forest alone?

"We're grateful that you're here," Nyssandra, a Potioner, offers kindly. She crosses the room to grasp Mathilde's elbow in welcome. "It's our custom to conduct a Ceremony of Blood and Ashes when a new witch arrives—to honor your fallen coven. We'll arrange one for you, when you—"

"That won't be necessary."

Confusion undulates through the gathered witches, including me. Why would Mathilde reject the chance to bestow a parting blessing on her lost sisters? Rhea's ceremony was difficult, but I'd been grateful for it, in the end.

"It doesn't need to take place right away," Nyssandra amends, patting Mathilde's arm. "Give yourself a few days to settle and then we can—"

"I have no coven," Mathilde cuts her off. "Nor have I ever. I'm Wayward."

Wayward? The word drops into the room like a stone, surprise and alarm rippling outward in waves. The witches sitting nearest to Mathilde noticeably inch away from her.

It's one thing for a witch to willingly break her bond with a coven, or even to be cast out. But a *Wayward* witch is one who never joined with a coven at all. In some instances, the Spirits might have rejected the witch's offering at her Ascension. But typically, Wayward witches are those who never desired to bind themselves to the Spirits. They're like the witches before the forging of the Veil. Their power is unpredictable, susceptible to being tainted by Malum.

"I understand these are unusual circumstances." Mother puts her hands up in a vain attempt to quell the churning suspicion. "But for the time being, I feel it best that Mathilde remains with us. Wayward or not, we cannot leave her to the wolves."

That's not how Mother felt when the coven split, I think bitterly. A memory rises up—a line of witches crossing through the gaping portcullis, their crimson cloaks littered on the ground behind them like pools of blood.

"Oh, I'm not so frightened of wolves." A slight grin quirks Mathilde's lips. "In fact, I find them better company than most."

Most? Does she mean witches? The hushed mutterings increase, but Mathilde ignores them. Her thick-knuckled fingers toy with a strand of tiny objects hanging from her belt. *Teeth*, I realize. Most are small and pointed, like they belonged to various species of animals, but some appear similar enough to my own that I shudder.

"Eat." Mother gestures at the untouched food on the tables, clearly changing the subject. "We're here to celebrate."

Her hazel eyes lock with mine and another memory emerges— the last dinner before Rhea's Ascension. Mother had spoken nearly the same words then: *We have much to celebrate.* Except, on that night, her smile had been genuine. Now the lines around her mouth are tight, like she's willing her power to make the words true.

"Adopting the life of Order Sisters and keeping the company of Wayward witches," Sindony comments, tearing off pieces of her bread and dropping them into her soup. "What other surprises might your mother have in store for us this visit?"

I bristle. Mother insisted that I continue *entertaining* the two Seconds tonight. After the incident with Nettle, it's going about as well as Nesta boiling fireroot. Perhaps I should let my cat loose on Sindony's wardrobe as well.

"I suppose we'll find out," I say, smiling.

Sindony only raises an eyebrow and strikes up a conversation with Della, one I'm obviously not invited to join. I pick at my food, forcing down tasteless bites to distract myself from the storm of worries and questions swirling in my mind.

But every now and then, my attention flits back to Mathilde. She remains in her place, but she doesn't eat, or even converse with the other witches. All she does for the rest of the night is work her fingertips along that strand of teeth.

CHAPTER SIX

THE FOLLOWING DAYS ARE AN ENDLESS BARRAGE OF PREPARATION for my Ascension. The last two Heirs finally arrive with their Seconds, which necessitates even more *entertaining* on my part. At least these witches aren't as unnerving as Sindony. But I catch them looking at me, analyzing me, like they don't find me a suitable replacement for Rhea.

They're right. And all I want to do is hide away in the south tower. But after what I overheard between Mother and the other Heirs, even that once-sacred place is ruined. The impossible plan to reforge the Bloodstones haunts me in the night, as does the mirror's cryptic words:

Your daughter's worth is yet unseen.

Will anyone ever see it? Will I?

On the day before my Ascension, I'm supposed to be tending to the Seconds. But when I stop to check on them, they're huddled together in Rhea's room. At my entrance, their conversation abruptly ceases. The following silence is so thick and awkward that I immediately retreat, steering my steps to the fresh air of the garden with Nettle.

Aside from the kitchen, the cloister's garden is my favorite place in Stonehaven. I settle myself in the patch I've been minding of late, pinching a spotted leaf off of a hyssop's stem and admiring the purple flowers as they sway in the cool breeze. Before the war, the Elementals and Blesseds used their magic to create perfect conditions for keeping our gardens. Many did the same for nearby towns and villages: Witches would teach mortals how to cultivate the land, as well as to identify healing herbs and other non-magical aspects of our craft.

But those days are long over. Mother's rules forbid spells in the garden, not that I mind. The grit of dirt between my fingers, the satisfaction of watching a seed sprout and flourish, carries a magic all its own. I run my hand over a rosemary bush, releasing its crisp, clean scent. Some of the knots of tension in my shoulders begin to untangle, and I close my eyes, breathing deep the autumn smell of—

Juniper.

Damn everything. Where had *that* come from? During one of the first miserable nights after my humiliating return to Stonehaven, I'd clawed up all vestiges of the shrubs in a blind rage. But the stubborn things keep growing back. I root amid the other plants, hunting for the spiny, green-frosted leaves. This time, I'll tear out every root. Every—

A piercing yowl shatters the quiet. Nettle springs from where she'd been trapping toads between her paws and bounds across the cloister.

"Nettle!" I call after her. "What are you—"

A flurry of clucking and feathers erupts as my cat plows into a flock of chickens. Not just chickens, though. Standing in the center of the chaos is the new witch—Mathilde.

By the Spirits, that cat will be the death of me.

"Nettle, stop!" I hurry over, shooing her away.

She slinks off, twitching her tail in annoyance at my spoiling her fun. The chickens cluck and fuss, lodging their complaints at being so rudely disturbed—like I have any control over my cat. I deal Nettle a glare. She perches on the low wall surrounding the cloister, her golden eyes glinting. And I'm fairly certain that she's smirking.

"I'm so sorry," I apologize to Mathilde. "Did she scare you?"

Those sightless eyes rove in my direction. *Wayward.* A little thrill runs through me. I'm not sure if it's curiosity or fear or ... something else.

"Takes more than feisty cats to bother an old witch like me." Mathilde straightens her clothes. "She your familiar, then?"

"Not quite," I say, doing my best to keep my tone casual, like I would when speaking with any other witch.

"Not *quite*?" Mathilde echoes, raising an eyebrow.

"I never bound her."

When I stumbled upon Nettle—a stray kitten abandoned in the forest—and brought her home to Stonehaven, Mother opened a grimoire to the binding ritual, one that connects an animal's soul to our latent magic. The bond between witch and her familiar is second only to that of a heartmate. If I'd gone through with the spell, Nettle would heed my commands even if she were far away, and she would live as long as I do. But as I studied the words of the binding ritual, I realized that the ritual required *taking* part of Nettle—the tip of her ear or a claw—in order to seal our connection. After Rhea died, I understood exactly what it meant to be robbed of part of myself, forced into a role I never wanted. I couldn't do that to someone else, even a cat.

"Did you not?" Mathilde asks, a touch of amusement in her voice.

"I wanted her to stay with me because it was her own choice," I explain, feeling somewhat foolish.

Mother certainly never agreed with my decision to forego the binding, which was hardly a surprise. After all, she suffered no guilt in feeding a raven's heart to her mirror.

A shadow swoops overhead, coupled with the flap of wings. A splotch of black descends, and I yelp and duck, assuming one of those wretched crows decided to attack.

"No need to be frightened," Mathilde says as the bird settles placidly on her shoulder. "This is Cornelius. I never bound him, either. Choice, I've found, is a magic in and of itself."

Cornelius squawks and gobbles down a treat Mathilde fishes from her pocket.

"But that's . . ?" I splutter. "It's a *crow*."

"Is it?" Mathilde asks dryly. "I hadn't noticed. Don't tell me you're afraid of him."

I picture the seven crows watching me from the window of the south tower. Had *he* been one of them? Had he brought the others?

"I'm not afraid," I lie, banishing the image. "It's just . . ."

"It's just that they're associated with Malum?" Mathilde's lips quirk. "I suppose I'm accustomed to such company, dreaded Wayward that I am."

A flush prickles up my neck. "I didn't mean to suggest—"

She waves me off. "Keep your excuses. But I do find it interesting that the witches here seem less than thrilled at the prospect of someone like me living among them, but they're perfectly content to parade about as Order Sisters."

"We had to do what was necessary." Mother's refrain automatically spills from my lips.

"Necessary." Mathilde offers another treat to her crow. "I suppose that makes sense. We're all just trying to survive. And living as a Sister is better than facing a pyre."

"That's what Mother thought."

Not everyone agreed with her, though. It didn't help that Mother announced her decision on the night of the Hunt's attack. With our dead sisters' bodies still warm, few could stomach the idea of the false goddess's Eyes staring down at us from the eaves and alcoves, where our runes should be. Wearing Meira's emblem was even worse. Sometimes I wonder how things might have been different if Mother had waited, or at least attempted a discussion before she levied her orders. Would the others have left? Would *she*?

She did *leave*, that voice reminds me. *And that's all that matters.*

"Your *mother*?" Mathilde asks, interrupting my thoughts. "That must make you the one that all the fuss is about. Irene, is it?"

"Ayleth," I correct.

She nods. "Descendant of one of the Five."

As always, the comparison to my ancestress makes me itch. It's like I'm trying on someone else's clothes that don't fit properly. "Millicent."

"Ah, yes. I should have guessed it would take a Caster to accomplish such a ruse as this." She gestures around the Sanctum. "Do you know how she did it?"

How could I forget? The enchantment is one of Mother's favorite stories—at least when the other Heirs aren't around.

"Mother's specialty is illusion magic," I explain. "Glamours and such. After the raid, she spelled the remaining members of the Hunt to believe that they'd won. They went back to the palace claiming that we were all dead."

"A glamour." Mathilde nods, though I can't tell if she's impressed. "But did the Order not send their own people? That's what I've gathered they've been doing anyway. Converting the Sanctums to honor the false goddess."

They did send their own. About a month after the raid, the sentries spotted the wagons transporting the real Sisters. There weren't many. Stonehaven is secluded. The nearest village is days away. I doubt the Order wanted to deal with the upkeep of such a remote location—that's part of why it took the Hunt so long to find us in the first place.

"Mother spelled the Sisters as well," I explain. "She jumbled their minds. We took their uniforms and belongings and sent them away."

It was strangely sad, watching the women depart. Mother might not have killed them, but they all looked so *lost*. Perhaps, after my own life was so irrevocably upended, I understood what the Sisters were experiencing. The difference was that the Sisters weren't aware that they'd left another life behind. Sometimes, I wish I weren't either.

"And then your mother assumed the identity of the Sanctress," Mathilde surmises. "Clever, I'll give her that. And she's a strong witch to accomplish such a spell."

Incredibly strong. Cornelius calls again, ruffling his feathers.

"And what of you?" Mathilde asks, petting her bird. "Do you aspire to follow in the great Ancient's footsteps?"

Aspire is all I'll ever do. "I'm . . . not sure."

"Not sure? In my experience, you coven witches love to boast about your abilities."

I'd have to *possess* abilities to boast about them. "Not me."

Wind sweeps through the cloister, stirring the ash of the coven fire.

"You're an interesting one." Mathilde fixes her white eyes in my direction. "Come here. Let me know you better."

Her hand goes to her belt, where the strand of teeth hangs, ivory and yellow bones glinting in the afternoon light. She's a Diviner, then. Or something like it. Wayward witches don't have affiliations. And I still can't shake the feeling that some of those teeth belonged to witches. What did Mathilde do to get them?

"No, thank you." I take a half step back. "I don't like readings."

After Rhea's death and the raid, the Diviners descended on me, eager to determine the Spirits' plans for the next Second and Heir. But their efforts always revealed more questions than answers. Soon enough, Mother put a stop to the practice.

Things will become clear after your Ascension, she'd tell me.

Even then, she sounded as though she were trying to convince herself more than me.

"I don't bite," Mathilde coaxes, beckoning. "My power is exactly the same as yours."

That isn't true. Cornelius squawks what could pass for a laugh.

I start to refuse again, but a thought swirls in my mind. Mathilde's magic *isn't* like mine. What if she can see something, like the mirror did?

She must reach. The unsettling voice resonates beneath the breeze.

Reach for what? Could Mathilde know? I'm not brave—or foolish—enough to mention the mirror. But desperation gets the better of me. After a quick glance to make sure we're alone, I extend my palm out to the elder witch. Nerves flutter in my belly as she snatches it up, the fingertips of her other hand working through her string of teeth.

"Ah." Her thumb presses down firmly in between my tendons. "You were not the first daughter to face the flame."

My stomach twists. "I had a sister. Rhea."

And I suddenly realize how strange it is that Mathilde didn't already know this about me. That she has no idea who Rhea was. It's freeing, in a way, that she can't compare me to her.

Mathilde makes a noise in her throat. "She's gone."

An image of Rhea's face—my face—blooms in my mind, her skin riddled with rust-colored veins as the iron poisoning took root.

Stay with me, I begged that night. *If you go, I'll be alone.*

But she didn't stay. No one stays—not for me.

"She died." The words catch. "In the raid."

And I was supposed to have been there. Supposed to have been helping.

"You have my sympathy for that," Mathilde says kindly, though she couldn't possibly comprehend the depth of my guilt and shame. "It's a terrible way to lose someone."

It was more than just losing Rhea, though. My whole life changed that night, the trajectory of my future yanked in a direction I never expected . . . or desired.

"There's someone else too." Her grip traverses my hand, along the slender bones of my fingers and the meat of my palm. "A loss that inflicted even greater pain."

Without warning, the smell of juniper hits me, strong enough to steal my breath.

The stars are singing.

Jacquetta's voice resurfaces, clear enough that she could be standing right behind me, her cobalt-blue eyes glinting with a secret. My heart slams against my ribs, and I yank my hand away.

"What's wrong?" Mathilde asks. Cornelius grumbles. "Did I upset you?"

I check over my shoulder. There's nothing, of course, and I scold myself for letting my imagination get the better of me. "No. I'm fine."

"It's merely a reading," Mathilde adds. "And I can see only what's there."

Jacquetta shouldn't *be* there at all, I think vehemently. She's gone. She left me alone in the forest after I'd risked everything to follow her.

"It doesn't matter what you saw," I snap. "Your magic is—"

I stop myself, but it's too late.

"Tainted?" Mathilde finishes for me, her expression unreadable. "*Dangerous*? Perhaps. But where was this concern when you offered your hand? It was only *after* you didn't like what I had to say that you questioned my gift."

Shame scalds my cheeks. "That's not—"

"If what's inside of you frightens you, it's no fault of mine." Mathilde waves me off. "Go on, Daughter of Millicent. Face your precious coven fire and claim your birthright. Don't pay any attention to a Wayward witch like me."

I deserve the bite in her tone, and that only fuels my frustration.

"Why did you stay here if you hate us so much?"

"Who said anything about hate?" Mathilde fingers her strand of teeth. "You're the one lashing out at an old witch."

The breeze picks up and I swear I can smell juniper again. That ancient chamber of my heart pulses. Would that I could carve it out.

"I'm sorry I bothered you," I say, turning on my heel and making a note to never repeat the mistake.

Cornelius calls behind me, his cry mixing with the memory of Mathilde's words.

If what's inside of you frightens you . . .

I clench my teeth. There's nothing inside of me.

Nothing at all, that voice whispers.

CHAPTER SEVEN

T HE DAY OF MY CEREMONY DAWNS BRIGHT AND CLOUDLESS, THE fair weather interpreted as a good omen by our Diviners— not that I can enjoy it. As is custom, I'm sequestered in my room for the day, to meditate and decide to which Ancient I'll make my vow. As if I have a real choice.

But at least I don't have to spend more time with the other Seconds. Dinner last night was particularly painful. It's not that the others are cruel, it's just that they know their places. They've always known. They've always been real Seconds, ready to face the flames. For years, I've waited for the same certainty to bloom inside me. Legend says the Ancients themselves were just twenty-three years old when they came together to forge the Bloodstones—which is why Ascensions typically occur at that age. But I'm not like them. I'm just . . . me.

They'll see right through you. That horrible voice again.

A chill snakes between my ribs. The steam from my bath has long since died away and the water is growing colder by the minute. At least it still smells nice, seasoned with purifying herbs and oils—rowan and rue and feverfew, a mixture that dyes the water as red as our cloaks. I cup a handful and let it fall back into the tub, the droplets creating ripples on the surface.

If I didn't know better, I'd say it was blood.

A soft knock startles me into the present. Aside from the Elementals who brought the bath, I've been alone. I can hear the other witches, though—the sound of music and laughter drifting in through my window, along with the unsettling crackle of the coven fire. Nettle, who has been batting at a feather that she dug out of my pillow, meows as Mother opens the door. She's already dressed for the ceremony. The green and black embroidered runes glimmer on her crimson cloak. And she's carrying a small slender box.

"What's that?" I ask.

"Get dressed and I'll show you." She sets the box on the bed. "You should have been ready ages ago."

I ignore her chiding and push myself up, stepping carefully over the rim of the tub as I reach for the drying cloth. Mother opens the shutters, amplifying the sound of celebration in the cloister and letting in the scent of sage and rosemary and the other herbs used to prime the coven fire. I tug my shift over my head, the only garment I'll wear to face the flames—as if I need any more reasons to feel exposed and vulnerable.

"This is for you," Mother says, handing me the box. "For your Ascension."

The corners of her lips lift, but the expression is awkward and stiff. Nothing like the smiles I remember from my years as a witchling. Nettle lopes over to investigate as I unlatch the lid of the box. Sunlight shimmers on the blade of a knife, its steel etched with the elegant lines of runes. Some of them I recognize—symbols for strength and swiftness.

"It's Dwarvian," Mother explains. "Which, as you know, makes it especially well suited for carrying our runes. And I enchanted it myself."

I lift the golden handle, set with glittering garnets and opals and citrines, their facets cold against my palm.

"It strikes true, should you need it," Mother goes on, pointing out a rune. "And it's also connected to your mirror. You'll use this knife to make your initial offering to the glass, then to wake it."

Offering. I picture the raven and its silvery eyes, its heart trapped inside Mother's mirror. A chill that has nothing to do with the bath shivers down my spine.

"Sacrifice, you mean. Whose heart do you suggest I give? Nettle's?"

Nettle growls. Mother glances at her. "That's not what I said."

"But you'd support it."

"No, believe it or not." Nettle evidently does not. She hisses, and Mother crosses her arms, her usual armor locking into place. "You *will* have to make an offering, Ayleth. That mirror is a priceless gift. You should be grateful it survived to be presented to you."

"You take it, then." I practically throw the knife back in the box and slam the lid closed. "That way, you can have another in your arsenal—better to spy on me."

An argument simmers behind Mother's eyes and I brace myself for her to lash back. What will she say this time? Blame me again for trying to run away? For not being there when Rhea was struck? Finally admit that she wishes it were me who died instead of my sister? Part of me wants exactly that. At least then we'd have some honesty between us.

"We'll discuss this later," Mother says instead. She points to a nearby stool. "Sit. I won't have you late for your own Ascension."

What would the illustrious Heirs think then? But I settle myself on the stool. Mother starts working a comb through my damp hair. A charged silence hums between us. It wasn't like this on Rhea's

Ascension day. I was just a witchling then, continually underfoot, but I recall Mother's laughter. The pride brightening her eyes as she braided Rhea's hair, threading it through with crimson blossoms. There are no flowers today. Only snarls and knots.

"Remember what I taught you." Mother yanks the comb through a stubborn tangle in my hair. I wince. "Stand tall as you face the flames. Make your vow firmly, as if Millicent herself stands in front of you."

If Millicent stood in front of me, I'd beg her for my sister back.

"And another thing." Mother starts a braid on one side of my head, taking no pains to be careful. I grit my teeth. "I don't want you speaking to that Wayward witch again. Not until you're more established. It sends the wrong message."

"Talking to—"

Comprehension jolts through my mind. The only way Mother would know that I spoke to Mathilde is if she'd been there—or been *watching*. She was employing that silver-eyed raven again. Fresh anger kindles behind my sternum. Is it not enough that she's controlled every hour of my life for the past seven years?

"I'm not a prisoner here," I snap. "I can speak to whomever I choose."

"You are my daughter." The hem of Mother's cloak swishes against the floor as she places herself in front of me. "Soon to be my Second—next in line to lead this coven. That position carries expectations."

"And showing kindness isn't one of them?"

"Like the kindness you showed to the *other* witch?" Mother asks, arching an eyebrow. It's been a long time since she's directly referenced Jacquetta, and I curse the wave of shame that rolls through me. "I warned you about *her* as well."

She had warned me. Everyone had, in their way. Jacquetta was a bad influence, they said, encouraging me to sneak off to the south tower or to the forest instead of attending lessons. She didn't respect the craft. Neither did her mother, Nerissa. The two of them never left offerings at the shrines to Millicent. By the end, it was rumored that Nerissa was secretly a Wayward. I didn't care about any of that. All I wanted was to laugh and dance and *live.* Look where it got me.

"That was seven years ago," I protest.

"Covens hold long memories." Mother leans closer. "Everything you do from this day on will be weighed and measured—your choices for inner council and patrol assignments. Even the witches who sit next to you at dinner. All of it will be judged."

My head pounds with the intricacies of this coven, a delicate web I'll only tear apart with my clumsiness. "I'm doing my best."

"And you must do better," Mother says simply. "Being a descendant of one of the Five requires sacrifice. Just as Millicent and the other Ancients sacrificed to create the Bloodstones and the Veil. Your sister understood that."

Yes, Rhea understood everything. Much as I loved her, sometimes I hate her as well—that I'll never live up to her memory.

"I'm *not* Rhea."

Mother looks at me, the years pulling taut between us. Despite all the evidence to the contrary, I hold my breath, desperate for her to say that of course I'm not Rhea. That I'm Ayleth, and that's exactly who she wants me to be.

You are my heart.

I was once. But now . . .

"I know you're not" is all Mother says instead.

The words dig between my bones, prying up a forgotten memory. Mother, wild-eyed with grief on the night Rhea died.

I've lost everything, she'd whispered, her shadow wavering in the candlelight, Rhea's iron-riddled body going cold under my hands. *Everything.*

Because that's what Rhea was—everything. And I'm nothing.

Without another word, Mother resumes her work on my hair. She pulls the braids even tighter than before, like she's trying to lash me down. My eyes sting, but I blink the tears away before they fall.

Just like Rhea would have done.

The coven fire is blazing by the time I reach the cloister, the late-autumn air thick with the scent of cedar-sweet smoke. Beneath the bruise-colored clouds, I spot flashes of the blood moon, like a welling puncture wound against the deepening twilight. Is it as bright as it was on the night of Rhea's Ascension?

How could it be? that awful voice asks.

I drag my focus away, taking in the mountains of food waiting on the trestle tables lining the cloister—roasted meats and stewed fruits, fresh bread and pies. Nettle lifts her nose and sniffs, then trots away to further inspect the offerings. But I can't even look at the feast without my stomach turning. Several witches call out their congratulations. The Seconds are huddled in their own group a short distance away. Della and a couple of the others wave. Sindony only watches, those depthless Diviner eyes seeming to peel back the layers of my skin.

"Ayleth!"

Eden emerges from the crowd, her crimson cloak flapping in the breeze. The courtyard is a sea of such cloaks tonight, which only heightens my sense of exposure as I stand among them in my simple white shift. I can't even hide behind my hair, secured as it is in an intricate—and excruciating—nest of braids on the crown of my head.

"Are you ready?" Eden loops her arm through mine.

Not in the least. "About as ready as any of us can be, with a fire looming in front of us."

She laughs. "As soon as you make your vow and the crimson smoke rises, you won't feel that way. An Ascension is like . . . coming alive. Everything is brighter and louder, but in a good way. It's hard to explain."

Rhea had described her own ceremony in a similar manner. I press my thumb against that place on my palm, below my left ring finger—Rhea's mark. More than anything, I wish my sister were here. The blaze of the coven fire sparks and snaps. In this moment, it doesn't appear as our sacred gathering space, where the flames will transform me into the witch I'm meant to be. It looks like a pyre. Smoke curls in sinister tentacles, reaching for me. My breathing shortens. I need to get away from here—from this.

"Eden . . ."

Don't tell her, that voice warns. *She'll see through you. She'll know.*

The truth tumbles out of me anyway. "I can't do it. I can't Ascend. I can't be Mother's Second. I'm not . . ."

Not Rhea. Not enough.

"Ayleth." Eden grasps my shoulders. "It's just nerves. That's normal, like Mother said."

"It's not," I insist, shaking my head so hard that I feel my pulse pound beneath my braids. A wild thought wings into my mind. "What if I just left? Would you come with me?"

"Leave? Ayleth, you can't be serious." Her horrified attention twitches over to the Seconds. "Does this have something to do with what Sindony said about you running away? We all know that was just a misunderstanding."

It wasn't, though, and I almost tell her that I'd *wanted* to run—to be somewhere, *someone* else. But the pleading look in Eden's lavender gaze smothers the confession. I've worn the same expression myself, when I used to sit in front of mirrors and beg my sister to appear to me. Eden needs me to be Rhea now—they all do. Painful clarity drums alongside my racing heart. I can never admit how I really feel, to Eden or anyone else. They wouldn't understand. And so I force my lips into a smile, hiding the parts of myself she does not wish to see.

"It's nothing to do with Sindony," I say. "You're right. It's just nerves."

The deep line of her brow instantly smooths.

"You'll be fine," she insists. "And I stashed away a plate of your favorites for after, plus a bottle of wine for each of us."

The wine, I will need. In fact, I could drink that entire bottle right now. Bells begin to chime, not those of the Sanctum, but the smaller ones used to clear the air and purify our space. Conversation dulls as the other witches gravitate toward the coven fire. Eden winks, then hurries after them, throwing me a final wave over her shoulder.

As I stand there alone, watching the coven gather beneath the red-tinged light of the blood moon, I can't help feeling that the fabric of my world is ripping apart. I would give anything to hold on to the fraying threads. But how can I?

There's nothing left for me to do but face the flames.

CHAPTER EIGHT

THE COVEN FIRE IS A BLAZE OF MOLTEN GOLD AGAINST THE INDIGO of twilight. For the final time, I stand outside the ring of crimson cloaks with those witches who have not yet Ascended. Nesta is among them, her eyebrows still somewhat singed from the fireroot incident. She waves at me and I muster a smile in return.

"Sisters." Mother steps out from her place in the circle.

The other Heirs, along with their Seconds, wait just behind her. My chest tightens at the prospect of making my offering in front of their hawklike attention.

"An Ascension is an important night for any witch," Mother goes on, the runes on her cloak glimmering as she spreads her arms wide. "It is the night she proves herself to the Spirits—honors the Ancients and their sacrifice. But tonight is even more than that. Tonight, we name a Second—a successor of Millicent herself."

Witches cheer and every nerve in my body tingles. Nettle, who has apparently lost interest in the food, nudges my ankles and gives me what I perceive to be a supportive trill. I'll accept all the help I can get.

"I need not describe how difficult times are for us," Mother goes on. "Covens burned. Witches lost. But we are a coven of survivors. And despite the mad king and his edict, despite this brutal war, we are *still here*. With each new power, we add strength. And with that strength, we will restore all that we have lost."

High above, the blood moon seems to shine brighter.

"Ayleth." Mother beckons. "Daughter. Heir of Millicent, one of the Five. The Spirits summon you forth."

This is it. No more hiding. Somehow, I compel my leaden limbs to propel me forward. The circle parts to allow me through, witches whispering their welcome. Their encouragement should bolster me, but it does the opposite. And it seems an eternity before I reach Mother, the jewel-handled knife of Ascension, one that has been passed down through centuries of witches, in her outstretched hands. It's the same blade Rhea held when it was her turn to face the flames. The rubies on its hilt glimmer in the firelight like freshly shed blood, and that place below my left ring finger tingles.

"Make your vow," Mother instructs. "Bind yourself to the Spirits and continue our line."

There's no gentleness in her words. It is the command of a High Witch to her charge. Of an Heir to her Second. I swallow, throat dry, and turn to the flames.

This close, the heat of the fire grazes my skin. Within the depths of the blaze, I imagine that I glimpse flashes of coal-bright eyes and grinning mouths. Black smoke billows and wreathes itself around my body, and I half expect it to wrap tighter. Squeeze until there's nothing left. Around me, the faces of the other Heirs and the Seconds swirl together, like the world itself is tilting on its axis.

Focus, I tell myself, heart slamming against my ribs. *Get it over with.*

A low note hums, the coven beginning its song to call the Spirits. The air thickens, carrying that metallic essence of magic. It's time.

My hand trembling, I dig the blade of the knife into the flesh of my palm. A slash of red blooms against the white of my skin. The fire whips back and forth, sparks dancing up toward the blood moon as the coven's song swells. My pulse thumps in time to its rhythm and, fighting the fear coiling in my chest, I extend my hand closer to the flames. The words of my vow, those I've recited hundreds of times at Mother's command, press against the back of my teeth. Blood leaks from my wound and tracks down my wrist. All I have to do is tilt my palm so that it falls into the fire. Speak the vow. And yet . . .

A cloud of smoke untangles itself from the tongues of flame. Not black smoke but *red*. I hesitate, confusion snarling my thoughts. What is that? It can't be crimson smoke. I haven't offered my blood yet. The nebulous shape shifts, elongating and morphing until it almost looks like . . . a *person*. The figure drifts nearer, shades of red and shadow. My entire body tenses. Is that a Spirit? No one warned me about seeing Spirits in the fire. The figure's features begin to sharpen and solidify. I can make out a long nose and a small mouth, almost like—*mine*.

Rhea.

The name drops into my mind like blood onto the fire. The scent of honeysuckle lingers beneath that of the burning wood and herbs. That spot on my left hand, where my sister carved our rune all those years ago, thrums.

She must reach. The mirror's words crackle beneath the snap of flame.

Is this what it meant? That I need to reach for Rhea? Pull her back from the Realm of the Spirits? I'm not going to waste time with second-guessing. Ignoring all logic and sense, I throw my hands into the fire, bracing myself for the searing pain of the flames licking my skin. It doesn't come. Instead, Rhea reaches *back*. Her hands, though nothing but smoke, lock around my own. I gasp at her strength, and at the life blooming on her skin. Color races over her fingers and up her wrists. How is this possible? I watched Rhea die. I stood by the pyre as we burned her body in a Ceremony of Blood and Ashes, salt stinging my lips. And yet she's here. I'm touching her. And I am *not* letting her go.

Driven by a primal impulse, I muster every ounce of my strength and pull. Rhea emerges several more inches from the flames. If she comes back, everything can be as it was before. I don't have to be Second. I don't have to die trying to forge another Bloodstone. Mother will stop hating me. I'll finally prove that I'm more than my mistakes. Perhaps the Spirits understand that I'm not meant to be named Millicent's successor. Perhaps they are returning Rhea to me, like they did with the Ancients, so that I don't ruin everything.

My sister's lips move, but I can't hear her.

"What is it?" I call.

She squeezes my hands tighter, and fire ignites in my veins.

It must be undone, her voice echoes in my skull, like it's coming down a long tunnel. *It must be undone.*

"What?" I shout over the roar of the flames. "What is *it?*"

Thunder cracks overhead, wrenching my attention away from my sister and toward the sky. Lightning rips a seam through the stars, headed straight for us. Witches scream, scattering as the jagged white blade lances the heart of the fire. Red-hot pain sears into my palms where I'm holding Rhea. An invisible force knocks me backward. I land hard on my shoulder, bellowing in fear and rage as I scramble to my feet, a single thought whipping in my mind.

Get Rhea. Get Rhea.

I'm too late. The flames have guttered out. Smoke curls in lazy tendrils from the blackened wood. And Rhea—Rhea is gone. Again.

"No!" I fall to my knees, scrabbling at the ashes in a delirious attempt to dig her out. "Rhea, I'm here! Come back!"

I cannot lose her twice. I *cannot.* I'll do anything to—

"What's going on?" Mother's voice stops me cold. It's only then that I register the whispers swarming around me. The other witches are huddled together, muttering and casting me furtive looks. And my palms *burn.*

Bewildered, I turn my hands over. My latent magic has already begun to knit together the small knife wound I carved into my flesh as part of the ceremony. But two new spots have appeared. Three crossed lines. Triangles, exact copies of the rune Rhea drew below my ring finger on the night before her own Ascension. Except, now I carry one on each of my hands.

"What are those?" Mother demands, pointing at the marks, which glow red with heat against my white skin.

I'm not sure. But I know where they came from. "It was *her.* Rhea."

Mother's face shades paler.

"Rhea?" another witch echoes. Selene. Her crimson cloak billows behind her as the crowd parts to allow her through. "Ayleth, are you certain? Your sister is beyond the Veil."

They hadn't seen her, then. She'd appeared only to me.

"I know what I saw," I insist. "She was there. I held her hands."

Witches begin to murmur. One word shivers in the night.

Malum.

Cold leaches through my blood. "No. It wasn't—"

"You're tired," Mother rushes to interrupt. "The strain of the day has overwhelmed you. You'll rest now. Whatever happened, we will mend it."

She drags me to my feet, and I'm too stunned to resist.

"Your daughter didn't offer her blood," Selene calls. "She didn't make her vow."

"She still has time to do so," Mother replies, clipped, as she steers me away.

My senses finally come back to me at the crushing pressure of her grip. "Let go of me! I'm not a witchling."

"Then what are you?" Mother flings me away as soon as we're out of earshot. "Inventing outrageous stories about seeing dead witches."

Fury balls in my chest. "Rhea is your daughter. I saw her. I held her hands. I almost—"

A sharp pain cracks across my cheek. It takes me a moment to register that Mother struck me. She's never struck me before. She might be cold and demanding, but never violent. I touch my throbbing face, dazed.

"How could you be so careless?" Mother seethes. "In front of *everyone*?"

Tears sting in my eyes, and I hate myself for them. Hate that I'm not stronger.

"I *saw* Rhea" is all I can manage. "She wanted to come back."

Mother steps closer. "Have I taught you nothing? The Veil is thinning. Malum is seeping into the realm again. Whatever you saw was not your sister."

Malum. The word is laced with the low rumble of thunder.

"No," I insist, refusing to believe it. "It was Rhea."

"And do you not believe that a force fueled by Malum could disguise itself?" Mother asks. "That it could use your own memories against you?"

Like the village that was driven mad and walked into the sea. The old tale slinks through my mind. Had the figure been Rhea? Or something more sinister? The shadows of the night swirl and thicken.

"This is why you're marked." Mother gestures at my hands, disgusted. "You meddled with the Veil. You could have brought something out. It could have touched you."

Cold rain seeps through the thin fabric of my shift. And I'm not entirely sure, but I think I might feel a nudge against the inner side of my left ribs—like something is *there*. No—I'm imagining things. Letting Mother dictate my thoughts.

"And what was I supposed to do?" I demand. "Leave her? You wouldn't have. If you'd seen Rhea, you would have reached for her, no matter what she might have been."

"Don't be ridiculous."

"It's the truth," I barrel on. "I remember the night she died. You said you lost everything. Would you have said the same if *I* was the one who was struck by the Hunt's arrow? If you could have traded us that night, would you have?"

Lightning flashes.

Heavy silence follows, broken only by the falling rain. Oily despair settles in my stomach like silt, thicker with each moment that Mother fails to answer. The truth shouldn't come as a surprise, but it hollows me out all the same.

"Go to your chamber," Mother says at last. "I will deal with this. The blood moon lasts another night. There's nothing that says you can't make your offering tomorrow, or at the next rising. And you will, Ayleth. You will *fix* this."

With that, she turns and stalks off. I watch her go, wishing that Rhea had pulled me into the coven fire with her, even if it would have burned me to ash.

Fix this. Mother's words resonate in my ears.

For a brief, shining moment, I thought I could. If I'd managed to drag Rhea out of the fire, no one would—

An idea hits with the next clap of thunder: Rhea came to me once. Perhaps she'll do so again.

She must reach, the mirror said.

And that's precisely what I'm going to do.

Chapter Nine

LIGHTNING GLAZES THE SHELVES OF THE LIBRARY IN WHITE. Nettle pads silently along beside me, the glow of my candle cutting through the gloom. As a witchling, I spent hours in this chamber. It was here that I learned about the Ancients, like Millicent, and how they'd sacrificed their latent magic to forge the Bloodstones and the Veil. Here where I memorized spells and rituals until my brain couldn't hold any more. It's time to make that knowledge count for something.

Nettle keeps close as I make my way toward the section in the back, an area I've visited only once before.

Like summons like, Mother warned when she showed me the ancient books. *Dark intents reap dark rewards.*

A caution against carelessness with our magic. A hex or curse returns to a Caster threefold. A storm conjured in rage falls worst upon the Elemental. A poison brewed for vengeance sickens the Potioner's soul.

Tonight, I don't care what price I pay. I just want Rhea back.

As thunder crashes against the Sanctum, I pull out one of the heavy grimoires, my eyes hungrily scanning through spells that call for ingredients such as nightshade and mandrake picked under the light of a full moon. Grave dirt and shards of bone. Lightning illuminates a rendering of a bloody heart, and I shiver. What am I even looking for? A spell to pull a Spirit from the Veil? To resurrect the dead? Even if I did find something, could I manage to cast such a spell? I've never—

Nettle trills a warning, her golden gaze pinned on a spot in the shadows. Shadows that, to my horror, appear to be creeping closer, like a sinister tide.

It could have touched you, Mother's words replay in my mind.

Again, I sense a nudge—a slight pressure against the inner side of my left ribs. *It's your imagination,* I repeat. Or I'm losing my sanity. But . . . what if I'm not? I study the triangles on my hands, Rhea's marks. They have to mean something. And I've always wondered if we were connected through the Veil. Could the feeling inside me be . . .

"Rhea?" I call, hesitant. "Is that you?"

The shadows slink nearer. A figure emerges from the darkness. I swear I detect a hint of honeysuckle wafting around me.

"Rhea?"

"Afraid not."

A pair of rheumy eyes shine like polished stones in the light of my candle. Mathilde. I let out a short breath, disappointed and suddenly irritated—but more at myself than at the other witch. "What are you doing in here?"

"Am I not allowed to visit the library?" she asks archly. "I assume that's where we are. I smell books . . . and a wet cat."

Nettle meows, offended.

"Sorry," I say, chiding myself for being rude again. "I assumed everyone was in the dining hall after the feast got rained out."

"I went there, but it didn't strike me as much of a party. Not with all the muttering and whispering. Did something happen?"

Something. I could almost laugh. "Were you not at the Ascension?"

She cackles. "A Wayward witch attending an Ascension? I'd rather not. Don't take it personally, mind."

That's right. I forgot that Mathilde wouldn't have been invited—and that she wouldn't have even wanted to join us. At first, I shy away from confessing the truth of what occurred. But what's the point of keeping it back? Everyone is talking about it—my second failure.

"Here." I nudge Mathilde's hand with my own. "I'm sure you can see for yourself."

Mathilde grips my palm the way she did in the garden, her strong fingers kneading along my knuckles. When she finds the spot below my ring finger, she pauses. "Well, well. That is interesting. Do you know where it came from?"

My dead sister. Thunder rolls through the room. "You wouldn't believe me."

"Yes, you're right." She shrugs. "I'm three hundred years old, and a Wayward witch. There's a narrow limit to my sphere of belief."

I scowl at her, the stubborn witch. Still, a thought itches in my mind. Mathilde isn't bound by the same rules as the covens. Much as I'm suspicious of her magic, her reading in the garden was eerily accurate. Lightning flares, shining white against the string of teeth hanging from her belt—a row of macabre pearls.

"Do you really want to know?" I ask.

"I'm still here, aren't I?"

Nettle winds herself around Mathilde's ankles, which I take to mean that my cat trusts her. That settles it, I suppose. In any case, I'm tired of holding back secrets. Tired, and cold. I haven't changed from my rain-soaked shift. There's mud drying on my feet and my braids are plastered to my head. I find a chair and Nettle leaps into my lap.

"I saw my sister," I begin at last. "In the flames."

Mathilde absorbs that information, but she doesn't seem suspicious or repulsed, as the rest of the coven had been. "Her Spirit appeared to you?"

"It was more than that." I hold Nettle tighter. "I reached for her. I *felt* her. I started pulling her out of the fire, but—"

Thunder cracks again, cutting me off.

"You . . . reached beyond the Veil?" Mathilde asks, her expression unreadable.

"I don't know what I did," I admit. "Mother said it wasn't Rhea. That the vision was a manifestation of Malum. But I know it was my sister."

Wood creaks as Mathilde feels her way to a chair and sits down. "It might have been. Spirits can be lured to the border of our world, given the proper motivation."

It must be undone.

What did Rhea mean by that? I turn my palms up and trace the three crossed lines below my ring fingers. They're not glowing anymore—just creases, like my Fate and Life lines. Was Rhea trying to tell me that her own *death* must be undone?

"I think she wanted me to bring her back."

"Ayleth." Mathilde fusses with her strand of teeth. "I'm sure I don't have to explain how dangerous it is to meddle with what lies beyond the Veil, Spirits or otherwise."

Malum. Wind whistles outside.

"But you're Wayward," I argue. "That means you don't care about the Veil."

"Oh, are you an expert on Wayward witches now?" she asks, crossing her arms. "Just because I didn't make a vow to one of your Ancients doesn't mean I don't respect the craft. I didn't live to see three centuries by being reckless, and neither will you."

Thunder rattles the window casements.

"I don't care what happens to me. I have to get Rhea back. Do you know how?"

"I can see where your cat gets her stubbornness."

Nettle twitches her tail, proud. I wait. Either Mathilde will tell me how to summon Rhea, or she won't. And if she doesn't, I'm no worse off than I was before.

Eventually, the elder witch sighs. "I don't know any more than you do. Witch souls need anchors. We carry that anchor with us in life in the form of our latent magic. Rhea's magic is expended. End of story."

The wheels of my mind work. "It's not the end, though. Not if she had another anchor."

"Theoretically," Mathilde allows. "But you would need an *enormous* amount of power to hold her here. And your mother is right. You don't know that what you saw in the flames was your sister. It could just as well have been Malum, taking advantage of the thinning of the Veil. It could have been seeking its own source of power—*you.*"

It might have touched you. Mother's words skim the curves of my skull.

The shadows of the room swell and lengthen. Again, I might feel a tremble behind my left ribs. I ignore it. "No. It was Rhea."

Mathilde grumbles under her breath. "All right, fine. It was your sister. Like I said, if you want to keep her here, you'd have to find the proper anchor."

"Like what?"

"Don't ask me." Mathilde shrugs. "I'm just a Wayward witch—not an Ancient."

And it *would* require a power like an Ancient's. My attention travels to a portrait above the hearth, one depicting Millicent in all her glory. This is the only image of our ancestress that Mother didn't order removed when we adopted our disguise. I must have studied it a thousand times over the years, tracing the constellations on her starry robes and wondering how I could possibly be related to such a witch.

Another flare of lightning washes the room, catching on the red jewel of Millicent's Bloodstone, glimmering on her first finger. The stone itself is a unique, roughhewn oval, flecked with bits of green and black. Our cloaks are designed to match the color, in honor of the Ancients. Millicent died for that stone—drained every drop of her latent magic. And a rush of anger bubbles up inside me. If the Spirits saw fit to bring *her* back from the dead, why not Rhea? Why can't my sister have her latent magic restored when—

A thought lands in my mind with the next boom of thunder.

"The Bloodstones," I whisper.

"What about them?" Mathilde asks.

"They're living vessels. And they contain the latent magic of the Ancients. One of them would be enough to anchor Rhea, wouldn't it?"

Mathilde hesitates, rubbing the strand of teeth hanging from her waist. "Probably. But last I checked, those stones were stolen at the start of the war. Also, they're a bit busy holding the Veil, are they not? How exactly do you plan to use one for your sister?"

I frown at her point. But if the Bloodstones are as powerful as they're said to be, they could hold Rhea *and* the Veil. Couldn't they? I stare at the portrait, at the Bloodstone, like a tiny beating heart in and of itself. A heart Rhea needs.

Nettle complains as I rise and cross to the shelves, hunting for another book, one that contains dozens of maps of Riven. I used to explore them for hours, curious as to what lay beyond our walls. The well-worn volume practically falls open to the section I need. The White City sprawls across two full pages, streets webbing like veins through the labyrinth of buildings and homes. And there, on a mountain overlooking it all, is the palace itself. Home of the mad king, where the Bloodstones were taken.

Wind whistles through the cracks in the Sanctum.

"I could go to the palace," I say.

"And do what?" Mathilde asks, gesturing vaguely. "Stroll into the throne room and request those stones back? Have you lost your mind, young witch?"

Probably. "The stones are there. They have to be. The Veil would have fallen if they were destroyed."

"Perhaps," Mathilde allows. "But the White City is littered with the bones of witches far more powerful than you."

She's right. I don't possess any ability beyond my latent magic, and even that is less than inspiring. I frown, thumbing the edge of the map. My attention falls on a bright silver patch nestled inside the city—the Sanctum.

"Longest Night," I mutter, the meager threads of a plan weaving themselves together. "The High Priest sent an invitation for Sisters to receive his blessing at the royal Sanctum. It won't get me into the palace, but it will get me into the city."

"Oh, yes, that sounds like fun," Mathilde replies dryly. "What about the fact that you don't have the faintest idea where those stones might be hidden? And you don't even know if the stones *would* anchor your sister."

A hundred other similar doubts and questions churn in my mind. This plan is reckless, and I'll almost certainly die in the attempt. But insane determination is all I have left.

"I have to try."

"And if you never come back?" Mathilde presses. "This is your home."

Home. Pain knocks against my sternum. The last years here have been difficult, but I don't hate Stonehaven. I love Eden and Willa and all the rest. I'd even love Mother, if she'd let me. But they'd all seen what happened tonight. More important, I'd seen *them*, the horror and suspicion etched on their faces at my Ascension. Covens hold long memories, Mother warned. They won't forget my failed ceremony—and they haven't forgotten Rhea. She's the Second and Heir this coven needs. This isn't my home anymore, not without my sister. If I bring her back, I can finally set things right. Prove that I'm worth more than my poor decisions.

"I'm going," I say. "There's nothing else for me here. Not after tonight."

Mathilde sighs, exasperated. "Fine. Get yourself killed if it suits you. But take Cornelius, at least."

"You want me to take your *crow*?"

"He knows the way to the White City—unless a guide doesn't interest you."

Her lips quirk up at my silence. Crow or not, I'd be daft to refuse the help. Even so, I can't help but recall the line of crows from the south tower. Seven of them, all watching me.

A curse, that voice whispers. I shove it down.

"How will I find him?"

"I'll tell him to find you." Mathilde waves me off. "And he'll be able to bring you back along the way—should you come to your senses."

But I won't be coming back. Not alone, anyway. I stare out the window, just able to glimpse my own distorted reflection in the sheets of rain sluicing down the glass. For an instant, it's as though Rhea herself is looking back at me. I hope she is—that my sister knows that I'm coming for her.

I'll either drag her through the Veil, or I'll burn trying.

CHAPTER TEN

R AIN SOAKS ME IN SECONDS AS I SPRINT ACROSS THE COURTYARD and into the small stable. Nettle yowls her displeasure, shaking her wet paws and sulking.

"You'd best get used to it," I tell her. "It's a long way to the White Palace."

She ignores me, grooming herself. The fury of the storm roused the horses, their eyes huge and watchful as I take stock of the array of weapons hanging on the far wall. It's been years since I've hunted, but I have to take *something* to keep me from starving. I select the lightest bow and strap it to my back. My satchel is already bulging with as much food and as many spare clothes as I could fit. The knife Mother gifted me, however, I've left behind. The open box is sitting on my bed, the only message I've left for her. Let her interpret it as she will.

A squawk startles me out of my thoughts. I glance up to discover a black bird perched in the eaves, one I recognize from the cloister.

"Cornelius?" I venture.

The creature flaps lower, settling on a stall door and earning an irritated chuff from the horse inside. But Cornelius isn't bothered.

He tilts his head at me, obsidian eyes expectant. Had Mathilde already communicated with him?

"You're . . . coming with us?" Another squawk, sharp enough to pass for impatience. Wonderful—it's a crow *and* it has opinions. "All right, then. Let's go."

Nettle meows at Cornelius as the bird follows us to the door. He'll be wise to stay out of my cat's reach. I pull up my hood, planning my escape route. There's no hope of raising the portcullis, so the side entrance is my best bet. Through the sheets of rain, I'm barely able to discern the shapes of the witches in the guard towers. If they catch me, they'll march me straight to Mother. But I don't let myself think about that.

After the next flash of lightning dims, I make a break for it, skirting the walls and ducking behind whatever shelter I find. By the time I reach the door, my heart is pounding, and I'm certain that the sentries have spotted me. But aside from the howling wind, the night is quiet—no bells or shouting from the guard towers. Water drips from the edge of my hood. I lift the bolt on the side door and hurry through it, fumbling my way toward the forest.

The woods at night are transformed into a scene from Willa's stories. The trees are like towering trolls, bending and reaching for me in the raging storm. Silver eyes seem to leer at me in the black. Rain lashes against my face, blinding me to the point that I'm tripping over roots and stumbling over fallen logs. Low-hanging branches claw at my skin and snag my cloak. I'm scratched and sore and terrified by the time I reach the stream, its current rushing in a frenzy.

Was it just a few days ago that Eden and I raced here? It feels like a hundred years have passed since then. Lightning forks a jagged spear across the sky. For what might be the last time, I turn in the direction of the Sanctum. What will happen in the morning, when everyone discovers that Mother's only surviving Second has vanished—again?

It doesn't matter, I tell myself, swallowing the lump in throat. They never wanted me anyway. Not really. They want Rhea. And I'm going to bring my sister home. Then everything will be fixed, the gaping holes of my failures knitted together as if they'd never been.

It must be undone. Rhea's words from the flames loop through my mind, and I clench my fists against the triangles stamped into my palms. Rhea's marks. *Our* marks.

"I'm coming for you," I whisper, my voice buried under the storm.

Thunder booms, and Cornelius squawks, annoyed. There's no turning back now. Shutting down every screaming instinct, I inhale a breath and leap over the stream. The cold shock of breaking through the wards hits me like shards of glass. But I don't let myself stop, or even think about what I've done. Cornelius's cry resonates beneath the wrath of the storm, and I follow after the barely perceptible blur of his body, leaving Stonehaven and the witch I used to be behind me.

Two days later, I realize what a fool I am.

Everything hurts. Even the heightened healing ability of my latent magic fails to ease the strain of our endless hours of travel. Sleeping on cold, wet ground is far more uncomfortable than I ever imagined it would be. My muscles throb and complain at every slight movement. My feet ache and my stomach is continually growling, demanding more food to keep up with the physical exertion of the journey.

Cornelius caws from where he perches on a nearby branch, as if to herd me along.

"You have wings. I don't," I grouse back at him.

He doesn't have to slog through freezing river crossings or sink ankle-deep in mud on impassible roads. In fact, sometimes I suspect that damn bird is routing the most difficult course, just to spite me.

The crow clacks his beak in what is unmistakably amusement. I'm starting to despise that creature. Nettle trills, evidently agreeing. My stomach rumbles again and I dig through my satchel for what's left of my rations. I'm already down to my final crusts of bread.

"We're stopping here," I announce. "I have to hunt. And it will be dark soon."

I'm still not sure how much the bird can understand me, but he ruffles his wings and turns his back, unimpressed.

"Were you this rude to Mathilde?"

Cornelius declines to reply.

Feckless creature. I dump my satchel, unstrap my bow from my back, and set off into the trees, Nettle loping alongside me. My last hunt was before Rhea died, when I still enjoyed the freedom of traipsing after the Elementals on their excursions. Back then, I was a decent enough shot to nab a few grouse or other small game. My stomach groans at the prospect of a real dinner. Perhaps I'll be lucky enough to flush out a rabbit or even—

Wind pushes through the trees. The bare branches clack together, the hollow sound like fragile bones creaking. Nettle's hackles raise, and she drops into a predatory crouch, her golden eyes trained on a spot behind me.

Someone's there.

Every muscle in my body tenses. Too many witches arrived at Stonehaven with stories about what can happen to women alone in the woods. My lessons with the Elementals come crashing back to me. Gripping my bow, I slowly turn, so as not to startle the threat. At first, I don't see anything—just trees and brush. Still, I sense an *otherness*.

The sun is setting, lengthening the shadows of the forest. A cold breeze gusts through the clearing, stirring my skirts and carrying the faint scent of . . . *honeysuckle*?

Ayleth, I swear I hear. *Ayleth*.

"Rhea?" I whisper.

Is it my sister? Or is it...something *else*? That faint pressure nudges behind my left ribs. *It's not real,* I tell myself. It can't be.

A dark shape springs out of the trees. I shriek, scrabbling for an arrow. Nettle hisses and pounces, but the intruder isn't a manifestation released from beyond the Veil. Instead, a Spirits-damned *raven* lands nearby. It tosses its head up and emits a clicking sound through its beak, thoroughly pleased with itself for causing such disruption.

"Wretched animal," I mutter, snatching up a stone to scare the bird off.

Dying sunlight flashes in its eyes. Eyes, I register, that aren't black, but *silver.* Like twin mirrors. Unwelcome recognition ripples down my spine. This isn't an ordinary raven. It's Mother's creature.

"Shit."

The bird squawks, as if in confirmation. It's carrying some message, no doubt. All ravens can be used for such communication between witches. Our magic makes certain that they always locate their intended recipient. Well—I have no interest in hearing whatever Mother has to say. I shoulder my bow and stalk down the path. The raven follows, flitting from branch to branch. I glare at it and quicken my pace, but the raven zigzags in front of me, forcing me to pull up short.

"For Spirits' sake."

Maybe I should just shoot it. Then again, I doubt I'd be lucky enough that it would die—which means the bird would simply keep following me. Given what I know of its mistress, the silver-eyed menace will probably start harassing me in my sleep.

"Fine," I snap, yanking my knife from my belt and pricking my finger. Blood wells and I extend my hand. The raven flaps to my wrist and pecks at the wound. An instant later, those unsettling eyes glow crimson, like embers. When the raven opens its beak again, a too-familiar voice fills the clearing.

Scry. Immediately.
Mother.

If I were a braver witch, I would simply send the raven on its way. Better yet, send it back with a reply so scathing that Mother would never dispatch another. But I know Mother. She'll keep sending her minion after me, then enlist another if I ignore it. Soon, I'll have a whole conspiracy tailing me before I reach the White City, and then what? I roll my shoulders back. Better to get this conversation over with.

We passed a stream a short while ago, and I trudge in that direction. Ravens can only carry one-sided messages, so enchanted mirrors are the preferred method of direct communication between witches. In the absence of a mirror, water will achieve a similar end. It's a small kind of magic, one even a witch like me can accomplish. Nettle trots ahead as I locate the stream and kneel at its edge. My cat grumbles, twitching her tail.

"I'm not thrilled about it either," I tell her, unsheathing my knife and slicing the skin of my palm. "*Departed sisters, hear my plea. Let this stream a vessel be. Water churn and current flow, the will of my Mother I would know.*"

My blood drips into the silver ribbon of the water, blooming like roses before the current ferries my summons away. For a few moments, I let myself hope that it won't work. Perhaps I'm even less gifted than I assumed, or Mother is busy, or—

The air begins to hum with the metallic charge of magic. Wonderful. Wind moans through the trees, low and sinister. Wisps of scarlet steam curl from the surface of the water. When it clears, Mother's face stares back at me.

"Where *are* you?" she demands. Even through the watery barrier, I sense her fury.

That part of me that has always folded beneath Mother's anger shrinks. But I force myself to sit up straighter, ignoring how hungry I am, or how much I miss my warm bed at Stonehaven. "I'm not coming back. Not yet."

After my botched Ascension, I assume it's better *not* to tell her where I'm going or what I plan to do. She'd probably send a party of witches to drag me home.

Just like last time, that voice reminds me.

"This is ridiculous," Mother snaps. "The entire coven is in an up-roar. You can't just leave, Ayleth. You're—"

"What am I?" I all but shout. "I'm not your Second. I'm not even Ascended. I'm—"

Nothing.

The word rips a hole through me. Even more painful is Mother's answering silence.

"We will mend this," she continues at last. "There's still time for you to Ascend. Whether it's now, or even in a few more years. There's nothing wrong with a delayed Ascension. Selene and the other Heirs believe—"

The mention of Selene only kindles fresh fire in my blood. "Why do you care what the other Heirs believe? They don't respect your opinion. I know about the spell to forge new Bloodstones. They decided to attempt it without even consulting you."

I can likely count on a single hand the number of times I've witnessed genuine surprise in Mother's expression. This is one of them. A strange sense of power builds at having caught her off guard. Wind rattles the branches, carrying the call of a crow.

"Then you understand," Mother says, regaining her composure, "how important it is for you to return."

"So I can participate in a spell that will kill me?"

"You don't know that it will," Mother argues, but she sounds like she's attempting to convince herself as well as me. "The Spirits—"

"Have shown no interest in me at all," I interrupt. "Why should they gift me with power in death, if they won't when I'm alive?"

"Your power will come," she insists, a refrain that gets feebler every time I hear it. "But not if you're off—wherever you are. You belong *here.*"

No, I don't. Not like this. I clench my fists against Rhea's marks and a question rises up, thorny and unwelcome. But I need to hear the answer.

"If I were any other witch, would you be scrying with me right now?" I ask. "Would you even care that I left?"

Mother huffs. "Must everything be such a production? Your sister never—"

I am so *tired* of this.

"No, Rhea never made any mistakes, did she? But I'm not her." I hardly know where the words come from, but I don't fight them down. "Say that you want me to come home for me, not because of my position, and I will. Tell me that you forgive me for leaving after the raid—that you'll never mention it again—and I'll start back right now."

Silence again. An owl hoots in the distance, low and knowing.

"You are a descendant of Millicent," Mother replies. I wait, expecting more, but that's apparently all the answer I'll receive.

Emotion tightens in my chest, and I hate myself for feeling it. Haven't I learned Mother's priorities by now? "That's what I thought."

"Ayleth—"

But I'm done with her. Done with all of it. "Don't worry, Mother. Soon enough, I won't be your problem anymore. You'll have everything you wanted."

And after tonight, I know it isn't me.

PART II

The realm of Riven upholds its name. Blight poisons the land and petty squabbles splinter the ranks of the nobility. War remains a constant threat. And then there is Malum. Shadow creatures stalk the night. Plague sweeps through our borders. Some even claim that Malum is what dried up the former royal line—that the old king was driven mad by it. It is a curse, they say, one that will gnaw at our realm until there is nothing left.

But if there is a curse, I intend to break it. And it might be the unlikeliest of allies who can help me do so—the witches.

My council will not hear of it. Witches are evil. They're responsible for Malum. But I am not so certain. And if the witches could banish that malevolent force, this realm would at last be healed.

But could the people look past their fear and understand the benefits of such an alliance? Today, perhaps not. But if Malum were to recede . . . If witches and mortals could achieve such a miracle together . . .

Riven could be reborn—a new world. One that would never be torn apart.

—*From the private writings of Braxos, White King,*
date unknown

CHAPTER ELEVEN

THE WHITE CITY GLOWS GOLD IN THE DAWN.

The sprawling ramble of roofs and streets and buildings spreads below me, the scene like someone breathed life into the ink and paper of the map at Stonehaven. It all seems too huge to be real, like I'm standing in front of Mother's mirror and glimpsing another world. Even the White Palace itself, perched on its mountain above the main city, appears as a dragon from one of Willa's stories, guarding its treasure.

The entire journey has seemed spun from Willa's tales. Over the span of a couple of weeks, Cornelius has guided us along the shores of mirrorlike lakes and around craggy mountain ranges. Given that I've spent my entire life within Stonehaven's borders, such sights were as terrifying as they were wondrous. Was one of the lakes, with its sapphire-blue water, the same place where Isolde, the first Elemental, forged enchanted glass? Did Sorcha, the first Blessed, work her magic on a grove of trees so enormous that they could have swallowed half of Stonehaven? Did Millicent journey along these paths, our footsteps crossing through the centuries? What would she think of her descendant?

It's no mystery what Mother thinks. I expected her to dispatch that silver-eyed fiend again, or perhaps a party of Elementals to drag me home, like last time. But the miles and days stretched on and, aside from Nettle and that obstinate crow, I remained alone. After the years I endured suffocating under Mother's demands, I assumed her absence would come as a breath of fresh air. Instead, I feel . . . hollow. Unmoored, without the tether of my coven.

None of the others at Stonehaven have attempted to make contact with me—not even Eden. Perhaps, given the disaster of my Ascension, she doesn't want to be associated with a witch like me. A failure. Or perhaps Mother told the coven that I'm dead. Did they already burn my cloak in a Ceremony of Blood and Ashes? Or have they merely swept me away, erased all trace of my existence, like Mother did with Rhea's room? Am I no more than the furniture and books and clothes, packed up and stored in a drafty attic because they're no longer wanted?

Cornelius caws, bringing me back into the present. A breeze wafts around me, one distinctly colder than those at Stonehaven. It's no surprise, given that we've traveled so far north. Frost glazes the trees, the ice sparkling in the sunlight.

"I suppose this is where I leave you?" I ask the crow, rubbing my arms for warmth.

He flares his wings in what I interpret as confirmation. Unexpected sadness balloons in my chest. The crow was a stubborn creature—and rude—but I'm accustomed to his company.

"Well," I say, adjusting my satchel, "give my thanks to Mathilde."

Cornelius chuffs and clacks his beak. Nettle meows, watching him hungrily. The bird takes the hint. He lifts into the air, circles once, and then soars off in the other direction.

As I watch the black splotch of his body disappear over the trees, I realize just how alone I am now. Cornelius was my last link to Stonehaven. My final bit of help before facing the rest of this mad plan on my own. On the side of the mountain above the city, I can just discern a path, like a dark vein through the woods, tracking all the way up to where the palace waits. Its dozens of turrets glint like spears in the rising sun.

Mathilde's words resurface beneath the whistle of the wind: *The streets of the White City are littered with the bones of witches.*

My bones will likely soon join them. Fear licks at my insides and I turn my palms up, studying the faint triangles etched below my ring fingers. *Rhea's* runes—ours.

No matter how distant we may become, we'll always find our way back to each other, she'd said.

It's true—I know that now. Not even the Veil can keep us apart.

Even so, that same premonition from the night of my Ascension tugs at me. There's a rip in the fabric of my world. A line approaching, one that cannot be uncrossed. A single question pulses alongside the thrumming anxiety in my chest.

What will be left of me on the other side of it?

Just keep your eyes down, I instruct myself as the gates to the White City loom ahead. *Don't give them any reason to suspect you.*

Easier said than done. But I've journeyed too far to give up. Shaking out my nerves, I file in with the line of people heading toward the entrance, repeating my scraps of a plan under my breath like a spell.

"Get through the gates. Hide. Find a way into the White Palace. *Don't* die."

Someone jostles my shoulder and I flinch. Cornelius had been careful to steer us around any towns or villages, so I'm still unaccustomed to mortals. Especially the men, who are almost shockingly large and intimidating. Male witches exist, of course, but they're exceedingly rare. I've never heard of one living in Stonehaven, even before the war. Witches usually visit mortal lovers who reside outside the coven, or they cast a glamour to disguise themselves and attract a coupling partner, which is how most witchlings are conceived these days. Apparently, I've inadvertently cast such an attraction spell, for a man leers down at me from where he drives his wagon. Nettle hisses in return. I tug my hood down and navigate deeper into the crowd.

At long last, the gates are within reach. My hands tremble as I approach one of the armored guards. He's a smaller man, with light-brown skin and a rounded face. His thick eyebrows draw together beneath his helmet as he looks me up and down. I shrink against the weight of his attention, reminding myself that I appear just like the other mortal women. There's no reason for him to assume I'm anything else.

"Present your business." He sighs and holds out his hand, clearly expecting me to place something in it. But what?

"I'm . . . here for Longest Night," I fumble.

He barks a laugh. "You and everyone else. But you can't just—" His attention pauses on the front of my dress and his expression softens. "Ah. A Sister, are you?"

Thank the Spirits I hadn't changed out of my uniform. I nod furiously. "Yes. I am."

"Why didn't you say? Go on then." The guard waves me through. "Follow the main road until it turns right. Can't miss the Sanctum from there. And take caution, mind. People are feeling *festive.*"

I'm not sure what he means, but I won't waste time by asking questions. Nettle and I hurry off before the man can think better of it. I don't get far. As soon as I step through the city gates, all thoughts of the guard, or my plan, or anything else, are instantly smashed by a wall of noise and activity. By the Spirits, there are so many *people.*

Some are richly dressed, riding about in elaborate carriages, their wide wheels clattering down the streets. Those in plainer clothes or uniforms weave their way on foot between the closely packed buildings. On either side of us, merchants display racks of ribbons or chests of baubles. Women call out from the street corners, selling white winter roses with blooms the size of my fist. Enormous windows display towers of pastries or gowns in shades I never believed possible, bedecked in feathers and jewels and impeccable embroidery. A sweet-spicy scent permeates the air. *Food.* Nettle meows, her tail twitching as she catches sight of a rack of roasted turkey legs waiting in a stall a short distance away.

Hunger gnaws at my insides. It's been weeks since I've eaten anything better than scorched grouse or dry rabbit. Still, while I may not comprehend much regarding mortal life, I know about coin. And coin is not something I currently possess. The merchant in the food stall turns away to assist another person. The turkey legs glisten with juice.

"Do you think you can cause a distraction?" I ask Nettle, who blinks at me as though she'd been waiting for me to suggest such a plan.

Giving a last swish of her tail, Nettle trots over and leaps onto the food stall's counter, then begins batting items onto the ground. The merchant yells and attempts to shoo away my cat, but Nettle deftly evades his attacks, continuing to wreak havoc. Seizing my chance, I rush forward, focus pinned on the closest turkey leg. Just a few more steps and then—

Several bodies slam into mine. I yelp, toppling backward. Pain shoots up my hip as I hit the cobblestones, and I utter a curse as a pack of children stampede around me, laughing.

"Easy there." A hand grips my elbow.

I instinctively jolt at the contact and wrench my arm free.

"Meant no offense," the person says. "You looked like you could use the help."

It's a woman. She has deep-brown skin and kind hazel eyes. Wisps of her gray hair peek out from her starched cap. And she's smiling at me—like I'm just another person.

Because that's what she thinks you are, I tell myself. *Don't make a scene.*

"Thank you," I say to the woman awkwardly as I get to my feet and brush off my clothes.

"Don't mind them." She jerks her thumb in the direction of the children. "They're just excited. It's not often that we get a traveling group of players. Come, how about you watch their show with me?"

"Oh, I'm afraid I have to . . ."

The rest falls away as I see that the merchant has finally managed to fend Nettle off and is now closing up his stall. So much for a turkey leg.

"Hungry, are you?" The woman laughs knowingly and fishes something out of her pocket. "Here, I brought enough for two."

She offers me an apple. Fruit is not nearly enough to satisfy my appetite, but my mouth waters at the thought of its tart juice.

"I have no coin," I tell her.

"None needed." The woman presses the apple into my hands. "You can pay me with the company."

I start to object again—I don't have time to waste—but the woman steers me over to where a group of people are surrounding a wooden platform. Others peel themselves away from their activities to join the crowd. Nettle meows, having returned from her ruined mission, and blinks up at me in what I expect is reproach.

"Sorry," I mutter, feeling a bit guilty as I bite into the apple. It might not be a turkey leg, but it's a feast compared to stringy grouse.

At the blast of a horn, my attention returns to the platform. Several people tromp noisily up the steps. Unlike the audience, the party wears bright colors, their clothes cut in unusual fashions. Their faces are caked with paint, reddening their cheeks and darkening their eyebrows.

"Ah, finally." The woman claps. "My sister saw this group in her village. Says they're quite good."

"What are they doing?" I ask.

The woman looks at me like I've asked her the color of the sky.

"Have you never seen a pageant before?"

I shake my head and she smiles broadly.

"You're in for a real treat, then."

I'd just as soon have another apple, as I've already devoured mine. The woman gestures back at the platform, where one of the performers bows with a flourish.

"Long ago," he begins, spreading his arms in a wide, elegant gesture, "in the time of the old kings, there lived a goddess. Her power was the brightest of lights in the realm. Her kindness, beauty, and wisdom made her known as *fairest of them all.* Meira."

A woman, dressed in gold, dances onto the platform to loud applause. The taste of the apple sours in my mouth. I *know* this story. And it is a lie.

"For years, our realm worshiped Meira and followed her Light." Other players kneel and bow around the woman representing the false goddess. "But there were those who grew jealous of our goddess and her power. Those who plotted in secret, lying in wait for their chance to strike. The *witches.*"

He hisses the word, and a storm of jeers ensues as several other performers swarm the stage, red fabric flapping from their shoulders in a mockery of our cloaks. My hackles rise. They've no right to wear that color. No right to steal our identity—our lives. But the crowd doesn't care. They boo and shout and laugh. A few go so far as to throw a shoe or a piece of rotted fruit at the false witches. It takes every ounce of my self-control to keep from reacting.

"Meira attempted to reason with the covens—to bring them into the Light," the leader of this farce continues. "But the witches refused to hear her. They desired to rule this realm with their own villainous hands. And so, using their Malum, they wove a spell of deception."

A spell of . . . *deception*? I've never heard this part of the story before. I glance around, expecting the audience to be similarly confused, but they're enraptured, drinking in the man's words like honey.

"The witches trapped Meira inside their vile enchantment." The players dressed as witches dance around the false goddess, wrapping her up in black fabric as she writhes and struggles against them. "With the goddess thus imprisoned, the witches turned their Malum upon the first White King, Braxos, blinding him to their wickedness. And their terrible enchantment webbed throughout the entire kingdom—spelling us all—so that none suspected the witches' treachery."

Our *treachery*? My blood roils. I knew that the mortals had turned against us. That the Covens' War started because the White Kings desired to control us, but *this* is what the Order is spouting? That our power is *Malum*? If witches used Malum, how do the mortals explain the years of prosperity during the Age of the Covens? Was it *Malum* that held back invading armies or mitigated the spread of plague? Covens may carry long memories, but mortals evidently hold none at all. Nettle trills, her tail twitching as she feeds off my energy.

"But during the time of the late King Reginald," the heretical man continues, "the Order at last awakened. The followers of Meira discovered the truth of the witches and their Malum. Driven by their faith in Meira, they devised a plan to free our goddess from the covens' clutches. And, at long last, they succeeded. The Order lifted the haze of Malum that ensorcelled the king, guiding him back to the Light."

Utter nonsense. And how, exactly, did the Order lift this supposed sorcery? With another spell? How convenient that such methods aren't called magic when the Order is involved. The audience, however, is oblivious to the hypocrisy of this tale. A cheer rises as a man wearing a crown gallops onto the platform, riding a wooden horse.

"Released from the witches' enchantment, King Reginald vowed to rid the kingdom of the covens and their Malum once and for all," the narrator calls with a sweeping gesture. "He dragged the leaders of the witches here and executed them for their crimes."

More cheers as the crimson-cloaked players wilt under the pretend king's sword. My stomach twists in disgust. The death of those witches was a massacre—just like every other raid carried out in the name of this so-called goddess. These people treat it like a celebration. Like we *deserved it*.

"At the witches' deaths, Meira was liberated from her prison of Malum." The pretend king slices at Meira's bindings. The scraps of black silk fall away and the player in gold emerges, wide-eyed and beaming. "King Reginald restored our goddess to her rightful position, thus returning the realm to the Light of Meira's protection."

The woman representing the false goddess extends her arms. Beams of light burst from her palms, earning delighted gasps and cheers from the audience. But it's not magic. It's just a trick. A farce, like everything else in this Spirits' forsaken realm.

I'm about to turn away, put myself as far from this atrocity as possible, when the pretend witches toss several small objects into the crowd. One of them lands a short distance away and I maneuver through the audience to see what it is. A stone, I realize. A rough-hewn, oval shape, glinting red in the sunlight. Is that intended to be a *Bloodstone*?

"Watch out!" someone yells.

I don't see the horse until it's practically on top of me. The beast whinnies, front legs rearing back and exposing the broad expanse of its belly. I scramble away just before its enormous hooves, which are roughly the size of my face, squash my head like a grape. The stone, however, is not as lucky. It's crushed beneath the horse's foot, red shards spinning in every direction. I pluck one of the glittering pieces from the cobblestones. It's only dyed glass, a cheap replica, as fragile and hollow as the players' story. Fury flashes in my veins. The mortals take our sacred relics, our history, and turn them into baubles and trinkets for their own perverse amusement. I clench my fist around the bit of false stone so hard that the edge cuts into my palm and my own blood trickles down my wrist.

"Are you all right?" The woman from before hurries over. "You're bleeding!"

"I'm fine," I say quickly as she helps me to stand, hiding my hand in my skirt and cursing myself for being careless. The cut will heal faster than anyone can tend it.

Others begin to congregate around us, whispering. It reminds me enough of the night of my Ascension that panic beats behind my eardrums. I'm too exposed out here. What if they guess what I am? Where is Nettle? I search the crowd, but my cat has vanished.

"Fine? That horse nearly smashed your head like a pumpkin. You're lucky to be alive. Where are your people? Did you—" She stops, noticing my uniform. "Oh, you're a *Sister*. And you look a fright. Of course you do, lost little thing. Come with me. I'll get you to the Sanctum."

I don't want to go to the Sanctum. "I can find my own way, thank you."

"Nonsense." The woman drapes her arm around my shoulder and steers me down another street. "What kind of Follower would I be if I didn't offer aid to a Sister in distress?"

The only distress I'm experiencing is from being prevented from getting to the palace. But I don't need to make more of a scene, especially with so many others watching. The woman leads me around another corner and a shadow falls over us. My breath halts—the Sanctum.

Even having lived as a Sister at Stonehaven for the last seven years, I'm unprepared for the sight of this place. It must be several times the size of Stonehaven, and impossibly tall. Five huge, square towers climb into the sky, birds wheeling above them. Unlike Stonehaven and most other Sanctums, which were built to honor a single Ancient, the White City's Sanctum was dedicated to all Five. But any trace of those witches has been eradicated. Instead, dozens of Eyes glare at me from where they're molded into the stone or set into the rich colors of an enormous circular stained-glass window. Small figurines of the false goddess line the arching eaves and others are carved into walls. There must be hundreds of them, their faces tilted downward like they're observing my approach.

"No, this is no trouble at all," the woman prattles on as she herds me up the wide steps. I can hardly feel my feet touch the stone. "And you must be exhausted from your journey. The Sanctress will get you a bath and a hot meal."

A hot meal. The words alone are like a spell, fighting through the haze of my stupor. My stomach growls, the apple already forgotten. Where else might I get a full meal? Certainly not from the merchants. And I haven't had a bath since I left Stonehaven. I'd probably have a bed inside the Sanctum as well. My whole body aches at the thought of sleeping on a mattress instead of the ground. Even so—I glance over my shoulder at the White Palace, towering on its mountain in the distance. That place might as well be a whole world away. And what if I get caught here? The doors to the Sanctum loom like the jaws of a waiting beast.

They'll see right through you, that voice says.

Before I can land on a decision, the woman swings the large bronze knocker on the Sanctum door. A few moments later, hinges squeal as the massive thing opens, revealing a figure standing on the other side. For a heartbeat, given her Sanctress robes, I almost mistake the person for Mother. This Sanctress is older, though, with dark eyes and silver hair tucked into her cap.

"I found this poor thing in the street," the woman who helped me explains, clicking her tongue. "She nearly got herself trampled by a carriage."

The Sanctress sweeps an appraising look over me. "You're not one of mine. Are you here for Longest Night?"

I pause. This is my last chance to escape. I could bolt down the steps and never look back. But where would I go? And where is Nettle? The sounds of the city float around me—wheels against cobblestones and shouting. I'm so *hungry.* I've nowhere to hide and no idea how to get into the palace. Perhaps it's not a bad idea to take some rest. A day or two at the most. After all, I've lived nearly a decade pretending to be a Sister. I can go a while longer. And Nettle, wherever she is, can fend for herself for a time.

"Yes," I say, banishing my doubts. "To receive the High Priest's blessing."

The Sanctress smiles, but I'm not sure if it's entirely friendly. "Another. Wonderful."

"It's so nice to see such devotion to the Light, is it not?" the woman asks.

"Indeed," the Sanctress agrees. "And thank you for your service in escorting her here. I'll take care of her."

She beckons for me to step inside.

The woman gives me a last pat. "Blessings for the season."

Blessings, indeed. I throw one last look at the White City and the palace beyond, and then trudge inside.

CHAPTER TWELVE

AS SOON AS THE HEAVY OAKEN DOOR CLOSES BEHIND ME, I REAL-
ize that I've made a mistake. Stonehaven might bear the
trappings of the false goddess, but it's nothing like this
Sanctum. Gone is the low hum of magic, a faint pulse of witchcraft.
The seemingly endless stone halls are cold and lifeless. The vaulted
ceiling is too high, causing our every footstep to echo, eerie and
haunting. Meira's Eyes appear almost alive as they stare at me from
the eaves and alcoves—and there are dozens more of them here than
at Stonehaven. I imagine the witches who used to walk these
corridors—the runes and shrines that were pried out and replaced—
and a heady mix of sadness and anger churns in my gut. This place
was built to honor the covens, and now it serves to glorify those who
hunt us. I rub the triangles etched below my ring fingers.

Just a day or two, I tell myself. *Get a few meals, fresh clothes, and
leave.*

"The dining hall and chantry are that way," the Sanctress says as
she points down the east wing. Dust motes glimmer in the dull sun-

light filtering through the arched windows. "Prayers are before breakfast. We greet the dawn with our goddess."

A line of young women passes us on the other side of the hall, their hands folded in front of them and their eyes downcast. I mimic their posture, attempting to blend in.

"The washroom is up ahead. Usually, baths are before prayers, but you'll take one immediately, given your circumstances." Her nose wrinkles. I probably do smell. "But I should warn you. As I'm sure was evident during your brief excursion in the city, some Followers hold to the misconception that Longest Night is a time of celebration and frivolity. An excuse to let darkness into their lives, as before the Age of the Light. They're wrong. This season is a time of penitence and reflection. *We* hold to the Light. Just like Meira herself."

The Sanctress's robes whisper against the floor as we pass a small statue of the false goddess, her motto engraved into the alcove behind her: *Fairest of Them All.*

"I understand," I say, gritting my teeth against the effigy.

"Good." The Sanctress directs us down another corridor. "In the meantime, clean yourself up and I'll get you a fresh uniform. This will be your room."

The Sanctress pauses at a row of doors and opens one of them, revealing a chamber about the same size as my own room at Stonehaven. But it's not mine. Everything here is sparse and drab. My chest tightens, missing the quilt Nyssandra stitched for me and the pieces of the forest I collected over the years—jewel-toned autumn leaves and interesting rocks. Will I ever see that place, or my home, again?

"Given our increased number of visitors," the Sanctress continues, "you'll have to share this chamber with several other girls. We'll get the last bed made up for you."

It's then that I notice the young woman who's changing the linens. She turns, sunlight spilling through the open window and over her features, a pointed chin and high cheekbones. But it's her eyes that catch my attention, a bright, cobalt blue set against her olive skin. Pain knocks through me before the realization fully hits—I *know* those eyes.

Every muscle in my body goes rigid as the scent of juniper wafts around me. This time, I'm not imagining it.

The young woman—the Order Sister—is *Jacquetta*.

Questions crash together in my mind, so loud and sudden that I'm dizzy with them. In fact, it seems the world itself is tilting on its axis. What is she doing here? Where has she been? Does she recognize me? She must, for Jacquetta's lips slacken and the color drains from her face. What will she say? What do I *want* her to say?

My heart beats a frantic rhythm, instincts muddling in my mind. But Jacquetta's shock abruptly hardens. She clutches her laundry tighter, and then, without so much as a second glance in my direction, pushes past me and out the door.

Like I didn't exist at all.

The rest of the day passes in a hazy blur. I complete my required chores and pray to the false goddess, but I hardly feel the sting of lye soap against my skin or hear the words of the absurd Illuminations falling from my lips at service.

All I can think about is Jacquetta.

For the first few years after that ill-fated night in the woods, I wondered if Jacquetta regretted what she did. If she might come back for me. Fool that I was, I probably would have forgiven her.

Now I hate myself for those wasted thoughts. Clearly, Jacquetta regrets nothing. Still, I can't stop picturing her face when she saw me. Her features have changed, become more angular—harder. More . . . *beautiful*.

No, I scold myself. I will not think of her that way. Not after what she did.

A memory surges up—the battle that had been deadlier than the Hunt's raid, witches slicing open old wounds and gouging fresh ones as they blamed one another for what had happened and fought over what we should do next.

Let's just go, I'd begged Jacquetta, the coven crumbling around us. *I can't stay here.*

Even then, I was certain that I couldn't be a Second. And Jacquetta was leaving. My life before I met her seemed colorless in comparison to our nights in the forest. I couldn't lose her after I'd just lost Rhea.

I'll be in our clearing, she'd promised, our hands clasped together, her pulse thudding against mine. *Tomorrow night. I'll wait for you.*

But she didn't wait. She didn't even come. And I was forced to return to Stonehaven, alone and disgraced. A Second who nearly abandoned her bloodline and betrayed her coven. And I spent the next seven years living under the shadow of that mistake. And for what? A witch with blue eyes who held my heart in the palm of her hand—and then crushed it.

It doesn't matter why she did it, I decide. I will not let her ruin my life again.

By some small miracle, Jacquetta isn't among the Sisters sharing my room. As soon as the others in the room are sleeping, I pack up my satchel and slip into the hall. The Eyes of the false goddess glimmer in the dimness. The front door would be the swiftest exit, but the Sanctress keeps it bolted. The only other way outside is through the laundry courtyard. I sneak through the too-quiet corridors and am relieved to find the back door unlatched. Moonlight gleams against the metal of the wash pumps and bathes the assortment of plants in the small garden as I let myself into the night. Keeping close to the outer wall, I follow the side of the Sanctum until I discover a wrought-iron gate, one that leads to the streets. It's locked.

"Damn," I mutter, rattling the handle.

I could attempt to pick the mechanism, but I've never done so before. I'll have to climb the bars. I'm already shrugging off my satchel and passing it through to the other side when a noise interrupts the quiet, one too close to have drifted in from the city. I drop my satchel and crouch behind the nearest bush. Is it the Sanctress? It sounds more like an animal. A growl, actually, low and rumbling. The wind picks up. Shadows seem to peel themselves from the far reaches of the courtyard and wind toward me, like vines.

"Rhea?" I whisper.

But that growl could not be my sister.

You could have brought something out. Mother's words resurface, and I feel a slight tremble behind my left ribs. *It's not real,* I tell myself. *It's not—*

A shape leaps out of a nearby bush. I jump, bracing for a Nevenwolf or some other manifestation of Malum. Instead, a pair of golden eyes gleams in the darkness.

"*Nettle.* Are you trying to kill me? And where have you been?"

She winds herself around my ankles, then starts to purr. I'm glad to know one of us passed an enjoyable day.

"Come on." I snatch up my satchel. "We're leaving."

Nettle meows, evidently approving. But the faint whine of hinges pulls me up short. Am I to have no luck at all? Fumbling with my bag, I crouch behind the bush again. A figure slips through the back door of the Sanctum and into the glow of moonlight.

Jacquetta.

That same treacherous jolt from earlier spears through me, like the lightning strike hitting the coven fire. I smother it, cursing myself for feeling anything at all. The last time Jacquetta came into my life, she ripped it to shreds. She means *nothing* to me. And judging from her earlier reaction, I obviously mean nothing to her.

But I can't shake the question . . . what is she doing out here in the middle of the night? What is she doing *here* at all? Jacquetta and her mother, Nerissa, were among those who left the coven because they disagreed with Mother's disguise. A Sanctum, wearing the very uniform she rejected, is the last place I'd think to discover her. Jacquetta rounds a corner on the other side of the building. The mystery nags at me. What if there's something I should know before going to the White Palace? It's better that I find out.

Nettle trills, dubious. I ignore her, slinking along the walls toward where Jacquetta disappeared. Eventually, her hushed voice fills the quiet.

"I'm handling it."

Who is she talking to? I angle myself to get a closer look. Jacquetta is kneeling, her attention fixed on a spot on the ground—a puddle. A shaft of moonlight shimmers on the surface in a way that isn't quite natural. It's the same way the water appeared in the stream when I spoke with Mother. Which means Jacquetta is *scrying*.

"It's been weeks and you don't have a plan," the other voice says.

"I will," Jacquetta retorts. "I can do this."

"But you don't *have* to. Your mother will understand—"

"I'm staying."

So Nerissa is still alive. Are the others with her? And what are they doing?

"And what about us?" the other voice asks, hitching slightly.

"I've told you," Jacquetta replies. "This is something I have to do. You can either choose to accept that, or not."

A tense beat passes.

"Fine." The word lashes sharp enough that even I flinch. "I *don't* accept it. And I'm tired of worrying about you, waiting and wondering if you're going to get yourself killed."

Understanding smacks me in the face. Jacquetta is *involved* with this witch. Or they were involved, until this moment. Discomfort writhes in my stomach. I banish it. What do I care about Jacquetta's . . . entanglements?

"That's fine with me," Jacquetta returns icily. "You were only ever a distraction anyway."

There is the Jacquetta I know. The one who abandoned me in the woods. The other witch shouldn't feel too sorry. She's saving a lot of heartbreak by—

Water splashes and footsteps crunch. Too late, I realize they're headed in my direction. I pivot left and right, scrambling for a hiding place, but I'm not quick enough. Jacquetta's body plows into mine. She trips, sprawling face-first onto the flagstones. Jacquetta snarls a curse, flipping over and pulling something from her waist. A *knife*. Cold, white rage blanches her features as she registers that it's me.

"You *followed* me?"

Embarrassment flames in my cheeks. Jacquetta's scrying was private, a moment I had no business in overhearing. The words of an apology swoop into my mind, but I catch them before they escape my lips. Why should I care about *Jacquetta's* feelings? She gave no consideration to mine. Anger builds again and I let it lock on to me like armor.

"So what if I did?" I demand. "What are you going to do? Stab me?"

For a terrifying moment, I think she might. Jacquetta stalks closer, knuckles white on the knife's handle. "What are you *doing* here, Ayleth?"

It's the first time she's uttered my name since the night of the raid, and I smother the ache in my chest with a harsh laugh. "So you do remember who I am. It didn't seem that way earlier."

"What did you want me to say?" Jacquetta pokes the knife in my direction. "Oh, hello, Ayleth. Fancy meeting you here. How's your coven?"

By the Spirits, she's insufferable. How did I ever believe otherwise? "No, I suppose I shouldn't have expected *anything* from someone like you."

Her jaw tightens and I revel in the flash of her blue eyes.

"Just go about whatever errand your mother sent you on like a good little Second and leave me alone."

Second. I flinch and nearly correct her, but pull myself back. Of course Jacquetta assumes that I'm here for Mother and the coven. Why wouldn't she? She has no idea what the last seven years were like for me—that they ruined me. That *she* ruined me. And she doesn't need to know. Let Jacquetta believe that I'm proud to be a Second. That she did me a favor by leaving.

"Fine by me," I tell her, lifting a shoulder. "The sooner I'm done here, the sooner I go home—to the witches who matter."

Jacquetta blanches. Good. Let her feel an ounce of the pain I've carried since she left me behind. Her pulse beats at her throat, matching the furious cadence of my own. But then, in one fluid motion, Jacquetta steps closer and presses her knife against my side, just hard enough that I can feel the edge of its blade through my bodice. My breath hitches at her nearness. At the thought of what she might do next—of what I might want her to do.

"I see you've turned out to be just like your mother," she says, pushing the blade deeper. "Congratulations."

That wounds me worse than her knife ever could have done. Jacquetta deals me an unnerving grin and stalks off toward the Sanctum, leaving me seething and alone.

Just like that night in the clearing.

CHAPTER THIRTEEN

THE SHOCK OF COLD WATER HITS ME LIKE NEEDLES AGAINST MY skin, stealing my breath as I sink into the wooden tub of the communal bathing room.

I didn't leave.

It's not because of Jacquetta, I insist, teeth chattering as I scrub myself with the harsh soap—a poor substitute for what Willa makes with lavender oil. Well, it's not *entirely* because of Jacquetta. The conversation I overheard last night served as a glaring reminder that a plan is essential. I might not know what Jacquetta is doing here, but if she's been at the Sanctum for weeks with no success, I can't expect to waltz into the White Palace without a strategy.

And what *is* Jacquetta doing here? I wonder for the thousandth time, stepping out of the bath and fumbling with the scratchy drying cloth.

It doesn't matter, that voice insists.

No—it doesn't. Soon enough, I'll leave this place—and Jacquetta—far behind me.

For now, I pull on my uniform and follow the others into the dining hall. Like at Stonehaven, trestle tables line both sides, with one at the head of the room, where several large bowls hold what I assume to be breakfast. *Unlike* Stonehaven, the scent of this breakfast is less than appetizing. But it is food. I take my place in one of the single-file lines stretching the length of the room. I spot Jacquetta waiting in the other one, her face pointed straight ahead as the Sanctress makes her way down the aisle.

"This evening at vespers," the Sanctress announces, "we will be visited by His Illuminance himself. He'll be lighting Meira's candle with a flame from the sacred brazier in the palace, which will guide our path through this season of darkness."

My blood chills at the mention of the High Priest, head of the Order itself.

"I expect all of you to exhibit impeccable behavior," the Sanctress continues. "You will represent our goddess with the grace and dignity she deserves."

A chorus of "Yes, Sanctress" answers. I don't join in.

"Go on then." She indicates the food. "The faster you eat, the faster you can be about your chores. Don't let the Darkness catch you idling. I expect this Sanctum to be spotless for His Illuminance's arrival."

And how long had it taken them to scrub away the *witch* blood smeared on these walls? I wonder bitterly as the line starts to move. When it's my turn, I slop a ladleful of what is allegedly porridge into my bowl. Better than nothing, I suppose. Mourning the absence of warm bread, I carry my breakfast to an empty dining table. But I've not taken two steps when my foot catches on a solid object and I fall face-first to the floor, my bowl clattering against stone. Porridge splatters in all directions—mostly on me.

"Do be careful," a young woman calls, feigning sympathy. Three others snicker around her. "Filth will drag you into Darkness."

Indignation smolders in my belly. If this mortal wants to see darkness, I will—

"Here." Someone kneels beside me, a Sister about my age, with blue eyes and red hair. Freckles smatter her white skin. She offers me a rag. "Clean it up before the Sanctress catches you. She'll have you scrub the whole room otherwise."

"It wasn't my fault," I mutter, wiping the splotches of porridge from my face.

"Oh, I know." She glowers at the Sister who tripped me. "I'm Eunice."

I'm hesitant to reveal my own name, as I shouldn't draw attention to myself. But Eunice doesn't strike me as a threat. And it might attract more notice if I ignore her.

"Ayleth," I offer.

"Welcome to the Sanctum." She throws me a wink, helps me finish cleaning up the mess, and then fetches me another bowl.

"What's wrong with them?" I ask, jerking my chin toward the foursome as we find a seat at the back of the hall.

"Personally, I think they're bored." Eunice settles into her place at the table. "I call them the Sanctress's Magpies. They like to collect bits of information and feed it back to her, spiteful creatures."

Excellent. "Why?"

"Why not?" She shrugs, spooning up her porridge. "Not much else to do here. And I've heard that the Sanctress gives them extra portions and such as payment. A *reward* for bringing the Light to the Sanctum or some other nonsense. Their room is always a good bet for finding contraband, if that's of interest to you. And Agnes—she's the one with the long nose who tripped you—hasn't stopped crowing about the fact that she gets to represent the Sisters at the pageant."

"Pageant?"

"You know, the play about how Meira was freed from Darkness and the witches were vanquished. Have you never seen one?"

Images from the White City flash back. The mockery of the witches' cloaks and the shattered Bloodstone. "Only recently."

"This one is put on by the palace. It's supposed to be very well done. His Illuminance has invited a few of us to watch. It's no surprise who the Sanctress picked." Eunice rolls her eyes. "Can't deny that I'm a bit jealous, though. Sitting in the palace sounds better than minding the Light, which is what I'll be doing."

My ears prick at the mention of the palace. "Can't we all go?"

"Don't let the Sanctress hear you asking such questions. Earlier, a girl mentioned a stroll through the city and she had to write each Illumination a hundred times." Eunice shudders. "We're stuck in here, I'm afraid."

I frown, spooning a bite of porridge into my mouth. It's little better than the watery soup that was served last night. And the lifetime of Willa's cooking only makes it taste worse.

"Better get used to that." Eunice laughs, reading my expression. "Rich food tempts the Darkness, after all."

She winks again. And I have to admit that I'm surprised. I imagined that the women in this Sanctum would be similar to the citizens of the White City, devoted to the lies of their false goddess. Eunice seems . . . less than reverent.

"You don't appear to be worried about Darkness."

She tucks a stray curl back into her cap. "As worried as anyone. But you know how it goes—it's marriage or the Order for us women. At least since the war."

What does the war have to do with it? "I don't understand."

"What Sanctum did you come from?" Eunice points her spoon at me. "You really don't know anything."

I curse myself for being careless with my words and scramble for an explanation. But Eunice only continues eating.

"Used to be, women had options. They could go to school. Some of them even owned land, or at least that's what my grandmother claims." She shrugs. "But after the war, it was decided that women were too close to . . . well, you know."

Witches. The word hangs between us. The wheels of my mind turn, processing this information. I didn't realize that anyone other than the covens was affected by the king's edict.

"Can't you do something about it?"

"Like what?" she asks, finishing off her bowl. "This is the way things are now. If serving the Order gets me a roof over my head and a meal that won't kill me—*without* having to marry one of the dolts in my village—I can't complain too much."

This is the way things are now.

She says it so simply. Matter-of-factly. What about the *witches*? Eunice might have been robbed of opportunity, but our very lives are being stolen.

"Where *did* you come from anyway?" Eunice asks.

Before I can invent an appropriately vague answer, I notice someone on the other side of the hall. Jacquetta stacks her bowl with a pile of others in a washbasin and glides back to her seat. Other Sisters sit around her, but she doesn't talk to them. *Why* doesn't she talk to them? And what is she doing here? The unceasing question itches in my brain. And a thought occurs to me—according to the other witch, Jacquetta has lived at the Sanctum for weeks. Eunice also seems to have been here a while. Perhaps she can provide some insight.

"Do you know her?" I ask, pointing near the middle of the hall, where Jacquetta is sitting. "The Sister with the blue eyes?"

The one who smells like juniper.

Eunices's brow scrunches. "I've seen her, but I don't know much, sorry. She keeps to herself. Why do you ask?"

A memory descends, crushing and intoxicating at once—my hands clasped with Jacquetta's as we danced in the south tower. The feeling of her body against mine when we tripped over each other's feet and tumbled to the floor, the room ringing with our laughter.

You don't care about her, that voice insists. *She doesn't care about you.*

"No reason," I say.

A bell begins to chime, and the others immediately start to rise. Eunice sighs.

"That's breakfast. Time for chores. I'm sure the Sanctress showed you where the rotation is posted." Eunice stacks her bowl with mine. "But you're still new enough to claim ignorance. Come with me to the garden. I could use the extra hands. The place is overrun with baneweed."

Baneweed.

The name is familiar, and I comb over all the plants Mother forced me to memorize. It's not one I encountered often . . .

Because it's a poison, or it can be. It derives its name from the stomach-curdling illness it inflicts on those who consume it. I know because I'd once confused it with valerian in a tincture and paid horribly for the mistake.

The Magpies file past, laughing about some inane joke, and an idea sparks in my mind. Eunice said those Sisters hide contraband in their rooms. Some of that contraband is bound to include food. If I can manage to add a little baneweed to their treats, Agnes and the others won't be able to go to the pageant. Which means *I* could take their place.

A smile curls at my lips. For the first time in my life, Mother's lessons are proving useful.

CHAPTER FOURTEEN

THE BANEWEED IS EASY TO SPOT, CURLING IN HEMLOCK-GREEN tendrils around what's left of the garden's meager autumn harvest. I jam my pockets full of the stuff when Eunice is distracted, planning to store it under my bed until I can find the opportunity to dose the Magpies. But I'll have to be quick—the pageant is in a few days.

Garden duty is short-lived as well. After just an hour, the Sanctress calls us to wash a veritable mountain of laundry and then to scrub the halls and the chantry from top to bottom in anticipation of His Illuminance's visit. By the end of the day, my arms and shoulders are aching and my skin stings from the strong soap. All I want to do is crawl into bed, but I'm expected to file into the chantry with the others, stomach still growling after a dinner that offered nowhere near enough sustenance to satisfy my appetite.

"Do not embarrass me in front of the High Priest," the Sanctress reminds us before the service that evening.

She should be more concerned about us falling asleep. If I didn't despise Jacquetta so much, I might admire her. I don't know how she endures all this, day after day. I notice her take a seat on the other side of the chantry. Our gazes meet and she glares. My lips twitch up. The one bright spot to the afternoon was when Nettle made an appearance in the laundry courtyard and promptly shredded Jacquetta's linens. I love that cat.

A bell rings, signaling the start of vespers. My smirk wilts. I'd wash another mountain of laundry if it meant I didn't have to suffer through prayers. Before the war, the chantry at Stonehaven was a place for witches to practice quiet meditation, or to seek guidance from the Spirits. Sweet-smelling incense drifted among the shrines to Millicent, which were adorned with runes for protection and wisdom. *This* chantry is no place for such solace.

Meira's effigy stares down at us from behind an altar, her all-seeing Eyes glimmering in the candlelight. Tallow candles, I might add, which leave a musky, animal-like smell hanging in the air. My attention lingers on various sections of the stone walls, lighter than the rest, where our sacred runes have been dug out or sanded over, replaced with the Order's Illuminations. But even worse than these desecrations is the impression of what I can only describe as *wrongness*. As I sit here, surrounded by the evidence of the Order's butchery, I suddenly understand what Eden had meant when she said that the tree in the forest died of sadness. I may not be a gifted witch, but I can sense an undulating grief in this room, as if the Ancients themselves are present, mourning all that we've lost.

Wood creaks as the Sisters rise, and I reluctantly stand with them. Measured footsteps progress down the aisle. The back of my neck prickles—it's the High Priest, Ignatius. He's younger than I anticipated, middle-aged with only a few strands of silver in his reddish-brown hair. Set against his white skin, his eyes are bright and sharp, a unique shade of hazel that's closer to amber—like fire. It's similar to the color of the gradient silk of his robes, which are dyed to mimic the flickering orange, yellow, and red hues of a flame. A potent mixture of anger and fear churns in my stomach. How many witches has this man killed, my own sister among them?

No one could guess that Ignatius is a murderer now, though. His hands are clean, not stained with blood, as he places his candle beside the jewel-encrusted book of Illuminations on the altar. A large ruby pendant, fashioned to represent the Eye of Meira, dangles from a chain draped across his shoulders. The huge jewel glitters in the candlelight, and I shiver with the unsettling impression that it can see me.

"Sisters." The High Priest's voice is rich and warm as it fills the chamber. "It brings Light to my heart to stand among you this season. First, I welcome those of you who journeyed from all corners of our kingdom to serve with us during this sacred time. It is your prayers, your devotion, which herald the dawn at the end of Longest Night. You alone will shield us from the dangers of Darkness during this period of temptation."

Lies. The High Priest draws the sign of the Eye in the air. I glance around at the other Sisters. Some appear bored. Perhaps, like Eunice, they joined with the Order because they had nowhere else to go. But others lean forward, intensely focused. Have they no minds of their own? Does no one remember what the witches did for this realm?

"One question I often receive during this time of year," the High Priest goes on, "is *why* did it take so long for us to free our goddess from her prison? How did the White Kings not sense that they were being deluded by Malum?"

Probably because there *was* no Malum deluding them. The *covens* were holding it back. I ball my skirts in my fists, willing my expression to remain neutral as hatred simmers inside me.

"To that, I present an opposing question: Is it not easier to hide the truth? Is it not simpler to mold ourselves into who we assume others expect us to be rather than shining a light on the deepest chambers of our own hearts?"

That touches a nerve.

"Darkness is comfortable," Ignatius continues. "Preferable, even. After all, what we cannot see often causes no harm. But remember the beast that lurks in such Darkness. Malum. It will devour you whole, and you will not even see it coming."

A shiver races down my spine as I recall the growl in the courtyard. Just like then, a faint pressure nudges against the inner side of my left ribs. It's not *real.*

"But our goddess offers refuge." Ignatius indicates the statue of Meira behind him. "Unlike the covens, *she* does not hoard her power. She does not demand gifts or tribute from her Followers. All she asks of us is that we carry her Light and embrace who we truly are."

The High Priest selects a long match from a gilded cup on the pedestal and lights it with the flame of his candle.

"This fire has been carried here from the sacred brazier. It is Meira's Light." Cupping his ringed hand around the flame, he transfers the lit match to a candle positioned at the base of Meira's statue. There's a soft pop as the flame catches on the wick. "And as long as it burns, there is hope for this realm. Please, join with me in prayer."

The High Priest spreads his arms wide and bows his head as he begins reciting a chant. Voices fill the chantry, but mine isn't one of them. Instead, my focus remains on the statue. In the glimmering candlelight, I could almost mistake the false goddess for Millicent.

The High Priest's words loop through my mind: *Embrace who we truly are.*

But who is that? How would Millicent judge the last descendant in her line? Would she be as disappointed in me as Mother is? Probably. Again, I wonder if Millicent is the reason Rhea appeared to me on the night of my Ascension. My ancestress preferred someone worthier to carry on her legacy. I don't blame her. I knead at one of the triangles etched into my palms, wishing I could—

The rest of my thought falls away, my brow furrowing as movement near the statue snags my attention. But not *near* the statue, I realize—the stone effigy itself seems to be *trembling*. I blink, convinced that the illusion is nothing more than the haze of the tallow smoke or a trick of the light. But no—a tiny fissure races up from Meira's stone feet. With his back turned, the High Priest hasn't noticed anything amiss. Neither has anyone else. Except—

Jacquetta. Her gaze is pinned to the statue, sharp as a blade. Her lips move, but I'd bet my life that she's not reciting a prayer. She's working a spell. Which means Jacquetta is . . . a *Caster*? She made her vow to Millicent? I can hardly believe it possible after—

A dull scraping sound yanks my attention back to the statue, which has started to wobble and tip forward. Sudden clarity lights in my mind. The damn thing is going to fall on top of the High Priest. It will crush him. Jacquetta's going to kill him, right here in front of everyone.

"By the Spirits," I mutter.

What is she thinking? Statues don't just collapse of their own volition. Someone is going to guess that this wasn't an accident. Someone might *see* her. I shouldn't care if Jacquetta gets caught, I know that, but something inside me snaps.

I'm racing toward the front of the chantry before I fully know what I'm doing. Stone groans as the statue loses its battle with Jacquetta's magic. I barrel headlong into Ignatius. He cries out and stumbles to the side, narrowly missing Meira as the false goddess's effigy collides with the altar itself, exactly where the High Priest had been standing mere moments before. At the shatter and crunch of stone, chaos erupts. Sisters scream, leaping up from their seats and fleeing, everyone talking and shouting at once.

"Your Illuminance!" The Sanctress rushes toward us, horrified. "Are you injured?"

The High Priest regains his footing, his mouth slackening as he assesses the damage and realizes what might have occurred. "No. I'm unhurt, thanks to—"

"Ayleth," Eunice calls from the crowd. "Her name is Ayleth."

Damn everything. The High Priest's amber gaze pivots to me.

"You saved my life." Revulsion knots in my stomach at the touch of his hand on my arm. It's everything I can do to keep from flinging him off. "You are a true Follower. An embodiment of Meira herself."

I am a witch. "No. I only—"

"Please." The pressure of his grip increases. "I owe you a debt."

I want nothing from him and take an instinctive step back. "That won't be—"

"The pageant!" Eunice again, grinning at me. "She should go to the pageant."

The Sanctress turns, her robes billowing. "We do not invite ourselves . . ."

"No." The High Priest stops her, never taking his unnerving gaze from mine. "That's a wonderful idea. In fact, I think our Ayleth should be part of the production. I want the whole of the court to understand the service that she's done for the Light."

A bolt of fear digs between my shoulder blades. Be *part* of the pageant? Does he mean like the performers in the city?

It's the palace, I remind myself. *This is what you wanted.*

Yes. Once I'm through the palace gates, nothing else matters. Even so, Ignatius smiles at me, and a deep instinct whispers that I've made a horrible mistake.

As soon as I'm able, I make a swift exit out of the chantry, determined to hide until the activity and attention dies down. I'm not fast enough.

A hand shoots out and grabs my arm, yanking me into a secluded alcove. The smell of juniper hits—Jacquetta.

This is the first time we've touched since Stonehaven, and I'm momentarily stunned by the contact. Sparks shoot through my blood. But no. Jacquetta doesn't get to touch me like this—not anymore. Not after what she did.

"Let go of me." I wrench free of her grasp.

"What were you thinking?" She seethes, blue eyes livid in the dimness.

"Me? I'm not the one who just tried to murder the High Priest in front of a room full of Followers."

"I didn't ask for your help."

"You clearly needed it. What would have happened if you'd succeeded? You think those sycophants would have simply declared it an accident? That they would have been content to believe that a stone statue just casually flattened the head of the Order?"

Her nostrils flare. "He deserved it. When would I get that chance again? You ruined it."

She ruined *me*. I shove that thought down.

"I did you a favor, not that I owed you any. Even if they didn't suspect witchcraft—and they would have—what do you suppose would have happened next? No more Order? It doesn't work that way. The king would have appointed another High Priest, then another after that."

It's a topic I heard discussed often enough at Stonehaven. Plenty of witches had made attempts on the king's life over the course of the war. All of them failed. Even if they hadn't, Mother reasoned, another ruler would come after him. Kings, she said, are like snakes who can grow new heads. It's perhaps the only topic we've agreed upon.

Jacquetta points at me. "I warned you to stay out of my way."

"And if I don't?" I challenge. "You'll kill me, like you threatened to do last night?"

I picture the knife in the courtyard, blade pressed against my side, and a thrill lights in my veins—one not entirely unwelcome.

She raises an eyebrow. "Are you so sure I wouldn't?"

The Jacquetta I knew in the forest wouldn't. That witch loved novels and stolen pieces of pie and dancing. An overwhelming sadness sweeps over me, thinking of the witches we used to be. Both of them are gone.

"What happened to you?" I whisper.

Why didn't you come?

For an instant, Jacquetta's icy exterior thaws. Is it possible that the witch I cared about is still in there somewhere? Do I even want it to be possible?

No, that voice whispers. *Let her go.*

"I grew up," Jacquetta says at last. "And I suggest you do the same."

And then she's gone, leaving me with nothing but a ghost of a memory.

CHAPTER FIFTEEN

THE DAYS LEADING UP TO THE PAGEANT ARE SOME OF THE WORST of my life. Whispers chase me down the corridors or swarm around me while I eat meals or slog through my chores. When they're not gawping at me, the Sisters who share my room won't stop peppering me with questions about what happened or how I knew the statue was falling. I offer whatever vague answers I can cobble together, but it's never enough. Especially not for the devout followers of Meira, who slide me bits of ribbon or other trinkets, murmuring their gratitude for my saving the High Priest's life. Would that they knew how badly I wanted to see the man squashed like a bug beneath a stone. I still can't believe that no one guessed the incident was the result of magic. Had the distraction been part of Jacquetta's spell? And what spell was it? I'd never seen—or even read—anything like it before. Given the depth of Mother's lessons, surely I should have.

It doesn't matter. And not everyone views my actions as being heroic. When I return from chores one day, my bed has been ransacked and all my clothes are soaked in a putrid, sticky substance. I suspect Agnes did it, as I've stolen her place in attending the pageant. I have a good mind to crush baneweed into Agnes's meal in retaliation, but even that has been pilfered. Does Agnes know how to use it? I decide to start dishing my bowl from the same tureen as the Magpies, just to be safe.

As for Jacquetta, I hardly see her, save for brief snatches when we're working in the garden or wringing laundry in the courtyard. The distance is fine with me, especially after our last encounter. Even Nettle senses the need to leave the other witch alone. Occasionally, my cat appears, twitching her tail as she perches on the wall of the courtyard, but she refrains from attacking Jacquetta's linens.

Any free moments I manage to gather are spent in attempting to flesh out my plans for the night of the pageant. I may have gained entry into the palace, but after that . . . Various options tangle together in my mind as I lie awake in the night. I could try to sneak off before the pageant begins, or during, but where would I go? I'm ignorant of the layout of the palace, let alone the location of the Bloodstones. My head throbs. I haven't enjoyed a decent night's sleep since leaving Stonehaven, and I sorely need it. I trace the faint triangles etched into my palms, wishing I had more of Rhea than just these thin lines.

"What do I do?" I whisper to her in the dark.

Wind groans against the Sanctum. Shadows thicken, dulling the moonlight. My heart beats harder.

"Rhea?" I whisper.

I close my eyes, open them, and the darkness is gone. But so soft I almost don't hear it, I detect the faint rumble of a growl.

The place behind my left ribs trembles.

"Hurry up now, come along."

The Sanctress ushers me through the front door of the Sanctum and down the steps, where a small wagon is waiting to take us to the palace on the evening of the pageant. Night is falling, a deep purple twilight blanketing the city, and it's cold. Winter is certainly cutting its teeth—sharp ones. I shiver and pull my cloak closer around me.

"Is there not a carriage?" one of the Sisters asks, pulling herself into the wagon after me.

"A carriage?" the Sanctress scoffs. "And who do you think you are? A countess? A wagon will get us to the White Palace just as well. And it would do you good to remember your Illuminations: *Believe not in the illusions of the world, for they will lead you into Darkness.*"

"Carriages are real enough," the Sister, one of the Magpies, mutters under her breath. She deals me a glower as she settles into her seat, a gift from Agnes, I'm sure. Better scowls than baneweed.

And I have bigger problems to worry about—like what to do after this wagon drops us off at the palace. I've agonized over my strategy until my brain buzzed, but I'm still no closer to a viable plan. I'll just have to think of something in the moment.

Because you're very good at that, the voice in my mind whispers.

"There should be one more," the Sanctress says, frowning. "Where is—"

Another Sister hurries down the steps, her dark braid draped over one shoulder. I glimpse the flash of a familiar pair of cobalt-blue eyes beneath her hood and sit up straighter. By the Spirits, what is Jacquetta doing here?

"Ah, there you are." The Sanctress herds her onto the wagon.

"Where's Martha?" the Magpie asks, voicing my own question.

"Ill" is all Jacquetta offers.

"But she was fine this morning."

"Well, now she's not," Jacquetta replies, clipped. "You can remain with her if you like. Last I checked, she was retching her guts out."

The Magpie snaps her lips closed. Suspicion tingles at my nape. I'd assumed it was Agnes who filched the baneweed from under my bed. But perhaps it was someone else. Maybe that same person doused all my clothes in the sticky liquid as well. Anger builds be-hind my sternum. It took me hours to wash out the mess, and my uniform still smells. As if she can read my thoughts, Jacquetta glances in my direction. So quick I almost miss it, her lips quirk up in a grin.

It was definitely her. By the Spirits, I *hate* this witch. And what does she want at the White Palace? Is she plotting another murder? Fine. I won't be coming to her rescue this time. Even so, a long-forgotten chamber of my heart twinges. If they do catch Jacquetta working a spell, they'll burn her.

Let her burn, that voice urges. *She would do the same to you.*

The wagon jolts, wheels clattering down the streets, and I fix my attention forward, where it belongs.

The White City is empty and quiet. Torchlight flickers against the façades of homes and shops. Only the plainly dressed citizens are about now, loading crates onto wagons or locking doors before dis-appearing between the buildings.

Occasionally, our wagon trundles past a statue of Meira, her three Eyes following us. I wonder which of the Ancients this statue has replaced. Does anyone living in this city remember a time when the witches watched over them? Or, like Eunice, have they all simply ac-cepted the Order's false history and moved on with their lives? I sup-pose I can't entirely blame Eunice—or any other mortal—for her complacency. She's never lived through a raid. She's not even old enough to remember the covens, or the blessings we spread across this realm. No one remembers, it seems.

In fact, the more time I spend among the mortals, the more I think of Nerissa and the other witches who left Stonehaven. Snatches of their arguments on the night of the raid float back to me. A few of them claimed that it was a mistake for the Ancients to have forged the Bloodstones. Such power, they said, only divided the covens. At the time, I was too terrified and heartbroken over Rhea to give their opinions much consideration. Now I'm beginning to see their point. Not entirely. We need the Bloodstones to uphold the Veil. But I suppose it's also true that the Veil itself lulled the mortals into a false sense of security. The citizens of Riven have never encountered the true horrors of Malum.

We'll all encounter them soon enough, I think bitterly. Should the Veil fall, no false goddess will be able to hold back the Nevenwolves, blights, plagues, and other manifestations of Malum. Perhaps the mortals deserve such a fate for their disloyalty—perhaps they'll all be driven mad and walk into the sea, like that old story. But what about us witches? What do *we* do when our connection to the Spirits falters and our power is at risk? I press my thumb against one of Rhea's marks. She'll know what to do—she always did. I just have to bring her back.

The wagon jostles as it pulls to a stop. Gates loom above us, fashioned to look like towering apple trees. Ruby-like gems the size of my fist glitter among the sculpted leaves.

"We're here on His Illuminance's invitation," the Sanctress explains to the guards, who wave us through.

The road to the palace is lined with torches, so that it appears like a vein of fire snaking up the mountain. The White Palace itself glows against the backdrop of stars. And I might be imagining it, but a few of those glittering points seem to shine brighter than the rest. Seven, I count, scattered roughly in the shape of an oval. It takes me a moment to place why I recognize them—

The Spirits' Mirror.

Jacquetta showed me the constellation during one of our secret nights in the forest. Before I can stop myself, my focus drifts across the wagon. Jacquetta's face is tilted up. Does she see the Spirits' Mirror? Is she recalling that same night? Sparks crackle in my veins at the memory of her hand guiding mine as she traced the stars' pattern—diamonds against a velvet sky.

And what else did she teach you? that voice whispers.

Yes. There is only one lesson I should take from Jacquetta, and it has nothing to do with stars.

The wagon lumbers up the path and I shift my attention to the White Palace, which looms larger with each passing second. Trees sway and creak in the biting wind.

Ayleth, I imagine I hear beneath the susurration of brittle leaves. *Ayleth.*

If I didn't know better, I'd say it was coming from the palace itself. Like the behemoth of glass and stone is welcoming me—or perhaps warning me away.

CHAPTER SIXTEEN

"M EIRA'S LIGHT," ONE OF THE MAGPIES MURMURS, FISH-mouthed as we follow the Sanctress through the stagger-ing display of wealth that is the White Palace.

Even with all the books I read at Stonehaven, all the stories Willa told, I never imagined that such a place as this could exist. The pal-ace's wide halls are designed to give the impression that we're walk-ing through a forest. Columns fashioned like trees stretch up to the arched ceiling, where the marble branches interlock in a latticed canopy. Miniature renderings of birds and other forest creatures are nestled within the branches. Instead of candles or torches, glass ap-ples dangle from sculpted boughs, emitting a soft, amber glow. Tall stained-glass windows depict former White Kings, posed in battle or on horseback. The royal sigil, an apple ringed in a crown, is pat-terned on rugs and woven into tapestries.

The false goddess, of course, is also present. Her Eye gleams where it is engraved into columns or molded onto eaves and awnings, the lighter patches of stone or wood betraying the areas where our runes were pried out and replaced. Again, a slow, smoldering rage simmers inside me at how easily we witches were erased. Being surrounded by such riches only makes it all worse. Everything in this despicable palace is dipped in gold or crusted in jewels—especially those items relating to the Order. Whatever Ignatius claimed about the *tribute* paid to the covens, our Sanctums never boasted such blatant gaudiness. Does the White King think to conceal his crimes behind this gilded façade?

Let him do as he likes. I have far more important matters to contend with—namely finding a hiding place. I've been waiting for an opportunity to break away from the group since we stepped off the wagon, but the Sanctress herds us along like chickens.

"Don't dawdle," she chides. "And remember, the honor bestowed on you by His Illuminance does not grant you permission to behave as though you're a member of court. You're Meira's daughters."

If only she knew whose daughter I really am.

The Sanctress ushers us through a set of enormous doors. The hall inside is at least five times the size of Stonehaven's largest chamber. Crowned apples are engraved into the paneled walls. Rows of stained-glass windows offer scenes of blooming apple trees, or episodes from the Order's lore, all picked out in jewel-toned color. People I assume to be the pageant's performers swarm like bees in their costumes, shouting about masks being misplaced or silks not pressed or laces not tight enough, their voices echoing against the vaulted, hammered-beam ceiling.

"Ah—" A lithe man with a rich black complexion and a cloud of dark hair extracts himself from the flurry of activity. "Sanctress. How delightful to make your acquaintance. I'm Master Foulton, the director of this . . . whatever it is at the moment."

He twirls his cane to indicate the room. A ruby apple the size of a fist sparkles on top.

"May the Light shine upon you." The Sanctress dips her chin in greeting. "These are my charges, appointed by His Illuminance."

"Yes, of course." He sizes us up and I'm not sure if he approves of what he sees. Still, it's better than some of the looks I received in the White City. "I promise to take good care of them."

"Please see that you do." The Sanctress's attention drifts pointedly to two players who are taking turns pouring wine into each other's mouth. "These young women represent our goddess and are unaccustomed to ... frivolity. I will not have them tainted by Darkness."

I suppress a groan, glancing over at Jacquetta to see what she makes of this ludicrous situation. But her expression gives nothing away. In fact, she hasn't uttered a word since leaving the Sanctum. What is she thinking?

Forget her, that voice urges.

"Fear not," Master Foulton assures the Sanctress. "I give my personal oath to shield our dear guests from any *Darkness.* And we've selected the most appropriate and modest of costumes for them."

Costumes? Damn everything. I was supposed to be gone by now. Horrified, I scan the room. Players lounge on benches or stand on stools, their garments being pinned and stitched. Some of them are hardly wearing more than scraps of silk or the paint smeared across their bodies. I can't wear anything like that. I won't.

"Come, come," Master Foulton says.

Before I can object, we're herded behind a privacy screen and descended upon by a veritable army of servants. Hurried hands untie the laces of my uniform and yank off my sleeves.

"Wait," I say, attempting to fend them off. "I can do this myself."

"This will only take a moment." The nearest servant roughly tugs at my braid.

"That hurts!"

She merely continues prodding and pinning and stuffing until I'm strapped into a gauzy, golden-colored gown. My hair is bound into a matching net, and then the servant fastens a glittering, spiked headdress into place, the horrible contraption pinching into my scalp.

"Stop that!" Jacquetta attempts to yank her own headdress off.

"That's no way for a beam of sacred Light to behave." Master Foulton reappears and swats her hand down. "And here are the final touches."

He drapes a length of silk around the Magpie's front. It's a sash. *Mercy* is spelled out in embroidered letters across her chest. Jacquetta's reads *Temperance*. I hold in a snort—there couldn't be a worse word to describe her.

"And for you"—Master Foulton guides the silk sash over my head—"*Perseverance*."

A charge tingles down my spine.

"Now." The director taps his cane on the floor. "The three of you will stand at the back of the stage until Meira is freed from her prison. Then, upon my cue, you will swan in and fawn over her. Don't be shy about it."

He walks and gestures in a manner that I assume is *swanning* and *fawning*. I've never made such movements in my life, especially not in front of others, and have no plans to do so now. I need a way out of here.

"Master Foulton!" Someone hurries through the curtains. "The apple tree's collapsed."

"Again? That damn thing is conspiring against me." The director pinches the bridge of his nose. He waves dismissively to us. "The three of you may remain in here. The servants will guide you to the stage when it's time."

He strides off, spewing more vitriol about how no one ever seems to get what they pay for anymore. I peek around the privacy screen. Servants are collecting the debris and arranging chairs in front of a large platform like the one I saw in the White City. It must be the stage. Where is the nearest exit? Probably the doors we entered through, but the Sanctress is standing near there. I'm not daft enough to try to slip past her. Perhaps there will be a door behind the stage. I can sneak out during the pageant.

And go where? that voice asks.

I'll figure it out—I have to. On impulse, I press my thumb into one of the triangles etched into my palm, yet again wishing Rhea were with me. Restless, I peruse the offerings laid out on a nearby table. There are delicate pastries like those on display in the city, as well as cheeses and sweetmeats. One of the Magpies is currently inhaling several tarts topped with sparkling flowers. I select a blue-veined wedge of cheese. Its buttery texture melts over my tongue, but I'm too agitated to appreciate it.

"You look quite dour for a . . . what is it you're meant to be?"

The question is spoken close enough that I jump. A man leans against the table next to me, a half-eaten apple clutched lazily in one hand. He's wearing plain clothes, and I can't tell if it's a costume or if he's a servant. Either way, he looks to be about forty years old, with broad shoulders and a strong jaw. His black hair is swept back, and his white skin is unlined. But it's his eyes that hold my attention. A light, arresting gray, like quicksilver.

"I'm not sure," I say, keeping my answer as discouraging as possible.

"But you must know." He bites noisily into his apple, tilting his head as he studies me. "Let me guess. A star, perhaps? For you do shine so brightly."

Is this actually the manner in which mortals speak to each other?

"Please, excuse me." I attempt to turn away, but he steps into my path.

"Did I offend you? Strange. I find that most women enjoy flattery."

My patience with this man is at an end. "I'm not most women."

I'm a witch.

"Oh, I can see that." He grins. "You must at least provide me with your name."

I'd rather not. I dodge out of his way again, but the man catches my wrist. Lightning fizzes in my veins at the contact, so quick and sudden that it steals my breath. That feeling starts again—something nudging against the inner side of my left ribs. The pressure swells and grows, like whatever is inside me is reaching, straining to burrow up through my flesh.

It's so foreign, so *unnatural,* that I yank free of the man's grasp, my pulse racing. The pressure instantly eases, reeling back into itself like a snapped tether. Soon, I can't sense it at all.

It was your imagination, I tell myself. *Nerves.*

"Ayleth?" The sound of my name startles me into the present. Jacquetta stands a short distance away, making a show of fussing with her costume. "Will you come and help me?"

"*Ayleth.*" The man's gray eyes light up. "So that's who you are. Well. Enjoy the pageant. I do hope to see you again—soon."

He bows before disappearing into the crowd.

"Who was that?" Jacquetta asks, throwing a scathing look at the man's back.

"I don't know. Some idiot performer."

I wipe my hand on my dress to rid myself of any trace of him. But I can't stop thinking about how the sensation behind my left ribs expanded at his touch, like it was taking on a life of its own. Like it was . . . *pulling* me.

It wasn't real, I insist.

Even to me, that sounds more like a wish. I turn my left palm up, studying the three crossed lines below my ring finger. In the library at Stonehaven, I thought the feeling might have been Rhea's presence, our connection through the Veil, but now . . .

It could have touched you. Mother's voice rolls through my mind, raising the hair on the back of my neck. *You're marked.*

"What is it?" Jacquetta asks, nodding at my hand. "Did he hurt you?"

She starts to reach for me, and my traitorous heart speeds up.

Don't let her close, that voice warns.

I step back, ignoring the knock of pain in my chest. Jacquetta's fingers curl away, and I might glimpse disappointment—or even hurt—flash across her expression. I probably imagined it though. After all, I don't know her anymore.

"It's time!" Master Foulton's announcement rings through the hall.

Servants swarm us. In a matter of moments, the three of us, along with the rest of the players, are assembled behind the closed curtains of the stage. Bodies rustle as the audience takes their seats. And then—long before I'm ready—Master Foulton gives his signal.

As the curtains whoosh open, I'm frozen to the spot. There are fewer people here than in the White City, but this is infinitely worse. Dozens of eyes stare back at me, their attention pinning me down like I'm a specimen on a board.

Focus, that voice commands. *Find a way out.*

I shake myself out of my stupor and latch on to the task. Master Foulton begins narrating the pageant—the same lies I heard in the White City. And as the players move about the stage, acting out the so-called history, I stay out of their way, scanning the set.

The main focal point is the apple tree that Master Foulton had been bemoaning. I can see why it would topple over. The thing is massive, far larger than any typical apple tree would be. The branches are bedecked with jeweled leaves and fruit, rendering them too heavy to be properly supported by the flimsy-looking material comprising the trunk. Whoever mended the tree attached a few of its limbs to the wall, but they'd done a hasty job—one branch has already broken free of its bindings. A thought glimmers in my mind. The tree is large enough that it could prove a suitable hiding place. I could stay there until the pageant finishes and then—

A shape blurs by in my peripheral vision, little more than a flash of red, which vanishes behind the apple tree. What was that? And where had it gone? Unless . . .

Could there be a door back there? Is *that* my way out?

The audience roars with laughter at something Master Foulton says. I use the distraction to edge closer to the apple tree. Sure enough, there's a gap between the tree and the wall, one wide enough for someone to walk through—like whomever I just saw a moment ago. Keeping one eye on the performance, I creep behind the trunk. There *is* a door back here. It's only about as high as my shoulder, which is odd, but it's a way out and I'm going to take it. As for what I'll do next . . .

"What are you doing?"

I freeze, anticipating the Sanctress or a palace official. It's Jacquetta—of course it is.

"Go away," I whisper, shooing her off.

Her eyebrows jerk up as she registers the door. "Is that unlocked?"

"I'm trying to find out. And stop talking—they'll hear us."

Jacquetta scowls, then gestures impatiently for me to try the door. The last thing I want is to bring her with me, but I suppose there's nothing for it. Besides, just because we leave together doesn't mean we have to stay together. I twist the door's handle, eager to leave this place behind, but it sticks. Damn. I turn it harder, pressing my weight against the wood. Nothing.

"Let me," Jacquetta whispers.

"There's no room."

She maneuvers herself into the narrow space anyway. The smell of juniper tickles my nose. Jacquetta extracts a pin from her hair and shoves it into the lock, then wriggles it back and forth. Where did she learn to do that? Evidently, she didn't learn very well, because nothing happens.

"Why isn't it working?" She jiggles the handle, frustrated.

"Maybe the lock is too complicated."

"It shouldn't matter. The pick is enchanted."

She's using magic again after what happened last time? "You're going to get us caught."

"No, I'm not." She wriggles the pick harder. Too hard. There's a brittle snap and then part of it falls to the floor. "*Shit.*"

She tosses the rest away, mumbling more curses.

"Don't just leave it," I scold her. "Someone could find it."

I bend to collect the slender pieces of metal, which I assume are runed. Spirits help us if anyone recognizes those markings. But as I root around, Jacquetta bumps against me and I stumble, tripping over the hem of my impractical costume. I flail about for something to catch myself and wind up tumbling backward—directly into the giant tree.

The massive prop groans as it pitches forward, the poorly secured limbs snapping free of their bindings. Flimsy branches smash against the stage and glass pops as the ruby-like apples shatter. Screams echo against the high ceiling and the stage rumbles with the cadence of fleeing feet. I watch in horror as several players barrel headlong into other props, which promptly careen to the ground. By the time everything settles, most of the set is completely destroyed and the only two players left standing—in full view of the audience—are Jacquetta and *me*.

"What is the meaning of this?" Master Foulton is the first to break the thick silence, brandishing his cane like a weapon as he picks his way through the debris.

My heartbeat thuds against my eardrums. "I—"

"Girls." The Sanctress blusters over. "I *warned* you. Your Majesty, I am *so* sorry."

She curtsies low, her gray robes billowing around her.

Majesty?

In all the commotion, it hadn't occurred to me that the king would attend the pageant. I scan the crowd, searching for a monster wearing a crown. Instead, a player dressed in orange robes pushes himself to his feet near the front of the stage. He tugs his hood down, revealing a pair of quicksilver eyes. Recognition flashes cold in my veins. This is the man from earlier—

He is the *king.*

Time itself seems to slow as the man's—the *king's*—gaze finds mine. Instantly, that feeling starts again—something stirring behind my left ribs. There's no denying it exists now. I may not fully understand what it means, but I know that it is dark and sinister and *wrong.* Instincts crash together in my mind—*run, hide,* do *something.* But I can scarcely breathe.

A slow clap interrupts the moment. A man with dark-brown skin and a roguish slash of a smile climbs onto an upturned prop. "*That* was the most memorable Longest Night pageant I've seen in years. Well done, Foulton."

"No one solicited your opinion, Sir Weston," a woman counters.

Judging from her costume—a blue gown littered with jewels— I assume she represents the false goddess. The king offers her his hand to help her to her feet. Even after her fall, the woman's raven-feather hair is swept elegantly over one shoulder, and her light-brown skin is luminous, like she bathed in crushed pearls. Given what I've experienced of the wealth of this court, she probably did.

"But I am the Lord of Misrule, my good Lady Marion." The man, Sir Weston, feigns being wounded. "My opinion is *always* solicited during Longest Night."

He winks and the audience laughs. The king, however, does not join them. Instead, his attention returns to *me.* Yet again, something nudges against the inner side of my left ribs, more insistent now. I grit my teeth against it, willing the sensation away.

"Mistress Ayleth," the king says. "We meet again."

Dread pools in my belly. I wish we'd never met at all.

"Did you say Mistress *Ayleth*, Sire?"

Courtiers trace the sign of the Eye over their chests as a set of flame-colored robes cuts through the crowd—the High Priest. By the Spirits, this night just keeps getting worse.

"This is the Follower I was telling you about." The ruby Eye pendant glimmers on its chain. "The Order Sister who intervened during the accident with the statue."

I cut a scathing glance at Jacquetta and think I might detect the hint of a flush creeping up her cheeks. Good. I hope she feels guilty. This is her fault.

"Well, it certainly seems the lady has a penchant for attracting falling objects." Sir Weston gestures at the disaster of the tree, earning another round of laughter.

I shift on my feet, hating this.

"Is that so, Perseverance?" The king brushes one finger lightly against my sash. Even that indirect contact causes the pressure behind my left ribs to build and expand, like something straining to break free. What *is* it?

"I'll return them to the Sanctum at once," the Sanctress announces, sinking into another curtsy. "Again, I cannot apologize enough for—"

"For providing the best entertainment I've seen all season? Nonsense." Sir Weston snatches up a wineglass. Burgundy liquid sloshes over the rim. "In fact, given that this Ayleth saved our esteemed High Priest from certain peril, I say she should be rewarded. Let her stay as maiden in the queen's household."

I don't know what it means to be part of the queen's *household*, but I can tell from the audience's reaction that it's the last thing I should do. They gasp and clap, gobbling up this proposal like it's one of their tarts. A few exclaim at what a wonderfully absurd idea it is. Everyone, that is, except Lady Marion.

"Absolutely not," she says flatly. "The queen's service is an honor, not an extension of the princess's menagerie."

Sir Weston gestures in my direction. "And does she not deserve to be honored? She saved the life of our High Priest, the representative of Meira."

Why did I have to do that?

"The queen isn't even present tonight," Lady Marion argues. "Shouldn't it be Her Majesty's decision?"

"This is Longest Night, is it not? A time for the world to turn upside down. When even kings and *queens* must dance to the beat of someone else's drum. *My* drum." Sir Weston seizes the crown from the player who represented Braxos and places it on his own head.

Several people cheer. This situation is spinning out of my control, and I resent the fact that I'm being spoken about like I'm an object and not a person. Like my voice doesn't matter. It's *exactly* the way Mother treats me. Rage climbs up my throat and my next words tumble out before I can reel them back.

"Shouldn't it be *my* decision?"

The attention of the audience lands on me like an iron weight. Damn my impulsive tongue. The king steps even closer, near enough now that I can smell him—wine and smoke and the deepest, most dangerous part of the forest. That unnerving feeling behind my ribs intensifies with each of my shallow breaths.

"And what do you say, Mistress?"

I say I want to run and never look back. This was a mad, reckless plan and I have no hope of succeeding. But I clench my fists against the marks on my palms—*Rhea's* marks—and can hear my sister's voice in my mind.

You have to be strong now.

Strong enough to get the Bloodstones anyway. And then I'll have her back. Much as I detest the idea of remaining among these awful people, I know I'll never get this chance again.

"I'll stay," I say, hardly feeling the words leave my lips.

The king smiles, wolfish. "Excellent."

"Your Majesty." The Sanctress's voice cuts cautiously between us. "I beg you to consider—Ayleth belongs to the Order of Light. It would be improper for her to remain *alone* at the palace."

"Surely you do not question the integrity of my court, Sanctress?"

A beat of silence passes. She blanches. "No, of course not. I only—"

"I'll stay with her."

My attention whips around. *Jacquetta.* By the Spirits.

Absolutely not, I scream at her with my eyes. She ignores me.

"There you have it." Sir Weston snaps his fingers. "It's settled. They'll both stay."

Both of us. Here at the White Court, hiding among those who will burn us if they discover what we are. And Jacquetta has already demonstrated how careless she intends to be with her power. As if she can sense my thoughts, Jacquetta finally looks at me. An impish smile tugs at her lips.

I hate her even more.

CHAPTER SEVENTEEN

A FTER A STERN—AND INFURIATING—LECTURE FROM THE SANC-
tress regarding our decorum while we're in the queen's service, Jacquetta and I are escorted to the area of the palace
where the queen's maidens reside. Our room—because of course
we have to share—is small, but infinitely nicer than the one in the
Sanctum. Flames crackle in the fireplace, filling the chamber with
pleasant warmth. There are four beds, two on opposing walls, each
dressed with thick counterpanes and expensive-looking fabric.
Small wooden chests rest at the foot of each one. Curtains shield
the tall windows, patterned not with the sigil of the crowned apple,
but with a crowned pomegranate instead. It must be the queen's
symbol.

"Someone will be along shortly with nightclothes," the maid who
guided us here explains. She, like everyone else, hasn't stopped ogling
us since we left the pageant. "And your things will be sent up as soon
as they arrive from the Sanctum."

After another few moments, in which she clearly expects us to say
something, the girl reluctantly slips out. As soon as she's gone,

Jacquetta heads for the nearest trunk and starts rifling through its contents.

"What are you doing?"

She pulls out a book and flips through it. "What does it look like? I'm getting acquainted with our new roommates. They'll do the same to us."

"Yes, and what will they find?" I jerk my chin at the door. "She said they were bringing our things from the Sanctum. What if they search yours?"

"I could ask you the same thing."

"No, you couldn't." I cross my arms. I'd had the common sense to leave anything related to our craft at Stonehaven. "I don't have any *lockpicks* or whatever else you brought."

Jacquetta tosses the book back into the trunk, maddeningly un-perturbed. "I don't see why you're still fixated on that. No one would have recognized it."

Does she think I'm daft? Maybe she does. After all, I believed her lies easily enough before.

But not again, that voice whispers.

"That pick had to have been runed. I saw you with the High Priest. You're a Caster."

She digs out a hand mirror, considering her reflection in the glass. "Am I?"

I should have used the baneweed on her when I'd had the chance.

"What are you even doing here? Have you come to take another shot at the High Priest? Don't expect me to rescue you this time."

Jacquetta lowers the mirror and looks at me. The blue of her eyes is touched with gold from the firelight, and I despise myself for the tiny thrill that runs through my blood.

"We might be stuck here together, but that doesn't mean I owe you answers—or anything else, for that matter. Let's just stay out of each other's way, shall we?"

Yet again, her dismissal stings far more than it should. Jacquetta wants it to hurt—I can see it in the twist of her lips. But I won't let her watch me bleed again. I lift my chin, matching her stony expression.

"I'd like nothing more."

"Good. Then—"

The door opens and someone else walks in. Jacquetta drops the mirror back into the trunk, but she's not fast enough to avoid being caught.

"Oh," a young woman says, her brow furrowing as she registers Jacquetta and the trunk. She's a little person, with bright-green eyes and auburn hair braided into an intricate arrangement on top of her head. "I'm afraid those are my belongings."

"Sorry, I . . ."

Jacquetta scrambles away, tugging on her wide sleeves—a nervous habit I'd forgotten she possessed. A highly satisfying flush climbs up her neck. Serves her right.

"No harm done, I'm sure." The young woman smiles, far more gracious than I would be. "I don't blame you for being curious. I'm Joan."

"Ayl—" I start.

"Ayleth, yes." Joan laughs, setting her armful of linens that I assume to be our nightclothes on one of the beds. "And Jacquetta. The whole court is buzzing about you both."

Wonderful.

"Those beds are free." She indicates the two on the other side of the room, which are—predictably—next to each other. I suppress a groan.

"Are you all right?" Joan goes on. "That tree might have flattened you."

At this point, I would hugely prefer if it had.

"I'm fine," I say, though my head is pounding. The torturous head-dress isn't helping, and I try to wrestle myself free of it.

"Here, let me." Joan crosses the room. Her fingers deftly loosen the fastenings. "I'm so glad they placed the two of you in here. Please do come to me if you need anything—headdresses or otherwise. I'm sure we'll be great friends."

Jacquetta makes a face that says she's sure we will not, then starts yanking at the laces of her costume. One sleeve slips down her arm, revealing the olive skin of her bare shoulder and the delicate ledge of her collarbone. Heat prickles in my cheeks and I can't help but recall the incident earlier, when the man—the king—had been bothering me before the pageant. Jacquetta had reached for me, like she wanted to . . .

A log collapses, sending sparks dancing up the chimney.

Don't let her in, that voice warns.

I know full well what will happen if I fail to listen.

"No—not that one," Duchess Poole corrects in a syrupy tone the next day. "Try again."

Metal clacks as I set the fork back down. Duchess Poole, the queen's Lady of Honor, doesn't notice—or ignores—my frustration, smiling benignly at us from her perch on a silk-upholstered chair. She's a tall, middle-aged woman, with a rich black complexion and a long, slender neck. A plate of cheeses and fruits waits on a table beside her. She has not offered us any of it.

"This one?" Jacquetta selects a slender fork.

"Yes. That's it." Duchess Poole nods, approving. "A utensil de-signed specifically for picking between the delicate bones of fish. His Majesty is fond of elaborate dishes. You may even be lucky enough to sample cockentrice during your stay."

My brow furrows. "What's a cockentrice?"

"It's His Majesty's invention," the duchess explains. Jewels sparkle in her elaborate crown of braids. "The upper half of a pig sewn onto the bottom of a capon. All roasted and gilded—with edible gold, of course."

I stare at her, my stomach rolling at the unnatural image. Then again, I suppose I'm not surprised that the White King would conceive of something so macabre.

And food is the least of my worries. This morning was a nightmare. We were roused at sunrise and practically dunked into washtubs. The water was warm, a small mercy, but I was scrubbed so thoroughly that I'm likely missing a layer of skin. After being flayed, we endured the horrendous experience of a gown fitting, a process that involved much fussing and pinching and some tortuous device called a *corset*—the main function of which I assume to be preventing women from properly breathing. Once we were unceremoniously strapped inside such contraptions, we moved on to *etiquette*, a practice I'm now convinced is the actual definition of insanity. Apparently, at the White Court, there is a correct manner of walking and sitting and even *passing* an object to another person. If that weren't ludicrous enough, each rule evidently varies depending on the rank of the person with whom we're interacting. How anyone keeps such details straight—or why anyone even cares about them—is utterly baffling.

"Now," the duchess goes on, dragging me unhappily back to the lesson, "do you recall the utensil I showed you for dessert?"

"I thought it was this one." I hold up a spoon.

"No." The duchess laughs, high and condescending. "That utensil is for *jellied* dishes. You wouldn't want to use it for anything else. That would be . . ."

"Ridiculous," Jacquetta mutters.

I entirely agree.

"Precisely." The duchess nods. "Now, try again."

Sunlight glints against the polished cutlery. Each piece is slightly varied, some curved and others serrated. I can't even begin to guess the purpose of a long, needle-like utensil sitting above my plate. Perhaps I might use it to gouge out my own eyes.

"This?" Jacquetta lifts a fork with three tines.

"Very good, Mistress. You're a quick learner." The duchess grants her a rare smile, one I find immensely irritating. Why is Jacquetta so much better at this than I am? "As I explained, there are many delicacies to be enjoyed at court. But you must both guard against overconsumption, especially where sweets are concerned. Above all, it is important that the queen's maidens appear modest in all areas, even with food."

I inwardly roll my eyes, immediately resolving to eat as much dessert as possible. Perhaps exclusively.

"Let us discuss your schedules." The duchess plucks a piece of cheese from her plate. "The majority of your time will be spent in the queen's rooms, or wherever else Her Majesty sees fit to send you. Queen Sybil is fond of the arts. Do you play any instruments?"

Some of the witches in Stonehaven were skilled with a lute, but I was too busy with Mother's lessons to indulge in any creative pursuits. "No."

"No, *Your Grace*," she corrects, wrapping a strand of grape-sized pearls around her long fingers. "What of singing?"

I can't carry a note to save my life. Jacquetta shakes her head as well, which is odd. I've heard her sing. She possesses a rather pleasant voice, in fact—low and resonant.

And she used it to lie, that other voice whispers.

"What a shame." The duchess clicks her tongue, as if our lack of talent has personally let her down. "But no matter. Perhaps you could read aloud to the queen. And there's plenty of sewing to be done—especially during this season. Her Majesty donates linens and shirts to the poor. I'm sure women of your station would enjoy such meaningful endeavors."

Enjoy is a strong word. But I don't care what chores we're assigned. As soon as the fuss about our placement dies down, I plan to ignore these inane duties as much as possible and scour the palace for the Bloodstones.

"Since it is Longest Night, however," the duchess goes on, "our days will often be interrupted by festivities. Jousts are popular, as well as banquets—whatever the Lord of Misrule organizes to honor our goddess. Sir Weston is quite the expert at inventing amusements. Like the pageant where you were . . . discovered."

"We're amusements?" The question surfaces before I can think better of it.

The duchess's dark eyes snap to mine.

"You are being *honored*." Her brocade skirts rustle as she rises, each step slow and deliberate as she crosses the room. "While I'm aware that this court owes you a great debt for your service to our High Priest, even you must understand that many women go to great lengths to secure a position within the queen's household. It is a privilege."

What she's really saying is that we don't belong here. We should be grateful for the scraps we're thrown from her table. Anger, the same I felt with Mother, flickers behind my sternum. I clench my back teeth, tamping it down before I say something else I'll regret.

"And who knows," Duchess Poole goes on, fussing with her pearls again. "Perhaps the two of you might even attract the eye of a gentleman. A lesser noble, of course. One who won't mind overlooking your . . . unique backgrounds."

Those men would do well to keep their distance, which is exactly what I intend to do—especially when it comes to the king. My hand travels surreptitiously to my left side, fingertips brushing my rib cage through my bodice. I haven't sensed the ominous feeling since my encounter with King Callen. Perhaps it really was my imagination, heightened by the anxiety of the night. Still, it can't hurt to remain as far from the White King as possible.

"But I must warn you." The duchess's train whispers against the floor. The pomegranate-colored fabric is embroidered in gold thread, miniature swallows flitting among a design of flowers and branches. "Not every man at court is *worthy*. Do not be led astray by empty promises and flattering lies. Do you understand? It is up to you to protect yourselves when a man gets . . . carried away."

"What are we supposed to do?" Jacquetta reaches for the mysterious, needle-like utensil. "Use this if someone gets too close?"

Duchess Poole gapes at her. "Absolutely not. This court does not condone violence."

Except for the murder of witches.

"Just . . . remain with the rest of the maidens or ladies at all times. And do *not* stab anyone. With anything." She swallows a mouthful of wine, presumably to fortify herself.

Jacquetta reluctantly replaces the utensil, not having promised a thing.

"Now." The duchess smooths her bodice. "I'd like to see a demonstration of your dancing skills. You may use each other as a partner."

"No!" Jacquetta and I answer at the same time.

I flush, an uninvited memory rushing up—Jacquetta and I spinning in the forest until we fell down, dizzy. Her body pressed against mine.

You taste like roses.

"Sisters aren't permitted dancing," I say, inventing the lie as a way to smother the image.

I may be forced to eat gilded pigs, but I will *never* be compelled to dance with Jacquetta. Judging from her icy silence, the other witch feels the same.

CHAPTER EIGHTEEN

ANY HOPE THAT OUR NEW UNIFORMS WILL CURB THE COURT'S
unceasing attention instantly dissipates the moment that
Jacquetta and I step out of our room the next morning. The
White Court evidently harbors the opinion that the two of us are
living dolls or pets, brought to the palace for their own amusement.
Gawks and condescending smiles follow us as we navigate the halls.
Even the false goddess's glittering Eyes seem to track our every step,
like they know what we are—that we don't belong here. The stiff
fabric of my gown is too confining and I continually tug at my bodice, desperate for a real breath.

But nothing is *real* in this palace—it's all like a manufactured
dream. Wealth oozes from every crevice. It's early winter, but vases
teem with huge white roses. Jewels sparkle and silks shine in the
light of the apple-shaped orbs dangling from marble tree branches.
Women parade about in elaborate headdresses spun with what's
probably real gold. One wears what appears to be a red-tailed fox
draped around her shoulders. We pass several card games, the tables
piled carelessly with stacks of coin. Clusters of people—called cour-

tiers, according to the duchess—are clumped in front of the arched, stained-glass windows. It's morning, but the smell of wine mixes with that of the various cloying perfumes, making it even more difficult to breathe.

For her part, Jacquetta doesn't seem affected by our surroundings, or even bothered by the attention thrown our way. She glides silently along beside me, her gaze fixed straight ahead. We haven't directly spoken since the night of the pageant. No matter how fiercely I command myself to focus on my own plans—or lack thereof—my traitorous mind keeps drifting back to her. Why is she *here*? The question refuses to be squashed, along with another—*Where has she been?* And, most uncomfortably, *Why didn't she come that night?*

Pointless though it is, I find myself sifting through the years Jacquetta and I spent together at Stonehaven. There aren't many. Jacquetta was young when the Hunt raided her first coven. After that, she and her mother, Nerissa, wandered the realm alone. According to what they told us, it took them years to find Stonehaven. I first spoke to Jacquetta in the library, after I discovered her tucked away in a corner, absorbed in my favorite novel. Maps were her real passion, though, and we'd lose hours tracing the boundaries of Riven or the other realms, inventing stories about what life might be like in different parts of the world. When we weren't buried in our books, I taught Jacquetta a few tricks from my arsenal of pranks. She was especially talented in trapping toads, which we slid into other witches' boots. I liked that about her—that she preferred to spend the day in the forest rather than in lessons. Like me.

She wasn't like you, though, that voice reminds me.

No—not in the end. And now I wonder how much of our time together was a total fabrication. Did Jacquetta ever care about me at all? Or was I just a *distraction*, like what she said to the other witch?

Jacquetta notices me looking at her. "What?"

"Nothing."

And it *is* nothing. We're different witches now. The Jacquetta from Stonehaven is gone. And the witch I was died in the clearing, like that barren tree where we'd carved our initials. A question unspools in my mind: Were we the ones who killed it? Our initials, carved together into its bark, were poison.

Even the forest knew we were cursed.

The low current of chatter dies as soon as we enter the queen's chambers. A dozen faces swivel in our direction and a wave of cold washes over me, like when I broke out of the wards at Stonehaven. This situation, however, is far more perilous.

They'll see right through you, that voice promises.

"Ah, here you are." Duchess Poole bustles over. She circles us, inspecting our uniforms. "You look ... acceptable."

Judging from my previous interactions with the duchess, I assume that such is the highest compliment we'll ever receive from her.

"Come," she beckons. "We don't keep the queen waiting."

Rustling skirts and raised eyebrows greet us as we pass through a set of double doors and into the next room. I do my best to ignore the sidelong stares, concentrating instead on the surroundings to distract myself. Like the rest of the palace, the queen's suite is extravagantly furnished. The crowned pomegranate, the same symbol embroidered on the front of our gowns, is molded into the eaves and patterned into the thick rugs. Colors of pomegranate and gold are reflected in cushions and chairs and drapes. Tall windows grant a view of the palace's manicured gardens, the steely winter sky streaked with thin clouds.

Rich tapestries and gilt-framed paintings crowd the walls, but I'm surprised to find that they don't portray scenes from the Order's lore—or even Riven's history. Instead, these works depict women, and not the typical mortal women I've come to expect. Rather than wearing ornate gowns or gaudy jewels, these women are dressed in armor. One is even brandishing a sword as she charges toward enemies on horseback, her mouth screaming a battle cry. Such scenes remind me more of the stories of the Ancients than any episode in mortal history. Why had the queen chosen to display them?

There's no time to puzzle it out as the duchess herds us into the innermost room of the suite. "Your Majesty. I present your additional maidens."

Duchess Poole sinks into a curtsy, watching us askance to make sure we're following suit. Queen Sibyl smiles at us from where she's seated in front of an enormous stained-glass window, a stunning rendering of an apple tree in full bloom. Pomegranates are scattered at the base of the tree, sparkling in the sunlight. Like the duchess, the queen is a middle-aged woman, perhaps even a bit older than the king. Where most courtiers clearly pride themselves on their appearance, the queen is refreshingly . . . ordinary. Instead of being piled into an ornate, and doubtless painful, arrangement, her waist-length, dark hair is loosely braided and threaded with jeweled pomegranates. Her white skin is etched faintly with fine lines, especially around her eyes and mouth. But the queen does not disguise the signs of age with powder or paint. In fact, the only real indication of this woman's status is the crown of intricately woven white-gold branches resting on her head. Tiny garnet apples glimmer among the metalwork like drops of freshly shed blood.

"Mistresses Ayleth and Jacquetta, if I'm not mistaken. Of the Order." The queen sets her embroidery on her lap. It's a raven stitched in black thread. Like the paintings, I find the pattern another surprising choice, given a raven's association with witches. "I'm so pleased to have you both joining us, Mistress Ayleth in particular. I learned of your recent service to the High Priest. We are very grateful to you."

"It was nothing," I reply automatically.

"Nonsense. Such bravery indicates strong character. We should all—"

A series of high, yipping barks interrupts the queen, followed by the frantic patter of tiny feet. Ladies yelp and leap from their seats, yanking their skirts out of the way as a blur of brown fur carves a haphazard path through the chamber.

"By the Light, what is this?" the queen asks.

She gets her answer when an animal careens between us, still yipping.

"It's a . . . dog!" Duchess Poole cries out, barely managing to dodge as the creature zooms around her skirts.

"Where did it—"

"Oh, here you are! Naughty thing."

Another woman emerges from the cluster of babbling ladies and promptly scoops the dog into her arms. Immediately, I recognize the raven hair and stunning features as belonging to the player who represented the false goddess in the pageant. The woman who vehemently protested our placement with the queen.

"Lady Marion." The queen's tone is kind, but I catch the hint of an edge beneath. "As you are aware, pets are welcome in my chambers, but they must be well behaved."

"I beg your pardon, Your Majesty." Lady Marion bobs a curtsy. The dog growls, its little ears laid flat. "I'm afraid I've not yet had the opportunity to train him. He's a recent gift, for Longest Night, you see. From a very *dear* friend."

So quick I almost miss it, a muscle in the queen's jaw twinges. "Indeed. Well, please make sure the dog—"

"Fitz, Your Majesty." Marion scratches between the dog's ears. "I've named him Fitz."

Startled gasps ricochet around the chamber. The queen's face shades momentarily paler. Why would a dog cause such a reaction?

THE CRIMSON CROWN   165

Marion, it seems, understands what she's done, her sharp-toothed smile widening as she coos at her dog.

"A generous gift," the queen says at last, regaining her composure as she settles herself back on her seat. "Though I would encourage you to take him to the kennel master for training as soon as possible. The dog clearly has a penchant for running off. I wouldn't want you to lose such a valuable *gift*."

The words are spoken innocently enough, but tension hums like a plucked cord. Marion adjusts the egg-shaped sapphire at her throat.

"Thank you for that advice, Your Majesty. And speaking of animals . . ." Her attention pivots to us. "Our guests should be sure to visit the princess and her menagerie during their stay at the palace."

Menagerie. I vaguely recall Marion mentioning that word before, at the pageant, but I still don't know what it means. I'd bet my life that it's nothing good, especially given that several ladies near Marion fail at holding back their laughter.

The queen, however, brightens. "What an excellent suggestion. Blodwyn would greatly benefit from the acquaintance of such *unspoiled* maidens."

Marion's eyes glitter, but she sweeps another curtsy and melts away, her growling dog struggling to free himself from her grasp. As the room returns to normalcy, the queen turns her attention back to Jacquetta and me.

"For now, I'll allow the two of you to acquaint yourselves with the rest of my retinue." She indicates the other women. "I'm certain that everyone is eager to make you feel welcome."

Welcoming is not a word I would ascribe to this viper's pit, especially not after the exchange I just witnessed. But Duchess Poole signals for us to curtsy again, then steers us back into the main chamber. Embroidery needles pause mid-stitch and books thump closed as we stand at the threshold. My nerves hum. I glance at the doors to the suite. They're not far. If I run, would they chase me? Probably not. I could just—

"Are you the new ladies?" Someone steps into my path, a woman with dark-brown skin and freckles smattered across her nose. "From the Order?"

"Who else would they be?" Another woman interrupts, her white cheeks heavily rouged. "Aren't they adorable in their little uniforms?"

It's the same uniform everyone else is wearing, but the women begin to circle around us, murmuring about our clothes and our hair and how wonderfully odd it is that we're here. Jacquetta appears as uncomfortable as I am, constantly edging away from the onslaught of attention. But no matter where we turn, we're immediately boxed in by more ladies.

"Did you really save the High Priest's life?" one asks. "I heard the statue shattered and someone lost their eye. Is that true?"

"And you've *never* been to court?"

"Of course they haven't." Another rolls her eyes. "They live in the Sanctum."

The first touches my elbow. "Is it terribly boring there?"

"Show some respect." The other gives her a smack. "They're *Sisters.*"

The space around us is narrowing at a frightening pace. Jacquetta and I are pushed close enough that our skirts brush.

"Have you ever tried one of these?"

A woman stuffs something bright orange into my mouth. Sudden sweetness bursts over my tongue and aches in my teeth. I almost choke, but she merely laughs.

"Look, she likes it!"

Panic rings, high and tinny, in my ears. Jacquetta is fending off a woman who's trying to straighten her headdress. Another reaches for me, a ribbon outstretched. Is she going to strangle me with it?

"For Meira's sake, give the poor girls some room to breathe."

The cluster of ladies instantly scatters, and I finally manage to inhale. But my relief at being rescued instantly sours when the circle parts to reveal Lady Marion. By the Spirits—I should have just let the other woman strangle me.

"The *Order* girls," she muses, still clutching her demon of a dog, who snaps at us as she approaches. "Won't you allow me to show you around?"

Marion beckons for us to follow her, and I see no way out of refusing without being swarmed again. Even so, such a fate might be preferable to whatever Marion has in store. Jacquetta seems to agree. We trade brief, beleaguered glances as we trudge after the courtier.

"The instruments are over there." Lady Marion points to an assortment of lutes and other stringed contraptions in the far corner of the room. "But Duchess Poole informed me that you don't play. Pity, that. And you don't sing, either."

Her comments are casual enough, but something about Marion's delivery causes embarrassment to prickle up my neck. It's exactly how Sindony made me feel, with her probing, Diviner gaze and damning insinuations. But at least I possessed an idea of why the Second disliked me—she judged me a poor substitute for Rhea. Marion is another matter. Why does the courtier hate us so much? Because of what occurred at the pageant? It feels like something more.

"Perhaps I could provide you with lessons," Marion offers.

"No!" The word bursts out of me, sharper than I intended. "I mean—"

"You should address me as *Your Excellency*," Marion corrects, dealing me the same expression that a wolf gives a rabbit. "I'm sure the duchess would have taught you to refer to others by their rank. Then again, perhaps she tried. Perhaps any sort of lesson is wasted on you."

Like your lessons in the craft, that voice adds.

Shame—identical to what coiled in my belly in Stonehaven's workroom during lessons with Mother—resurfaces. For a moment, I'm back there, small and inadequate. A powerless witch. *Nothing*.

"The duchess did explain," Jacquetta replies coolly, pulling me from the thorny memories. "She never mentioned you, though, or your rank. Perhaps she assumed such details weren't important."

A few ladies within earshot choke back a laugh. Marion cuts them a venomous glare and they're suddenly intently focused on their embroidery. That sludgy feeling from moments ago instantly dissipates. But Jacquetta hadn't goaded Marion for my sake. Had she? Her expression reveals nothing.

"The duchess was likely correct." Marion scratches between her dog's ears. He bares his tiny teeth at us. "I doubt very much that our paths will cross in any meaningful way. Then again, the two of you do seem to have a habit of appearing where you don't belong. What, exactly, were you doing the night of the pageant to cause such a disruption? Was it another daring rescue, like with the High Priest?"

Jacquetta is silent.

"It was an accident," I say.

"I see." Marion sidles closer. The scent of her oleander perfume clouds around us. "Someone like you must be prone to such *accidents*."

Like you. It slithers between us, raising my hackles.

"In any case," the courtier goes on, "I encourage you to take better care in future. Do you see the Watchers?"

She points to the ceiling, which is crafted to look like the latticed branches of apple trees. But there's something else I hadn't noticed before. Amid the carved leaves and renderings of fruit are small, sculpted faces. They stare down at us, grinning.

"Quite lifelike, aren't they?" Marion asks. "The Watchers serve as an important reminder for us all: At court, nothing remains secret for long."

And if anyone discovers my secrets, I'll be burned.

A shiver races down my spine. I need to get out of these rooms—away from Marion and every other vapid member of this court. But movement in the ceiling snags my attention. My brow furrows. Was that . . . a *Watcher*? I blink, sure that I'd imagined it. But no. One of the sculpted faces shifts again—slight, but definitely real. And then, to my utter amazement, the small face winks at me, then vanishes with a flash of red.

Just like what I saw duck behind the apple tree during the pageant.

CHAPTER NINETEEN

SOMEONE IS FOLLOWING ME.

I lie awake in the night, details spinning in my mind. In the Great Hall, I assumed the person who ran past me on the stage had been a servant or a performer. But neither of those people would have been observing me from the ceiling. Who was it? And what do they want?

Nothing remains secret for long. Marion's words haunt me, laced with the whine of the wind in the chimney. Mathilde was right. The White Palace is far more dangerous than I ever perceived. What was I thinking, coming here? I'm just one witch and the Hunt has killed thousands of us.

The fire crackles, like a waiting pyre. In its writhing tongues of flame, I can almost imagine that I see a face, just like on the night of my Ascension. Just like when . . .

I sit up straighter. Rhea appeared to me in a fire once before. Could she do so again? Could she tell me where the Bloodstones are? By the Spirits, why haven't I thought of this before? I scramble to the edge of my bed, concentrating on the flames.

"If you're there, I need you," I whisper, clenching my fists against our marks and willing my sister to appear. "*Please,* Rhea."

Another gust of wind moans down the chimney. Embers hiss and spark.

Ayleth, I think I hear. *Ayleth.*

Smoke curls up in inky tendrils. Is it thickening? Changing?

A sharp tapping noise makes my heart leap up my throat. But it wasn't from the fire. I think it came from the window. Is it Rhea? I start to clamber off the bed, but another sound stops me. Fabric rustles and the closed curtains of Jacquetta's bed shiver, then part. I burrow back under my coverlet before she sees that I'm awake. Jacquetta pads across the room. A few moments later, I hear the latch of the balcony door unclick. Why is she going out there?

I wait a full minute in the silence before slipping out of bed and creeping over to the windows, pressing close to the wall so that Jacquetta doesn't see my shadow. I ease one of the heavy drapes open a sliver. Jacquetta is standing at the far corner of the balcony, a bird perched on the railing beside her. Its blue-black feathers gleam in the moonlight.

It's a raven. That must have been the tapping I heard—not Rhea. Disappointment whooshes in my belly, even as I scold myself for being silly enough to believe that my sister would have been drifting around knocking on palace windows. I'm about to return to bed and sulk when a muffled voice floats in from the balcony—not Jacquetta's. I pause, angling myself to get a better look, and notice the crimson sheen to the raven's eyes. Of course—it's a messenger. Who sent it? Holding my breath, I ease the window open just enough to allow the raven's words to reach my ears.

We're running out of time. The voice is vaguely familiar. Nerissa's, perhaps? *I do not need to remind you of the sacrifices I've made to put you where you are. You can do this, Jacquetta. You* must *do this.*

My stomach knots, having endured similar speeches from my

own mother too many times to count. And I find myself curious to know how Jacquetta will respond. I wait in the quiet after the raven's message ends, anticipating a version of the scathing reply she dealt the other witch when she scried at the Sanctum. But Jacquetta doesn't say anything. Instead, she taps the raven's beak and sends it soaring into the night.

For a long while, she simply watches it go. The wind billows her nightdress around her, but she doesn't seem to sense the cold. What is she thinking? Is she—

Abruptly, Jacquetta clamps both of her hands over her mouth, sinks to her knees on the balcony, and *screams*.

The sound is barely audible, but I *feel* it. Her rage and sadness and pain vibrate against my very bones.

She betrayed you, a voice in my mind whispers.

She did. But in this moment, I know exactly how she feels— vulnerable and alone. My traitorous hand twitches, half reaching for the door. But what am I going to do? Comfort her? How? And why should I?

I don't get the chance to decide. Jacquetta's scream drains away. She tilts her face up to the stars and exhales a long breath. Moonlight slides over her features, highlighting the angles of her cheekbones and the fullness of her lips. At sixteen, I remember thinking she was the most beautiful witch I'd ever seen. Now . . .

Beauty is dangerous, that voice warns.

Jacquetta rises and straightens her nightdress. I scramble to return to my own bed and bury myself beneath my coverlet. Jacquetta lets herself back into the room. Her footsteps shuffle across the floor. For an instant, she pauses near my bed. I hold my breath. Does she suspect that I saw her? She must not, for her bed creaks with her weight, and then it's quiet again.

But even in the silence, her scream echoes in the forgotten chambers of my heart.

"How are you settling in?" Joan asks as she escorts us to the princess's rooms the following morning.

The queen had sent word with breakfast, inviting us to visit her daughter and see the menagerie. I'm grateful for time away from the other ladies. With any luck, I can leave the princess early and begin my search of the palace.

"Everyone is making us feel right at home," Jacquetta answers dryly.

She's been in a sour mood all morning, which I suspect is related to the raven last night. Part of me wants to ask her about it. On the balcony, she'd looked so . . .

She betrayed you, that voice whispers again.

"Court takes some getting used to," Joan replies, reading Jacquetta's sarcasm.

Indeed, the novelty of our presence still hasn't worn off, and I'm acutely aware of every murmured comment and surreptitious glance.

"Have you gotten used to court?" I ask.

She tilts her head, considering. "I think so. Being here is better than at my family's country estate, at least. There's nothing *there* but sheep and horses."

"Far preferable company," Jacquetta mutters, scowling in the direction of a man I recognize as Sir Weston, the person who suggested that we serve the queen.

He's surrounded by a gaggle of courtiers, gesturing wildly with his wineglass as he recounts some evidently thrilling tale. His gaze catches mine from across the hall, and a corner of his mouth quirks up. I look away.

"Preferable to Lady Marion's company, perhaps." Joan laughs. "I saw what happened between you yesterday. Good for you, Jacquetta, holding your own with her. Not many do that."

Jacquetta receives the compliment with a half grunt.

"Luckily, she doesn't meddle with me. I'm not important enough, I suppose."

"But we are?" I ask, still unsure what we did to earn Marion's hostility.

"Lady Marion," Joan begins, hesitant. "Well . . . she tends to assert her authority, given her position."

"As what?" Jacquetta asks.

Joan pauses as two courtiers drift by, then lowers her voice. "Lady Marion is the king's mistress. She has been for years. Some say it's the longest he's been with a woman. Besides the queen, of course."

I'm vaguely aware of what "mistress" means, and revulsion ripples through me at the idea of anyone having to be in such close proximity to the king on a regular basis.

"Some even speculate . . . well, you heard that she named her dog *Fitz*, of all things." Joan waits, clearly expecting us to react, but Jacquetta and I only stare blankly at her. "Fitz means *son of the king*. A horrible slight. The queen has prayed to the Light for a son for years, but . . . aside from the princess, her pregnancies have ended in tragedy. Even for Marion, that stunt was cruel."

A sudden rush of clarity washes over me. *That* was what I sensed between Marion and the queen, some power play regarding the king.

"But don't speak of it," Joan adds quickly, drawing the Eye over herself. "Trust me. Lady Marion's husband raised a fuss a few years back, and the king sent him away on *business*. He's been gone ever since."

"No need to worry about that."

As far as I'm concerned, Marion can keep the king, preferably as far away from me as possible. Again, I recall his hand snatching mine—that feeling behind my left ribs, like something reaching.

Pulling. It was nothing, I insist. Or it will be, because I have no intention of encountering that man again.

Joan leads us around another corner, and Jacquetta pulls up short, hissing a breath.

"What—" I start.

And then I see it. A massive tapestry stretches from floor to ceiling on the wall ahead. But this isn't a piece of artwork honoring a White King or the false goddess. It depicts *witches.* Five of them, their bodies contorted in agony, their crimson cloaks shredded and hanging limply from their shoulders. On their feet, identical pairs of iron shoes glow red. These are the five *Heirs,* I register. This tapestry is a rendering of the Night of Flame, the act of violence that ignited the Covens' War. Indeed, each witch is missing a finger, where her Bloodstone was cut off by the Huntsmen's blades. One of those witches was my grandmother, I realize dully, though I have no idea which figure represents her. Mother never showed me any portraits—hardly ever even spoke of her own mother, save to reference the massacre. But here she is in front of me. A mix of horror and disgust churns in my stomach.

"Ayleth, are you well?" Joan grasps my elbow, then notices the tapestry. "Oh. *That.* Yes, it gave me nightmares when I first came to court. I still try to avoid it."

She says that so lightly—as if the tapestry is a mere inconvenience, not a representation of the night that shattered our world and splintered my family. I can't tear my gaze away from those red iron shoes, picked out in glimmering scarlet threads to give the illusion that the metal is livid with heat. Those witches, my own grandmother, must have clawed and fought as their magic drained out of them. The phantom sizzle of flesh meeting iron hisses in my ears. It is a horrible, barbaric death. But this tapestry is displayed in a place of pride. *Triumph.* Like those witches were prize stags taken down in the forest.

"Ayleth," Jacquetta says at my side, low enough that only I can hear. "Don't react."

She might as well tell me not to breathe. But I know she's right. We're supposed to be Order Sisters, unbothered by such atrocities. I shove my rage down until it's just a dull throb.

"There's a different way to get here," Joan says, leading us down another corridor. "I'll show you next time."

"That won't be necessary," I say tightly, meaning it. I want to look at that tapestry as much as possible—so that I never forget what they've done.

Joan frowns but doesn't press.

"The princess's rooms are just through here," she says, pausing at a set of double doors. "And you should know . . . Princess Blodwyn rotates through her ladies rather quickly. When Lady Marion suggested you visit her, she wasn't being kind."

"What do you mean?"

"You'll see," Joan says, opening one of the doors for us. "And I'm sure you'll be fine."

From the sympathetic expression on her face, I doubt that very much.

CHAPTER TWENTY

THE DISTANT SHATTER OF BREAKING GLASS GREETS US ALMOST AS soon as the doors close, swiftly followed by startled cries and racing footsteps.

"No." Jacquetta immediately pivots back to the door. "I have better things to do than waste a day with a feral child."

I'm inclined to agree with her. But something in Jacquetta's tone gives me pause.

Time is running out, Nerissa had warned through the raven.

Clearly, her message hit its mark. Much as I try to fight it, the sound of Jacquetta's scream still resonates in my own heart.

"Are you . . . all right?" I venture.

Jacquetta's hand pauses on the doorknob. "I'm fine. Why?"

I hesitate. The last time Jacquetta caught me eavesdropping, she pulled a knife on me.

"I thought I heard you get up in the night," I say, skirting as close to the subject as I dare.

She stiffens, but she doesn't bite back at me. In fact, for an instant,

I think a bit of Jacquetta's armor falls away. Will she tell me about the raven? Against all good sense, my pulse quickens. But then—

"Let's not pretend we care for each other, shall we?"

The question lashes like a whip, but I deserve the sting. That's what I get for trying to be *nice*. Let Jacquetta scream all she wants. It's not my problem.

"Fine. But be quieter next time. I need my sleep."

A crash of wood echoes from deeper in the suite.

Jacquetta nods toward the sound. "Have fun with that."

And then she disappears out the door. By the Spirits, she's intolerable. Selfish and rude. Why hadn't I seen it when we were younger? I might have saved myself—

The tinny clang of falling metal interrupts my thoughts. What is going on? Curiosity pulls me toward the sound of shouting. Princess Blodwyn's suite is large and comfortable, like the queen's, with huge windows and rich furnishings. And—I pull up short at the threshold to an inner room—every expensive piece of it is currently being toppled, crushed, or thrown.

"Over here!" a woman yells, hoisting up a chair.

"No, it's here," another calls, flinging away a canary-yellow pillow from a chaise longue.

"It bit me!" someone else screams.

The other women hurry in her direction like a flock of noisy geese. One trips on a half-curled rug and tumbles to the ground. What are they chasing?

"I've got him!"

A girl of about twelve triumphantly lifts her arm, gripping something in her hand. Short legs poke through her fingers, vainly fighting to break free. A chorus of relieved cries follows her announcement. Some of the women collapse onto nearby chairs.

The girl coos at whatever creature she's captured. "Silly Crumbs. Look at all the trouble you've caused."

Is she . . . *the princess*? I expected that the daughter of the mad king would be a younger version of courtiers like Marion, vain and spoiled. This girl seems like she sprung up out of the forest, fully formed. Her white skin is flushed with exertion, and her ebony locks are wild and loose around her face. Her fine dress is rumpled, and various types of flowers litter her hair. She spots me and halts. Her lips—the red of a witch's cloak—slacken.

"Who are you?"

The other women look up from where they have wilted onto the furniture.

"Ah," one says. Unlike the others, who must be servants, she's not wearing a uniform embroidered with the royal crowned apple. Her gown looks more like ours, with the queen's crowned pomegranate embroidered in gold on her bodice. "The new maiden?"

"I . . . yes," I manage, still distracted by the wreckage. Feathers float lazily in the air. Broken glass and porcelain glitter on the floor.

"Excellent." The woman's deep sigh suggests that she believes I'm here to rescue her. "I am Lady Margery, head of the princess's household. Highness, perhaps you might show your new companion around your menagerie?"

Lady Margery flaps one hand absently toward a set of glass doors on the east wall. The princess doesn't answer, just veers off in that direction, cuddling what I suspect is a hedgehog. The servants peel themselves up and start collecting debris. From their resigned expressions, I gather that these incidents are regular occurrences in the princess's chambers. And I suddenly have *no* desire to be alone with that child.

"Perhaps I should help out here?" I offer. "There's clearly much to—"

"No, no." Lady Margery steers me forcefully toward the other room. "It really is better if the princess isn't left alone for too long. Go on, then. Catch up with her."

I should have escaped when I had the chance. Lady Margery practically shoves me through the doors and into the . . .

Menagerie.

The meaning of the word blooms wondrously before my eyes. A vaulted glass ceiling towers above me, winter sunlight pouring through the panes. Birds flit among dozens of small potted trees, trading melodies. Bell-shaped contraptions mounted to the ceiling spit out puffs of misty air. The walls are glass, permitting foggy views of the rest of the suite through the fronds of ferns and stems of climbing vines. Flowers bloom on topiary bushes and loll from trellises.

Everywhere I look, there's a different animal. A goose with her goslings, bathing in a shallow fountain. A peacock struts with his brilliant feathers flared. There's even a doe poking her head around a tree, her white-flag tail flicking when she sees us. I let myself take a deep breath of the humid air, wrapping a stray vine of honeysuckle around my finger.

"This place is is—"

A bright-yellow warbler flits across my path, followed by a yowl and a smear of black and orange. I blink. If I didn't know better, I'd think that was . . .

An animal trots out from behind a large fern, the bird proudly in its mouth and its tail swishing in a satisfied tempo. Horror flashes in my veins.

"*Nettle!*" I rush over to her. "Put that down! And what are you doing here?"

With an annoyed twitch of her tail, my cat reluctantly drops the warbler.

"Here, let me see."

The princess nudges my elbow. With the surprise of the menagerie and the shock of seeing Nettle, I'd almost forgotten about her. And now she knows about my cat. Damn. I glare at Nettle, who only licks her paw and doesn't even pretend to be chastened.

"I'm so sorry," I say, slipping the bird into the princess's cupped hands.

She gently prods at the injured creature, then inspects its wings. "I think it's just stunned. I've seen much worse."

A moment later, the bird shakes itself and lifts into the air. It emits one reproachful call at Nettle and then flaps away. My cat sulks, watching it go.

"So, you know that cat?" Blodwyn gestures at Nettle. "I wasn't sure where she came from. I found her in the garden and decided to keep her."

Nettle blinks her golden eyes. So she'd swindled her way in here, clever thing. I might have guessed. And despite my irritation, guilt prickles between my ribs. I hadn't returned to the Sanctum after the pageant. Nettle must have been worried. In fact, now that I think of it, I'm more than a little impressed that she found me.

"I . . . knew her at the Sanctum," I explain, the only answer I can summon. "She must have followed me here."

Blodwyn kneels, stroking underneath Nettle's chin. My cat lengthens herself, purring like she's known the princess all her life. Interesting. She's never friendly with new people.

"She's a nice cat."

"When she wants to be," I add, throwing Nettle a pointed look.

Crumbs, who is indeed a hedgehog, reappears and scampers beneath my skirts, his tiny feet pattering across my slippers. "Oh!"

"Don't worry." The princess waves a hand. "No matter what they said out there, he doesn't really bite. Not unless I want him to."

Judging from the grin on her face, I assume that Blodwyn was hoping I'd be horrified by her veiled threat. I laugh instead and she frowns, then starts off down one of the paths. Nettle lopes over to me and winds herself around my ankles.

"I'm sorry I left," I tell her quietly, scratching between her ears.

She swishes her tail in what I interpret as petulance, which I suppose I deserve. Then, already bored of me, my cat flops down in a spot of sunlight. I follow after Blodwyn, still marveling at the menagerie. With so many plants and animals, I can almost imagine that we've left the White Palace far behind us.

"Are you here to spy on me?" the princess asks abruptly.

I blink. "No. Do people spy on you?"

A pale narcissus flower floats down from her hair. "My ladies are always reporting on me. Someone pays them, I think."

"I'm not a lady."

The princess considers this. "I suppose not. You said you met your cat at a Sanctum. It's true you lived there, then? I think I'd hate being a Sister. What do you do all day? Pray? That sounds boring."

I'm not sure which question or comment to respond to first. Blodwyn certainly isn't afraid to speak her mind, one seemingly as prickly as her hedgehog. Perhaps Jacquetta was wrong to leave. The two might get along.

"I studied a lot," I tell her truthfully.

"I despise study," she answers. "I prefer the garden."

"So do I. Well—the forest." Back before it was ruined for me.

A rabbit hops up to the princess and she fishes a carrot out of her pocket. "Ladies aren't allowed in the forest."

"I already told you—I'm not a lady. And our Sanctum was very remote. We had to go into the forest if we wanted to eat."

Blodwyn settles herself on a bench. The warbler lands beside her and she pets the tuft of fuzz on top of its head. Nettle reappears, crouching low and watching the bird with interest.

"Don't," I warn her under my breath. She grumbles.

"What do you mean, if you wanted to eat?" Blodwyn asks. "Didn't your Sanctum have kitchens?"

"We had to have something to *put* in our kitchen. The forest was filled with herbs and plants. Wild game."

"Wild game?" Blodwyn stops petting the warbler. "Does that mean ... you *hunted*? With a bow and everything?"

"Of course. No one else was going to do it for us."

A duckling waddles away from its fellows, clicking its beak at Blodwyn's skirts. The princess ignores it, fixated on me. "Have you ever seen a wolf?"

I think back to when I would accompany the Elementals on their hunts. I'd spotted plenty of wild boar, or foxes. But never wolves. "I don't—"

"Or a Nevenwolf?"

A *Nevenwolf*? How does a mortal child—*this* child—know about such creatures?

"Where did you hear about those?"

"I've seen one," she replies, matter-of-fact. "Prowling the grounds at night. I told my ladies, but they think I'm lying. They can't say that, of course, but I can tell."

A shiver races down my spine as I recall the spots of light I'd glimpsed in the forest at Stonehaven, those that I mistook for a pair of glowing red eyes. *Could* the princess have seen a Nevenwolf? If the Veil is thin enough, it's possible that one slipped through.

"When did you see it?"

Her brow scrunches. "A few days ago."

After I arrived at the White City, then. Dread knocks in my chest. It's just a coincidence, I tell myself. And the princess probably didn't even see a Nevenwolf. Just a large dog or some similar creature.

"I know what it was," the princess goes on, as if guessing my thoughts. "I've seen pictures in books in the library."

That catches my attention. "There's a library here?"

"Of course there is." She frowns. "Not that I get to visit it very much. I'm not allowed anywhere without an escort, and none of my companions ever want to accompany me. They'd rather play cards or gossip about stupid men."

"*I* would like to visit," I tell her immediately. If the palace has books pertaining to Nevenwolves, they might have information about the Bloodstones as well.

"Princess?" A voice carries through the menagerie. "Your tutor is here."

Blodwyn groans.

"Not that odious man again." But then she looks at me and grins. "You said you wanted to go to the library? How about right now?"

The footsteps are closer now. "Princess?"

"Are you sure we can—"

Blodwyn is already up and hurrying toward the back of the menagerie. I scramble to follow the flash of her skirts, disgruntled animals parting in my wake. The princess halts at the far wall—the only one that isn't glass. She lifts a curtain of climbing vines, revealing a door, then fishes a key out of a hidden pocket on her dress. With a deftness that suggests she's done this many times before, Blodwyn jams the key into the lock, yanks the door wide, and then rushes through it. I duck in after her. Nettle doesn't follow, probably hunting the warbler again.

"Just a minute," Blodwyn murmurs as the door closes behind us.

She rummages around in the darkness and then a match strikes. The princess's face is illuminated in the light of a half-burned candle. Gradually, our surroundings sharpen into focus. The walls are narrow and covered in cobwebs. A thick layer of dust carpets the floor and rusted sconces line the walls.

"Where are we?"

"Old passages." Candlelight bobs along the walls as she leads me in the other direction. "They were sealed off long before the menagerie was built."

It certainly appears that way. And a question occurs to me: How extensive are these passages? More important, could I use them?

"How do you keep track of all this?" I ask the princess.

"Mostly by exploring," she explains. "But there might be some maps in the library. We can ask the Keepers, if you like."

This is *exactly* the sort of help I've needed. "I'd like that very much."

She throws a glance over her shoulder. "You're different. Perhaps I won't mind having you around now and then."

Now and then. What a—

A draft billows down the hall, cold enough to needle through my uniform. Beneath the shuffling of our footsteps, I detect a faint moan, low and ominous and similar enough to a growl that the hair on the back of my neck prickles.

"Did you hear that?" I ask Blodwyn.

She pauses and tilts her head as she listens. "No. What did it sound like?"

Malum, my mind supplies. *A manifestation from beyond the Veil.*

Faint as the brush of a wing, I sense a tremble behind my left ribs.

"It was nothing," I say, as much to myself as to the princess. "I must have imagined it."

"I've heard rumors that these passages are haunted, but I've never seen a ghost," she says, sounding disappointed. "Anyway, here we are."

She stops at a wooden panel and maneuvers it loose, revealing an entrance. The other side is blocked by a tapestry. Blodwyn and I fight our way around the heavy fabric and then I'm blinking at the sudden brightness of—

My breath catches. *The library.*

Before this moment, the palace's Great Hall was the largest chamber I'd ever seen, but this place is even more massive. Shelves tower over my head, carved to resemble trees that stretch up into a second-story gallery. Light fixtures arch out from the walls, their bases fashioned to appear as boughs with lanterns dangling from the branches. And there are *so many* books. Our collection at Stonehaven is paltry in comparison. I could spend years here and never read every volume.

"It's wonderful, isn't it?" Blodwyn asks.

I turn in a circle, still absorbing the gold-latticed ceiling and glimpses of the upper floor. "Did you say that your other maidens don't like coming here?"

"That's right," Blodwyn confirms primly. "Fools, aren't they?"

They are indeed.

"Ah, Princess." A man in purple robes rounds one of the shelves, bowing when he spots Blodwyn. "I was wondering when you might grace us with a visit again."

Blodwyn pulls herself away from where she was admiring a rather gruesome-looking eel encased in glass. "Mother finally sent me a companion who isn't an idiot."

The man notices me. He has deep-brown skin and kind hazel eyes.

"A high compliment," he says, inclining his chin. "Any friend of the princess is a friend of the Keepers. Can I help you find anything?"

"Another novel," Blodwyn replies. "And nothing fluffy like last time. If I read about one more princess being rescued by a knight, I'll toss the thing out the window."

A smile twitches at my lips.

"Understood." The Keeper bows again, pressing a hand to his chest. He looks to me. "And for you? Are you as uninterested in romance as our princess?"

I'd like to know what happened to the Bloodstones after the Heirs were murdered.

I tug at my sleeves. This man seems nice enough, but I don't want to raise any alarms with my request.

"I'm not sure," I hedge. "Could you point me in the direction of your history texts?"

A record of the early events of the war might mention the Bloodstones. After all, there's a tapestry dedicated to the massacre.

"History?" Blodwyn makes a face. "Really?"

"Now, now," the Keeper chides gently. "It's a passion of mine as well."

"Passion," Blodwyn mutters under her breath. "More like *torture.*"

The Keeper shakes his head at her. "You'll find the histories in the back right, next to a rather hideous bust of an important person whose name I have forgotten. Let me know if you need help locating anything specific. Will you be occupying your usual place, Princess?"

"Probably." She waves as she traipses off into the stacks. "And if you happen to have any tarts on hand, I wouldn't object."

The man laughs. "I'll see what can be done."

CHAPTER TWENTY-ONE

BLODWYN'S *USUAL* PLACE, IT TURNS OUT, IS TUCKED AWAY IN A FAR corner of the library. An enormous window looks over the sea of trees spilling down the mountainside, a landscape so vast that I could almost forget that I'm in the palace at all. Blodwyn herself is nestled in the window seat, wrapped in a fur blanket, with a small pile of the promised tarts within reach.

"Yes, gut him," she murmurs to herself every so often.

I wish I was as satisfied with my own reading. Though I'd located the history section, as well as a dozen titles detailing the start of the Covens' War, none provide any information about the Bloodstones. In fact, my initial impression of this library is souring by the minute.

"Call these *histories.*" I slam another book shut after I come upon a passage that suggests the death of a witch is painless, as it releases their soul into the Light.

I snatch up a tart from my own plate and angrily bite into it, unable to appreciate the rich lemon flavor. What did I expect? After what I witnessed at the pageant, it's clear that the mortals care nothing for truth. Each account of the war is the same—witches used

Malum to spell Braxos, and every other White King, into believing their lies. They imprisoned Meira. It was only when the Heirs were killed that the false goddess's "Light" shone once again upon the realm. Every raid is described as a celebration, a banishment of Malum. But it's the Veil we *witches* forged that's really keeping that sinister force at bay. I think of how the Ancients *actually* died to create that barrier and my rage deepens. Would that the Five could see what their sacrifice accomplished.

Bells chime through the cavernous library, signaling that another hour has passed. That's two since we arrived, and I haven't discovered so much as a hint to what happened to the Bloodstones after the massacre. Sighing, I pull another book toward me and start paging through it. As with the other accounts I've read, this volume begins with the story of Braxos. Sunlight glimmers on the luminous ink illustration of the first White King, back when he was nothing but a mere apple farmer. As the tale goes, the line of the former royal family—those who originally worshiped the Order—was all but dried up. Without an heir, the realm would cede to the Rycinthian rulers and their ancient ties to the throne.

But rather than allow another realm to claim Riven, the dying king established a contest, one that would name its winner his heir. According to this record, nearly every man in the realm—women, predictably, were barred from participation—entered for the chance to inherit the crown. But it was Braxos who emerged victorious.

Another illustration depicts the future king standing triumphant on the steps of the old palace, still dressed in his peasant clothes. White rose petals float down around him, heralding the new age. To Braxos's left, a woman who is obviously meant to portray a witch lies in wait, her green eyes glimmering beneath her crimson cloak. A Bloodstone shines on her finger, a menacing tendril of red rising from the jewel and slinking toward Braxos. To his right, an Order priest lifts a hand, as if to shield the king from her wickedness. This book was evidently written recently, for the Order priest looks strikingly similar to Ignatius. I roll my eyes, unsurprised that Meira's supposed representative would immortalize himself in such a pretentious manner.

"Mistress Ayleth."

I jump, having been so absorbed in the text that I didn't hear anyone approach. Panic jolts up my spine. It's Ignatius. I hastily close the book, skin crawling at the idea that the High Priest's portrait somehow summoned the man himself.

"Your Illuminance." I dip my chin in greeting.

"What a pleasure to discover you both here." His amber gaze drifts between me and the princess, who tucks her own volume surreptitiously into the folds of her blanket. "I was just visiting the archives. What brings the two of you to the library today?"

Before I can answer, he picks up one of the books on my table and skims the title.

"An account of the war." He raises an eyebrow. "How interesting. In my experience, most in this court find such subjects to be rather dry."

"That's what I told her," Blodwyn chimes in.

Ignatius laughs. "May I ask what attracted you to the topic?"

I swallow, fisting my skirts. What would a real Order Sister say?

"The . . . illustrations" is all I can muster.

He opens the book. "Yes, I see what you mean. The detail is impeccable. Have you had the opportunity to view the tapestry on the second floor? I commissioned it myself."

A vision of the hot iron shoes sears in my mind. "Yes. I've seen it."

Ignatius returns the book, still open to an image of a witch strapped to a pyre.

"You know, I feel that I haven't properly thanked you for your act of selflessness on the night I visited the Sanctum."

"Selflessness?" Blodwyn asks.

"That's right, Princess." Ignatius smiles at her. "Are you aware of Mistress Ayleth's heroics?"

She winds an ebony curl around her finger. "I know she can shoot a bow."

Damn. I shouldn't have told her that.

"Is that so?" Ignatius studies me. "You surprise me again, Mistress. But no, Highness. Our Mistress Ayleth saved my life. She pushed me out of the way before I was crushed beneath a falling statue, with no regard for her own safety."

Blodwyn sits up straighter. "Truly? Weren't you afraid?"

Not as much as I am now. "I only did what anyone else would have done."

"I'm not sure that's as accurate as we would prefer to believe." The ruby Eye pendant glimmers on its chain. "We're all very fortunate that Meira's Light guided you to that Sanctum—and to court. In fact, why don't you join me at the High Table tonight at dinner?"

I'd rather eat that monstrous pig-capon dish. "Duchess Poole said I'm to stay with the other maidens."

"I'll send word to the duchess myself." He waves a ringed hand. "I'm eager to learn more about you."

Before I can devise some other excuse, the High Priest traces the sign of the Eye between us and sails away, his flame-colored robes billowing like a pyre.

Marion's words loop through my mind: *At court, nothing remains secret for long.*

"Lucky you," Blodwyn comments, retrieving her book. "I only get to sit at the High Table on my birthday or when someone special is visiting. You'll have the best food. And you'll be sitting with Mother and Papa as well."

Sitting with the *king*? A memory of those gray eyes blooms. That is the *last* place I need to be.

"In fact, will you bring me some dessert?" Blodwyn asks around a bite of tart. "I'm never served anything half as good in my rooms."

Judging from the sludge churning in my stomach, the princess is welcome to my entire dinner. I rub at my temples. What have I gotten myself into?

Footsteps patter nearby, too light and quick to belong to the High Priest. I swivel in my seat just in time to catch a flash of red blur past on the other side of the aisle, one that instantly registers. I'd seen that color in the Great Hall and again in the queen's rooms. It's the person who's been following me. This time, I'm going to find out what they want.

"Where are you going?" Blodwyn asks as I push up from the table.

"I'll be right back," I call over my shoulder.

Picking up my skirts, I hurry into the stacks, chasing after that smear of red. Whoever it is, they're fast. I break into a trot, cursing my too-tight slippers as I veer right and then left through the aisles. I round the next shelf. There—a scarlet cap.

It's a little person. Male, and about a head taller than Joan. He spots me and panic twists his features. I was right—he *has* been following me. I urge my feet faster. There's a small statue up ahead—a marble rendering of Braxos sitting under an apple tree—and the man darts around its base. I dive just before he disappears, nearly colliding with the pedestal, and manage to close my grip around his ankle.

He kicks at me. "Let go! Let me *go,* damn you!"

"Not until you explain why you've been following me."

I grunt, struggling to keep hold of him. He's all muscle, with deep-brown skin. His cap falls from his head to expose wispy white hair beneath. Creases bracket his mouth and fan out from his eyes. Eyes, I notice now, that are a striking kaleidoscope of colors, like sapphires and turquoises and emeralds that have been crushed up together. Recognition hits like an arrow striking. I've seen illustrations of eyes like those. This isn't a mortal man.

"You're a *Dwarf,*" I gasp.

My mind combs feverishly over the details I learned of the

Dwarves and their Guilds. Like the witches, the Dwarves were a re-spected magical community within Riven. If I'm not mistaken, there was even a Guild here at the palace. But the Dwarves vanished after the king levied his edict. Most witches assume they went into hiding. Some, kinder, witches believe the king killed them. Evidently, we were all wrong.

"What are you doing here?" I demand. "I thought you were all gone—or dead."

"Do I look dead?" He kicks at me again. "And it's no business of yours what I am doing, *Mistress Witch*."

Everything in me goes still. He *knows*.

"Thought I wouldn't notice, did you?" He wrinkles his nose, which is roughly the size and shape of a turnip. "Bet you thought you were a clever witch, hiding yourself in the queen's service. Won-der what Her Majesty would think of it."

The panic thrumming in my veins congeals to anger. "Is that why you've been following me? You're going to turn me in? My sisters were right about you. You left us to die. We're kindred and you—"

"Kindred?" He hoots. "Answer me this—if it was the Dwarves who were hunted, what would you witches have done? Swooped in with your magic spells to rescue us?"

"Of course we would have."

He barks a laugh. "Well, that's interesting news. If my recollection serves, the covens keep to themselves, holed up in those Sanctums of yours. Never did see one of mine invited in there, did you?"

I open my mouth to argue with this infuriating Dwarf, but the words don't come. Because he's right. Only witches live among the covens. That's just how things are done.

It's the way things are now, Eunice's words in the Sanctum float back to me.

I'd been so frustrated with her—how she and the other mortals had been focused only on their own lives and not what was happening to us. But I suppose the covens weren't much different. A guilty flush prickles up my neck.

"Aye, thought so," the Dwarf grumbles at my silence. "Just like a witch to barge in here, hurling accusations when all we've done is keep our heads on our shoulders. I deeply apologize, Mistress Witch, if our survival inconvenienced the covens."

"Inconvenienced?" I echo, dumbfounded. "We're being murdered. And you're here, living a comfortable life in the palace."

"Comfortable?" He cackles. "Take a look for yourself what *comfort* we Dwarves enjoy."

He jerks his chin to indicate his left leg. The hem of his trousers is pulled up, exposing an inked image of crossed pickaxes, with a crowned apple in the middle. It matches the gold pin on his cap. But I notice that the skin around the mark is pink and puckered, suggesting . . .

"Is that . . . a *brand*?"

"Clever witch indeed," he replies dryly. "It's a Guild Mark, to show all the world where we Dwarves belong. Not to the Mines, as is our right, but to the king. Anyone outside the palace sees it on me, they know what to do. Hefty reward for returning a *lost* Dwarf these days. King can't live without his baubles and trinkets, after all."

Understanding begins to stitch itself together in my mind. Dwarves possess a crafting magic, skilled in jewelry and weapons and fixtures. The White Palace is dripping with such wealth. I must have seen a hundred examples of Dwarvian craftsmanship in the last days without even registering it. I study the Guild Mark again, fresh guilt digging between my shoulder blades with the knowledge of what it really represents. The king might not have passed an edict against the Dwarves, but he certainly devised a method to control them—one just as sinister as the raids.

"You're prisoners."

"Observant, are you?"

My grip on his ankle loosens and he scoots away from me, muttering about permanent damage.

"I didn't know." Even to me, the excuse sounds flimsy. "None of us did. I told you—we thought you were gone or dead. We would have helped you, if we understood. *I* would have helped you."

Though I'm not sure how.

The Dwarf grunts, brushes off his cap, and jams it back on his head. "Big words from a small witch."

And a powerless one at that, that voice whispers.

"My name is Ayleth," I tell him, extending my hand.

For a moment, he just looks at it, unimpressed. But then he heaves a sigh and accepts. His skin is rough and calloused against mine. And I can feel a faint vibration through our contact, like rocks rolling down a mountain. Perhaps it's his connection to the Mines.

"Roland," he offers, gruff.

"It's nice to meet you. Though I wouldn't call it our first meeting. You *have* been following me. Are you going to tell me why?"

He shrugs, the barest hint of color blooming in his cheeks. "Curious, I suppose. This is the last place I'd think to look for one of your kind. What are you doing here? Got a taste for the flame?"

I hesitate. Can I trust Roland? Or will he turn me in? But he hasn't reported me yet, and he's had plenty of opportunity to do so. And then there's the matter of his Guild Mark. Roland's obvious—and perhaps understandable—resentment of the covens aside, I doubt he harbors any loyalty to the White King. Perhaps I can take advantage of that. Roland might hold the answers I'm looking for.

"I'm here for the Bloodstones," I tell him at last.

"Bloodstones?" he echoes.

By the Spirits, have even the Dwarves forgotten our history?

"Those that hold the Veil?" I ask, irritated. "They were stolen when the Hunt captured the Heirs."

"Oh, *those* Bloodstones." Roland snaps his fingers. "Why didn't you say so? I've got them down in the Mines. Let me just pop down and fetch them for you."

I cross my arms, glaring. "Do you know where they are or not?"

"'Course I don't." He waves me off. "Everything related to the covens was burned in the Great Cleansing. I expect the Bloodstones were with them."

Great Cleansing. I shudder, envisioning a huge pyre stacked with grimoires and crimson cloaks and *witches*. But the Bloodstones couldn't have been there.

"No, they weren't."

He arches an eyebrow. "And how do you know? Did you attend?"

"I know because the Bloodstones are what hold the Veil, and the Veil hasn't fallen."

Roland frowns. "Don't know about that. Strange enough things have happened of late."

"Strange?" My heart kicks. "Like what?"

He lifts a shoulder. "Shadows acting like they shouldn't. Noises. And just a feeling I get. Like something's off. It's been getting worse too."

"How long has it been worse?"

"A week or so. Maybe less."

That would fit with when Blodwyn claims to have seen the Nevenwolf. When *I* came to the palace. Could those events be related? I don't let myself look at that question too long.

"If the Veil had really fallen, you would know," I say, as much to Roland as myself. "It's holding, but barely."

"Aye, if you say so." He tilts his head at me. "And let me guess— you're here to find the stones and fix things. Save the realm from certain peril?"

And to pull my dead sister out from beyond the Veil. I decide it's better that Roland doesn't know all the particulars just yet. "Something like that."

"I see." He straightens his jacket and starts to turn away. "Well, good luck to you, Mistress Witch. Hope you don't die, but you probably will."

"Wait," I call after him. "Don't you want to help?"

He snorts. "Why in the Mines would I want to do that?"

"Because . . ." I fumble to find a reason for what should be obvious. "It's the *Veil*. When it falls, it threatens all of us. Surely you've heard of what Malum brings—blights and plagues. Madness."

"Do things not seem *mad* already?" He gestures around him. "I live in the White Palace, home of the *mad* king. Veil, no Veil—it makes little difference to me. Unless you have some secret weapon at your disposal, I'll thank you to leave me out of it."

By the Spirits. Secret weapon? Who does he think I am, an—

An Heir.

No. *No.* I can't use that—won't use it. It's not even true. But Roland starts tapping his foot, impatient. In another moment, he'll leave and I'll be utterly alone.

"I'm Millicent's descendant."

He gapes at me. "You're an Ancient's *Heir*?"

Not even a little bit. "My mother is. I'm her Second, next in line."

Roland leans in so that his face is inches from mine. "Are you lying, Mistress Witch?"

"No." But I very much wish that I were.

If I hadn't been born into this bloodline, I'd probably be off in some other coven. Or I'd be dead, killed in a raid. Right now, either sounds better than my current situation.

"*Millicent.*" Roland looks me up and down. "Thought all the Heirs were dead at this point. And what do you need me for, then? Can't you find the stones with your power or something? Blast this palace to pieces?"

That too-familiar feeling of inadequacy settles over me. "It's . . . complicated."

"Nope. Don't like complicated. Simplicity is the way for me." He presses his hands to his chest. "Air in my lungs and my neck on my shoulders. Goodbye, Mistress Witch. Give my best to your ancestress when you meet her."

He heads for the statue.

"Please," I beg, desperate. "I need help. Don't you want to escape? If the witches have the Bloodstones again, we can mend the Veil. Strengthen our power. No more war or mad kings or Guild Marks. Riven will be different."

None of that is the actual reason I came to the White Palace, but I'll figure out the details later. Besides, it's true. I could get Rhea *and* return the Bloodstones. Then I'll have more than erased the shadows of my past. I clench my fists against Rhea's marks.

Roland eyes me, dubious. "You really think you can manage it?"

"Not alone."

He grumbles something under his breath. "And what do you need, exactly?"

"Just point me in the direction of the stones."

"Oh, a simple request, is it?" Roland rubs his chin. "Fine, then. I'll see what I can do. But I make no promises. And when I say I'm done, that's it. No more."

"Of course." I'm grinning with relief. "I understand. Thank you."

He only shakes his head, muttering about his own lack of sense and impending doom.

"Wait," I call as he ducks behind the statue. "How do I find you?"

"You don't," he replies without so much as a backward glance.

And then he's gone. I hurry over to peer behind the statue's base, curious as to how he gets around the palace, but there's nothing there.

CHAPTER TWENTY-TWO

B LODWYN AND I SPEND THE REMAINDER OF THE DAY IN THE LI-
brary, but—aside from my encounter with Roland—my
search for the Bloodstones is maddeningly fruitless. I didn't
even locate any maps of the servants' passages, not that I'd have a clue
what to do with them if I had. The princess makes me promise that
we can return for more books soon, but what's the use of combing
through thousands of pages of the Order's lies? All the factual accounts of the war have obviously been erased, probably in the *Great
Cleansing* Roland described. Whatever is left has been distorted to fit
the Order's narrative. Hopefully Roland finds information about the
stones soon. If not, I'm not sure what I'll do. And then I'll have failed
at something else.

After enduring another prayer service in the evening, I trudge
back to our chamber, deciding to skip dinner and sulk in bed. But
Joan flies at me as soon as I step through the door, flapping a piece
of parchment in one hand.

"Oh, Ayleth!" She shoves the paper at me. "This just came. You're
to have dinner at the High Table. Can you believe it? Not even

Lady Marion has received such an honor. Come, I'll help you get ready."

Damn everything. I'd all but forgotten the High Priest's invitation.

"What's going on?" Jacquetta asks as she enters the room.

I'm not sure where she spent her own day, but—judging from the cloud of frustration following her—it wasn't productive. Also, her fingertips are stained with a dark purplish substance. What had she been doing? Not that it's any of my business.

"Ayleth is invited to the High Table," Joan effuses as she steers me to sit on a stool and begins rearranging my hair. Her movements are surprisingly gentle, not like the harried servants who yank and pull.

"What does that mean?" Jacquetta asks.

"According to the princess, it means I'll have the best food and enjoy the company of the king," I say dryly. Something flashes across Jacquetta's features. Concern?

Stop being an idiot, that voice scolds.

"The princess is correct about the food," Joan confirms. "And you'll also be seated in front of the whole court. So, it's important to look your best."

In front of everyone. Again.

"Can't someone else take my place?" I practically beg. "You seem like you want to go."

Joan only laughs as she slides a pin into my hair. "My mother would be thrilled, but I'm afraid not. A specific invitation is required to sit at the High Table. And it would be a huge slight to refuse."

Which means doing so would attract even more unwanted attention. I let out a sigh, a headache already twinging at my temples.

"I know it's nerve-wracking." Joan pats my shoulder. "But you might enjoy yourself."

There's no possibility of that. But I don't argue as Joan finishes with my hair and then fusses with my dress. This won't be any different from dinner with the Seconds, I attempt to convince myself. In fact, it might be easier, as I won't have Mother breathing down my neck and I'm not expected to entertain anyone. I just have to sit there and eat. Still, my jittering nerves refuse to settle. I'm a witch, about to share a table with the man who hunts us. And I can't help feeling like *I'm* being served for dinner.

Long tables run the length of the Great Hall, already filled with courtiers who—judging by the wine-soaked smell—are deep in their cups. The decorations from the pageant have been removed, replaced by rich tapestries that display scenes from Riven's history picked out in glimmering thread. Banners hang from the hammered-beam ceiling, each bearing the crowned-apple sigil, which shines like a beating heart in the torchlight. Dozens of mounted stag heads line the walls, their empty eyes and branched antlers appearing ghoulish in the shadows. How typical of the White King to decorate his palace with creatures he slaughtered.

Reluctantly, I present my invitation to the servant at the door. He checks it and then leads me to the raised platform of the High Table. A few other people I don't recognize are already seated, their unspoken questions grating against my nerves.

Who is she?

What is she *doing here?*

Desperate for a distraction, I busy myself with the cutlery surrounding my plate, trying to recall Duchess Poole's lesson. Where's the long, pointed one? I highly suspect that I'll need it.

"Ah, Mistress Ayleth." The ripple of flame-colored robes warns me of the High Priest's presence. "I'm pleased to see you've accepted my invitation."

Summons is a better word for it. Ignatius takes the seat next to mine, and a servant pours wine into both of our glasses.

"I do hope the food won't be too rich for you this evening." The High Priest sips his wine, red slick on his lips. "I'm sure you're accustomed to much simpler fare at . . . which Sanctum was it again?"

Instinct screams at me not to tell him. But lying is more dangerous. "Stonehaven."

"That's right." He nods. "Quite remote, isn't it? I confess, I've never ventured to that part of the realm. Perhaps I should visit."

I flinch. "The journey is quite long."

"That may be so." He raises his glass to me. "But one clearly worth the effort, if such a place is where we can find the most devoted Followers of our goddess."

I already hate this night and take a healthy swallow of my own wine. It's a dry vintage, stronger than what we kept in our cellars at Stonehaven, and it goes down smoothly. There's something odd in the aftertaste, though. I don't care—not if it makes the time go by faster.

"Tell me," Ignatius adjusts his ruby-Eyed pendant. "What drew you to our faith?"

"Safety." It's near enough to the truth.

"I understand. The world is a dark place beyond Meira's Light." The High Priest pauses, picking up a knife and examining the blade. "My own village was poor. I witnessed firsthand how Malum was ruining this realm. The rot beneath the veneer, so to speak."

I swallow more wine. It might be going down *too* smoothly, for half my cup is gone.

"But even I—a mere butcher's son—heard the call of our goddess," Ignatius goes on. "Once I followed her Light, I never looked back."

Would that I could stuff that *Light* down his miserable throat.

"What of your own life?" he asks, amber eyes gleaming as he studies me. "Where did you come from before answering Meira's call?"

I am a witch. Some wild part of me wants to tell him, just to see the look of shock on his face. But that must be the wine.

"I—"

"All rise for King Callen," a herald announces, saving me from having to cobble together a believable answer.

A wave of curtsies and bows travels through the chamber as the king and queen enter and ascend the platform to the High Table. I instruct myself to keep my attention fixed on anything *besides* the king, but my gaze is drawn to him nonetheless. Any hope that I'd imagined what I felt on the night of the pageant instantly dissipates as the king's gray eyes lock on mine and I sense that nudging against the inner side of my left ribs, growing stronger with every breath.

Damn everything. This is more than just nerves. But what *is* it? Nothing good, if it keeps happening around the king. But that doesn't matter. If nothing else, I inherited Mother's stubbornness. I focus on controlling the unnatural sensation, inwardly tamping it down. After a few moments, it ebbs, shrinking to a dull pulse. There—that wasn't so difficult.

This time, that menacing voice comments.

"Mistress Ayleth." The queen assumes the other empty seat beside mine, sparing me from having to sit near her husband. "I wasn't aware you'd be joining us."

"I invited our guest," Ignatius explains. "I assumed that we'd all appreciate the opportunity to become better acquainted with Ayleth, given her recent service to the Light."

"Yes," another voice agrees. Sir Weston's. "I myself am simply brimming with curiosity. Won't you recount your version of the tale, Mistress? Rumors abound. Some would have us believe that you lifted the statue with your own two hands."

Everyone laughs, and I bristle. Would that I had known how

much trouble it would cause me to interfere with Jacquetta's spell. I look to the place where the other maidens are sitting. Jacquetta's cobalt-blue eyes are already on mine, and I startle a bit at their intensity. What is she thinking?

Ignore her, that voice reminds me.

And Jacquetta isn't the only one watching. Marion is staring daggers at the High Table. There's no need to guess the thoughts in the countess's mind. I drain my cup.

"I saw the statue falling and intervened" is all I offer Sir Weston. If I'm boring, maybe they'll lose interest in me.

"You must be quite the dancer, to be so quick-footed." The king's oil-smooth voice slinks across the table.

He leans forward, gray gaze finding mine, and that feeling inside me sharpens.

"I don't dance," I reply, fighting it back. It's easier this time.

"Oh, you'll not convince me of that," Sir Weston replies, twirling a fork in one hand. "After all, you found your way up here, didn't you?"

His wolfish grin has me missing that needle-like utensil even more. And I'm relieved when our conversation is interrupted by the arrival of food. Blodwyn wasn't exaggerating. Dishes of glazed turkey legs and entire hens are paraded in front of us. I accept a portion of fish and some roasted vegetables, though I doubt I could keep anything down.

"So," the king begins after a few courses. "How are you finding court, Mistress Ayleth? If you do not dance, then how do you pass your time?"

"I serve the queen," I answer, nodding to the servant when he offers more wine. It's my third cup, and the room is slightly swimming, but I gulp it down anyway.

"Mistress Ayleth is a companion to the princess as well." The queen spears a bite of venison. "Our Blodwyn is quite fond of her. I consider my daughter's affection as a high compliment to Mistress Ayleth's character."

The queen smiles at me and I smile back. However much I despise the White Court, my afternoon with the princess was enjoyable, even with the frustration of the library.

"It is indeed a compliment." Sir Weston lifts his glass in my direction. "But I've heard the princess can be most fearsome. What's your opinion of her, Mistress? Is the princess as sharp-toothed as some of those creatures she keeps?"

My hackles rise on Blodwyn's behalf. I don't appreciate the way this man speaks of her as though she's not a real person. "She's kind and clever."

"Too clever by half," the king mutters.

The queen stiffens slightly, but her expression remains neutral. "Is such a thing possible? Our daughter has the makings of a formidable ruler."

The king grunts into his wineglass. I recall the tapestries in the queen's chamber, those warrior women from ages past. I may not be well acquainted with the princess, but I could easily envision Blodwyn as following in their footsteps.

"That reminds me." The High Priest points with his knife. "I've received several recent inquiries pertaining to the princess's eventual marriage. Your Majesty's privy council has suggested Rycinthia, for one. Uniting our realms through such a union could do much to soothe ongoing tensions."

"Not Rycinthia," the king says flatly. "They'll use her as their pawn."

The queen saws off more venison. "Or perhaps our Blodwyn will prove herself a skilled diplomat in such an environment."

The king doesn't respond to that, but Sir Weston laughs.

"She certainly has the imagination of a diplomat," he says, gesturing with a half-eaten turkey leg. "I heard she recently complained of a *wolf* prowling the grounds near the castle."

But it wasn't a wolf. I picture the sinister red eyes in the forest. Beneath the music and chatter of the hall, I can almost hear a low growl. "It was a Nevenwolf."

I don't realize that I've spoken those words out loud until the laughter stops and the full attention of the table falls on me like an iron weight.

"A *Nevenwolf*?" the High Priest repeats. The ruby Eye of his pendant glints.

Damn everything, especially this wine. I push my glass away. The fuzziness in my head seems to be intensifying with every second. "I'm . . . sure I misheard."

"And where would our daughter have learned about such creatures?" the king demands of his wife.

"I have no idea," the queen replies smoothly. "Perhaps you should inquire with her tutors. You selected them yourself, if my memory serves."

Even beneath the warmth of the wine in my veins, I feel the air chill between them.

"I *shall* make inquiries," the king promises.

Queen Sybil dips her chin. "Do let me know what they report."

"Now, Majesty," Sir Weston says, breaking the hum of tension. "If the princess claims she spotted a Nevenwolf, I'm inclined to believe her. In fact—"

He sweeps up his glass and climbs onto his chair, his outline a bit blurry around the edges. How much wine did I drink?

"Attention please!" Liquid sloshes over the rim of Sir Weston's glass. "There's been a Nevenwolf sighted near the palace. Drawn here, no doubt, by the forces of Malum."

Gasps ricochet around the room and echo against the high ceiling. *Ayleth*, I'm sure I hear beneath the hissing whispers. *Ayleth.*

"It's our sworn duty, as Followers of the Light," Weston goes on, "to flush the creature out and banish it beyond the Veil where it belongs. Therefore, I propose a hunt!"

Hunt. Images of green uniforms and flaming swords slosh together in my mind. Weston cannot be serious. I don't know a single Elemental who would pit herself against a Nevenwolf. But the room is cheering. *Laughing.* As if—

Understanding finally fights its way through the haze of wine. This so-called hunt is merely a game. These people don't believe the Nevenwolf is real any more than they do that our Bloodstones are sacred, or that witches crafted the Veil. This is all just a farce—

Just like we are.

The dark parts of the room start to shimmer, shadows peeling themselves away and slithering toward me. The faces in the crowd become manic. Noses sharpen into beaks and feathered headdresses expand into black wings. They're crows, all of them, come to peck at me—rend me to ribbons. I cannot breathe. That feeling churns behind my left ribs, expanding against my bones, straining to break free.

Run, instinct screams. *RUN.*

Stumbling out of my chair, I bolt down the platform and out the first door I find. My clumsy feet don't get far before my stomach lurches and I vomit into a nearby vase. The taste of regurgitated wine is awful. There's something else too. Bitter and earthy.

"Ayleth?"

Who is that? Please don't let it be the king. Another round of retching has me leaning into the vase again. Cool fingers touch the back of my neck, and then I register the smell of juniper.

It's my favorite—like winter.

"That's it," Jacquetta says. "Get it all out."

My sides ache and my mouth tastes like death. But finally, the wave passes. I sit back on my heels, forehead beaded with sweat.

"How much of that wine did you drink?" Jacquetta asks.

"I don't know," I mutter.

But I didn't think it was enough to affect me so quickly. Not like this, anyway. I've experienced my fair share of drunken nights, but I've never hallucinated. I yank my handkerchief out of my sleeve and wipe my mouth, that bitter taste lingering. It's familiar somehow, but my sluggish mind can't place it.

"Here," Jacquetta says, passing me a glass of water.

I swallow a grateful sip. "How did you know I'd need this?"

She shrugs. "This isn't the first time I've seen you intoxicated."

The stars are singing.

Memory hangs between us, delicate as spider's silk.

Both of us, however, seem to prefer to pretend that it's not there. I drink more of the water, distracting myself with identifying the strange taste that came up with the wine. Had I encountered it in one of Mother's lessons? Maybe.

"Come on." Jacquetta offers her hand. "Let's get you up."

I hesitate, sliding her a sidelong look. "Why are you helping me?"

She crosses her arms. "I'm happy to leave you here, if that's what you'd like."

Part of me wants to say yes out of spite, but my head is pounding and I doubt I could even remember how to get back to our rooms. "No."

"That's what I thought." She offers her hand again and I take it. Tiny sparks fizz in my blood at her touch. "Why did the High Priest invite you up there, anyway?"

The tiles on the floor blur together and I lean hard against Jacquetta, struggling to put one foot in front of the other. "I ran into him in the library, and he said he wanted to thank me."

Jacquetta snorts. "This wouldn't have happened if you'd let me do away with him."

"I'm starting to agree with you."

My stomach rises again, so swiftly that I clamp a hand to my mouth and hobble over to the nearest bust—that of a former White King—and vomit behind it. This time, there's no remnants of wine, only that awful bitterness. It's close to mandrake, but not quite. And it's not hemlock . . .

"Thornapple," I gasp, the answer ringing clear. "It was thornapple in the wine."

"What's that?" Jacquetta asks.

"An herb," I explain, my muddy thoughts still churning. "A rare one. It's mostly used for potions relating to the mind, but it can be poisonous when brewed properly."

That's why I'm vomiting. Not because of the alcohol but because my latent magic is rejecting the toxin. That must be why I hallucinated as well.

"Do you mean—" Jacquetta's brow furrows. "Someone *did this* to you? Who?"

I shake my head. "I have no idea."

She glances around and lowers her voice. "Could they suspect us?"

The back of my neck prickles.

"If they thought I was a witch, there's an easier way to get rid of me," I reason. "Plus, if anyone knew, they wouldn't have tried to poison me. They should have realized that my latent magic would fight it off."

"Unless they were idiots," Jacquetta says, frowning as she thinks.

There's no shortage of those around here. I attempt to stand, but I lose my footing. Jacquetta catches me.

"Easy." She guides my arm around her neck. I can feel the heat of her skin through my gown. "Let's get you back to the room. Sounds like you have a long night ahead of you."

My stomach roils again, as if to agree with her.

"How do you know what thornapple tastes like anyway?" she asks.

"Mother insisted I memorize everything by sight, smell, *and* taste," I explain, grimacing at the memory of my countless blindfolded tests, most of which I had to attempt twice when I got the answers incorrect. And I wasn't even going to be a Potioner.

Jacquetta doesn't respond to that. In fact, we're both quiet as she leads me the rest of the way to our room, then helps me get into bed.

It is, indeed, a long and agonizing night. The retching, mercifully, ceases. But my dreams are filled with swirling darkness and flapping crows' wings and shadow-wraiths reaching out at me from beyond the Veil. I thrash, nightclothes sticking to my skin as I sweat out the poison. But occasionally, I imagine that I feel cool hands on my forehead or the back of my neck. Soft murmurs that the sickness will pass, that I'm safe, coupled with the lingering scent of juniper.

CHAPTER TWENTY-THREE

HOOVES THUNDER ON THE PACKED EARTH, THE VIBRATION LIKE a hammer against my tender skull. I still haven't fully recovered from the previous night, but staying in bed wasn't an option.

The entire court witnessed me fleeing the Great Hall, the rumor being—as Jacquetta initially assumed—that I was drunk. I've already received a stern lecture from Duchess Poole regarding the dishonor I showed the queen with such behavior.

"If you are unwell today, I suggest you take that as a lesson," she'd said, then further stated that such a grave breach of conduct was only to be forgiven due to my lack of experience. I am, however, forbidden from drinking wine in future. Given what I suspect truly occurred last night, such a directive isn't the punishment the duchess intends it to be.

Being forced to attend this event, however, is *absolutely* a punishment. A barrage of cheering slams into my brain as two horses charge toward each other on a long stretch of what Joan described as the *tiltyard*. There's nothing tilted about it, save for my lingering dizziness and the sheer ridiculousness of the situation. Armored riders heft huge, pointed weapons—*lances*—aimed at their opponent as the crowd goes positively feral. What they're cheering for is a mystery to me, however, as Joan explained that the desired outcome of this sport is *not* for one rider to impale the other. Why else would they be charging with pointed sticks?

Honor and bravery, she supplied.

Utterly baffling. But the ladies in the queen's box, perched on stilts high over the yard, don't share my opinion. They wave their handkerchiefs in wild support of one rider or the other. Wood cracks as the lances collide and splinter. The riders teeter in their saddles, but don't fall. The crowd groans in disappointment.

"What did you say this was called again?" I ask Joan, massaging my temples.

"Jousting." Joan pulls her fur blanket around her legs. "It's the king's favorite."

Somehow, that doesn't surprise me. The riders trot off and another pair readies themselves on the sidelines. Armor gleams silver and white-gold and black. The horses are bedecked in similar colors, feathers pluming from elaborate helmets. Those poor animals look as miserable as I am.

"How long does it last?"

"Oh, all day," she says brightly. I hold in a groan. "Especially the joust for Longest Night. It honors Meira's triumph over Malum. Riders sport either the colors of the Light, or those of the Nightbringers."

I flinch at that name, one the Order invented to vilify the covens. I'm tempted to ask Joan if she really believes in all that nonsense. Was it *Light* when the Heirs were brutally murdered? When our Sanctums were burned? But Joan, like the rest of this court, likely cannot see past the glittering confines of the White Palace.

Wood explodes as the riders meet. This time, the opponent wearing bright silver goes flying from his saddle. Metal crunches sickeningly as he lands. He moans, unmoving, and stretcher-bearers immediately rush to carry him from the field. The rider wearing black steel raises his lance in victory, sunlight glinting off his dark armor. The crowd boos and hisses.

"It's good to see Meira doesn't *always* win," Jacquetta comments under her breath.

A breeze stirs around us, carrying her scent of juniper. Foggy memories from last night resurface—reassuring words and soft hands brushing my face. Had that been real? I'd woken up alone and Jacquetta hasn't said anything, which means it was probably a dream. A crow flies over our heads, its shadow flitting over the box, and I pull my blanket closer.

"How are you feeling?" Joan asks, throwing me a sympathetic look.

Like I'd be grateful if the earth opened up and swallowed me whole. "Better."

And I *should* be better, but the thornapple is clearly interfering with the healing properties of my latent magic. My gaze skims over the crowd. Who could have put the poison in my wine? I drank from the same pitcher as the others at the High Table. No one else was affected.

"You shouldn't feel too embarrassed," Joan goes on. "We've all endured similar ordeals."

"Not according to Duchess Poole."

Joan laughs. "Really? Once, at a ball, I watched her drink practically a whole pitcher of wine by herself. She was in bed for the next two days with a 'cold.' And Lady Marion is always 'indisposed' the morning after a banquet."

That sounds about right. Marion and her cadre are sitting a few rows ahead of us. The courtier flashes me a sharp-toothed smile over her shoulder.

Jacquetta leans close. "Do you think it could have been her?"

The thornapple? I mull over the possibility. Joan did say that it was an honor to be invited to the High Table, one Marion has never enjoyed. And the countess has made it abundantly clear that she doesn't want me around. Still, *poison* seems an overreaction, even for her.

"I don't know how. She wasn't sitting nearby."

"She could have put it in your cup before you got there."

That's true, I suppose. Then, "You seem to be well versed in poisoning."

"Well enough."

Enough to dose one of the Magpies with baneweed. I'm sure that's how Jacquetta secured her place at the pageant. And if she would do that to the Magpie . . .

A hazy thought begins to sharpen in my mind. Jacquetta also tried to kill the High Priest, who happened to be sitting beside me at dinner last night—and she'd been staring at us so intently. I study Jacquetta's profile as she watches the riders gear up for the next match. Her hands are folded on her skirts, fingertips still carrying traces of the stain that I'd noticed yesterday. Thornapple is sometimes a violet flower, isn't it? And I still have no idea where Jacquetta went after leaving the princess's rooms. Could she have . . .

No. Jacquetta didn't even know what thornapple was when I mentioned it. Then again, maybe she pretended to be ignorant. Maybe she was trying to poison the High Priest, or even the king, and the thornapple got mixed up with my own wine. Perhaps that's why she came after me in the corridor. Not because she really cared but because she felt guilty.

"Where were you yesterday?" I ask Jacquetta.

"That's none—" Her brow creases at the look on my face. "What's the matter with you?"

I point to her hands. "What's under your fingernails?"

She looks down and blanches. The last dregs of my doubt evaporate, replaced with smoldering anger. Jacquetta poisoned me. Perhaps it wasn't even an accident. Maybe she decided to finish what she started in the Sanctum's courtyard. Too bad she didn't brew the poison strong enough.

"It's thornapple, isn't it?" I hiss at her under my breath. "Marion didn't poison me. It was *you.*"

Her blue eyes snap to mine, bright in the winter sunlight. "You think I would do that?"

The question throws me off guard, but only for an instant.

Don't let her distract you, that voice warns.

"Wouldn't you? You seemed eager to get rid of me that night at the Sanctum."

My blood heats, recalling her knife pressed against my side. But I can't tell if the fire in my veins is from rage or . . . something else.

A cheer rises as the match begins. Jacquetta leans close.

"If I wanted to kill you"—her words brush my ear—"you'd be dead."

A charge shoots through me, both at her nearness and her threat. Without another word, Jacquetta rises and stalks to the stairs, leaving me spinning in my own fury. It's wasted anger. Honestly, I should have guessed about Jacquetta as soon as I tasted the poison. I know who she is. She destroys everything around her—like she destroyed *me.*

Lances smash as the riders slam into each other. The ladies in the box leap to their feet, screaming so loudly that my head *pounds.* I need to leave. Duchess Poole is distracted by the match. Perhaps if I just—

"Mistress Ayleth."

A frantic hand grabs my elbow.

"Look!" Joan points. "It's the queen."

Queen Sybil stands at the front of the box. She gestures to the empty seat beside her. "Will you keep me company?"

I can think of no worse torture than spending another moment out here. But after what happened last night, I know better than to refuse. Several ladies slide me pointed glances as I maneuver my way to the front row of the box. Marion grins at me like a cat who finally trapped her mouse. Would that *she* was the mouse. Maybe Nettle should find her way to the countess's rooms.

"I've been hoping for the opportunity to speak with you." The queen passes me a fur-lined blanket as I settle myself onto the cushioned seat beside her. "You rushed off so suddenly last night. Were you unwell?"

Surely Duchess Poole reported the incident, or the rumors have reached the queen. It's kind of her to pretend otherwise.

"I've recovered," I tell her.

"Good. Court can be overwhelming for those who aren't accustomed to it." The queen observes another pair of riders. "It was for me when I first arrived here—a young princess from a foreign land. I imagine that you must feel the same homesickness that I did. Did you leave family behind when you joined the Order?"

I press my thumb into one of the triangles etched into my palms.

"A sister," I say, picturing Rhea's face. My face.

"Then we have that in common." The queen smiles softly. "I have several sisters, though I haven't visited them in years. What of your parents?"

"I never knew my father," I tell her, which is true. "And my mother . . ."

I trail off, the memory of our last conversation pricking like thorns.

"You may speak freely, Ayleth," the queen prompts.

Much as I know that I shouldn't divulge too much personal information, the queen possesses a certain warmth, like Willa or Nyssandra. Maybe it's the lingering thornapple, but I realize how much I *need* to confide in someone. Perhaps I'm more homesick than I realized.

"My mother wanted me to be someone else," I say at last, my eyes stinging at the truth of those words. "I'm not sure she even knew me. If she did, she was never proud of me."

The queen squeezes my wrist. "I'm sorry, Ayleth. That's a terrible pain, and one I understand. Sometimes I'm convinced that the single instance in which my own mother was ever proud of me was when I secured my match with King Callen. Even then, I suspect that she was prouder of herself."

In the dark of the queen's eyes, I sense a hollowness that matches my own, a void I never expected to share with anyone, much less a mortal queen.

"She should have been proud of you," I say.

"And *your* mother"—the pressure of the queen's grip increases—"should have seen your worth. You're a strong and capable woman. One I'm honored to have serving in my household."

Honored. When was the last time anyone ever said that about me?

"You don't know me very well, Your Majesty," I say, shifting in my seat.

She raises an eyebrow. "I know you spoke up for my daughter last night, in front of the most powerful men in the realm. That takes bravery."

Or stupidity. "I simply told the truth."

"Honesty, unfortunately, is not a common trait at this court."

A shadow swoops over us, followed by the haunting laughter of a crow, which reminds me too much of the hallucinations at dinner last night. All that had been the poison—hadn't it?

"Presenting Sir Weston," the herald announces from the yard.

The ladies in the queen's box applaud like their lives depend on it. Some even appear close to fainting as Sir Weston waves in our direction, sporting black armor.

"And"—the herald pauses—"an unnamed knight."

Excited chatter swells as the other horse, a massive white charger, trots onto the field. The opponent is armored in a stunning suit of gold, with intricate designs embossed on the breastplate and helmet. But unlike Sir Weston and the other riders, this man bears no standard to hint at his identity. He circles the yard and rides up to our box.

"Mistress," he calls, his face hidden behind his visor. "Might I be so bold as to request your favor?"

It takes me a moment to realize he's talking to *me*. "I don't . . ."

"Your handkerchief," the queen prompts.

Why on earth would anyone want that? I think I used it earlier. The ladies around me whisper, their heads bent close. The longer this man remains here, the worse the attention will become. With no other way to get rid of him, I yank my handkerchief from where it's folded into my sleeve and toss it down to the rider. He snatches it out of the air and tucks it into his breastplate before trotting off to take his place.

I cannot for the life of me comprehend why such an exchange would provoke interest, but the ladies are practically buzzing behind me. Marion, especially, appears as though she would impale me with the nearest sharp object. I'm about to ask the queen what I've done, but the thunder of hooves drowns me out. Wood splinters as the lances collide. Sir Weston is unhorsed, his armor clattering as he sprawls in the dirt. But he's otherwise unharmed, wobbling to his feet and lifting his helm. The stands erupt as he deals the audience his signature roguish smile, which incites an even louder storm of cheering from the ladies. And then the other rider—the unnamed knight—removes his own helmet. Sunlight gleams on his raven-black hair and glitters in his gray eyes, the exact color of the sky behind him.

It's the king.

The crowd cheers and gasps in one breath. Understanding hits me like a lance cracking against a shield, draining the blood from my face. No wonder the other ladies, especially Marion, were acting so strangely. King Callen's steel-gray eyes lock on to mine and that feeling behind my left ribs expands, like a vine of midnight flower unfurling beneath my skin. The king tugs my handkerchief from his breastplate and displays it like a trophy. Like *I* am a prize to be won.

"Remember what I told you about truth, Ayleth," the queen says, still smiling as she applauds her husband. "Nothing at this court is ever as it seems."

Above us, that single crow wheels in the sky.

One for sorrow.

Chapter Twenty-Four

OVER THE NEXT FEW DAYS, THE PALACE HUMS WITH ACTIVITY AS the court prepares for Sir Weston's ludicrous "hunt." In a rare stroke of luck, I'm not selected as one of the maidens to accompany the party and will remain behind with the queen. Jacquetta isn't going either, though I'm not sure what she plans to do instead. She makes herself scarce among the queen's retinue, appearing only when absolutely necessary. Even then, she's silent and sullen— probably plotting which poison to brew next.

If I wanted to kill you, you'd be dead.

Much as I hate to admit it, her words winnow through the steel of my certainty. At the joust, I'd been utterly convinced that Jacquetta had poisoned me. But there had been plenty of other opportunities for her to do me harm. Why would she have waited for a dinner? And why help me afterward? She could have easily dosed me with the poison again while I was recovering. But if she doesn't want me dead, what does Jacquetta want? Too often in the night, I find myself watching the closed curtains of her bed, questions knotting in my mind. When the wind whines against the palace, it carries the phantom echo of Jacquetta's scream. One that, though I try to smother it, still echoes in my heart.

"I don't understand why I can't attend," Blodwyn complains in her menagerie.

It's late afternoon on the day before the hunt and we've just returned from the library—yet another exasperatingly ineffective trip. The third, to be exact. I haven't discovered so much as a sentence that mentions the Bloodstones. It's becoming increasingly apparent that I'll never get anywhere with the Order's stilted histories, and I can practically feel the hours slipping away. I need help—Roland's, preferably. But I haven't glimpsed so much as a flicker of red since my last encounter with the Dwarf. What if he never comes back?

"If I was a prince, they'd have invited me," the princess grumbles, bringing me back into our conversation. "Boys aren't cooped up in the palace all day."

Nettle stalks a stray duckling and Blodwyn scoops it up before my cat can pounce. Nettle flattens her ears, disappointed, and lopes over to me.

"If it's any consolation, I'm not going either," I tell the princess.

"It's not." Blodwyn pats the duckling's fuzzy head. "Sometimes I wish boys didn't exist at all. There weren't any in your Sanctum, were there? Was that better?"

"Immensely," I tell her, stroking Nettle.

"Maybe *I* should join with a Sanctum."

I imagine Blodwyn among real Sisters. She would drive them utterly mad. It would be wonderful. Nettle trills in agreement.

"If you left the palace, you wouldn't have your menagerie," I point out. "Or the library."

"Don't Sanctums have libraries?"

"Not like yours." Though I expect they're filled with just as many false histories.

Blodwyn frowns. "Perhaps not, then."

A wise decision for everyone. Blodwyn busies herself with her duckling. For a few minutes, I sit back and allow the gentle sounds of the menagerie to wash over me—the soft, cheerful calls of the animals and the pleasant gurgle of the water in the fountain. After the constant strain of being among the court, this peace is welcome. Even Nettle curls herself in my lap, and I smile at the vibration of her purring against my body.

"She's ruined another one." A voice carries from the outer chamber. It's one of Blodwyn's additional maidens. We're close enough to the fogged windows that I can see two of them walking together.

"Spoiled thing," the second comments. "I'd give my eyeteeth for lace like that and she just traipses about through the mud. And did I tell you that I had to clean up after one of her *pets* yesterday? I swear, she trains them to leave messes."

The first clicks her tongue. "Well, give it a few more years and she'll be some other realm's problem. I heard there's a few potential betrothals being bandied about."

"*That* blessed event can't come quick enough." The other points. "But mind you don't get sent off with her."

"Could you imagine . . ."

The voices fade into the next chamber. I look to the princess, sympathy needling between my ribs. Blodwyn hasn't moved, but she's gripping the duckling hard enough that the creature whistles in alarm. She sets it free and it waddles away, shaking itself.

"I'm sorry, Blodwyn. That was cruel of them."

"I don't care." But she blinks, banishing the glassy sheen to her eyes. "Do you know what they meant, about the betrothal?"

At first, I'm shocked that Blodwyn isn't aware of such details herself. Then again, I suppose her ignorance fits with what I've experienced of this court. Why *would* Blodwyn know about a proposed marriage? Why would the princess, or any other woman, possess even an ounce of control over her own future? The unfairness of the situation is similar enough to my own life with Mother—how my status as Second was thrust upon me without any consideration of my own desires—that fresh anger kindles on the princess's behalf. She deserves to know.

"The High Priest mentioned Rycinthia," I tell Blodwyn.

She picks the petals off a flower. "I'm not surprised that they want to send me away. They all hate me."

"You don't know that. Just because they complain about your pets—"

"Not my pets." She dismisses me. "They hate me because of the curse."

Even Nettle lifts her head at that. "Curse?"

"Don't you know?" I shake my head, and the princess glances toward the menagerie doors before continuing. "It's said that the witches who were killed here cursed Papa's father. That's why my uncles died and why Papa hasn't had a son—just me."

I'd almost forgotten about the king's older brothers, each killed in the witch raids. As far as I'm concerned, such a death was too kind for them. A vision of the tapestry and the red-hot iron shoes resurfaces in my mind. If my grandmother was anything like Mother, I have no doubt that she would have levied a curse against the king before she was murdered. But she couldn't have done so—none of the Heirs could have. The iron would have poisoned their magic, the same as it did to Rhea on the night of Stonehaven's raid.

"There's no—"

"It's true," Blodwyn interrupts, sharp and vehement. "I see the way

Papa looks at me sometimes, like I did something wrong. He thinks I'm cursed. That's why he wants me to go away. That's why he built this menagerie—to keep me locked inside it."

The bitterness in her voice resonates in my own soul. We might be on opposing sides of this war, but, in the hard lines of Blodwyn's expression, I glimpse the same pain that winnowed between my bones during every lesson with Mother, when each mistake I made only highlighted the fact that I wasn't Rhea. Wasn't good enough. I reach for Blodwyn's hand.

"There's no curse."

She shies away from me, fidgeting with a climbing vine. "Then why does everyone say there is?"

"Because people are idiots. Don't let them dictate who you are. Decide for yourself."

Blodwyn drops the vine, and her dark eyes are like windows into her soul.

"I'm glad you're here," she whispers.

I tuck a lock of her ebony hair behind her ear. "So am I."

Against all odds and sensibility, I mean it. Blodwyn may boast a fierce heart, but she's fragile as well. Wounded. I wish I could smooth over the princess's hurt—help her the way no one helped me.

"And . . . just so you know"—Blodwyn fusses with her skirts— "I *do* train my pets to make messes."

I laugh. Of course she does. "I taught Nettle to do the same."

My cat trills and swishes her tail in what I interpret as pride.

Blodwyn grins. "Let me show you what I—"

But the rest is cut off when a set of strong footsteps echoes through the menagerie.

"Where is my daughter?" a now too-familiar voice calls. "Has she managed to sprout wings and fly away?"

It's the king, damn everything. Blodwyn scrambles up, already rushing to greet her father, but I have no desire to join her. Neither does Nettle. She scampers off and I hide myself behind the nearest potted plant, watching through the veil of brightly colored blooms.

"Papa!" Blodwyn exclaims, throwing herself into her father's arms.

And now I'm doubly grateful for my hiding place, for King Callen isn't alone. Lady Marion clings to his side like a barnacle, dressed in gray silk and wearing the most bizarre hat I've ever seen. It's fashioned to resemble a bird's nest, with a stuffed starling perched in the center. Jeweled eggs surround the glass-eyed creature, glimmering in the winter sunlight. What would possess someone to wear—or even *make*—a hat like that?

"Here she is." The king spins his daughter around.

I have to admit that I'm taken aback at his overt show of affection. This is not the man from dinner who barely looked at his wife and spoke of the princess as if she were a piece in one of the court's pointless games. *This* man plants a kiss on the top of Blodwyn's head, a proud father. It's terrifying, watching the king shed one skin and slide into another—like a snake.

"She's becoming so pretty," Lady Marion comments, tilting her head at the princess. "Soon, she'll be fairest of them all—just like our goddess."

"But Meira is called *fair* because of her sense of justice," Blodwyn corrects primly. "Justice is far more important than beauty, isn't it, Papa?"

I press my lips together to stifle a laugh.

"You've been spending time with your mother." The king thumps Blodwyn playfully on her nose. She grins at him. Marion fumes, silent. "Here, I've brought you an early gift for Longest Night."

The king motions for a servant, who steps forward and offers Blodwyn a long, shallow box. The princess lifts the lid and gasps. "Really, Papa? For me?"

She extracts a small bow and a slender quiver of arrows. Again,

I'm surprised. Given what Blodwyn told me, I didn't think women were permitted such activities here.

"I heard of your displeasure in not being invited to Sir Weston's hunt," the king explains, gesturing at the bow. "But I suppose there's no harm in allowing you some sport—at least with this. Sir Weston devised the thing. It's harmless enough."

Blodwyn inspects the weapon, completely enthralled. "Thank you, Papa. It's wonderful."

"You'll have to be careful." The king points at her. "The arrows are blunted, but I don't want to hear about shattered glass or you threatening to pick off your tutors."

A fair concern.

Blodwyn laughs. "I promise, Papa."

"Good." The king beckons. "Here, let me teach you how to use it."

Blodwyn clutches the bow to her chest. "Mistress Ayleth can help me. She hunted at her Sanctum, didn't you—"

She stops short as she discovers that I've gone. Shit.

"Ayleth?"

I remain as still as possible, hardly even daring to breathe. If I just stay here, they'll think I left. I won't have to—

"There she is." Marion squints in my direction. "She's . . . I don't know, roosting?"

I really do need to send Nettle to Marion's rooms. Grudgingly, I emerge from behind the plant. The king spots me, and that feeling stirs behind my left ribs, something growing and reaching. Something that doesn't belong.

Control it, I command myself, forcing the sensation down. Eventually, it lessens.

"Mistress Ayleth." King Callen glances at the plant and back at me, his brow creased. "Were you hiding from us?"

"I . . . no." A flush creeps up my neck, betraying me.

"Then what were you doing?" Marion asks, smirking.

"I was . . ."

"In truth, I'm glad to find you here," the king says, stepping uncomfortably nearer. "I've been meaning to thank you for gifting me with your favor at the joust. Such a prize undoubtedly contributed to my victory."

Would that my handkerchief had done the opposite—that the king's head were knocked off by a lance, or that he were trampled to death by a horse.

"You exaggerate, Majesty." Marion loops her arm through the king's. "Your skill is unmatched on the tiltyard, as it is in so many other areas."

Like killing witches.

The king extracts himself from Marion's clutches, those gray eyes like hooks drawing me in. That feeling stirs again, brushing against the inner side of my left ribs. I clench my fists until it calms.

"But I'm interested in hearing of Mistress Ayleth's skills," the king says. "My daughter claims that you hunt?"

Blodwyn beams proudly at me, and I try not to be irritated with her. She didn't know.

"Only by necessity," I explain. "And I can boast no significant skill."

"Really? I'll be the judge of that." He motions to Blodwyn. "Please. Assist my daughter."

"An excellent idea, Sire." Marion settles herself on a nearby bench. "I was so hoping to enjoy some proper entertainment today."

She adjusts the rope of sapphires settled across her collarbones and I picture how satisfying it would feel to strangle her with her own jewels. But another idea sprouts in my mind. A bad one—but deliciously so.

Ignoring my own good sense, I walk over to Blodwyn and whisper in her ear. "Do you trust me?"

She throws me a bewildered glance but nods.

"Over here." I steer the princess a short distance away and help maneuver her body into position. "Draw your arm back. There. Take your aim. Then . . . let go."

Just as Blodwyn releases the arrow, I pretend to stumble, disrupting her aim so that her bow veers to the left, toward Marion.

"Look out!" Blodwyn calls.

The arrow whizzes straight for the courtier's face. Blunted or not, it will surely harm her—perhaps even take out one of her eyes, if the angle is right. That wasn't what I meant to do. I'd only intended to scare her, as a prank. But instead of panic, a deep urge rises inside me like a wave—to hurt. To wound. *More,* it whispers, stoking that feeling behind my left ribs. *More.*

Marion shrieks and ducks, shattering the moment.

The blunted arrow impales the stuffed bird on her hat, knocking it from her head.

Twin splotches of crimson explode on her cheeks as she gapes at the ruined thing, then back at me. "You tried to *kill* me."

"She couldn't have killed you," the princess manages, practically vibrating with suppressed laughter. "The arrows are blunted."

Marion's nostrils flare. She reaches for her hat, but a blur of dark calico pounces from a bush with a yowl. Feathers fly.

"No, you horrid thing!" Marion flails at Nettle, but my cat only picks up the hat in her mouth and trots off with it. One of the jeweled eggs detaches and rolls away. I love that animal.

The countess wheels on me. "Look what you've done, you stupid fool! I will—"

"I'm quite certain that you possess the means to replace a mere *hat*," the king interjects smoothly. "This was an accident, after all."

A tense beat passes.

"An accident," Marion echoes eventually, her jaw tight.

And while it is immensely satisfying to watch the courtier be put in her place, it seems the king is not yet finished with me.

"And Mistress Ayleth." I catch his scent as he steps closer—leather

and smoke and the deepest part of the forest. That unnerving sensation vibrates. "You will join us at the hunt."

No. "I wasn't appointed. And I—"

"Then I officially appoint you." The king's gray eyes pin me in
place. There seems an entire ocean behind them—one that will drag
me screaming into its depths.

With that, the king beckons to Marion and strides toward the exit.
But the countess pauses before following him.

"I'd take care, if I were you," she says, the words brushing my ear.
"Who knows what might happen to a lost little Order girl in the
woods?"

CHAPTER TWENTY-FIVE

I LEAVE THE PRINCESS NOT LONG AFTER THAT, MARION'S THREAT still hounding me. I'd known better than to antagonize her. Now I've gotten myself roped into yet another avoidable situation. Even so, my mind keeps returning to that moment when the arrow was sailing toward Marion's face—the horror scrawled on her expression. Horror *I* put there. Even with all my pranks at Stonehaven, my battles with Mother, I've never done anything like that before. It felt *good* to taste such power.

But who's wielding it? that voice in my mind whispers. I'm not entirely sure, especially not when I consider how it stirred that feeling inside me. Terrifying and yet . . . *intoxicating.*

You were marked, Mother's words resound in my mind. I shove them down.

"Mistress Witch."

I stop short, discovering a pair of gemstone-colored eyes glittering in the dimness of an alcove. Roland. Thank the Spirits. A weight lifts from my chest and I hurry to join him, checking to make sure no one has noticed us.

"You're back," I say, resisting the urge to throw my arms around the Dwarf.

He shrugs. "Told you I would be."

Actually, he didn't. But he's here now. "Does this mean you found information about the Bloodstones? Do you know where they are?"

I look him up and down, half hoping he has them stashed in his pocket. He doesn't, of course. A few courtiers glide past the alcove and Roland waits to continue until they've gone.

"Turns out we were both right," he starts when we're alone. "Most things associated with the witches were burned in the Great Cleansing—except the Bloodstones. Royals paraded them about like trophies, apparently. Some say the fingers were still attached—for a while, at least."

My stomach rolls at that image. "Monsters."

"Aye," Roland agrees. "And it doesn't get much better. My brothers said the White King ordered that one such stone be set into his sword. He commissioned the same for the princes."

My rage deepens at the idea of our sacred stones—our tie to the Spirits—being used as embellishment for weapons that likely slaughtered witches.

"So that's where the Bloodstones went? Swords?"

"The king's commission is the last time they were seen in the Mines, anyway," he confirms. "And that's only three of them, maybe four."

It's better than none, which is exactly how many I've located since coming here. "Where are the swords now?"

"That's the tricky bit." Roland grimaces. "Such weapons are usually housed in the armory. But the White Kings insist on being buried with theirs."

Understanding clicks into place. "And the king is dead."

As are two of his sons.

"Right," Roland agrees. "If I were you, first place I'd search is the crypt."

Crypt. A draft snakes down the hall, raising gooseflesh between my shoulder blades. I stand taller, banishing my fear. If I have to pry the Bloodstones out of the dead king's skeletal hands, nothing will stop me. But that doesn't mean I want to go alone.

"Will you come with me?" I ask Roland.

He taps his chin. "Funny—I have this strange aversion to dead things. Don't like imagining myself as one of them."

"Please," I beg. "I don't know the way to the crypt, or what I'm looking for. The longer I search for the Bloodstones, the more chance I have of getting caught. That's bad for us both."

Another chattering group of courtiers sails down the corridor. Roland watches them, muttering to himself.

"Fine," he grunts. "But don't get used to this. I'm not your personal escort."

"Just this once," I promise, sincerely hoping it's true. If the Bloodstones are in the crypt, I won't need Roland to take me anywhere else. Surely even a few stones will be enough to both get Rhea and mend the Veil.

Roland grumbles, unconvinced, and removes a ring of keys from his belt. They're all different sizes and metals—some brass, and others silver or gold. A few even appear whittled from what is suspiciously similar to bone, and I shudder, thinking of Mathilde and her string of teeth. Roland selects a slender wrought-iron key and then jams it into the wall. To my astonishment, the wood sucks the key inside itself. An instant later, a small door materializes. It's shoulder-height, exactly like the one I'd found behind the apple tree at the pageant.

"*That's* how you've been getting around."

Roland bows with a flourish. "Aye. Now, are you coming or not?"

He replaces the ring of keys on his belt and opens the door. With a last check over my shoulder, I follow him, praying to every Spirit listening that these are my last hours in the palace.

I expect Roland's door to lead into a maze of halls—cobweb-covered stone and rotting staircases, like the passages Blodwyn uses. Instead, there's ... *nothing.* Even when Roland fishes a lantern from some invisible corner, all I see is darkness beyond the orange glow of its flame. I'm certain that there's a floor only because I can feel it beneath my feet. And I sense walls on either side of us, but there aren't any forks or turns. It's like the tunnel is carving itself through the palace, unfurling with every step we take.

"Where are we?" I ask, bewildered. "There aren't any halls or stairs or ..."

Roland laughs, long and echoing in the depthless void. "You witches aren't the only ones with power. Dwarves have our own magic, thank you very much. We don't need *halls* or *stairs.* A Dwarf can navigate or operate anything crafted by their own."

I flinch at his tone, one that suggests I should have known such information already. I probably should have. As witchlings, we'd learned about our own history and magic, but never anyone else's. It was as if our stories were the only ones that mattered. But of course there were others, Roland's among them. And not just the story of his magic but his whole life and history. I suddenly feel incredibly selfish for never having shown an interest.

"Have you always lived at the palace?" I ask now.

"I came from farther north." He gestures in what I assume is that direction. "But that was some fifty years ago. My mine specialized in the mirrors. Enchanted ones. I'm sure you're familiar with them."

Too familiar. I shiver at the memory of Mother's mirror. I haven't seen her silver-eyed raven again, but I wonder if it's haunting the gardens, spying. "A little."

"Aye—hard to come by now, I gather. Used to be, there was a whole hall of mirrors here in the palace," Roland goes on. "Before the edict, witches would use them for the Crown. Suppose they all were shattered—destroyed in the fire."

I'm not as sad about that prospect as I likely should be. A hall of mirrors, especially witch's mirrors, is the last place I'd want to visit.

"Ah, here we are." Roland stops and detaches the ring of keys from his belt. He sticks one into the stone wall and another door appears. "Right this way."

The crypt must be located in the deepest part of the palace, for the darkness here is thick and tangible, laced with the distinctive staleness of death. The glow of Roland's lantern spills over rows of coffins. *Glass* coffins. It's an unsettling custom, to house the dead with the living, letting their bodies rot and decay beneath our feet. We witches do not believe in burying our dead. Instead, we return them to the coven fire, freeing their souls to join with the Spirits. That's another reason the raids are so horrific. If our dead aren't burned in the flames of a Ceremony of Blood and Ashes, our spirits are trapped between our bones for eternity.

Roland rubs a window on one of the grime-covered coffins, revealing a glimpse of hollowed eye sockets and tufts of white hair beneath the glass.

"This is the older section," he determines.

How many sections are there? The line of White stretches back thousands of years, and it seems all their royal dead are entombed here. Roland's lantern carves a dim path as we shuffle through the aisles. Pillars carved to look like trees climb into the murky expanse of the ceiling, which must be high because even the slightest sound echoes. Water drips in the distance, and every surface is slick and silty. Shadows undulate outside the safety of Roland's light, the darkness seeming to slink and creep, pooling around my ankles as we walk. I keep looking over my shoulder, unable to shake the prickling sensation of being observed. That feeling starts again—something nudging the inner side of my left ribs. I tamp it down.

Finally, we reach an area where the bodies are less decomposed. Through the gauzy fabric of their shrouds, I can make out the gleam of jewels on bony fingers and the delicate embroidery stitched into fine gowns. All this wealth, left to rot.

"Even the dead here are richer than we are," I mutter.

"Aye," Roland agrees. "Welcome to the White Palace."

He brings his light closer to the engraving on a casket.

Queen Islabet, it reads.

The former king's wife, if my mortal history serves. Unlike the other corpses here, the dead queen's body is positioned beneath the glass with her palms turned up, a pose that mimics that of the false goddess. The queen's natural eyes—or what's left of them—are sewn shut, and a jeweled Eye of Meira is fixed to her forehead. Even the decaying corpses uphold the Order's lies.

I move on to the next coffin. This one is larger and more elaborate. The crowned apple sigil is engraved in the glass.

King Reginald.

This is the man who levied the edict against the covens. The man responsible for countless burnings and deaths. Worse than that, for extinguishing our way of life. Rage simmers inside me. He likely died in his bed, surrounded by his family. Such an end was too good for him—too clean. A deep, primal urge stirs—that delicious sense of control I felt in the menagerie. I want to drag out the dead king's bones and grind them to dust. I want to summon his spirit and make him watch as I tear his realm down, piece by piece. I want to—

"Mistress Witch." Roland's voice jolts me out of my imaginings. "Look. The sword."

He dips his lantern lower, illuminating the weapon resting on the dead king's chest. Only the top of its pommel is visible beneath a gilded blanket. If the Bloodstone is there, I can have Rhea with me again—perhaps even tonight. We can return to Stonehaven. It will be like the last seven years never happened. We could even stop the war. My pulse kicks up.

"Help me with the lid."

Roland sets his lantern down. It takes both of us to pry open the coffin, releasing a cloud of stale, death-scented air. My stomach roils.

"By the Mines." Roland coughs, covering his mouth. "Can't believe they leave weapons down here. Waste of proper craftsmanship is what it is. All that good metal just . . ."

He continues complaining about the White Kings' disrespect of Dwarvian work, but I'm not listening. My hands tremble as I reach for the blanket. The gold fabric is stiff and cool as I pull it back. The sword is massive, its blade stretching all the way to the dead king's knees. Jewels glimmer on the pommel—tiny rubies cut to represent the crowned-apple sigil. The gleaming steel blade is etched with an Illumination:

TO BURN A WITCH IS TO FREE A SOUL

I hardly register the spark of anger that ignites at seeing those words, my focus pinned to the place where the sword's blade meets the pommel. There's a setting—a large oval, exactly the shape of the Bloodstone in Millicent's portrait at Stonehaven.

Except nothing is there.

"No," I whisper, touching the empty space as if the stone might appear. It doesn't. "*No!*"

"Damn." Roland scrubs the back of his neck. "They must have removed the stone before they buried the king."

Which means the Bloodstone could be anywhere.

"Don't lose hope just yet." Roland indicates the next coffin. "Check the princes' coffins. The king commissioned swords for them as well."

That's right. I hurry over to where the first prince—Prince Arthur—is laid out inside the glass. His sewn-shut eyes stare at me as we heave open the lid and I yank the blanket back. The prince's sword is just as ostentatious as the dead king's, studded with jewels and forged of fine steel. And just like King Reginald's weapon, the Bloodstone has been pried out.

I step back, raking my hands through my hair. "This can't be happening."

Desperate, I wheel around in search of the final glass coffin—my one remaining chance. I stop short. There *is* another casket, but it's carved of stone.

"That's odd," Roland comments, approaching it. "Royals always insist upon glass."

"Are you sure it's the prince?"

He lifts his lantern, light striking against the inscription on the lid: *Prince Tiergan.*

"Why would they put him in there?" I ask.

"No idea." Roland rubs his chin. "But now that I think of it, there was some strangeness surrounding the prince's death. Rumors and such."

The air in the crypt seems to grow colder.

"Rumors about what?"

"Madness, if I recall," he replies, darkly. "Aye. They found him running around the palace, screaming that something was chasing him."

Chasing? A long, low sound echoes in the distance.

Pull yourself together, I chide myself. It's just a story the mortals made up. And it doesn't matter why they buried the prince in stone—not if he has what I need. Rolling my shoulders back, I brace myself against the coffin's lid.

"Sure you want to do that?" Roland asks, dubious.

"Don't tell me you're afraid."

He makes a face but reluctantly sets down his lantern and joins me. The stone lid is ten times heavier than the lids of the glass coffins. My muscles burn after just a few seconds of pushing. Even Roland grunts with the effort. Finally, stone grinds as the lid slides open an inch. Then another and another, until—

The smell hits, pungent and horrible and *wrong*. Years ago, Nettle killed a rat and hid it in Mother's room at Stonehaven. The smell thickened for days before she discovered it. *This* stench is a thousand times worse than that, and a hundred thousand times worse than the fetid reek of the other bodies. I turn away from the casket, gagging. Roland curses and coughs.

"What *is* that?" I croak, covering my nose and mouth.

"Nothing I want to know about." Roland backs away.

But I *have* to know. Holding my breath, I peer over the edge of the casket, then immediately wish that I hadn't. Where the other royals are still somewhat recognizable, the prince's remains could best be described as a black, stinking sludge. It's as though he . . . *melted,* leaving nothing but a tarlike substance congealed at the bottom of the casket. There's absolutely nothing left of him, not even the flash of a jewel. What could have done something like this?

As if in answer, an unmistakable moan sounds from deep within the crypt, followed by a clicking, like claws against stone. The temperature drops even lower.

The place behind my left ribs vibrates. "We need to leave. *Now.*"

Roland's face pales in the lantern light. "Aye."

Without bothering to close up the prince's coffin, we sprint to the nearest wall. Roland fumbles his keys from his belt. The clicking sound is louder now. Closer. That feeling behind my ribs intensifies.

"Hurry," I urge Roland.

"What do you think I'm doing? Having a nap?" Metal jangles as he attempts to jam a key into the wall. Nothing happens.

"Why isn't it working?"

"I don't know," he snaps, jabbing the key at the stone. It only scrapes and scratches the surface, leaving frantic white streaks. "You're a witch, can't you do something?"

No. I can't. And I have no desire to delve into *why* at the moment. "Come on. Just run!"

My breath puffs in front of my face as we tear through the crypt, stumbling over loose bricks and colliding with caskets. Relief floods me when the outline of the main doors emerges from the gloom. I urge my clumsy feet faster, throwing myself against the handles as soon as they're within reach.

They stick.

A high note of panic builds in my ears. I thrust my shoulder against the door again and again, but it refuses to budge. "It won't open!"

The clicking of claws is even closer, and slower. Like whatever is chasing us has decided to take its time. Toy with us, like Nettle and her mice. The place behind my left ribs *throbs*, pressure straining beneath my skin, like whatever is there wants to break free. We need to get *out* of here. I clench my fists against the triangles stamped into my palms. If anyone can help us now, it's my sister.

Please, Rhea, I beg. *We need you.*

"Together," Roland says, positioning himself beside me. "One, two, *three.*"

Whether it's our combined strength or my sister's intervention, the handle gives and we stumble into the light of the palace, scrambling to slam the door behind us. A deep, disappointed moan leaks through the paneled wood, one that resonates in my very bones.

"What was that?" I gasp between frantic breaths.

"I don't know." Roland pats himself, as if to make sure he's still in one piece. "I've never seen anything like that. It's like it was . . . from another world."

Or from beyond the Veil, a voice in my mind whispers, followed swiftly by Mother's: *You could have brought something out.*

Fear oozes down my spine.

"What did you say the prince claimed before he died?" I ask Roland. "He was being chased?"

"Aye." He confirms. "But no one knew by what."

I might know. Because I'm starting to believe the same thing is chasing me. And, as the feeling behind my left ribs settles, I think I know why.

CHAPTER TWENTY-SIX

I T'S NOT *MALUM.*

I repeat the words in my mind like a spell, like saying it enough times will make it true, as I pace the balcony in the dead of night. After what happened in the crypt, sleep was all but impossible. When I did manage to slip into a fitful doze, my dreams were filled with curling shadows and images of the dead prince's sludge-like remains. Every pop of the fire sounded like the click of claws against stone. Every sigh of the wind like the low moan of whatever creature had been stalking us. Eventually, the very walls of the chamber became too suffocating to endure and I snuck outside in the hope that the cold night air would clear my head.

It hasn't. No matter how much I try to explain away the shadows and the noises and that awful sensation behind my left ribs, my mind keeps circling back to Mother's words on the night of my failed Ascension:

It could have touched you.

It—*Malum.* I've been denying it this whole time, but was she right? When I reached for Rhea, had Malum winnowed beneath my skin and wound itself between my bones? I picture it, like a vine of midnight flower intertwined with my ribs, burrowing deeper with every breath.

Like summons like. Mother's lessons come back to me. *Dark intents reap dark rewards.*

I may not have intended to summon Malum, but I did reach beyond the Veil. Is this the price I'm paying for meddling? I press my hand to my side, against the spot where I first felt the tremble of something that didn't belong. Something stirred by shadows and whatever was following me in the crypt—even the king himself, a man whose dark heart might well have been carved from Malum. Is the force inside me calling to him? Is it drawing more Malum from beyond the Veil, sending it to haunt me? *Claim* me?

Wind gusts over the balcony, its chill needling under my thin shift. Another crow calls, settling on the lip of a fountain. It's swiftly joined by a second, then a third. They keep coming, winging out of the shadows, beady black eyes shining like polished stones in the moonlight.

"Seven," I whisper. Just like before my Ascension.

A secret, mystery, or curse.

The hair on the back of my neck prickles. Had they known? I wonder wildly. Did the birds' connection to Malum alert them to what I would do? Or, a far more ominous question slithers through my mind: Is there something about me that has *always* attracted them? Is that why Malum latched on to me in the first place?

Like summons like, that horrible voice taunts.

Perhaps it's right. There's a darkness in my soul—a *wrongness*—that invited Malum. That's why no one from Stonehaven tried to find me after I left, not even Eden. Perhaps that's even why Jacquetta never came for me in the woods after the raid. She sensed the fatal flaw that marked me as different. Other. Beneath the rustle of leaves,

I swear I can hear the prowling of an invisible beast. Spots of light dance amid the shadows in the distance, like eyes.

"Enough," I mutter to myself.

I throw my arms wide, scattering the birds, who caw at me and soar off into the night. Even if Malum has touched me, once I pull Rhea back, we'll devise a way to fix the Veil, and then that sinister force will be banished, its dark hooks removed from me forever. I just have to locate the Bloodstones—and quickly. Roland promised to look for clues as to where the stones might have been taken after they were pried out from the royal swords. If he doesn't find anything, I will, even if it means scouring every book in that Spirits-forsaken library.

I turn back to the door, leaving the crows and their ominous message behind. Rhea never felt that there was anything wrong with me. And there isn't. Soon, everything will be as it was before the raid.

Even so, beneath the biting wind, some strange, foreign part of my heart whispers, *Is that what you really want?*

Of course it is. What else is there?

The palace courtyard teems with activity the following morning as Sir Weston's hunting party readies itself to depart. Horses stamp their feet, breath steaming from their nostrils. Dozens of hounds bay and bark, straining at their leads. Servants haul crates and boxes onto wagons. The whole scene has me thoroughly perplexed. At Stonehaven, the Elementals packed only the supplies and weapons that they could carry for their hunts. Judging from the sheer amount of food—and wine—currently being loaded, it appears as though we'll be traveling for weeks, not just a day. And the clothing is even more impractical.

I tug at what Duchess Poole deemed a *riding habit*, yet another torture device invented for mortal women. The bodice is tighter than our typical gowns, with buckles marching down the front. The skirt isn't as full, which is preferable to my regular uniform, but it's a stiff and unwieldy burgundy wool. And the hat is even worse. It's too small to provide any shade, and huge, plumy feathers protrude from the top, constantly drooping down to tickle my nose. Yet again, I curse myself for being reckless enough to get myself wrapped up in this madness.

A cart rumbles past, laden with bows. *Finally*, something I recognize. I may not be the best shot, but considering the company I'll be keeping, I'd prefer to enter the forest armed. I pull a bow down from the rack and frown. It's far lighter than it should be, as well as a good deal flimsier. At Stonehaven, our bows were carved from maple or ash or yew. This one is of such poor construction that I doubt it's wood at all. I pluck an arrow from a quiver. The tip is blunted—just like the set the princess was given. Vaguely, I recall that the king said Sir Weston had devised the weapon. But I thought his invention was only for Blodwyn. Are we really going into the forest with nothing but children's toys?

"Planning on skewering someone else's wardrobe?"

I cringe at the voice—Marion's. She and her cadre are congregated a short distance away, dressed in some of the most extravagant outfits I've seen yet. The embroidery on Marion's gown is stitched with golden thread, and her hat is decorated with pearls the size of grapes.

"You won't do much damage with these, I'm afraid." She walks over to the weapons cart and selects an arrow. "Hasn't Sir Weston outdone himself? I can't wait to see what the rest of his game entails."

That makes one of us.

"Really?" I ask, unable to resist the jab. "You seemed rather frightened of those arrows yesterday."

And she should have been. If Marion had been a second too slow, the arrow might have taken out her eye. The same intense desire from the menagerie thrums in my veins. I shy away from it, unsure where it comes from—especially after yesterday.

"Was I?" Marion frowns. "I don't recall. And there's no need to worry. Sir Weston assures me that the weapons are harmless. Then again, blunting so many arrows is such an overwhelming task. I do hope they didn't miss any by mistake."

A crow calls overhead.

I'm about to turn away and leave Marion to her veiled threats when there's a whoosh of air and a faint whistle. Something whizzes between me and the courtier. She cries out, stepping back as it thunks into the side of the weapons cart. The shaft of an arrow vibrates where it's caught between two slats of wood. I turn to see who fired it, and my breath hitches. Jacquetta.

What is she doing here? She wasn't on Duchess Poole's list. Jacquetta's blue eyes, made brighter against the deep burgundy color of her riding habit, meet mine, and my feckless heart kicks in my chest.

"Look at that," Jacquetta says to Marion. "They did miss one. How negligent."

Rage rolls off of Marion in waves. But she doesn't bother to answer. The courtier spins on her heel and storms off, with the other ladies trailing behind her.

"You looked surprised to see me," Jacquetta comments dryly as she returns her bow to the cart. "Aren't you going to ask who I poisoned to secure my place?"

The ridges of my ears burn, and I fidget with my weapon. Despite my earlier certainty, I'm finding it increasingly less likely that Jacquetta put thornapple in my wine on the night of the dinner. After all, if she wanted to kill me, she could have simply shot me just now. Marion probably would have awarded her a medal for the service.

"About that—" I start, having no idea how to finish. And Jacquetta isn't interested.

"Save it." She dismisses me with a wave. "We don't have to be friends, Ayleth. Let's just get through the day."

She rehangs her bow and walks off. Some insane part of me wants to go after her—but what would I say? That I *want* to be friends? That I'm sorry? I don't and I'm not. Instead, I roll my shoulders against the nagging tension settled there and head to the stables. Jacquetta is right. We just need to get through the day. And judging from how it's started, I can tell it's going to be one of the longest of my life.

CHAPTER TWENTY-SEVEN

I F THERE WEREN'T ALREADY A PATH THROUGH THE FOREST, WE'D BE carving one. Horses' hooves squelch in the mud. Wagons lumber down the trail, rattling and creaking so loudly that birds startle, their irritated cries mixing with the party's laughter and the baying of the hounds. It's barely midmorning, but the scent of wine lingers beneath the cedar-sweet tang of early winter. Sir Weston's dreaded game has yet to commence, but before we departed the courtyard, all the women were handed quivers of blunted arrows. All the men carry the flimsy bows. The riders are chattering excitedly about what the difference might mean. Whatever it is, I'm going to hate it.

At least my horse is tolerable. A kind-eyed stable hand introduced me to Honeywine, a dappled mare named for her docile nature. He wasn't exaggerating. I could probably let go of Honeywine's reins and she would continue plodding contentedly along after the rest of the party. The steady, gentle motion of her steps is actually rather comforting, and I don't resist as my mind starts to wander. My attention travels into the latticed forest canopy, spindly branches glittering with frost. Again, I'm reminded of how much I love forests. How much I miss—

A blur of black swoops past, close enough that I duck and Honeywine chuffs. I swivel in the saddle just in time to watch a crow land on a nearby branch.

One for sorrow.

"Mistress Ayleth."

I would rather be visited by a hundred crows than hear *that* voice. The king's white stallion pulls up beside me, its bridle adorned with jeweled crowned-apple sigils. That feeling behind my left ribs stirs.

Call it what it is, that voice taunts. *Malum.*

I ignore it. Even if it is Malum, I've controlled it before. I can do so again.

Granting the king the barest dip of my chin, I keep my attention fixed ahead, gritting my teeth until the sensation dulls.

"How are you enjoying the day?" King Callen asks. "Have you shot any *birds*? Or hats?"

Without thinking, I glance at him. Dappled sunlight patterns the king's face as he grins at me. I grip Honeywine's reins tighter. "That was an accident."

"So you claimed. But *I* think"—leather creaks as the king leans in his saddle, close enough that I catch his scent of leather and smoke and the dark heart of the forest—"that you knew *exactly* what you were doing."

A crow calls overhead again, and that invisible force thrums.

"Here." The king reaches over his shoulder and withdraws an arrow fletched in bright-gold feathers. Strange—I thought only the women carried quivers. "It will bring you luck during Weston's game, like your favor did for me at the joust."

He slides the arrow into my own quiver with a wink. Whatever the king touched will bring me the opposite of luck. As he finally nudges his horse and begins to move away, I reach for the thing, determined to throw it into the bushes. Before I get the chance, twigs snap nearby. Several courtiers gasp at a rumbling growl. The horses nicker. My pulse kicks up. Had the creature from the crypt followed us out here—followed *me*?

Brush rustles and an animal springs out of the forest.

"The Nevenwolf!" someone shouts.

But it's not. This creature is nowhere near large enough to be confused with such a beast. I'd say it was closer to the size of a dog, with shaggy black fur and a long snout.

"I've got it!" The king fires off one of his gold-fletched arrows, which sinks into the creature's body.

The animal howls and rears up on its hind legs, but there's no blood. In fact, its moaning and writhing are so exaggerated that it's almost comical. This is no beast, I realize as the creature wilts dramatically to the ground. It's another trick. Sure enough, the so-called Nevenwolf rises, pulls off its head, and reveals a pair of dark-brown eyes and a roguish grin. Sir Weston.

Applause swells as the Lord of Misrule bows. "I have been slain."

Laughter. I roll my eyes. Can these people really find nothing better to do with their time than parade about the forest in costume? Would that a real wolf had mistaken Sir Weston for a midday snack.

"What's all this, Weston?" the king calls.

"Our hunt, Majesty," Weston replies with a flourish. "For I am not the only Nevenwolf loose in these woods."

On cue, growls and barks surround us from all sides. The actual dogs begin to whine and strain at their leads. Honeywine whickers, nervous. I pat her neck.

"It's not real," I whisper close to her ear. "They're just idiots."

She snorts, evidently agreeing.

"How are we supposed to kill the beasts with these?" a man calls, brandishing his bow.

"Ah." Sir Weston points at him. "But you must ask our *ladies*."

More applause and cries of delight.

"For the remainder of the hunt," Sir Weston continues, "the ladies in our retinue represent our goddess, Meira. Just as we must earn the protection of *her* Light, you men will have to earn their arrows. The ladies will only bestow one upon you if they deem you worthy to receive it."

The women begin to chatter excitedly. I don't join them.

"Men, once you find yourself in possession of an arrow, you may use it to slay a Nevenwolf—as did our brave king." Sir Weston yanks the arrow from his costume with a grimace. "And don't worry about us wolves—the costumes are padded. Softer than Rathburn's backside."

The rest of the party laughs, but I only stare around at them. Do they not understand the insanity of this plan? I think of how Jacquetta's arrow, even blunted, stuck in the weapons cart. Someone could actually get killed out here. No one else seems bothered by that possibility, though. A few men are already suggesting what they might do to earn a lady's arrow.

"The hunt ends when you hear the horn," Sir Weston says, displaying the curved wooden instrument. "Prizes await any man who returns with a slain Nevenwolf, as well as for he who collects the most arrows. And, as a special bonus, if any of you daring hunters receives an arrow from the *king*, you shall have the honor of requesting a favor from His Majesty."

The king waves to the party, who cheer even louder. His gray eyes fall on me and he winks. I sense another maddening nudge against the inner side of my left ribs.

Like summons like, that voice whispers. I shove it down.

"And what are the prizes?" someone calls.

"Is that Rathburn?" Sir Weston shades his eyes as he peers into the crowd. "Greedy as ever, I see. You still owe me after our last game of Castles."

The man answers with a rude gesture.

"The bounty will be well worth your effort, I assure you." Sir Weston indicates a nearby wagon stacked with crates. "We have some *very* rare items to bestow upon our winners. But nothing, of course, that can compare to the favor of our ladies."

Rare items. How rare? Could one of them be a Bloodstone? Is that why they were missing from the crypt, because they'd been pried out to be used as trinkets for Longest Night? Revolting as the idea might be, it's exactly the sort of antic I've come to expect from this court. Scraps of a plan begin to cobble themselves together in my mind. I already have a horse. I could find the Bloodstones and just keep riding. I could have Rhea back with me before the sunrise.

Sir Weston is blathering on again about rules, but I'm already steering Honeywine in the direction of the wagon. All I need is a few moments after everyone leaves to—

"Let the game begin!" Sir Weston shouts.

The horn bellows and the party lurches into motion. Courtiers spur their mounts and bound into the trees, and—to my horror— Honeywine whinnies and gallops after them. It's everything I can do to keep myself in the saddle as she barrels into the forest.

"Wait!" I shout, yanking on the reins. "Stop!"

But my frantic commands only seem to increase her breakneck speed. Honeywine, who has until this moment seemed content to keep the pace of a snail, leaps effortlessly over fallen logs and weaves her way between the tree trunks, every thud of her hooves resonating in my bones. Branches snag at my hair and clothing as the forest blurs past me. I'm probably going to die, my head knocked off by a low-hanging tree limb.

"Stop!" I yell again as she veers perilously close to a wide oak.

For whatever reason, Honeywine finally obeys—sort of. She lurches to a halt so abruptly that I'm thrown from the saddle and onto the ground. Pain lances through my joints. I curse and roll to one side, chest heaving. There's a taste of copper and earth in my mouth. Grimacing, I push myself up to sit. A leaf flutters in my peripheral vision and I pluck it out of my hair. I hear a far-off crash of thunder. Wonderful. It's going to rain. I'll be soaked on top of everything else. Damn Sir Weston and this ludicrous game. No prize is worth—

The Bloodstones. My plan comes crashing back to me. How far am I from the wagons? I scramble to my feet, ignoring the aches in my limbs. I need to return to the cart while the rest of the party is still occupied.

"Do you know where we are?" I ask Honeywine, my own sense of direction jumbled.

She only flicks her tail. Perfect.

"Come on." I take her reins. "Let's just—"

A twig snaps nearby.

"Mistress," a cloying male voice calls.

Between the trees, I catch glimpses of black fur and a long snout. One of those pretend Nevenwolves. *Shit.*

"You needn't be afraid of me. I'd never harm one of Meira's own."

He laughs, slurring, and my blood chills, recalling Marion's threat in the menagerie.

Who knows what could happen to a lost little Order girl in the woods?

Had she sent this man to find me? Today's excursion is the perfect opportunity to do me harm. After all, no one would actually care if I died out here. It would just be a tragic accident, instantly forgotten.

Panic rings in my mind. Honeywine is my fastest option out of this situation, but what if she bolts again? I might wind up at the border to Rycinthia. Brush rustles, the man edging nearer. By the Spirits, I am the unluckiest witch alive. I won't be able to outpace him on foot. I scan my surroundings. There's a huge oak nearby, its wide branches low enough for a relatively easy climb—not that any physical activity will be easy in this gown. But I can't just stand here.

Gathering a few rocks as additional protection, I make for the tree. Between the stiff fabric of my skirt and my corset, hauling myself into the branches is ten times more difficult than it should be. But I manage it—barely. By the time I finally settle myself on a thick bough, my breath is sawing through my lungs and my heart hammers in my eardrums.

"Come out, come out." Brush crunches as the man slinks into the clearing. He's about twenty feet below me. "Or no, stay where you are. Let me find you."

Just keep still, I tell myself. *He won't see you.*

My hand reaches for a rock anyway. The stone is too small to do him much harm, but perhaps I can use it as a distraction.

"I know you're out here." The man circles Honeywine, who shies away from him.

My palms are slick. The man turns in my direction. He pokes around in several bushes. Ice flows through my veins as his attention tracks right and left, then . . . up. *Shit.* I brace myself for him to spot me. One heartbeat passes. Two.

"By the Light, where could she have gone, slippery thing?"

He kicks at a fern. A rush of relief swoops in my belly. He hadn't seen me. I slump onto the limb, inhaling deep breaths of the chilly air. But then a sharp crack splits the clearing, followed by a whinny and the gallop of hooves. Honeywine charges into the trees.

"Good luck finding your way back!" the man calls.

He laughs again and trundles off. Damn *everything.* I despise these mortals. But I tamp down my anger. There isn't time to waste. As soon as the sound of the man's movements fades, I start to maneuver myself down the tree. If climbing up here was difficult, getting down will be nearly impossible. And I'm far enough above the ground that a fall would likely break a bone. My latent magic would heal it, but any injury will slow me down—and hurt. I don't let myself dwell on that possibility.

Keeping my movements small and precise, I edge myself off my branch and onto the lower one. My boot barely touches the bark when a maddeningly familiar laugh rings in the quiet. I freeze. Is that . . .

Two figures traipse into the clearing. One is definitely Marion, and the other—

Sunlight gleams on the gold stitching of the king's doublet. The feeling behind my left ribs shivers to life.

"By the Spirits," I mutter, scrambling back up the tree.

Of all the clearings in the forest, *why* did they have to choose this one? At least they don't know I'm here. With Honeywine gone, there's no trace of another person. Unfortunately, however, Marion and the king are happy to take full advantage of their solitude.

"If you want one of my arrows, Callen," Marion says, her voice low and sultry in a way that makes my skin crawl, "you're going to have to earn it, like Weston said."

The king prowls toward her, pinning her against the trunk of a tree. *My* tree. I should have just let the other man kill me. Death is far preferable to my current predicament.

"Callen," Marion breathes as the king bends his face to the curve of her neck.

No, no, no. This can't be happening. Marion groans in pleasure and I clamp my hands over my ears. Every fiber of my being screams to jump out of the tree, broken bones or not. But they're *right underneath* me. I'm stuck up here, witness to their . . .

Movement shimmers on the other side of the clearing. Is it the same man from before? I squint into the trees, just able to discern a figure crouching in the brush. But the person isn't dressed as a Nevenwolf. In fact, I recognize the same burgundy wool of my own riding habit, which means it must be someone in the queen's household. But who—

A pair of cobalt-blue eyes flashes among the tree trunks. It's

Jacquetta? What is she doing? I get my answer as she removes a bow from her back, then an arrow from her quiver. I can tell from the glint of silver that *this* arrow is not blunted.

And it's pointed directly at the king.

Time itself seems to slow as Jacquetta nocks the arrow and aims. That deep part of myself, the one that reveled in Marion's terror in the menagerie, rises up.

Yes, the voice in my mind whispers. *Let the king die. He deserves it.*

He deserves worse. I hold my breath, picturing Jacquetta's arrow striking true. The king slumped against the tree, those gray eyes cold and vacant. Jacquetta draws her arm back. My heart knocks against my chest.

No, the word drops into my mind like a stone.

I try to ignore it, but I can't. Because I know the truth: The king's death won't solve anything. Just as with the High Priest, someone else will simply take his place. And what if Jacquetta misses? What if the king sees her and lives? Or if Marion sees?

It's too much of a risk. Holding in a frustrated scream, I yank a rock from my pocket and hurl it as hard as I can across the clearing, away from Jacquetta. It lands loud enough to startle the king and Marion, who immediately untangle themselves from their embrace.

"What was that?"

King Callen scans the clearing. "One of Weston's wolves, no doubt. They'll stay away if they know what's good for them."

He leans into Marion again, but the courtier must possess some measure of intuition, for she stops him. "We should go back. It's going to rain anyway."

As if to underscore her point, distant thunder rumbles.

"But I've yet to earn your arrow," the king complains.

"Here." Marion snatches one out of her quiver and hands it to him. "Let's return before Weston drinks all the wine."

"Excellent point," the king agrees, offering her his arm.

The two walk together out of the clearing. My attention pivots to where I'd seen Jacquetta. Is she going to follow them, or—

She's not going anywhere. Those cobalt-blue eyes are fixed directly on mine, glittering with rage. Every muscle in my body goes still, like a rabbit spotted by a wolf. Jacquetta might not end the king's life today, but she very well may end *mine*.

CHAPTER TWENTY-EIGHT

M
Y FIRST INSTINCT IS TO REMAIN IN THE TREE.
But then I realize that doing so makes me a sitting
target, and I'm not convinced that Jacquetta won't start
shooting at me. I clamber down the branches, heedless of the way
the bark scrapes against my skin or how my ankle rolls when my
footing slips. Jacquetta is already waiting for me when I hit the
ground.

"What's the matter with you?" she seethes, cornering me against
the tree. "I warned you not to meddle with me."

"Meddle? I was saving you—again. Just like with the High Priest."

"This was different." She brandishes the bow. "It would have been
a hunting accident. No one would have suspected anything."

"Yes, they would have!" I throw up my hands. "He's the king. And
what if someone saw you? Marion was right there."

Her jaw tightens. "This is just like you, swooping in and deciding
what's right. Giving no consideration to anything other than your
own plans."

Like *me*? Frustration builds in my chest.

"At least I think those plans through," I seethe. "You just show up and destroy whatever is around you. Then you leave because you don't want to clean up the mess."

Like the mess she left of me. The ruined pieces she discarded on the forest floor.

Jacquetta only glares. "What are you talking about?"

She's actually going to pretend she doesn't remember. Perhaps this is how Jacquetta deals with the conflict in her life—Don't look at it and it doesn't exist. But I'm going to *make* her look.

"I'm talking about Stonehaven." I point at her. "When you left me behind. What *consideration* did you give to me?"

Jacquetta swallows, the only indication that my words have any effect on her. Good. I want them to hurt. I want to dig the blade deeper, even if it means I'm the one who bleeds.

Thunder booms in the distance. "And what did you expect me to do?" she says at last, low and vehement.

There's a bitterness beneath her anger. Like *I'm* the one who hurt *her*, not the other way around. How typical of her to try and turn the tables.

"Oh, I don't know." I cross my arms. "Keep your promise, perhaps?"

"*My* promise?" She huffs a laugh. "Did the thornapple addle your mind?"

"Stop pretending! I risked everything for you and you left me alone in the clearing. *Our* clearing. After you said—"

"And what about what I risked?" She interrupts. A twig snaps under Jacquetta's boot as she steps closer. "Do you have any idea what it took for me to go to that clearing? I was ready to abandon my mother, my whole life, all because of a promise *you* made to me."

I stare at her, the clouds thickening overhead. "What do you mean you went to the clearing?"

Jacquetta pauses, narrowing her gaze at me. Her eyes are bright against the coming storm. "Now who's pretending? You know I went."

No, I don't. And I search Jacquetta's expression for any cracks of deceit, but there aren't any. She can't be telling the truth, though. I *know* what happened that night—it shattered my whole world.

"Would that I saved myself the trouble," Jacquetta continues, vehement. "Don't speak to me of promises and risks when you're the one who suddenly changed your mind. Chose your duty as Second over anything else. You can point a finger at me all you like, but I left because you told me to go."

My duty? I never used that word when speaking of my place in the coven. And I wouldn't have told her to leave, not when I was so desperate to escape. It sounds more like—

"Mother," I whisper, the truth searing into my mind like a hot blade, poisonous and deadly. "It was Mother."

Of course it was. Her specialty is illusion magic. She spelled the Hunt and the real Sisters, jumbling their memories so that we could steal their identities. She crafts the glamours for the witches who fetch supplies. It would have been nothing for Mother to disguise herself as me, especially when she was so familiar with my expressions and mannerisms. Numbness bleeds over me and I slump onto a fallen log.

"What does your mother have to do with anything?" Jacquetta asks, still angry.

"It wasn't me that night," I tell her, the pieces of the puzzle still coming together in my mind. No wonder the Elementals found me so quickly the next morning. Mother knew exactly where to send them. "It was my mother. She must have used a glamour. Wore my face to meet with you—and convinced you to leave."

Silence stretches between us, laced with thunder.

"It . . . wasn't you?" Jacquetta asks softly.

I shake my head, the truth roiling in my veins. Honestly, it shouldn't be this much of a surprise. After Rhea died, Mother would have gone to any lengths to keep from losing another Second. That's all she's ever cared about. Not me, but what I stood for.

A slow-festering rage begins to eat through my shock. Mother let me wait in the forest all night, likely watching me through her mirror, that silver-eyed raven perched in a tree. She let me believe that Jacquetta didn't want me—that there was something wrong with me. And then Mother held that night over my head, wielding it like a weapon to punish me for my disloyalty to the coven. *She* is the one who is disloyal. Mother should be glad that there's a whole kingdom between us. If there weren't, I would . . .

The wind whistles, carrying the charge of the storm.

"I went to the clearing," I say to Jacquetta, voice rough. "I waited until sunrise. I thought you didn't come. I never would have . . ."

But I'm not sure how to finish. Years stretch between us, my long-held beliefs crumbling to dust. Jacquetta was there that night. She didn't abandon me—didn't break us. Where would we be if Mother hadn't kept us apart? And what does it mean that, despite everything, we were brought back together? Jacquetta steps even closer. What is *she* thinking? Her blue eyes glimmer. I'd forgotten until this moment that there are flecks of silver spangled within them, like tiny stars. And as that gaze flits to my lips, I forget again. I forget everything, save for the thrum of her nearness.

"Ayleth . . ."

A low snarl interrupts her.

The roots of my hair rise and a cold, instinctual sweat breaks over my body. That noise did not come from one of the costumed men. Brush crunches behind me and, against every screaming instinct, I turn. The largest animal I've ever encountered stares back at me, with raven-black fur and crimson eyes. Its teeth are bared—long, daggerlike things that will rend flesh to ribbons before you can even think to scream.

A Nevenwolf.

The world itself seems to halt as the beast prowls into the clearing. There's no question as to its origin. Shadows curl up from its black coat and trail behind its footsteps. Its eyes—the red of a witch's cloak—glitter. This is a creature of Malum, brought forth from beyond the Veil.

And I know what brought it here—me.

The Nevenwolf growls, and I can feel the vibration in the place behind my left ribs. Any remaining doubt that Malum touched me burns away. That terrifying force reached through the coven fire. It sunk its hooks into me and now I'm luring things out from beyond the Veil. This is the same beast from the crypt. It's been hunting me. Tracking me. And it's not going to stop until it pulls me back through the Veil with it. That force inside me shivers, as if to agree.

"Run," I murmur to Jacquetta, hardly daring to move my lips. "It won't follow you."

She stays where she is. "How do you know that?"

Because I summoned it. The Nevenwolf stalks closer.

"*Go*, Jacquetta," I urge. "*Now.*"

She hesitates a second longer, but her common sense must kick in, for she bolts into the trees. The Nevenwolf doesn't even glance in her direction. Some selfish part of me wishes that she'd stayed, and I won't have to face this beast alone. But it was always going to be the two of us in the end. As if in answer, the creature growls.

Focus, that voice in my mind insists. *You're not dead yet.*

No. Instincts crash together in my mind as I evaluate my options. There aren't many. A few rocks are scattered around, but I might as well throw apples at the beast for all the good those will do. I spot a fallen tree branch that's as thick as my leg, but I doubt I could lift it, much less use it as a weapon. By some miracle, Sir Weston's quiver is still strapped to my back, but the arrows are blunted. Maybe I could—

A piercing yowl cuts through the clearing, followed by a blur of dark calico.

Nettle.

How did she get here?

My cat lands on the Nevenwolf's back, stubbornly clinging to its haunches, hissing and scratching as the beast tries to throw her. I seize the opportunity to snatch an arrow from my quiver and break off the end, so that at least I have a sharp object. The Nevenwolf bucks again, and Nettle is tossed into a bush with a painful mewl. It takes every ounce of self-control to keep from running after her.

The beast returns its attention to me, clearly annoyed at having been interrupted. It circles me, one slow step after another, and I brandish my broken arrow like an idiot. Thunder rumbles, louder now. I inhale the Nevenwolf's scent—musk and fetid earth and something I can only describe as *wrong.* The same smell from the crypt. As if it knows I recognize it, the Nevenwolf's lips part in a hideous, haunting grin.

And then it lunges.

I duck, thrusting out the broken arrow and praying for just one hit before the beast rips me apart. Thunder booms and lightning splits the sky, connecting with the branches of a nearby tree. There's a sickening crack of wood and then—to my horror—half of that tree comes tumbling down on top of us.

A scream climbs up my throat and I cover my head with my arms, bracing for the crush of bone as the tree flattens me. It doesn't come. Instead, a deafening crash explodes in the clearing, followed by an agonized roar. Then ... silence. I lift my head, bewildered. The mess of branches from the felled tree smolders a short distance away. Beneath it—I blink to make sure I'm not hallucinating—the Neven-wolf is still.

"What in the—"

"Ayleth."

My attention whips to the right. Jacquetta emerges from the trees, looking weak and spent and exhausted. Like she . . .

Comprehension dawns. I gape at the smoking tree and then at her. "Was this *you*?"

How is it possible? If Jacquetta were an Elemental, she might be able to accomplish a spell like what I just witnessed. But it would still require years of training and an immense amount of magic. I've never seen a Caster command a storm.

"Can we discuss it later?" Jacquetta motions for me to follow her. "We need to go."

Right. I push myself up and hurry to the bush where Nettle was thrown, releasing a grateful breath that she doesn't appear to be badly injured. I scoop her into my arms and run toward Jacquetta. A cold rain is beginning to fall, the drops stinging against my face. But I'm not halfway across the clearing when another growl stops me in my tracks. It can't be—

With a roar that rattles my teeth, the Nevenwolf springs to life. It shrugs off the remains of the tree like a discarded cloak. But instead of targeting me, the beast turns its attention to *Jacquetta*.

"RUN!" I scream at her as the Nevenwolf bounds across the clearing.

Nettle fights her way free of my arms and we sprint after the beast. Jacquetta disappears into the trees, but too late. The Nevenwolf roars, there's a scream—one that stops my own heart—and then nothing.

"*No!*"

I urge my clumsy feet faster, desperate to get to Jacquetta, but the Nevenwolf reemerges, blocking my path. Rage pounds in my veins as I stare into the depths of its crimson eyes. I will *kill* this beast for hurting Jacquetta. I will tear it to pieces, or die trying. Gritting my teeth, I yank another arrow from my quiver—it's the last. My only chance.

You have to be strong. Rhea's voice skims the curves of my skull.

I have never been strong. Wind whips around me, the air crackling with the energy of the coming storm. Lightning flares again, glinting silver on the Nevenwolf's bared teeth. Shadows thicken around us, seeming to unspool from the distance and wend their way through the trees, reaching for me, ready to drag me beyond the Veil. That sensation behind my left ribs abruptly sharpens, pulling at me, as if it's shortening, reeling me in. And that's exactly what's happening, I realize dully—like is calling to like. The Nevenwolf is here for the piece of itself that lives inside me. I fight it with everything I have, clenching my fists against the triangles etched below each ring finger.

"Two lines drifting apart and then back together," I whisper, the words like a spell. Because I need us to be together now. "Please, Rhea. Help me."

It might be my imagination, but the triangles on my palms prickle. In the gathering darkness, the Nevenwolf's eyes glare red.

The eye. I can hear my sister's voice in my mind. *The cleanest kill is always the eye.*

The beast growls and something inside me snaps. I will not go without a fight. Ignoring the fear licking the inside of my body like tongues of flame, the panic swarming in my mind, and the churning of Malum between my bones, I let out a feral yell and charge the creature. It pounces, wicked teeth poised for my throat.

Seconds drag out as I arch my arm back and bring it down into the red target of the Nevenwolf's eye. Flesh tears and smoke hisses, like hot iron meeting water. Inky blood spatters my face, tasting of rust and rot and death. My stomach curdles. The Nevenwolf roars in agony. I'm knocked backward. White-hot pain shoots through my shoulder where I land.

Get up! that voice screams.

I scramble to obey, if only to run, because I have nothing left to defend myself with. But the Nevenwolf isn't chasing me. It stumbles drunkenly, then falls. Its entire body shudders once, and then—with a last whimper—goes still.

The force behind my ribs instantly settles, its connection to the Nevenwolf severed. In the quiet that follows, all I can do is stare at the smoke rising from the Nevenwolf's wound. I did it. I actually *did* it. As the surge of adrenaline ebbs, I register an ache in my right hand. I look down, surprised to find a burn mark stamped across my palm, one the same width as the arrow's shaft. The triangle below my ring finger prickles.

"Rhea?" I whisper.

The wind picks up, whistling through the branches.

Ayleth, I swear I hear. *Ayleth.*

It had been my sister. She'd answered me. Protected me, as always.

"Thank you," I whisper, pressing down on the triangle. It might be my imagination, but I think I feel a faint, answering pulse beneath my skin.

Nettle meows, directing my attention to the trees.

Jacquetta.

Heart pounding, I stumble toward the place where I last saw the other witch. She's sprawled on the ground, her limbs bent at awkward angles.

"No," I whisper. She can't be dead.

A thousand horrible images swirl in my mind as I roll her over—Jacquetta's throat torn out or her face clawed to ribbons. But no—her features are intact. Her chest is moving as she breathes. She's alive. Relief balloons inside me, followed swiftly by a shot of fear. Jacquetta's skin is too cold, and her shoulder is soaked in blood. There's a gash on the side of her neck where the Nevenwolf's claws grazed her.

A memory of Rhea rises up, the iron poisoning webbing beneath her skin. This isn't the same, I try to convince myself. But it could be, couldn't it? After all, the Nevenwolf is born of Malum. That's just as bad—if not worse—than iron. Panic drums in time with my heartbeat. I cannot lose Jacquetta as well. Not again.

Brush rustles deeper in the forest. Nettle trills a warning.

"I think it came from over here," someone shouts through the rain.

Damn everything. They cannot find us here.

"Jacquetta." I slap at her cheeks to rouse her. She moans. "We have to go."

Lightning flashes. Her eyes at last flutter open, fever-bright.

"It's you," she murmurs. "You're all right."

Her hand reaches weakly for me and every bone in my body turns to wax. But I can't think about that now. The voices are closer. I sling Jacquetta's arm around my neck and manage to haul her to her feet.

"Find the horse," I tell Nettle, who bounds off in another direction.

Half dragging Jacquetta alongside me, I follow my cat, leaving the smoking corpse of the Nevenwolf behind us. And I pray to every Spirit listening that this is the last time I ever encounter such a beast.

CHAPTER TWENTY-NINE

THUNDER BOOMS OVER THE FOREST, TREES SWAYING IN THE WIND as the storm lumbers over Riven. By some miracle, we locate Honeywine and I manage to haul Jacquetta into the saddle with me, but it seems an eternity before the palace walls are at last visible through the sheets of rain.

"Come on," I urge Honeywine, clinging to Jacquetta. She's so cold.

At last the mare plods through the palace gates. The storm has driven everyone inside, and the hunting party hasn't returned, which helps me to get Jacquetta out of the saddle before anyone asks too many questions about the state she's in. I guide her into the palace, racking my brain to recall what the healers had used for Rhea.

"Ironbane," I mutter to myself. "Feverfew and comfrey."

But where am I going to find them? Jacquetta groans, her head lolling against my shoulder as we stumble down the halls, dodging curious looks from passing servants. Hopefully, they'll all assume she just drank too much.

"You're back!" Joan looks up from where she's reading by the fire, then promptly drops her book when she spots Jacquetta. "What's happened?"

"She needs . . ." I'm not even sure what to say. Jacquetta mumbles unintelligibly. She's getting worse—just like Rhea. Panic drums against my skull.

"She needs a physician." Joan rushes over and helps me hold Jacquetta upright. "I'll help you get to the infirmary."

"No!" I all but shout, earning a bewildered look. "Not there."

Technically, it might be possible to hide Jacquetta's true nature from a mortal physician, but it's not worth the risk. Besides, I don't want to let her out of my sight.

"Ayleth, we really must—"

"Please." I grasp Joan's arm. "Trust me on this."

Joan purses her lips, but finally nods. Together, we guide Jacquetta over to her bed. To my immense relief, the bleeding has slowed, but most of Jacquetta's bodice is drenched in blood. And the claw marks on her neck haven't knitted back together yet. My throat tightens.

"What is that?" Joan asks, angling around me.

I cover the wound before she can get a better look.

"One of Sir Weston's arrows used for the game." I fumble the lie. "It wasn't blunted."

Joan clicks her tongue. "I knew something like this would happen. She's lucky she wasn't killed. Are you sure she doesn't need—"

"She needs bandages," I say firmly. "And medicine. Do you think you can help?"

"Let me see what I can scrounge up." Joan hurries off. "You get her undressed. She'll catch her death in those clothes. And we should make sure there aren't any other injuries."

Undressed? Fire climbs up my neck. But I give myself a swift shake. Joan is right. Jacquetta's sodden clothes are likely worsening her condition, and I need to tend the wound—one that was my fault in the first place.

"Sorry about this," I tell Jacquetta, my fingers fumbling on the clasps of her bodice.

I ease the fabric of her dress apart, and she murmurs as my hands brush the ledge of her collarbone. Her breathing is shallow beneath her corset. I'll have to remove *that*, too. By the Spirits, I think I will burst into flame.

Jacquetta groans again as I heft her up and lean her body against mine so that I can peel her arms free of her rain-soaked sleeves. Her face is close enough that I can feel the warmth of her breath against my neck, which sends gooseflesh prickling over my skin. I ignore it, focusing on the laces of her corset—which is a bad idea. Especially when, as I lift the garment away, there's nothing but the flimsy fabric of Jacquetta's shift between my hands and her skin. The shape of her is achingly visible—the rise of her breasts and the dip of her waist. My heart pounds harder.

The door opens and Joan hurries through, mercifully diverting my attention. "Hopefully one of these will do."

She dumps an assortment of bottles, jars, and wrappings onto the mattress. I swipe wet tendrils of hair out of my face and sort through her findings. One of the jars smells like it contains chamomile and feverfew. Another is probably a paste of willowbark. It's not iron-bane, but all of it is suitable for healing. I start slathering the paste onto Jacquetta's wound.

"Where did you get all this?" I ask Joan.

"I know how to find things," she says simply, carrying over a basin of water. "They're medicines, aren't they?"

Medicines our Blesseds taught the mortals to use. It seems not *everything* related to witches was burned in the Great Cleansing. Funny how we taught mortals the art of healing only to be thanked with a pyre. But I rein in my resentment, focusing on Jacquetta. She's still so pale. I pack additional herbs on top of the paste.

Please, I whisper in my mind. *Don't let her die.*

Not now. Not after we discovered that it was Mother in the clearing that night—not me. What was Jacquetta going to say before the Nevenwolf showed up? What did I *want* her to say?

"Did you learn about healing from the Sisters?" Joan asks.

"Yes," I hedge, concentrating on Jacquetta's bandage.

Joan sniffs the contents of a bottle. "I'd like to be a physician. But not like the ones in the palace. They never take me seriously."

Probably because they're all men.

Jacquetta mutters in her sleep and I dab her brow with a cool cloth.

"She's lucky to have you," Joan comments.

Lucky is not the word I would use—not when I'm the reason a Nevenwolf tried to claw her face off. "I'm not sure she agrees."

"Don't be silly. I saw her follow you on the night you were ill. She cares for you."

Some long-forgotten, shriveled part of my heart reopens at that. *Close it off,* my mind says. *It's not safe.*

Before today, I would have listened. Now though . . .

I reach for Jacquetta's hand. Her skin is like marble against mine and I try to squeeze warmth into her fingers. It might be my imagination, but I think I feel her hand twitch, like she's squeezing back.

I remain with Jacquetta through the night, grateful when no one asks too many questions about what occurred at the hunt. At some point, I must fall into a shallow sleep. Like the night before, my dreams are filled with swirling darkness. A Nevenwolf stalks me in the forest as I run, tree branches tearing at my flesh. The beast pounces, pinning me to the ground with its massive paws, but its eyes aren't red. They're gray—just like the king's.

I jolt awake, discovering that my arms are draped over Jacquetta's legs. I jerk back immediately, wiping my mouth and pushing my hair out of my face. Jacquetta stirs, mumbling as her eyelids flutter open. A weight lifts in my chest.

"What . . ." Jacquetta reaches for the binding at her neck.

"Leave that," I say, lightly catching her wrist.

She doesn't fight me, still groggy. "What happened?"

I glance around the room. The clock on the mantel tells me it's midmorning. Joan and the other girl are gone, but I hadn't even heard them get up. "The Nevenwolf."

Jacquetta's brow creases. "The . . ."

And then the memory hits her. Her eyes widen and she slumps against the pillows. "By the Spirits. I was sure it would kill me."

"So was I."

The echo of the panic I felt when I found her sprawled and bleeding in the woods ripples through me. I almost lost her—again.

There's nothing to lose, that voice whispers.

But Jacquetta's expression suggests otherwise.

"You saved my life," she says, the words rough.

"You saved mine" is all my clumsy mind can summon in return. "I told you to run. Why did you come back?"

Sunlight spills over her features, still pale but . . . *beautiful.* My heart stutters.

"Because . . ." she starts. But then she shifts on the bed and her brow creases. She lifts the blanket. "*Where* are my clothes?"

Heat explodes in my chest.

"Oh. Sorry about that. You were soaked and I had to make sure there weren't any other injuries. There weren't, but . . ." I cross to the other side of the bed, eager for a task to distract myself. "I should check this one, if that's all right."

Jacquetta hesitates. "Fine."

I carefully peel back the bandage on her neck. Relief wings in my belly. The wound is worlds better than it was last night. Only a pink scar remains, and that will likely be gone by tomorrow. The herbs worked.

"It's almost healed," I tell her. "But you'll want to wear the bandage for a while longer. Joan was here when I brought you in. I didn't let her see the wound, but she saw the blood."

"Joan?" Jacquetta repeats. "I thought that was a dream."

"Don't worry." I replace the bandage, fingers light against Jacquetta's skin. "She believed me when I told her it was an accident with one of those blunted arrows."

"Thank the Spirits for that," Jacquetta mutters, burrowing deeper under the blanket. "What was a Nevenwolf doing out there in the first place?"

Looking for you, that voice whispers.

I fidget with the jar of willowbark paste. "The Veil must be too weak to hold it."

But I *had* sent it back. I'd killed it, if such a beast can be killed. And now that I think of it, that place behind my left ribs feels ... different. I'm not as aware of it. Perhaps destroying the Nevenwolf slackened Malum's hold on me. Good. Hopefully, it will stay that way.

The door opens and Joan enters the room, brightening as she sees Jacquetta.

"You're up!" She holds out a plate of fruit. "I brought you some breakfast."

Jacquetta pulls her blanket higher. "I ... appreciate that."

"How is your wound?" Joan sets the plate beside Jacquetta and starts reaching for the bandage. "Shall I check it?"

"I've already dressed it," I say, heading her off. "It's looking much better."

Joan frowns, I suspect disappointed at no longer having a patient.

"That's good news. And don't worry about your duties. I made your excuses to the queen. You're not the only ladies indisposed for the day. The whole palace is buzzing with talk of what happened." Joan looks to me. "Why didn't you tell me there was a *Nevenwolf*?"

So they did discover the beast. A foolish part of me hoped its body would simply vanish beyond the Veil where it belongs.

"I didn't know," I lie.

"Count yourself lucky," Joan says with a shudder. "It's dead now anyway. But that's the peculiar thing. They don't know what—or who—killed it. I heard they tried to bring the carcass back, but it *melted*."

Melted. That's precisely how Prince Tiergan's body appeared in his casket. My spine tingles. "You're sure?"

"It's what everyone is saying. And that's not all—there are rumors of a witch nearby."

Jacquetta and I exchange a panicked glance.

"Here at the palace?" she asks.

"No." Joan shakes her head. "But close. His Illuminance believes that the witch must have summoned the beast yesterday, as an attempt on the king's life. The Hunt is searching the woods now. No one is permitted outside until they discover the truth."

The truth. And what is that? The walls of our chamber seem to shrink closer.

The clock chimes, signaling the hour.

"I should go," Joan says with a sigh. "If I'm late again, I'll never hear the end of it. You're sure you don't need anything else?"

I'm not sure about anything anymore. "We're fine."

Joan nods and hurries off. The door snicks softly behind her.

"A witch didn't summon that Nevenwolf," I say to Jacquetta when we're alone, keeping my voice low as I imagine ears and eyes lurking in every corner.

"No." She picks at the blanket. "But I'm less worried about what the Hunt is looking for outside the palace than how long it takes them to realize there are two witches *inside* of it."

A log in the fire collapses, sending sparks dancing up the chimney.

"You could leave," I suggest, though the idea of her absence stings more than it should.

"So could you."

But I can't. Not without Rhea. I press the pad of my thumb against one of the triangles etched into my palm. "Not yet."

Jacquetta arches an eyebrow. "And what is *yet?*"

Given everything that's changed between us, part of me wants to tell her. Jacquetta didn't abandon me in the forest at Stonehaven. She saved me from the Nevenwolf. Maybe she would understand about Rhea. Even so, revealing my plan means admitting that I lied about being a Second. That I'm powerless. Weak. Jacquetta isn't weak. She'd summoned a lightning strike, for Spirits' sake. What would she think of me if she heard the truth? I don't want to know.

"I came for the Bloodstones," I tell her instead, falling back on the story I fed Roland. "They're the only way to mend the Veil. Set things right."

"Set things *right,*" Jacquetta repeats, her expression hardening. "Yes, I suppose you would believe those magic rocks would hold the answers."

I see you've turned out to be just like your mother, her words at the Sanctum dig into my flesh.

"And your plan to kill the king is better?" I counter, bristling.

She throws me a glance. "You have your solutions, and I have mine."

"And yours is what? Becoming a rogue assassin? That's not who you are."

"You don't know who I am."

But I did once. Yesterday, I thought that witch was gone forever, but now . . .

"I know you came to the forest," I say quietly. "To our clearing."

Quiet hums. Jacquetta pulls her blanket closer around herself. I hold my breath, desperate for her to tell me what she was going to say before the Nevenwolf appeared.

It makes no difference, that voice insists.

But it does, especially after I spent the last seven years believing she'd rejected me. That there was something about me that pushed her away.

"That was a long time ago," Jacquetta says at last.

"And yet it's all changed. What my mother did—"

"She did us a favor," Jacquetta interrupts, swift and direct, like the sweep of a blade. "What did we believe was going to happen if we ran off, two young witches on our own? We're too different, Ayleth. We would have wound up hating each other."

She's right, that voice says. I ignore it.

"You don't know that."

"Yes, I do," she says without a moment's hesitation. "I might have gone to the forest that night, but I also walked away. And so did you. You could have run off—started a new life somewhere else—but you went back to Stonehaven. We made our choices."

Fresh cracks form on my heart and I curse myself for feeling them. I should be stronger than this. Smarter. I know how to lock my heart inside a cage. But as much as I want to deny it, Jacquetta *still* holds the key.

"Fine," I snap. "But you should consider the consequences of the *choices* you make here. Killing the king might be your solution, but it only complicates matters for me."

"You're not my problem," she says flatly. "And neither are the Bloodstones."

"Really?" I cross my arms. "Those stones are the only things holding the Veil. If it falls, all witches suffer. Even you."

She doesn't reply to that, just stares into the smoldering embers of the hearth.

"What makes you think they're even here?" she asks at last, her tone softer, pensive. Like she really wants to know.

"This is where they were taken after the massacre," I reason. "Where else could they be? After all, the Veil hasn't fallen."

"But it's close, isn't it?" Jacquetta asks, more to herself than to me. "If Nevenwolves and who knows what else are starting to emerge."

"Yes," I agree, picturing the beast, "it's close."

She thinks a few moments longer, and—for the hundredth time—I wish I could glimpse inside her mind. "All right, then. Where do we look first?"

We? I blink at her. "You want to help?"

She shrugs. "I don't want to get swallowed alive by Malum—which nearly happened yesterday. Two of us looking for those stones will be better than one."

She has a point. And my own attempts to find the Bloodstones have proved disastrous. Still, the last time I allowed Jacquetta into my life, she left it in ruins.

"You expect me to let you waltz into my plans after you threatened to gut me for interfering with yours?" A thrill jolts through me, recalling her knife pressed against my side. "And last I checked, you don't care about the *magic rocks,* as you deem them. Or the Ancients."

She and Nerissa made that abundantly clear when they left Stonehaven.

"I care about Nevenwolves ripping out my insides," Jacquetta says simply. "Besides, the sooner you find those stones and leave, the sooner you'll be out of my way."

I arch an eyebrow. "So you can kill the king?"

She deals me an icy glare. "I'm not going to argue. We can either put our differences aside for a time, or not."

Don't trust her, that voice warns.

I know that it's right. But my only ally at this point is Roland, and I'm not even sure I'll see him again. It would be foolish to refuse another, even if it is her.

"A *short* time." I point at her. "We work together to find the Blood-stones and then we go our separate ways."

Just like before.

Jacquetta sticks out her hand. "Deal."

This is a terrible idea. But what other options do I have? I take her hand, ignoring the jolt of fire that races up my arm and straight into my wretched heart.

PART III

Tonight, we reconvene to strengthen the Veil. I admit, my power—vast as it is—wanes. Soon, it will be time for me to pass my Bloodstone on to my successor, my Heir, who will stand sentry at the borders of our worlds.

Such borders are necessary. It has been an age since we forged the Veil. In that time, we witches have held more power than we ever dreamed possible. Riven is no longer a realm plagued by blight or war. The covens can live without risk of being hunted.

All this, and yet still there are those witches who refuse to join us. They prefer to live as they did before the covens. Wayward. Some, I've heard, claim that the Veil disrupts an ancient balance. That we witches have meddled where we shouldn't, and will pay a terrible price.

For the most part, I can dismiss these theories. Change, after all, is always resisted. But, sometimes, in the night, I dream of swirling darkness. Of crows and creatures spun from shadow—Malum straining to break free of its prison.

Should it ever do so, I fear the vengeance it would wreak would tear this world apart.

—From the lost writings of Millicent, one of the Five,
Age of the Covens 400

CHAPTER THIRTY

As NEWS OF THE NEVENWOLF SPREADS, THE COURT BUZZES WITH speculation of witches and Malum. Given the decimated condition of the Nevenwolf's corpse, the High Priest claims that it was Meira herself who destroyed the beast, and that the goddess is personally protecting the White Palace. Soon, the court's fear of a witch lurking in the woods shifts to mockery. Men leap out from behind corners, red blankets draped around their shoulders, to scare unsuspecting courtiers. Cries of *witch* echo through the halls, followed by screams and laughter. Part of me wishes the Nevenwolf were still alive and that it could show these courtiers exactly what's waiting for them if Malum returns to this ungrateful realm.

As Joan reported, most outdoor activities are prohibited while the Hunt conducts its search for the supposed witch. Large and sprawling as the White Palace may be, its walls soon squeeze around us, as confining as a cage. It doesn't help that Jacquetta and I are forced to spend all our time in the queen's rooms, surrounded by other ladies, making it impossible for us to strategize about our search for the Bloodstones. It's not until the fourth day after Sir Weston's hunt, when the queen insists that her guards allow her household a brief walk in the gardens, that we're able to talk.

"So it wasn't just the Nevenwolf that . . . what did Joan say? Melted?" Jacquetta asks, keeping her voice low as our footsteps crunch along the gravel paths. The sound of the other women's distant chatter drifts around us.

I've just described my visit to the crypt, including the discovery of the prince's tar-like corpse, along with the shadow creature, which I now suspect was the Nevenwolf itself, fighting to break free of the Veil. I sense a slight tremble behind my left ribs. But it's nothing like it was in the forest, when the Nevenwolf attempted to pull me with it beyond the Veil. In fact, in the last few days, I've hardly sensed that ominous force, which only solidifies my belief that banishing the Nevenwolf lessened Malum's hold on me. I just hope it stays that way.

"That's right," I tell Jacquetta. "Honestly, it makes more sense for the Nevenwolf's carcass to have decayed in such a manner, given where it came from. But the prince . . ."

She frowns. "What were you doing in the crypt anyway?"

I hesitate. This newly spun alliance between us is as fragile as it is complicated. No matter what we agreed, I still don't fully trust Jacquetta. But if I don't share information, I might as well be working by myself—which has proved about as successful as Nesta boiling fireroot.

"Searching for the Bloodstones," I tell her. "I heard that the old king ordered them to be set into the royal swords, so I went down there to find them."

Instinct advises me to avoid mentioning Roland's involvement. Judging from my experience with the Dwarf, I doubt he'd appreciate being named.

"But the stones weren't there?" Jacquetta asks.

"They *were*," I explain, still bitter about the empty settings on the sword pommels. "But someone had already pried them out."

Jacquetta's cloak flutters in the wind. "Any guesses as to who would have done that?"

"No. And no guesses as to where the Bloodstones might have gone either. I haven't discovered any leads since the crypt. Except"—I pause, recalling the hunt—"at Sir Weston's game, I had a thought that the stones might have been among the prizes, but I never got the chance to check."

"Prizes?" Jacquetta raises her eyebrows. "Could the mortals be so careless?"

I shrug. "I told you—the Bloodstones were brought here as trophies. The mortals believe Meira is holding Malum back—not the covens, and certainly not those stones. They've completely rewritten our history. The Bloodstones are little more than baubles to them now."

Like the glass stones from the pageant in the White City, our sacred relics reduced to mere trinkets.

"It's all so strange." Jacquetta fiddles with the edge of her sleeve. "I still can't believe the Nevenwolf got through the Veil. What spell did you use to kill it anyway?"

I flinch. We never discussed the details of the short-lived battle. Of course Jacquetta would assume I used magic against the creature. I'm supposed to be a Second. And a good one. Flashes of the attack come back to me in a blur—the arrow smoking where I'd driven it through the beast's eye. I touch the place on my palm where the arrow's shaft burned me. The mark has faded, but Rhea's triangles are still etched beneath my ring fingers. Because it hadn't been my magic that saved me—it was my sister's.

"A protection spell," I offer at last, which is close enough to the truth. If Rhea hadn't intervened, I'd be dead. "What about you? I'm not aware of any spells powerful enough to snap a tree in half. Honestly, I'm surprised you're a Caster at all."

"You think I couldn't be?" she asks, archly.

"Not that. It's just . . . I wouldn't have expected you to make your vows to Millicent after"—I pause—"everything."

The past hangs between us like a storm cloud, heavy and crackling. We walk by a row of rosebushes, those rare winter blooms a stark red against the dusting of snow.

"Well, I didn't vow to Millicent," Jacquetta says, plucking a rose. "I didn't swear to any of the Ancients. Why should I have? There's no need to devote my life to one of five witches who died centuries ago."

That touches a nerve. "You must have. How else could your gift manifest?"

"I made a vow to myself," Jacquetta replies simply. "To the earth and the sky and the magic in the world—the things that felt true to me. That's what counts."

My brow furrows. Witches don't get to *choose* our vow like that. We either swear to one of the Ancients, or we don't swear at all—like Mathilde.

"So . . . you're Wayward?"

"No," Jacquetta counters, a hint of irritation in her voice. "I'm part of a coven. I *made* a vow, just not the way you think is necessary."

"Then where does your power come from, if not the Spirits?"

"I told you—the world around me. I can sense things." She gestures at the rosebushes and trees, their frosted leaves sparkling in the sunlight. "Like the ancient roots of a tree or the beating heart of a storm—the elements connected to my vow. Sometimes, I can even hear them. It's hard to explain, like . . ."

A long-buried memory rises.

"Like the stars," I finish for her quietly. "You once said that you heard them singing."

Jacquetta's gaze snaps to mine, her blue eyes touched with silver in the winter day. "You remember that?"

How could I possibly forget? For an instant, we are two young witches again, spinning under the night sky, oblivious that our fragile world would soon be nothing but shards of glass.

A cold wind stirs the dry leaves.

"What does sensing magic have to do with snapping that tree?" I ask, pulling myself into the present.

Jacquetta fusses with her rose. "In the forest, I sensed the storm, the lightning within it, and . . . I'm not sure how to describe it, but I asked it to help. It answered."

It certainly did. Most of the witches in Stonehaven couldn't achieve a spell half as strong as what Jacquetta did. I comb back over the countless hours I spent memorizing spells until my head throbbed or practicing rune work until my fingers ached. What if the whole reason I never showed talent in those areas was because I was learning our craft the wrong way? Could I be like Jacquetta?

She's dangerous, that voice hisses.

"But I'll be honest, I didn't expect the spell to work," Jacquetta adds with a frown. "My magic has been acting strangely ever since I came to the city."

A crow wheels beneath the low clouds, its cry resonating over the garden.

"What do you mean—strangely?" I ask. "It seemed fine in the forest, not to mention at the Sanctum."

"Sometimes it is," she allows. "But I've been finding it harder to sense things. It's all . . . muffled. Like the magic is buried. The harder I try to reach for it, the further it seems to wriggle away from me. That's how it was with the statue at the Sanctum. My spell should have taken seconds, but I kept losing my hold on it."

Now I might understand why Jacquetta seemed so frustrated every time she returned to our chamber after being gone on her mysterious errands.

"That sounds maddening," I tell her.

She grunts her agreement. "For both of us. I assume you're affected as well?"

Right—because I'm supposed to have power. "Oh—yes. I mean, I haven't been able to cast properly either."

Now, or ever.

"Any idea what's causing it?" she asks. I shake my head. "I suppose it doesn't matter. All the more reason to leave this place as soon as possible."

On this much, we agree.

"So . . . you *are* a Caster then?" Jacquetta asks, a touch of skepticism in her tone.

Has she guessed? I pull myself up taller. "Why wouldn't I be?"

"I don't know." Jacquetta twirls her rose. "From what I recall, you were never interested in the craft, especially not in being Second. What changed?"

Everything. Some wild instinct urges me to confess. Admit how that night in the forest shattered my whole world. That I'm not a Second, not even gifted, and that I'd do anything to go back and run away.

Don't, that voice warns. *She will crush you.*

"Like you said before," I tell her instead. "I grew up."

Jacquetta looks at me a long moment, unspoken questions behind her blue eyes. Part of me wants her to ask them, to pull the details out of me. But she doesn't.

"What's next, then?" she asks. "Do we go rifling through every drawer in the palace, searching for those magic rocks?"

Magic rocks, really. "They're not—"

I stop short at the ripple of yellow robes in my peripheral vision. A young Order novitiate halts in front of us, blocking our path.

"Mistress Ayleth?" he beckons. "His Illuminance requests your presence."

My heart pounds as I'm led through the labyrinth of the White Palace. If I was suspected of being a witch, they would have sent guards, I reason. I'd be clapped in irons and dragged to the dungeon, not causally escorted to the High Priest's chambers. But a summons from Ignatius could never be casual. The novitiate, however, offers no indication of what Ignatius wants with me. The uncertainty is worse than any fate my own mind can conjure.

We turn another corner, and a set of huge doors looms ahead. They're fashioned of a special glass, textured and tinted so that they appear sculpted from fire itself—like a huge pyre yawns before me. Every instinct screams at me to run in the opposite direction. I clench my fists, my pulse thudding against Rhea's marks as I force myself to walk into the suite.

The High Priest's chambers are exactly what I would expect of the man who heads the Order—dripping with self-importance. The false goddess's Eyes are patterned on the rugs and embroidered onto nearly every scrap of fabric. Scenes from the Order's lore—its lies— are proudly displayed on huge tapestries and gilt-framed oil paintings. Even the floors of this horrible wing are veined in amber, like rivulets of fire expanding beneath my feet.

"Just through here." The novitiate knocks on a door and ushers me through it.

The room beyond is not gaudy and cavernous, as I anticipate, but threateningly small. Its ceiling is low. Windows line one wall, but the thick curtains are drawn, blotting out all light save for that of the fire in the hearth, which is flanked on either side by life-size statues of the false goddess. The dimness creates the illusion that the room is even narrower. More like a tomb.

"Mistress Ayleth." The High Priest sits behind a large mahogany desk, the red-tinged wood engraved with Meira's Eye, along with apples and other crests. "I'm glad to see you're in good health. I heard Mistress Jacquetta fell ill after Sir Weston's hunt."

Where had he heard that? Has he been watching us? "She's well now."

"Excellent." Ignatius sets down his scarlet-feathered quill and rises, gesturing to a sideboard, where a decanter of wine and a bowl of apples waits. "Are you hungry?"

My stomach turns at the memory of my ill-fated dinner. "No, thank you."

"Keeping a plain diet, I see." The ruby Eye winks. "That's likely wise. I did warn you about the richness of the food at court. But I see you've recovered after the . . . incident."

When I was poisoned. "Yes, thank you."

"Your health is very important to us." Ignatius selects an apple and examines the ruby skin. "But I did not invite you here merely to inquire after your well-being. I've been told you attended Sir Weston's hunt. Did you witness anything unusual in the forest?"

A vision of the Nevenwolf resurfaces in my mind, those glittering crimson eyes. "No."

Ignatius pauses, pinning me with that strange amber gaze. "Are you certain? You witnessed no signs of Malum?"

Something nudges against the inner side of my left ribs. Is it stronger than before? No, I tell myself. It can't be. The Nevenwolf is dead. And the High Priest doesn't know what really happened. If he did, I'd be in the dungeons.

"I'm certain," I say, willing the tremor from my voice. "I spent most of the day tending to Jacquetta. As you said, she was ill. I only learned of the Nevenwolf after we returned."

The High Priest hesitates a moment longer. The fire crackles.

"Well," he says at last, picking up a knife and peeling the apple. "I'm hardly surprised to hear of such selflessness. It was you who saved me from disaster at the Sanctum, after all. In fact, you and I share a special connection, do we not?"

We do not.

"We're both true Followers of the Light," he goes on. The knife glints in the firelight. "As such, it may not surprise you to learn that the Nevenwolf is not the first instance of Malum lurking near the palace. In fact, I'm beginning to suspect that what happened with the statue at the Sanctum was not an accident at all."

Not an accident? Damn Jacquetta's recklessness.

"Forgive me if I've frightened you." Ignatius bites into the apple. Juice glistens on his lips. "But I would request a favor, one I could only entrust to someone like you. Keep your eyes open, Mistress Ayleth—just like those of our goddess. If you glimpse even a hint of Malum here at the palace, come to me at once. Even if you're not sure."

Is he attempting to make me his spy? My skin crawls at the idea of reporting to this man. Then again, if he trusts me, perhaps that means I'll avoid his suspicion.

"I'll do what I can," I say, dipping my chin in what I hope passes for deference.

"I admire your bravery in upholding the Light." His robes whisper against the floor as he crosses the chamber. A scent of orange and clove follows him. "Your service will be amply rewarded—especially if you were to uncover any threats to our goddess, or the king."

Unless he's offering his own head on a platter, I'm supremely un-interested in any reward. But I bob the swiftest of curtsies before re-treating toward the door.

"Mistress Ayleth," Ignatius calls just as my hand touches the door-knob. "Do pay close attention to the queen herself. I know she har-bors some . . . *unique* ideals. We do not want Her Majesty to stray too far from the protection of our goddess."

CHAPTER THIRTY-ONE

T HE NEXT DAY, OUR NORMAL DUTIES IN THE QUEEN'S ROOMS ARE interrupted by a visit from Sir Weston. A swarm of ladies surrounds him as he narrates what is undoubtedly a bawdy story, gesturing with his wineglass. Despite the memory of the thornapple episode, I could use some of that wine myself. My nerves are still humming after my encounter with the High Priest. How long will his supposed *trust* last? How long until he discovers who's really responsible for what happened with the statue? Or even the Nevenwolf itself?

Not long at all, that voice whispers.

My attention flits around the room as I speculate about which of these women might also be his spies. Jacquetta is jumpy as well. I heard her tossing and turning all night.

"Damn," she mutters. A bead of blood blooms on her fingertip where she stabbed herself with her needle.

"Careful." I pass her a scrap of linen.

"*Careful.* In this court?" She presses the fabric over her wound. "I feel like an insect waiting to be squashed."

That makes two of us.

"You're sure he doesn't suspect us?" Jacquetta asks for the third time this morning.

"As sure as I can be, given the circumstances." Then, because I can't resist: "And I did warn you that the statue would end badly."

She shoots me a glare. "If you had let me finish what I started, he wouldn't be here *to* suspect us."

"Yes, because a dead priest would have been much easier to explain."

"I could have—"

A smear of brown fur and frantic barking zooms past us. Fitz. I yank back my skirts before they're trampled by his tiny feet.

"Horrible creature," Jacquetta grouses, watching as the dog steals a piece of cheese off someone's plate and scampers away with it.

"And his mistress," I add. "I've no doubt Marion trains him to be a terror."

The courtier and her cadre laugh, teasing the dog with a crust of bread so that it twirls around on its hind legs.

"Like you do with your cat?" Jacquetta asks archly. "Don't expect me to believe that she just *happened* to claw my linens to shreds at the Sanctum."

I'd almost forgotten about that. A smile twitches at my lips. "I haven't the faintest idea what you're talking about."

Jacquetta rethreads her needle. "I'm sure you don't."

"You can't pretend to be innocent." I point at her. "I seem to recall someone who used to make fireroot explode for fun."

"I did not."

But she did, and she knows it. I can tell from the mischievous glint in her eyes, one I haven't seen since our years at Stonehaven. In fact, I could almost . . .

"Good morning!" Joan approaches, shattering the moment. Jacquetta immediately refocuses her attention on her sewing, and I go back to my snarled embroidery. "Have you heard about the banquet?"

Unfortunately. Sir Weston announced the event earlier, yet another excuse for this court to drown itself in wine.

"I can't decide what to wear." Joan settles beside us. "Do you two have any ideas?"

The theme—whatever that means—is that of a menagerie, on account of the Nevenwolf, which means that we're all required to attend dressed as animals. Nothing sounds worse.

"Is invisibility an option?" Jacquetta asks wryly, evidently sharing my opinion.

Joan taps her chin. "You know, I might have a better idea for you. I heard of a recent addition to the princess's menagerie. Not a hedgehog but . . . what was it called? It has spikes."

I think I know. I've seen pictures of the creatures in books at Stonehaven.

"A porcupine?" I ask, struggling to maintain a straight face.

"That's it!" Joan points at Jacquetta. "You could go as a porcupine. It would suit you."

"What is that supposed to mean?" Jacquetta demands.

Joan hesitates. "Well, I don't intend this to be rude, but you *do* display a rather prickly nature at times."

Prickly nature. I picture Jacquetta walking around covered in spikes and nearly die.

She glares at me. "You think it's funny?"

"Absolutely not," I manage. "I'm sure you'd make a lovely . . . *porcupine.*"

Joan giggles, clapping one hand over her mouth, and that's all it takes for me to lose myself in a fit of laughter. Jacquetta tosses down her sewing.

"I'll just leave you two to plan, then," she says, getting up. "Enjoy yourselves."

She stalks off. I start to call after her, but I'm laughing too hard. I can't recall the last time I *have* laughed like this. I'd forgotten how good it feels.

"I shouldn't have said that." Joan gasps between breaths.

"Don't worry," I say, wiping my eyes. "She's just in a bad mood. Normally . . ."

But, actually, I have no idea what Jacquetta would normally do. Once, she might have slipped toads into other witches' boots or mixed around ingredients in the workroom. But that witch is gone. We're different now. *I'm* different.

"I'll help you think of costumes, in any case." Joan picks up the shirt Jacquetta had been sewing. "After all, the three of us should stick together."

"What do you mean?"

"We're the odd ones out," she says, then a flush heats her cheeks. "I hope that didn't sound unkind. It's just . . ."

She trails off, but I understand her meaning. Joan has never openly discussed it, but I've noticed how she's usually sitting by herself. She rarely even speaks to the other maiden who shares our room. And now that I think of it, it's rare to see *anyone* interacting with Joan.

"Why do they treat you . . ." I'm not sure how to finish in a way that isn't cruel.

"Like I don't belong?" Joan finishes for me. I nod, sheepish. "Because I don't. Typically, women of my station wouldn't be appointed to serve Her Majesty."

"Why not? You're nobility, aren't you?"

"It's more complicated than that." She snips her thread. "There were Dwarves in my family, ages back. Some of them might still be alive, I don't know."

Dwarves? My mind immediately goes to Roland. "Here, at the palace Guild?"

"Perhaps. Some served on a council for the king, but that was before the war. When the edict passed, other courtiers began to question our loyalty. We were desperate to prove ourselves before the old king decided to jail us or . . . worse."

A memory of Roland's Guild Mark resurfaces. "I'm sorry, Joan."

She shakes her head, but her green eyes glimmer with buried pain. "We surrendered most of our lands and holdings—save for the country estate. And we stepped down from all our positions. We have to save every coin to remain here at court."

"And you . . . *want* to remain?" I ask, genuinely curious.

"We're loyal to His Majesty. We always have been. And we follow the Light." But the words are rushed, as if they're rehearsed, and Joan pulls her next stitch too tight, puckering the fabric. "But none of our efforts mattered, in the end. The other nobles refuse to accept us—save for Queen Sybil, of course. She personally invited me to serve her, which is what allows us to reside at the palace. I owe her a debt."

I look to where the queen is sitting with Sir Weston and the rest. Winter sunlight filters through the stained-glass window behind her and shines on the threaded white gold of her crown. She may not be wielding a sword or riding a horse like the women in the tapestries, but I sense that Queen Sybil carries her own form of strength. So does Joan.

"I'm glad you're here," I tell her, surprised at how much I mean it. "And I'm sorry about what happened to your family members."

"So am I." She presses her lips together, like she's keeping herself from saying more. But then she waves the unspoken words away. "Enough of all that. Let's discuss your costume. You'd be beautiful as a falcon. Or perhaps . . ."

She's interrupted by a stir in the room—a wave of curtsies and bowing as someone else enters. There's only one person who would command such a flurry of activity. To my extreme displeasure, King Callen strides into the chamber, the ruby crowned-apple jewel sparkling on his doublet. That feeling behind my left ribs shivers to life, sharp and swift—exactly like it had done in the forest when the Nevenwolf appeared. Panic wings in my chest. I was wrong. Slaying the beast hadn't lessened Malum's hold on me. It had only been waiting. And, judging from how that unnerving sensation presses against the inner side of my left ribs, the king really is connected to that sinister force. I need to get away from him.

"Your Majesty." Sir Weston bows. "I've just been relaying the details of our banquet. And I've already claimed the fox costume, so don't think to steal it."

"If there's a thief in this room, it's you, Weston," the king comments. "You robbed me blind at our last Castles match."

Sir Weston produces a deck of cards from his pocket. "Care to test your luck again?"

The king plucks a wedge of cheese from a tiered plate. "Gladly."

At Sir Weston's signal, a servant rushes to set up a table. Marion immediately saunters over to join them. This is my chance.

"I'll be right back," I say to Joan.

Hiding myself behind clusters of women, I edge along the walls and toward the door. I'm *almost* there, when—

"And who is that I spot sneaking away?" I freeze at Sir Weston's voice, cursing my ill luck. "Ah, it's the Order girl, isn't it? Mistress . . ."

"Ayleth." My name on the king's lips makes that feeling behind my left ribs *sing.* His gray eyes lock with mine. "Don't lurk there in the doorway. Come and join us."

I would rather be facing down the Nevenwolf again than be sitting at this table. The force inside me throbs dully, like a second heartbeat. I focus on my breathing, insisting that I can control it—tamp it down, as I have before. But I'm starting to doubt that I'm in control of anything. As if on cue, a tiny snout snaps at me.

"I do apologize." Marion scratches the tuft of fur on the top of her dog's head. "He's simply incorrigible. Aren't you, Fitz?"

He barks, solidifying my suspicion that Marion encourages him to be a menace. But at least I'm not totally alone. The queen grants me a small, encouraging smile from her place across the table. She'd joined us as soon as I sat down, which I don't believe was a coincidence.

"The game is Castles," Sir Weston announces as he shuffles the cards. "Place your bets."

Metal clinks together as everyone else tosses coins into the center of the table.

"Mistress Ayleth?" Sir Weston gestures at the pile of gold. "Your bet?"

"I don't have anything."

"Everyone puts in *something*." A bauble dangling from Lady Marion's earlobe glitters. "It's only fair."

Frustrated, I tug out the only item in my possession that's not attached to my gown—the handkerchief in my sleeve—and toss it in with the coins. Marion smirks. Let her mock me. Maybe she'll insist that my offering is too small and then I can leave. But before Marion can utter a word of criticism, the queen removes her own handkerchief and adds it to mine.

"It's refreshing to see someone be so creative with their betting," she says, approving.

"Indeed," the king agrees. "In fact, that's a rare prize. Mistress Ayleth's handkerchief won me my victory against Weston in the tilt-yard."

Not that again. Marion looks like she swallowed a lemon, but I can't even appreciate her irritation. All I can think about is the dull hum behind my ribs as the king's attention brushes against me.

Just ignore it, I tell myself. *Get through the game and then leave.*

"I knew there was something working against me during that

match." Sir Weston selects a card from the deck, then chooses one from his own hand and lays it facedown on the table. "And how *have* you been enjoying life at court, Mistress Ayleth?"

About as much as one enjoys their teeth being removed. "Very well."

It's my turn, but no one bothers to explain the rules to me. I pick up a card and set one down without even checking what they are.

"It's been such a joy to have the Order girls with us," Marion effuses. Fitz growls. "Quite brilliant of you to suggest their placement, Weston."

That's not what she said on the night of the pageant.

Weston bows at his seat. "Yes, I can understand how such beauty would be a welcome addition to our ranks."

Why couldn't the Nevenwolf have found the two of *them* in the forest?

"Don't waste your efforts, Weston." The king flips down another card. "The lady does not care for flattery."

Weston scoffs. "A woman who doesn't care for flattery? Impossible."

"It's true." Wood creaks as the king leans back in his chair, crossing one leg over the other. "She prefers archery. I've witnessed her mastery of the sport with my own eyes."

The ridges of my ears burn. But I suppose I should count myself lucky that my entire body isn't on fire for the way Marion is glowering at me.

"Is that so?" Sir Weston asks, amused. "Well, I suppose we'll have to inform Lord Jasper that there's a new addition to the Hunt."

It's my turn again and I toss down a card, clenching my back teeth.

"Lord Jasper will be disappointed, I'm afraid." The queen takes her time as she considers her next play. "My daughter is much too fond of Mistress Ayleth to lose her now. In fact, no other lady has proved to be such a positive influence on my daughter."

The queen smiles at me again, and I manage to smile back. Despite my hatred of this court, Blodwyn is a bright spot at the palace. Part of me wishes the princess were here now. She'd be running this game, or she'd find some ingenious method of disrupting it.

"But the princess won't be needing a companion for too much longer," Marion comments, selecting a card. "Has there been a decision on her betrothal?"

She throws the question innocently enough, but I notice how the queen absorbs it like a dagger. "You are speaking of the heir to the throne, Lady Marion. My daughter's home is at the White Palace."

Laughter carries from the other side of the room.

"Forgive me, but I'm sure Your Majesty intended to say that the princess is heir to the throne *until* the king has a son. Unless . . ." Marion tilts her head. "Do you not believe that Meira will secure the future of our realm?"

"I hold no doubt of the future of this realm," the queen replies. "Or of my daughter's place within it. After all, a sovereign queen is commonplace in other parts of the world."

What the queen says is true—I've read about such realms in the books at Stonehaven. Rycinthia, for one, permits women to rule. Even so, the air at the table thins. The king shifts in his seat, his mood souring.

"You must all excuse my wife. Despite the years she's lived in Riven, she's not yet rid herself of such . . . eccentricities."

The queen herself remains silent. Just like at my ill-fated dinner, I sense a storm brewing between the royal couple, and I marvel at the queen's bravery. She doesn't take back her opinion, or even shrink—just like those women in the tapestries, charging headlong into battle.

"And what are your own thoughts on the subject, Mistress Ayleth?" Lady Marion's viper-like attention swivels to me. "Do you believe women should rule?"

I should stay quiet. The last time I tangled with Marion, I wound up hiding in a tree while some man hunted me. But again, the self-satisfied expression on the courtier's face reminds me too much of Sindony. I'm tired of being pushed around by people who believe themselves better than I am simply because of their position.

"Meira is a woman, is she not?" I ask. "If *she* can be worshiped, it stands to reason that a woman can rule."

The king watches me over the rim of his goblet. The feeling behind my left ribs intensifies, Malum nudging against my bones.

Sir Weston laughs. "I had no idea Order girls were so opinionated."

"Indeed," Marion agrees. "And ill-informed, apparently. Our Meira is a *goddess*, not a mere woman. Perhaps court life is proving too much of a distraction. You've been away from your Sanctum for too long, if you've forgotten such basic tenets of the faith."

"And what about you, Lady Marion?" the queen asks lightly. "Do you also find court life distracting? Perhaps you could benefit from the rest afforded at a Sanctum."

The courtier's eyes flash, and I catch the hint of a smile tugging at the queen's lips.

"You know, Her Majesty may be right." Weston flings down another card and points at Marion. "You could use a rest. Didn't I see you fleeing the princess's rooms not too long ago?"

The courtier's grip on her dog tightens. "You must have me mistaken for someone else."

"I never mistake a face like yours, Lady Marion." He winks. "You were screeching about how the princess ruined one of your gowns. She'd tried to use it to line a peahen's nest or something like that. By the look of you, she'd nearly succeeded."

Marion slaps down her next card. I may not possess any coin of my own, but I would give a thousand handkerchiefs to have been able to see the countess running through the halls covered in feathers and bird shit.

"You were mistaken," Marion repeats. "And speaking of animals, do tell me what you're planning to wear for the banquet, Mistress Ayleth. Or is it a secret?"

She deals me that courtier's smile, and I regret not shooting her in the face when I had the chance. "I don't have a costume."

"What a shame. But you should still attend the banquet. I know—" She sits up straighter. "Mistress Ayleth could judge which costume is best. It would be immensely entertaining to hear her quaint ideas about what's fashionable."

Does this game never end?

"Make the banquet a contest." Sir Weston rubs his chin as he considers the idea. "I like it. We'll call the winner . . ."

"Fairest," the king says, his gray gaze pinning me in place. "To honor our goddess."

"Perfect!" Marion claps, upsetting Fitz, who snaps at me. My head throbs.

"But it's unkind to devise a contest if our guests won't be able to participate." The queen sets down her next card. "I shall gift them something from my own wardrobe. It's the least I can do, considering their service to my daughter."

A much better gift would be to excuse us from the banquet altogether.

"Oh, do let *me* provide their costumes, Your Majesty." Marion leans in, as if this is the most important request she's ever made. "It would be such an honor. I insist."

No. Absolutely not. I cast the queen a pleading expression, one she mercifully seems to interpret.

"That won't be—" she starts.

"If Lady Marion is kind enough to extend the offer, I see no reason to refuse," the king comments, the order clear beneath his words.

Marion beams at him. Damn everything.

"Very well, Lady Marion." The queen glances at me in what I suspect is apology. "You are, after all, always so impeccably attired. Sometimes I wonder how you manage to afford a wardrobe that's often finer than my own."

The king grips his wineglass tighter.

"I am fortunate, indeed, Your Majesty." Marion adjusts the necklace at her throat, her gaze flicking to the king beneath her lashes.

"Fortune," the queen muses, selecting her next card. "It's like a wheel, is it not? It comes up and goes down. One never knows when the next turn will occur, but it's often at the most unexpected and . . . inconvenient moment."

The two women stare each other down, their claws wrapped in velvet.

"Perhaps you're right, Your Majesty," Marion says at last. "And let's see what fortune has in store for us now. I call Castles."

Weston groans and the king lets out a short, frustrated breath. Marion, however, smirks as she lays her cards face-up on the table.

"Swords," she announces, displaying a full hand of cards painted with the weapons.

"By the Light!" Weston tosses his own hand on the table. "That's it for me."

The king's gray eyes find mine. "And you, Mistress?"

I haven't even glanced at my cards since the game began. I lay them flat now and my breath halts. Five cards—each bearing an image of a shining, golden crown—stare up at me.

"Well, Lady Marion." Sir Weston drains the rest of his wine. "It seems Mistress Ayleth has taken everything you have."

But it's not Marion I'm worried about. My attention is fixed on the king. On the way that feeling inside me stretches and pulls like an invisible tether between us—just like it did with the Nevenwolf. This time, though, I know that not even Rhea will be able to save me.

Chapter Thirty-Two

I NEED TO GET OUT OF THE PALACE.

If Malum is drawing the king to me, I doubt I will live much longer. And it's not just the king who's a threat. Soon, I'll start luring things out of the Veil again. There's no more time to waste—I need the Bloodstones.

"Are we running from something?" Jacquetta asks.

We're on our way to the library with Blodwyn. Given yesterday's encounter with the king, I've been restless and jittery all morning. I'd hardly even allowed the princess a choice in our activity today, and I carve a path down the halls with single-minded purpose.

"The books aren't going anywhere," Blodwyn adds.

I'm not as certain. Between the king and Malum, it's starting to feel like this whole palace is conspiring against me. I round a corner and barely avoid crashing into a servant carrying a large pot of roses, the white petals limned in red—like they'd been dipped in blood.

"Watch where you're going," I snap at him, though I know full well that it was my fault. The boy grumbles under his breath and keeps walking.

"Is everything all right, Ayleth?" Blodwyn asks, cautious. "You seem . . . not yourself."

She sees through you, that voice whispers. *They all will.*

"I'm fine," I say, attempting to set off again.

Jacquetta blocks my path.

"Go ahead," she tells the princess. "We'll be right behind you."

Blodwyn frowns, doubtful, but finally trots off toward the library.

"What's the matter with you?" Jacquetta asks when we're alone. "You're drawing attention to yourself. Even the servants in her rooms noticed."

Because that's all she cares about—the attention. Not me. Never me. "I said I'm fine."

"You were fine *yesterday.*" She crosses her arms. "When I left you with Joan and your inane costume planning. What happened?"

Malum itself is reeling me in, getting stronger. "Nothing."

I try to step around her, but Jacquetta holds me back. The pressure of her hand on my elbow sends sparks shooting up my arm.

"Let go of me." I pull myself free of her grasp.

"Fine. But if there's a problem, you need to tell me. We agreed to work together."

Together. Her scent of juniper hits me and, for an instant, I'm thrown back to the south tower when we were sixteen. Then, I could have told her about how I reached beyond the Veil. I could have told her anything.

Not anymore, that voice whispers.

It's right. If Jacquetta knew what I'd done—what's following me—she'd leave. I may not fully trust her, but I can't afford to lose her help, not when I can practically feel the hours slipping through my fingers.

"It's just nerves," I insist. "I hate this place. Like you said—we need to get out of here as soon as possible."

The wheels behind Jacquetta's blue eyes work, weighing my answer. From the set of her jaw, I know she's not convinced. I lift my chin, daring her to call me out. After all, she doubtless holds plenty of secrets of her own. Whatever we agreed, I don't owe her anything.

"If you say so," she relents at last. "But maybe stop assaulting the servants."

"I'll take that into consideration," I say, then push past her, my footsteps echoing in the wide halls.

The princess has already disappeared into the stacks by the time we reach the library, likely hunting her next novel. I envy her.

"I've been focusing on the history section," I tell Jacquetta. "But I—"

"By the . . ." Jacquetta pulls up short, turning in a circle as she takes in the vast expanse of the room. "I didn't know this many books existed."

Some of my frustration melts away at her enraptured expression, the same one I wore when Blodwyn first brought me here. I shouldn't be surprised—Jacquetta loves reading as much as I do. In fact, we officially met in Stonehaven's library. I imagine the two of us as we were back then, let loose in a collection such as this, and the corners of my lips twitch up. They never would have found us again.

All that is over now, that voice reminds me.

"Don't get too excited," I tell Jacquetta, refocusing. "There may be a large number, but all the books I've read are filled with lies—at least the histories."

Jacquetta drags her attention away from where she'd been inspecting an ancient text displayed on a pedestal. "Is that the only subject you've investigated?"

"So far." I lead her down one side of the library. "I hoped there might be a mention of the massacre and I could trace the Blood-stones from there."

With the endless shelves of books towering over us, I realize the flimsiness of such a strategy. I brace myself for Jacquetta's criticism, but then—

"Smart," she says, simple and sure. Like she would have done the same.

It's silly, but a tiny flicker of pride glimmers in my chest at her approval. How long has it been since someone deemed one of my ideas *smart*? Before Rhea died, I was the High Witch's troublesome daughter, always avoiding lessons or instigating pranks. After Rhea, every aspect of my life was dictated by Mother's rules. Anytime I expressed a thought of my own, she instantly dismissed it.

"By the Spirits," Jacquetta murmurs, suddenly veering off in the other direction.

"What is it?"

I follow her toward an enormous table, where a map of Riven is spread beneath a glass case. But this is unlike any other map I've encountered. It's multidimensional instead of flat. The mountain ranges rise up from the surface, and the lakes and rivers are indented. Tiny facsimiles of buildings and homes dot the cities. There's even a small version of the palace itself, its minuscule turrets rendered in painstaking detail, complete with gargoyles the size of pinheads. And—I peer closer—it appears as though there are *lights* glimmering inside the palace. Every so often, shadows cross the windows, as if people were passing within its walls.

"Look." Jacquetta points to a river, which I now notice seems to rush with actual water. A dot that must be a fish leaps from the surface and then splashes back into the current.

Entranced, I bend so that my nose nearly presses against the glass. A figure no bigger than my fingernail lumbers along one of the mountain ranges. It has arms and legs, like a person might, but it's not a person. "Is that . . . a troll?"

Jacquetta leans closer, her forehead almost touching mine. "I think so. Who made this? I thought the king ordered all magical items burned."

"It must be Dwarvian," I say, recognizing their craftsmanship.

"Dwarves." Jacquetta huffs. "So, *their* magic is acceptable, but ours isn't. Typical."

I almost tell her about how the Dwarves are really treated here—Roland and his Guild Mark—but I stop myself. I'm not sure Roland would want me to explain, and it's better to be careful about what information I divulge. Even so, as Jacquetta's fingertips skim over the top of the glass, a memory resurfaces—the two of us exploring the maps in Stonehaven's library, tracing our way across the realm and into the neighboring kingdoms, guessing about what life was like inside the paper and ink. Had she found out?

"Where did you go?" I ask before I can think better of it. "After the raid?"

Jacquetta pauses. Probably she'll hedge with some vague answer or change the subject entirely. But her fingertip travels to a mass of trees sprouting from the map, their branches rustling almost imperceptibly in an invisible wind.

"Here, I think. That lake is familiar. And this village." She points to an area on the map on the south side of the shimmering body of water. "There was a festival and I snuck inside. Stuffed my face with the best pie I'd ever eaten."

"Better than Willa's?"

Jacquetta glances at me. "*Willa's.* Spirits, I'd almost forgotten her. Does she still mix lavender in with the blackberry?"

"Of course." My stomach complains at the memory. "And rosemary in with the apple."

Both are famous at Stonehaven, almost instantly disappearing as soon as they're baked. I should know. Jacquetta and I had stolen much more than our fair share of slices.

"Well. These came close." Jacquetta taps the glass. "I wish you could have . . ."

Been there.

Is that what she was about to say? My heart stutters and I scold myself for the weakness. I wasn't there, and I couldn't have been. Jacquetta left and I stayed—that's the way it was supposed to be.

"What of you?" Jacquetta asks, not taking her eyes from the map. "Did your mother go through with her plan about the Sisters?"

The disguise that saved us and split the coven in the same night. My attention drifts to the area of the map where Stonehaven should be. It's there—miniature towers poking up through the sea of trees. "She did."

"That must have been . . . different."

Awful, she means. A pang of jealousy knocks through me as I compare my own years to Jacquetta's. I'm not naïve enough to assume her life was easy after she left the Sanctum, but it was a *life*. What can I say about my own? For the last seven years, I've felt like I was an insect trapped in amber, unable to move or think for myself. But I can't admit to any of that. I'm supposed to be a proud Second. This is the life I chose.

"It kept us alive," I say, ending the discussion. "The history section is this way. We better get started."

And then I go, leaving the map and all the lives I might have lived behind me.

For the next several hours, Jacquetta and I comb through records of Riven's stilted history. Just as with my other visits, the texts are maddeningly one-sided and blatantly false. Every so often, Jacquetta scoffs at something she reads, or even tosses a book onto the floor in disgust.

"Can you believe this?" She jabs at a page. "Apparently, we used Malum to spell the mortals into believing we were keeping their crops alive and healing their sick, but actually we weren't. How, exactly, do they explain the literal centuries of prosperity?"

It's nice to have someone sharing in my rage.

"Illusion," I answer wryly. "And it gets better. Have you found any illustrations featuring an Order priest yet?"

She frowns, flipping back through the pages. "Here. Why?"

"Take a closer look. Who does it remind you of?"

Jacquetta's brow furrows as she studies the drawing. "Is that . . . Ignatius?"

"I assume so. He must have ordered that his own likeness be used to represent the Order, at least in recent texts."

"Vain snake of a man," Jacquetta mutters. That mischievous glint suddenly lights in her eyes. She snatches up the quill in the center of the table and dunks it in the inkpot.

"What are you doing?"

"If he can insert himself into history, then I can remove him," she says simply.

The nib of her quill scratches on the parchment.

"*Don't*," I whisper, glancing around in case a Keeper is nearby. "They'll—"

"There." She stops and considers her work, then swivels the book to face me. "Much better, wouldn't you say?"

Ink lines mar Ignatius's face on the page. Jacquetta has gifted him a long, forked tongue and a tail peeking out from beneath his robes. An Order snake, just as she said. I can't suppress the smile that sneaks onto my face. Jacquetta grins back, thoroughly pleased with herself.

"Do another," I tell her. "But give him horns."

Her grin widens and she searches for the next illustration. But as she dips her quill into the ink, bells begin to ring, signaling vespers.

"Damn." She pauses. A drop of black drips onto the page, blotting out Ignatius entirely. "I suppose that's it for today, then. Too bad. I was just starting to enjoy myself."

A thrill runs through me, imagining that I had something to do with that.

Keep her at a distance, that voice warns. *You know what happens if you don't.*

"I'll put these back," I say, stacking the books to distract myself. "You go ahead."

"I don't mind helping."

But I do. Because these last hours were too similar to the hundred others we shared at Stonehaven. Too easy to get lost in—dangerous. *Jacquetta* is dangerous.

Close up your heart, that voice whispers again.

"It's fine." I wave her off. "I have to fetch the princess anyway. No one will care that I'm late if I'm with her."

"All right," Jacquetta says. I don't let myself believe that it's reluctance I hear in her tone. "I'll see you later then."

I nod and disappear into the stacks, listening to the sound of her retreating footsteps.

Don't get caught up again, I command myself. *Don't lose yourself.*

But did I lose myself *with* Jacquetta? Or only after she left?

"Mistress Witch."

One of the books in my arms clatters to the floor. A pair of gemstone-colored eyes peers at me from the other side of the shelf.

Roland.

"By the Spirits." I fumble with the rest of the books, heart racing. "You have to stop calling me that. Someone might hear you."

I check the aisle to make certain the Keepers aren't nearby.

"No one's paying any attention. Not with all this talk of the Nevenwolf." Roland rounds the shelf to join me. "You've heard, I assume?"

The damn thing has been haunting my dreams. "I heard that it *melted*. Sound familiar?"

"Like the prince's body? Really?" Roland rubs his chin. "Don't suppose you found out what caused that?"

"No." And it's maddening. "But they have to be related. I don't think that *thing* that was following us in the crypt was coincidence either. I suspect it was the Nevenwolf, trying to break free of the Veil."

Roland shakes his head. "Dark times, these."

An understatement. "Why have you come? Did you find anything about where the Bloodstones might have gone?"

"Not specifically," he says. Disappointment swoops in my belly. "But I did have a thought. One I should have considered before, honestly. We Dwarves keep a record of what comes through the Mines— commissions and such."

"A record?" I repeat. "You think the Bloodstones might be mentioned there?"

"Should be," he confirms. "That's how my brothers knew about the swords. There might even be a mention of the weapons returning to us, and what was done with the Bloodstones—assuming they weren't outright stolen."

My mind whirs. This is good news. "Where are the records kept?"

"Here." Roland waves toward the back of the library. "Guild records are stored in the archives. But you'll need some luck getting in there. The Keepers are particular about visitors."

Luck—I've never known the meaning of that word. Vaguely, I recall running into the High Priest on my first visit here. He'd mentioned the archives. If Ignatius is the sort of person permitted into that section of the library, I doubt one of the queen's maidens shares the privilege.

My attention flits to Roland's set of keys. "Could you—"

"Oh no." He crosses his arms. "I'm not taking you anywhere. Not after last time."

"Roland, please."

"No." He points at me. "You're on your own with this errand. It was risky enough taking you to the crypt. If I get caught sneaking you into the archives, I'll be a head shorter."

Fair enough, I suppose. Still . . . the records are *right* here, and I can't get to them.

"Don't go making that face at me. Here." He reaches into his pocket and pulls out a small ring. "It's enchanted. Put it on and turn it, and I'll come."

He drops the ring into my palm. Silver glimmers in the candle-light, illuminating the Dwarves' crossed-pickaxe symbol etched onto the inside.

"You . . . want me to have this?" I ask, more than a little surprised that Roland would trust me with something so valuable. "That's kind of you."

"*Kind* has nothing to do with it," he snaps. "Can't have you getting caught and telling them about me when they torture you."

There's the Roland I know. "I appreciate your confidence."

"Aye. And I'll be wanting it back, mind. Don't go abusing the privilege either. I'm not your personal errand boy."

"Of course not." I slip the ring into my pocket. "For what it's worth, I really do appreciate everything you've done to help me. I know it hasn't been easy."

Roland grunts, surly as ever, though I detect a faint flush smearing on his deep brown skin. "You're right there—all this sneaking around, risking my neck. Well, whatever you do, take care, Mistress Witch. Something's coming. We can sense it in the Mines."

CHAPTER THIRTY-THREE

"REMIND ME AGAIN HOW YOU GOT US INTO THIS SITUATION?" Jacquetta grouses as we navigate the halls the following morning. We'd been summoned to Marion's chambers immediately after breakfast, which is the last place we need to be. But there's nothing for it. The countess will doubtless devise a worse fate for us if we fail to appear.

"It's part of the idiotic banquet," I tell her. "I was hoping Marion would forget."

"And miss an opportunity to torment us? Unlikely."

Torment is exactly what's waiting for us in the courtier's chambers. "Let's just get this over with and then we can go back to the library."

"Yes, I'm sure we'll have a much better day there." Jacquetta adjusts her headdress. "I must have skimmed through dozens of books yesterday. There wasn't even a drawing of the Bloodstones."

At least I'm not alone in my failure. "If you have a better idea, I'm happy to hear it."

"I don't," she admits. "But . . . isn't it odd? You mentioned the Bloodstones were brought to the palace as trophies. Shouldn't trophies be shown off?"

She has a point. "They *were* in the royal swords. But now . . ."

"Exactly," she says, tugging at her sleeve as she thinks. "What if they didn't just go missing, but someone is hiding them?"

Assuming they weren't outright stolen, Roland had said. What if they had been?

"But who would be hiding them?"

Her blue eyes meet mine. "I think that's what we have to figure out."

A feat that sounds about as simple as killing a Nevenwolf. I ignore that thought, as we have a bigger problem to face at the moment. We've reached Marion's chambers. Before I even get the chance to knock, a servant answers.

"We're here for—" I start.

"Right this way," the girl says, motioning us through. "The countess is expecting you."

Excellent.

Marion's thick oleander perfume hits us as soon as we enter the suite. The countess's rooms are almost as elaborate as the queen's. Honeyed morning sunlight pours through the stained-glass windows, all of which are decorated with motifs of blossoming apple trees. The furniture is polished and outrageously expensive. Plump chaises upholstered in burgundy silk, mahogany tables held up with legs carved like graceful-necked swans, chests engraved with forest scenes. A bowl overflowing with apples waits on a sideboard.

The servant leads us deeper into the suite, toward the sound of laughter.

"Ah, here they are," Marion says as we cross into what must be her bedchamber.

Evidently, we're to have an audience. Three other ladies are seated on cushioned chairs, nibbling on plates of cheese and fruit and observing us with a mix of amusement and curiosity. Fitz, who is perched on the courtier's lap, lays his ears flat and growls.

"I hope you don't mind that I've invited the others," Marion says, setting down her own plate of half-eaten fruit. There's more on a table nearby, but no one invites us to partake. "The additional opinions might prove helpful, given how daunting our task."

Daunting for us. My attention travels the room. A huge hearth swallows one wall, the marble sculpted to resemble a tree climbing toward the ceiling. The rugs, patterned with apples, are plush beneath our feet. But the bed is the most striking piece. It appears large enough to hold ten people, the mattress piled with a mountain of blankets and pillows. Blue velvet curtains hang from the frame, embroidered in gold to resemble the night sky. An unwelcome image creeps into my mind—Marion and the king in that bed.

"Isn't it magnificent?" Marion asks, nodding toward the bed. "It was a gift."

Her lips curl in a smile that suggests she knows exactly where my mind wandered. I curse the flush prickling on my cheeks.

"Let's not waste any more time," Fitz complains as Marion shoos him off of her lap. She claps, summoning three servants who descend upon us and begin unlacing our dresses.

"I can do that," I insist, vainly attempting to fend off their hurried hands.

"No modesty here." Marion selects a grape from the plate. "There's nothing we haven't seen before."

The others pick at their breakfasts, observing us like we're players on a stage. To make the experience even better, Fitz decides that our being wrangled out of our uniforms is a game. He zips between us, attacking and pawing at our discarded skirts, his nails likely tearing holes that will earn Duchess Poole's wrath.

"Every other lady at court will be dressed as a peacock or some such." Marion walks slowly in front of us after we've been stripped down to our corsets and shifts, her dark eyes traveling from the top of our heads to our feet. I have never felt more exposed in my life. "The two of you should wear something more . . . *unique.*"

She pauses and tilts her head at Jacquetta. "You're a quiet one, aren't you? I never can tell what you're thinking."

I can. Especially now. If the fire in Jacquetta's eyes were real, Marion would be nothing but a burnt ember.

"How about"—Marion points at her—"a mouse? Yes. Didn't Master Foulton direct a production with such costumes last year?"

"That's right," another of the ladies agrees. "The players wore masks with pointed noses and whiskers."

"Perfect. I'll have him send one over. And we must fashion something to serve as a tail." She gestures at a servant, who rushes off into another chamber. "And for Mistress Ayleth . . ."

My muscles tense as Marion adjusts the shoulder of my shift where it fell, the brush of her fingernails like claws against my skin.

"You're quiet as well. But I sense there's something . . . deeper within."

Darker, that voice whispers.

"I'll make you . . . a snake," Marion determines. "Fitting, I think."

She deals me that dazzling smile, and that deep urge from the menagerie rises up again, goading me to fight back. Show her what I really am. But I smother it. Whatever that feeling is, it's too close to Malum to trust. And lashing out at Marion won't do me any good right now.

"Come." Marion grips my upper arm. "We'll need to tighten that corset."

She steers me to face a full-length mirror on the other side of the room. The last time I've really looked at myself was at Stonehaven, when Selene gifted me the witch's mirror, and I flinch at my own reflection. Has it really only been weeks since I left? I appear so much older. My sleepless nights show on my face. Dark rings smudge under my eyes and my white skin is paler than it should be, especially next to the healthy glow of Marion's. What's happening to me here? Is it Malum, slowly eating me away?

"I recall when I first arrived at court," Marion tells me, giving my laces a swift tug. "It was all a glittering blur, especially whenever the king was near. But I suppose that's to be expected. It's said that when His Majesty looks at you, it feels like standing in the sun."

The corset creaks as she tightens the stays again. I wince, one hand going to my stomach. "I think that's enough."

"Not quite." Marion draws the laces even tighter. My next breath hitches.

Relax, I tell myself.

"But should the king look away," Marion continues, "I've heard it is like the darkest, coldest night."

She yanks hard enough to squeeze my ribs. My lungs constrict, and I can't get enough air. In the mirror, my reflection swims. For an instant, I'm sure that it's not me but *Rhea*. Her lips are moving, like they were in the fire.

It must be undone.

"What?" The word croaks. Rhea starts to fade away. "Wait. Don't . . ."

"I, for one," Marion's voice is strangely distorted, "will not be left out in the cold."

Another cinch of the laces sends a wave of dizziness over me. My knees buckle.

"You're hurting her!"

A pair of arms catches me as the floor rises. Something scrabbles at my back and, an instant later, air whooshes mercifully into my lungs. I suck down breath after grateful breath, inhaling the scent of juniper.

"By the Light, I had no idea she was in such a state." Marion presses a hand to her chest. "I assumed she would be accustomed to a snug corset."

"That was more than snug," Jacquetta snaps. "And she told you to stop."

She's still kneeling next to me, her hands bracing my shoulders. The heat of her travels through me, warming my blood.

"I'm fine," I manage. My focus, still a bit blurry, shifts to the mirror. Had it really been Rhea? Or was I hallucinating?

The silk of Marion's dressing gown whispers as she crosses to the plate of fruit.

"Perhaps, in future, it's better if you remember what you can and *cannot* handle. Wouldn't you agree?"

She takes a bite of a strawberry, the juice smearing on her lips.

Like blood.

"What is *wrong* with that woman?" Jacquetta seethes as soon as we escape from the countess. "And that dog. I'm going to hear it barking in my sleep."

I press at my sides, which are still slightly tender after the vise of the corset. "It's my own fault. I baited her at the card game."

"Whatever you said, I'm sure she earned it." Jacquetta throws a stony glare in the direction of Marion's rooms. "She might have killed you."

"It wouldn't be the first time she tried," I comment.

Jacquetta raises an eyebrow. "Have you decided to stop blaming me for the wine?"

"That's not what I meant," I say, ignoring my flush of embarrassment at the mention of the poison. "A man followed me during the hunt. I'm fairly certain Marion sent him."

"Followed you? Is *that* why you were up in that damn tree?" I nod and her eyes flash. "Why didn't you say something?"

She reaches out, but stops herself before her hand touches my arm. My pulse flutters at her nearness and at what might be genuine concern written on her expression.

No, that voice says. *It's dangerous.*

"I didn't exactly get the chance," I say, "seeing as I was avoiding being skewered by someone else's arrow."

This time, Jacquetta flushes. The rise in color suits her, highlighting the elegant angles of her cheekbones and the curve of her neck. She starts to reply, but a blotch of brown skitters past me. A pair of footsteps quickly follows.

"Crumbs!" the princess calls. "Crumbs, wait!"

Blodwyn barrels down the corridor, a storm of burgundy skirts and unbound ebony hair.

"Oh hello, Ayleth!" She waves over her shoulder. "I'm afraid I can't stop."

A small army of ladies and servants chases the princess, clucking and fussing like the hens in Stonehaven's cloister. I stare after them, utterly bewildered. Blodwyn is the unlikeliest princess I've ever met. She could run this whole realm if given half the chance. She certainly runs her corner of the palace, what with her secret excursions through the passages and ordering the Keepers about in the library.

The library.

An idea strikes, one I should have thought of before.

I know exactly how we're going to get into the archives.

CHAPTER THIRTY-FOUR

"THE ARCHIVES? THAT'S AN UNUSUAL REQUEST FROM YOU, PRINCESS."
The Keeper studies Blodwyn from over his half-moon
spectacles. Jacquetta and I stand behind the princess, doing
our best to appear nonchalant. I'm just grateful that it didn't take
much to convince Blodwyn to want to visit this place. As soon as she
heard there were forbidden books within reach, the princess practically bolted out of her chambers.

"Perhaps," she allows. "But I'd like to go. Is there a reason I
shouldn't?"

The Keeper's frown deepens. "Not explicitly, but . . ."

"This is the royal library, isn't it?" She crosses her arms. "And I *am*
royal?"

I have never admired this girl more. Honestly, I wish I had an
ounce of her brazen confidence. Beside me, Jacquetta ducks her head
to conceal what I suspect is a smirk. The Keeper, to my amazement,
smiles as well.

"You are, indeed." Amusement gleams in his eyes and he sweeps a
bow. "Follow me."

"That child could take on a Nevenwolf," Jacquetta murmurs as the Keeper weaves his way through the tree-like stacks. "It's somewhat terrifying."

"I know," I agree. "I love it."

The Keeper halts us at a pair of huge mahogany doors deep in the library. On one side of the paneling, there's a rendering of Braxos sitting under his apple tree. On the other, Meira holds out his crown.

"Let me know when you've finished," he says, unhooking a brass ring of keys from his belt. "And no tarts in there, I'm afraid. These books are too rare to risk any mishaps."

Blodwyn scowls, disappointed, but she doesn't argue as the Keeper unlocks the door and motions us through.

The smell of old books and papers is thick as we enter the chamber. Two torches are lit near the door, and Jacquetta and I each remove one from its holder. Rows of stacks and stone columns come into focus in the glow of our light. Tables are littered throughout the space, the wood worn and cracked. A draft winnows through my clothes.

"Which of these are the books I'm not supposed to read?" Blodwyn asks, lighting her own torch and heading off into the dimness. "I hope they contain lots of beheadings."

"Wait," I call after her, having no desire to have to explain that we lost a twelve-year-old princess in a restricted part of the library.

"Let her go," Jacquetta advises. "Better that she doesn't know what we're looking for."

I suppose that's true. And Blodwyn will be fine—probably.

Alone, Jacquetta and I wander into the shelves. The archives aren't as expansive as the main library, but still large enough that I'm beginning to regret leaving the Keeper behind. We could spend days searching here and never locate what we need.

"Where did you hear about this place again?" Jacquetta asks.

"The . . . High Priest mentioned it," I fumble, still judging that it's better to keep Roland's involvement a secret. "I thought there might be records here from the Mines."

Jacquetta nods. "Good idea."

That same warmth from the last time she complimented me blooms in my chest. I didn't realize how much it would mean to have my ideas respected instead of questioned. Now that I think of it, even those closest to me, like Eden, rarely took me seriously. Even when I tried to share my fears with her on the night of my Ascension, she wouldn't hear them. At the time, I assumed she couldn't understand my feelings. But perhaps she simply didn't *want* to understand. It was never like that with Jacquetta. She was the one witch who never judged me for my lack of interest in the craft. She never once compared me to Rhea.

And yet she still left you, that voice whispers.

I grip my torch tighter.

"The books must be arranged by subject," Jacquetta says, reading the spines. "These are all military history."

"Hopefully the Dwarvian records aren't far," I say, shivering. "This place is massive. And it's freezing."

"Better than Marion's chambers."

True enough. "The costumes she sends us are going to be hideous."

"We could skip the banquet," she suggests, turning down another aisle.

"Tempting," I allow. "But they'd look for us. Marion is clearly counting on a show."

"Too bad we can't return the favor. Wait—" She pauses. Her blue gaze glitters in the torchlight. "Do you happen to remember the recipe for contortion powder?"

A laugh escapes me. "Oh yes, that would go over well. No one would suspect anything if Marion showed up wearing the face of a lizard."

Jacquetta blinks innocently. "What? The theme of the banquet is a menagerie. Marion would blend right in. And I was thinking less lizard and more . . . rodent. Like we did with that one witch. What was her name? She'd caught us sneaking out and made us scrub pots."

"Gert." I laugh again, picturing the other witch's face transformed by the potion. Her small pink nose and long whiskers.

"That's right. It lasted for what, three days?"

Jacquetta laughs, and I realize that it's the first time I've heard her do so in years. I used to hear it every day, filling the south tower or ringing through the trees. I'd forgotten how contagious it is. How it lets sparks loose in my veins.

"We never got caught, though," Jacquetta goes on, still grinning. "Because Rhea—"

A wave of cold douses me.

Jacquetta instantly sobers. "I'm so sorry, Ayleth. I didn't think . . ."

I clench my fists against the triangles etched below my ring fingers. As much as the pain of my grief sears through me, irritation swiftly follows. All it took was the mention of Rhea's name to ruin the moment—send me spiraling back into the sadness of her death. I pull myself up, refusing to let myself be dragged down by it.

"Rhea said she'd done it," I say, fighting the hitch in my voice. "She said it was some accident in the workroom."

The stiffness in Jacquetta's shoulders relaxes. "She was always covering for you."

She was. She still is, for that matter. I press my thumb into the mark on my left palm, two lines drifting apart and then coming back together. *That's us*, she'd said. It might be my imagination, but the triangles prickle faintly.

"I was jealous of you sometimes," Jacquetta admits softly.

"Jealous?" I repeat, surprised.

"What you and Rhea shared was special," she says, not taking her focus from the books. "I wanted a sister."

I never knew she felt that way. "You and your mother seemed to get along well enough."

We turn down another aisle. Judging from their titles, these books seem to be related to the first White Kings—journals and such.

"We do," Jacquetta allows. "But it's different. Mother and I . . ."

My torch snaps in the draft. "What?"

Jacquetta's fingertip pauses in traveling along the row of books. "Sometimes I think she wants more from me than I can give. That I'm not enough as I am."

That resonates in a place deep inside me. A sudden urge bubbles up from the pit of my stomach—to confide in her about my relationship with my own mother. I'm *desperate* to talk about it, especially with someone who understands. But a sharp, insistent instinct restrains me.

No matter how it may seem, this *isn't* Jacquetta from the forest. And I'm letting myself get far too close. I'm falling back into habits that will be my undoing.

"I'm sorry" is all I allow myself to say, throat tightening.

So quick I almost miss it, Jacquetta flinches. Had I wounded her? *Good,* that voice whispers. *Keep her away.*

Awkward silence settles between us, broken only by the crackle of torches and the shuffle of Blodwyn's distant footsteps. Time passes, but, with no windows or bells, it's impossible to discern if it's been minutes or hours. I start to worry that we won't locate the records, or that the Keeper will come back and force us to leave, and quicken my pace.

As I round the next shelf, torchlight glimmers against the gold

foil of an emblem stamped into the book spines. It's a crossed pickaxe symbol, exactly like the one on Roland's cap. My heart beats
harder. The Dwarvian records.

"Jacquetta." I nudge her. "This is it."

I snatch a book off the shelf. The pages are filled with neat rows of
dates and names and objects.

> Gilded Mace, commissioned by King Reston, Age of the
> Covens 350

"Age of the Covens," Jacquetta reads, tapping the page. "These go
back before the war. They weren't burned."

Which means they should mention the Bloodstones. Exchanging
a hopeful glance, Jacquetta and I yank stacks of ledgers off the shelves
and dive into them.

> Enchanted Mirror, commissioned by High Witch, Coven
> Ravenwood, Age of the Covens 1113

> Glass Coffin, commissioned on behalf of King Archibald,
> Age of the Covens 1536

That's where my book ends. I reach for another, but then—

"Ayleth."

Something in Jacquetta's tone sends alarm bells ringing in my
mind. Her fingertip hovers over the middle of her book. And then I
see it. Short, ragged edges run down the inner spine, where several
pages have obviously been ripped out. Dread pools in my belly.

"Tell me it's not . . ?"

But the line of her mouth is tight and when I read the dates on
the remaining pages, I understand why—

Age of the Covens 2999. The last year before the war.

Age of the Light 3. The third year of the new age.

The years in between are missing. Years in which the royal swords, set with the Bloodstones, would have been commissioned.

"We don't know what was recorded there," Jacquetta says, guessing my thoughts.

But I do. I know it in my bones. I flip through the rest of the book, frantically searching for some mention of the stones being returned to the Mines, but there's nothing. Of course there isn't. The only record of the Bloodstones was written on the pages that were stolen. I grip the sides of the book, torn between throwing it and setting it on fire. Burn this whole palace down.

"Who would have taken those pages?" I shake the book. "And why those records and not anything else?"

Jacquetta shakes her head. "Perhaps it's the same person who's hiding the stones—maybe this is how they found them."

But who is *they*? And *why* do they want the stones? "I don't—"

My torch flame gutters in a draft, one far colder than it should be.

"Blodwyn?" I call, peering into the dimness.

Silence answers. The chill deepens enough that my breath frosts in front of my face. And then, just barely, I detect a faint clicking noise, one I've heard before—in the crypt.

No, I think. It's not possible. I killed the Nevenwolf. But the sound starts again, gaining strength. That place behind my left ribs, where that ominous force dwells, *thrums.*

"We need to go," I tell Jacquetta. "Now!"

She doesn't argue. Abandoning the books, we race through the aisles.

"Blodwyn?" I call. "Where are you?"

There's no reply. I can't leave her here. Not with some . . . whatever it is stalking the archives. A shock of frigid air whooshes past us, and we drop the torches. The flames sputter out on the stone floor, throwing us into darkness.

"What was that?" Jacquetta whispers.

A Nevenwolf, the voice in my mind whispers. *Malum, reeling you in.*

It's trying—I can feel it inside me, lengthening and reaching like a tether, pulling me toward the Veil. There's a pattern to the sensation, almost like . . . footsteps. The *thing* is getting closer. We need to *move.*

A glimmer of light in the distance snags my attention, but it quickly disappears.

"There!" I call to Jacquetta "That must be Blodwyn."

Blindly, we feel our way toward the direction where I'd seen the light. A low moan resonates deeper in the chamber, one that sounds frighteningly close to laughter.

"Hurry!" Jacquetta urges.

Our footsteps slap against stone as we break into a clumsy run. The clicking of claws matches our pace, louder with every panicked heartbeat. Whatever is haunting this palace, haunting *me,* is about to pounce. The force behind my rib cage strains against the underside of my skin. I'm not going to be able to hold it back. I'll wind up just like the dead prince and—

I round a corner and collide with something solid.

"By the Light, what are you doing?" The glow of the princess's torch washes over us.

"Did you hear that?" I ask, wheeling around. "Did you see anything?"

But the sound of the claws has abruptly vanished. The invisible tether attached to my left ribs slackens.

"What are you talking about?" The princess peers into the shadows. "Wait, did you see a ghost? I'll be so upset if I missed it. I *knew* this place was haunted."

Jacquetta's fingers tremble as she straightens her dress. "That wasn't a ghost."

No. It was Malum. But why had it stopped chasing me? Did the light scare it off? Or is the beast simply toying with me? I press my hand to my side. And I pray that it's my imagination, but I think I feel a slight rumble between my bones, as if whatever is living inside me is laughing.

CHAPTER THIRTY-FIVE

"I DON'T UNDERSTAND." JACQUETTA PACES THE BALCONY LATER THAT night, after Joan and the other girl have fallen asleep. "You killed the Nevenwolf."

The moon is high and full above us, and it's ringed in a halo—a sign of trouble coming, though I can't imagine how matters could be worse than they are now.

"It must be another," I say, envisioning an entire pack of crimson-eyed Nevenwolves straining to break free of the Veil.

To drag you back through it, that voice whispers.

The wind picks up, stirring the bare-branched trees. The brittle clacking of wood sounds enough like the click of claws on stone that I shiver. But, by some miracle, I don't sense the force behind my left ribs. It's been quiet since the archives.

But it will come back, that voice again.

Much as I try to ignore it, I know that it's right. How much longer do I have before something else escapes the Veil, drawn by the dregs of Malum inside me? Days? Hours?

"Did you ever see a Nevenwolf near Stonehaven?" Jacquetta asks, breaking me out of my questions. She leans against the railing as she looks out over the gardens. A fountain flows in the center of the manicured paths, the water silvery in the night.

"I don't think so," I lie, banishing the memory of the red eyes in the forest. "Why?"

"Because I never saw one, either, and we traveled half the realm. I've never felt the Veil as thin as it is here." She tugs at her sleeve. "I told you before—something strange is going on in this palace."

I'm the strangeness Jacquetta senses—the reason behind every stroke of ill luck or looming shadow. Yet again, some reckless part of me wants to confess. But then what? At my Ascension, even the whisper of Malum had been enough to drive witches I'd known my whole life away from me.

Because they saw the truth, that voice again.

A crow calls in the distance.

"We find the Bloodstones and it all goes away," I say, as much to myself as to Jacquetta. "Everything will be as it was before."

And I'll have my sister.

Jacquetta turns around. Moonlight brightens her nightdress and gleams against the exposed olive skin of her shoulder. "Maybe the way things were *before* is the problem."

"What do you mean?" My brow furrows. "I thought you wanted to find the Bloodstones—stop yourself from getting torn apart by a Nevenwolf."

"I do," she agrees. "But are you so certain that five magical rocks are the answer?"

Magical rocks. I cross my arms. "You're clearly not. Please— enlighten me. How else might we construct a barrier between our worlds? One strong enough to hold back Malum?"

A faint flush blooms on her cheeks. "I don't know."

"Well, that's a first."

She glares at me. "You don't know either."

"Because there's nothing to know," I throw back. "The stones hold the Veil—it's always been that way."

"Yes, which is exactly what the covens *want*." Jacquetta points at me. "They've staked their whole existence on those stones, on their precious bloodlines and hierarchy. And look where it got them in the end. Look where it got *you*."

Me? Anger crackles in my wrists. "Look at yourself. You take such pride in having sworn your 'special' vow, when it's the Veil—the Ancients themselves—protecting you. Or are you counting on the *stars* to swoop in and rescue you from another Nevenwolf?"

Her eyes blaze. "And where are your all-powerful Ancients now? Funny, you were never concerned about bloodlines or position before. When did you stop thinking for yourself?"

The jab lands as intended and I flinch. Because she's right— I never wanted to become a Second or lead a coven. I still don't. But what else could I have done? And I hate Jacquetta for suggesting that I had a choice, or at least an easy one.

"What do you care?" I grind out. "You walked away."

She lifts her chin. "At least I didn't go running back to a life I despised."

Rage smolders in my belly. How *dare* she judge me for what happened? *This* is the real Jacquetta, the one my sisters warned me about but whom I was always too blind to see. I see her now, though— selfish and arrogant, treating everyone around her like witchlings to be instructed.

"Oh really?" I tilt my head at her. "How different is your own life from Stonehaven? Is Nerissa the High Witch of your coven?"

Jacquetta's jaw tightens, which is all the confirmation I need. A bitter laugh climbs up my throat.

"That's what I thought. You blame the Ancients and Heirs and Seconds for this war, but you're exactly the same."

Her nostrils flare. "No, I'm not. I would never be part of something that consumes its own. Just look at Rhea."

This time, there's no hesitation or guilt at uttering my sister's name. In fact, Jacquetta wields it like a blade—like Mother does.

The wind picks up, the chill eating through my nightdress.

"You don't know what you're talking about."

"Or do you just not like what I'm saying?" Jacquetta advances. "I might have left Stonehaven, but I heard the rumors about Rhea's power being too weak to mend the wards on the night of the raid. My mother thinks it's true. That there was too much pressure on her, being a Second. It drained her. The *covens* drained her."

You drained her, she doesn't say.

Another crow calls in the night.

One for sorrow.

"That's not what happened."

"Are you certain?" she asks, a cruel twist to her mouth. "Maybe Rhea even *welcomed* the iron poisoning. Because then she was finally free."

A sob rises and I fight it down, along with the memory of the night Rhea died. She hadn't cried, not a single tear. In fact, she'd *smiled.*

No, I want to scream. Rhea wouldn't have abandoned me on purpose—and she didn't. She came back.

It must be undone.

I dig my fingernails into the triangles etched on my palms—two lines drifting apart and back together. Twin promises. Jacquetta wouldn't know anything about such promises. All she does is leave. All she cares about is herself.

That deep, dark impulse rises inside me.

Hurt her, it urges. *Hurt her like she's hurt you.*

This time, I don't care where it comes from.

"What do you know about freedom?" I all but growl. "I saw you out here, screaming into your hands after that raven came. You're not free. You're a *Second,* desperate to prove yourself. And you're failing."

Her face shades paler. A small voice whispers that this is too far. I ignore it.

"And I heard you scrying with that other witch at the Sanctum." Wind billows my nightdress. "Your lover, I take it? Or ex-lover. *I'm tired of waiting,* isn't that what she said? Even she could see that you're not worth it."

A long moment stretches between us. The pulse between Jacquetta's collarbones is rabbit-quick. She steps closer and the smell of juniper burns in my lungs.

"And what are you worth?" she asks, her voice low and lethal. "Do you know what I felt when I walked away that night in the forest? Away from you? *Relief.*"

The word plunges in and out of my chest like a hot blade.

Jacquetta doesn't stay to watch me bleed. She stalks back into the chamber and slams the door, leaving my foolish, wretched heart nothing but a smoldering pulp.

The days before the banquet pass in a blur of frustration and anger.

My nights are filled with dreams of writhing flames and swirling darkness. And *Rhea.* Just like at my Ascension, my sister reaches for me through the fire, her lips moving in words I can't hear. Rust-colored veins snake up her neck as the iron poisoning claims her.

It must be undone.

Rhea wouldn't have said that if she didn't want me to bring her back. She wouldn't have given me our marks, or protected me from the Nevenwolf, if she wished to remain beyond the Veil. Even so, Jacquetta's words will not leave me alone.

The covens drained her.

Did they? I always assumed that Rhea wanted to be Second. She was so talented, a natural leader. Everything I'm not. But while tossing and turning between nightmares, I begin to wonder how much I truly knew my sister. Could Jacquetta be right?

You're letting her get too close, that voice warns.

As the days drag on, I avoid the other witch as much as possible, our deal burned to ashes. I spend most of my time back at the library, slogging through useless texts. But there's no point in attempting another visit to the archives. The pages from the Dwarvian records are gone, and I have no idea who might have stolen them. Was the theft recent? Did the person know what I was looking for? Are they watching me? The uncertainty sets my skin crawling, leaving me jumpy and irritable.

On the day of the banquet, the queen's rooms are closed so that we can prepare our costumes. There's little for me to do, seeing as Marion will be sending mine. Unable to stand the thought of another mind-numbing hour in the library, I pass the morning in bed. At some point, I hear Jacquetta leave. What will she do now that she's evidently given up on the Bloodstones?

It doesn't matter, that voice whispers. *Forget her.*

I'm trying, but I can't seem to banish the lingering scent of juniper.

A knock shortly after four bells interrupts my sulking. Joan answers the door.

"Oh, thank you. Just put them there," she says. Then, "Ayleth. Your gown arrived."

Just what I need. With nothing better to do, I kick my way out of the bedclothes. Joan is already investigating one of the costumes, tossing a mouse's mask unceremoniously on the floor.

"Poor Jacquetta." She clicks her tongue, examining a swath of gray fabric. "Perhaps I can salvage it."

"Don't bother," I advise. Jacquetta deserves to wear the hideous thing.

But Joan is already committed to the task, ripping what I take to be a tail off the dress. I lift the lid of the other box, expecting to discover a snake's mask, as Marion promised. But the gown inside is a stunning arrangement of orange, red, and yellow silk, softer than any material I've ever touched. Bewildered, I lift it up. The bodice is studded with rubies, and the undersleeves are black, so that it appears as though the dress itself is flame rising from coals.

"That's gorgeous!" Joan gasps. "Marion can't have sent that."

No, she couldn't have. Was it the queen, taking pity on me? But it seems unlikely that Queen Sybil would have sent a gown for me and not one for Jacquetta too.

"A phoenix," Joan determines, fussing with the folds. "I admit, it's a bit unusual for the theme, but it is Longest Night."

The gown *is* unusual. And wildly ostentatious. Everyone at the banquet will assume I chose it on purpose to stand out. Who had sent me this? And why?

Phoenixes burn, that voice inside me whispers.

And so do witches.

CHAPTER THIRTY-SIX

THE GREAT HALL IS ENCASED IN GLASS.

Huge panes line the sides of the room and form a domed ceiling overhead, a near-exact replica of the princess's menagerie. The doors are thrown open, revealing what could be a scene from an enchanted winter forest. Columns are dressed as arching trees, brushed with a glittery powder that gives the impression of fresh-fallen snow. White and gold ribbons wind around frosted garlands. Candlelight dazzles on crystal goblets and shines on life-size ice sculptures of fawns, antlered stags, and other animals. A troupe of minstrels plays in a corner, the jubilant melodies of the lute and harps mingling with the courtiers' already slightly drunken chatter. Their costumes are even more elaborate than the decorations. One woman wears a gown entirely comprised of feathers. Another is dressed as a peacock, with thousands of jewels sewn into her train.

"I *told* Mother I needed to visit the dressmaker," Joan mumbles, fussing with her own costume, which is meant to be a swan—and it's lovely. The cut is flattering, and the bodice is crisscrossed with ribbons, giving the illusion of feathers.

But despite Joan's talent with a needle, her efforts are lackluster when compared to the others. Would that I could say the same. Just as I feared, my own gown is garnering far more attention than any costume Marion could have devised. Courtiers whisper as they pass us, their gazes lingering in a way that makes me wish I'd kept the mouse's head that came with Jacquetta's costume—at least then I'd have something to hide behind.

And where is Jacquetta now? She still hadn't returned to the room by the time we left. Maybe she's not coming, which is fine with me.

"Well." A too-familiar figure emerges from the crowd. "Mistress Ayleth."

Marion sails over with her cadre in tow. Her gown is a gleaming silver brocade, embellished with vine-like designs stitched in pearl thread. The sleeves and train are furred in white. A snouted mask with pointed ears covers the top of her forehead. I suspect she's meant to be a snow wolf—a creature as beautiful as it is deadly.

"I must admit that I'm surprised at such cunning." Marion's gaze rakes over my dress. "A phoenix. It's a bit brazen for my taste, but I suppose you would need something flashy—to distract from your *other* features."

The ladies standing behind Marion smirk. A flush smears across my cheeks, one I scold myself for feeling. It doesn't matter what Marion thinks of me. But her talent for digging *just so* under someone's skin is as uncanny as it is despicable. Again, that deep part of me rises up, urging me to dig back. Wound her.

"And what features might you be concealing?" Joan inquires, feigning innocence.

Marion looks at the other woman as if surprised to find her there.

"Me? Why, none at all. I dressed to complement His Majesty—at his request." Her dark gaze returns to mine, glittering with malice. "Enjoy the banquet. And good luck during the contest. I'm sure this court will judge you fairly."

With that, she disappears into the crowd.

"Good riddance," Joan mutters. "*Dressed to complement His Majesty.* Really. Her arrogance knows no bounds. If I—"

She stops short and motions behind me.

"Look!"

Joan points to another courtier near the front of the Great Hall. But no—not a courtier, I realize as the person turns so that I can see their face. It's Jacquetta.

For a few moments, the noise of the crowd dulls. Joan worked wonders on Jacquetta's gown. The gray color is striking against her olive complexion. The neckline scoops low enough to display the delicate ledges of Jacquetta's collarbones. The sleeves drape gracefully over her arms, showing off her wrists. A pearl silk ribbon is woven through Jacquetta's braided hair, and there's a band of matching jewels along her forehead. The pale gems bring out the blue of her eyes, which widen slightly as they land on mine. My foolish heart stutters.

"Come on," Joan says, tugging me through the crowd and toward Jacquetta.

"Oh," I protest. "No, I should—"

But the rest falls away as we draw close. Joan circles Jacquetta, admiring her own work.

"You look beautiful," she says. "It turned out better than I hoped."

"You did this?" Jacquetta asks, brow creasing.

"Of course." Joan adjusts a fold in Jacquetta's skirt. "I couldn't let you come wearing that awful thing Marion sent."

She throws a dark look behind her, presumably in the courtier's direction.

"I . . . thank you." Jacquetta's attention twitches to me. "Did Joan fix yours as well?"

We haven't directly spoken since our argument, and I shift on my feet, unsure what to do with myself. "No. I don't know where it came from."

"Perhaps the queen," Joan chimes in. "But she does look stunning, doesn't she? The color really suits her."

Joan nudges Jacquetta's elbow, but Jacquetta only mutters unintelligibly before becoming fascinated with a nearby decoration.

You don't care about her, that voice in my mind insists.

No. But then why is my pulse racing? Why can't I stop noticing the exposed area of her chest, just before her skin disappears beneath her neckline?

The blast of a horn mercifully shatters the moment.

"Presenting His Majesty, Defender of the Light, King Callen!" a herald announces at the front of the room. "And Her Majesty, Queen Sybil."

Applause swells at the royal couple's entrance. The queen is dressed in white. Silk roses are sewn into her gown, and a pair of delicate antlers grace her headdress, suggesting that she's a deer. But the king . . .

I suddenly understand what Marion meant when the courtier said she dressed to complement him. King Callen wears a black doublet littered with jet-colored gems. A snouted mask, similar to Marion's, is pushed up to the king's forehead. But *this* mask is not that of an ordinary wolf. Its eyes are set with crimson jewels. The Nevenwolf.

Dread winds between my bones in oily ribbons. As if pulled by some sinister force, the king's gray gaze locks with mine. The place behind my left ribs shudders. The king dips his chin in greeting, and a horrible sensation blooms in my belly—that I am *prey*.

Dinner commences shortly after that. Dish after dish surfaces from the kitchens. Glazed turkeys and entire hens. Whole fish and meat pies and—as Duchess Poole promised—a *cockentrice*. The gilded half-pig, half-capon is paraded about on a golden platter to overwhelming applause. Its eyes have been plucked out, replaced with cherries—red and bulbous and *wrong*.

My appetite instantly dies, not that I had much of one to begin with, seeing as Jacquetta is sitting beside me. The air between us might as well be a wall of ice, but I refuse to be the one to break it. For her part, Jacquetta ignores her food. She drains her wineglass, though, and continually flags down the passing servants to request more. By her third cup, however, the boy pretends to stop hearing her and she pushes herself up, wobbling slightly as she chases after him. Concern winnows through my resentment. Is she attempting to drown herself in wine because of our argument? Or is there something else?

She's not your problem, that voice admonishes.

And it's right. Let Jacquetta drink herself into oblivion if that's what she wants to do. I just hope she doesn't expect me to help her back to our room later.

"Did something . . . happen between you two?" Joan asks carefully, pointing her fork in Jacquetta's direction.

"What?" I ask, flustered. "No."

"Are you sure? Because I've had conversations with rocks that said more than you two did just now. And I thought I heard voices out on the balcony a few nights ago."

Damn. "We just . . . we had an argument."

"I'm sorry." Joan spears a quail egg. "You know, some people say I'm good at giving advice, if you want to talk."

I should keep it to myself. But snippets of my exchange with Jacquetta flow back to me and, against my better judgment, I swallow a mouthful of wine. Luckily, there doesn't seem to be any thornapple in it—this time.

"She thinks I'm someone I'm not," I tell Joan, keeping my answer vague. "And she's punishing me for things that aren't my fault."

Do you know what I felt? The words roll around my skull. *Relief.*

Did she mean that? Was she glad to walk away? I drown the questions in more wine.

"I am sorry, Ayleth." Joan frowns. "But are you certain she's punishing you? I don't know Jacquetta well, but that doesn't sound like her."

I huff a laugh. "You don't know her at all. And neither do I."

"You wouldn't be this upset about someone you didn't know." Joan slides me a look. "Or didn't care about."

"Jacquetta makes it impossible to care about her. She's stubborn and insufferable and . . ." I run out of words and stab at a boiled potato.

Joan is quiet for a few moments. Another dish is carted into the hall—a towering pastry dessert fashioned to look like a blooming apple tree, with marchpane fruit dangling from the limbs. Amber-colored filling oozes like sap down the trunk.

"I met someone like that once," Joan says, pitching her voice beneath the applause. "There—beside the flowers."

She points her knife toward the other side of the room. Near a huge vase of white roses, a woman is seated beside several other members of the queen's household. Like Joan, the woman wears a swan costume, though hers is much more elaborate. Her white gown is speckled with gems. A gauzy, winglike cape flutters from her shoulders.

"Lady Anora," Joan says. "We dressed to match. Swans mate for life, you see."

Understanding clicks into place, followed by surprise. They're a couple. I look to Anora and back to Joan. "I've never even seen you two near each other."

"And you won't." Sadness shines in Joan's green eyes. "Such relationships were common before the war. Now two women together are close enough to a—well, you know."

A coven. Rage kindles in my chest. "That's not fair."

"No," she agrees. "But there's little to do about it. I wanted you to know, though, in case you were feeling alone."

"Feeling . . ." The purpose of Joan's story registers. She thinks Jacquetta and I . . .

"We're not!" I insist. "I mean—the two of us aren't—we could never."

Not anymore, anyway.

Joan laughs and holds up her hand. "It's all right, Ayleth, I promise. I won't say a thing."

"But we *really* aren't."

She arches a skeptical eyebrow. "Well, whatever is between you, you deserve to be happy. We all do."

What would make me happy? When I came to the White Court, I thought the answer was Rhea. I press my thumb into one of my sister's marks. Is that still the case? Or do I crave something else? *Someone* else?

Close off your heart, that voice warns.

"Attention!"

Sir Weston's booming voice rises above the laughter and clink of silver on plates. He clambers onto his chair, tapping that needle-like dining utensil against his wineglass. His doublet is rust-colored, and a pair of golden ears peeks out from his unkempt hair. A bushy tail—one that is probably real—swishes where it's fixed to the back of his waist.

"As the Lord of Misrule, I declare that our contest must commence."

The court cheers, and I drain the rest of my cup.

"In just a moment," Sir Weston proceeds, "the men will begin circulating around the room, bestowing their favors upon the lady they deem *fairest.*"

"My favor cannot be so publicly *bestowed,*" someone shouts. The hall erupts into laughter and the pressure in my head increases.

"Then I suggest you keep the vile thing to yourself," Sir Weston calls back in mock reprimand, earning a storm of hoots and gasps. "Ladies, I urge you to be your most charming and beguiling selves. For she who earns the most favors at the end of the night will be crowned *fairest of them all*—just like our goddess."

Sir Weston snaps his fingers, and a servant hurries up, carting a box. He lifts the lid and extracts a crown. Candlelight catches on the jewels, and every muscle in my body stills. The stones are a deep red—the same color as our cloaks.

Bloodstones.

Are they real? Surely not. They're likely the same useless replicas that I saw at the pageant in the city. But what if I'm wrong? There's only one way to find out.

Sir Weston replaces the crown in its box. Music begins, fast and lively. Dancers form two rows down the hall, hopping and skipping to its tempo. Before Joan can ask any questions, I push back from the table and jostle my way through the room, avoiding men who try to *examine* my costume. The box that held the crown is sitting at the High Table. All I have to do is—

A figure steps into my path, and I'm met with a pair of glittering red eyes. The force behind my left ribs *jolts*.

"Mistress Ayleth," the king says. "You must do me the honor of a dance."

CHAPTER THIRTY-SEVEN

FOR A FEW PANICKED MOMENTS, THE CROWD BLURS AROUND US, AS if it is only me and the king in the Great Hall. Just as at the card game, I sense that unsettling tether—Malum—pulling taut between us. It pulses faintly with a heartbeat that is not my own. Is it *his*?

"I can't dance," I say, praying the feeble excuse is enough to throw him off.

"You can shoot, you can rob everyone blind at Castles, but you cannot *dance*?" The teeth affixed to the snout of the king's mask gleam white.

Damn everything. "I don't—"

"One dance, Mistress," the king insists, extending his hand. "Surely you can grant as much to your king."

He is *not* my king. But this is not a request. And, like Joan said about my invitation to the High Table, I'll draw far more attention by refusing.

A single dance, I tell myself. *You can survive it.*

Fighting the sense that I'm a rabbit caught in a snare, I allow the king to lead me among the other dancers. My skin crawls at the brush of their whispers and envious glances. The music changes, becoming slow and sinuous.

"Like this," the king says, moving behind me.

His hands rest on either side of my waist and I close my eyes against the sensation of that tether shortening, like it had in the forest with the Nevenwolf—dragging me toward the Veil.

I watch the other couples, trying to distract myself in finding a pattern to the steps. It doesn't help. The women are always reaching in the opposite direction of their partners, always leaning out of an embrace—relentlessly pursued. Possessed. Controlled.

King Callen circles me.

"The gown suits you." That gray gaze roves along the lines of my body. "My phoenix."

His phoenix? Understanding slams into me. I was wrong. The queen didn't gift me this dress. "It was you."

The king is behind me again. He bends close to the curve where my neck meets my shoulder. "Don't you like it?"

No. I don't. "You should have given it to someone more deserving."

"There *is* no one more deserving." The king's circle around me narrows. "Surely you can see that."

All I can see is that I need to be as far from this man as possible. I step back, but the other dancers box me in, as if I do not exist at all. Not one of them would help me if I cried out, I realize. If the king wants to dance with me, they will let him. They will let him do anything. That invisible tether vibrates like a plucked cord.

The king seizes my hand, spinning me wide. The manufactured menagerie smears into a blur of faces and colors, like the whole world is tilting on its axis. Shadows slink toward me. Darkness peels from the costumes of the other dancers, shades of midnight. Panic drums in my chest as the tether cinches even tighter. What's happening? Is it another creature emerging from beyond the Veil, come to devour me whole? I half wish it would.

"Is something wrong?" The crimson eyes of the king's mask glimmer. "You seem frightened."

He draws me back to him, holding me so that I'm pressed against his chest, drowning in his scent of leather and smoke. My heart pounds, and I sense that the horrible force inside me is feeding off of my terror, stronger with every breath. Something in the gray of the king's eyes tells me that he senses it too.

"What is this hold you have on me?" the king murmurs. "Who are you, Ayleth?"

I'm not sure I know anymore—if I ever knew at all.

"No one," I whisper.

Glass shatters, breaking the spell between us. The tether mercifully slackens, and my attention snaps to the High Table, where a servant has dropped a bottle. Wine spills like blood over the floor. A cloaked figure hurries around the mess. So quickly I almost miss it, they scoop up a box and rush away with it. Not just any box, my mind processes—the one containing the crown. The person is *stealing* it.

And that's when I know—the stones are real.

No. Not again.

Mustering my strength, I wrench myself out of the king's grasp and race after the thief. But I don't get far. The hall is overcrowded, its glass walls acting like mirrors, repeated reflections of myself staring back at me in an endless, dizzying loop.

Ayleth, I hear beneath the music and laughter. *Ayleth.*

I run away from it, plowing through the sea of courtiers, trampling hems and smacking wings out of my frantic path. By the time I stumble through the outer doors of the Great Hall and into the corridor, the only sign of the other person is the echo of footsteps against stone. I race after them, but hampered by my corset and skirts, the thief easily outpaces me. Before I even round the next corner, the hall is quiet.

Breathless, I pivot left and right, cursing as I throw open the nearest door in the wild hope that the thief is hiding behind it. But there's nothing—only an outer courtyard. An apple tree stands in the center, frosted with ice. The crown—the Bloodstones with it—is gone.

"Damn!"

Who'd taken it? And why? Had it been the same person who ripped the pages from the Dwarvian records? Are they following me?

Wind pushes into the courtyard, strong enough that the apple tree groans under its pressure. A murder of crows swoops overhead, their calls crashing together in a sinister chorus. I stare up at the dark cloud of their formation, heart thudding. That place behind my left ribs trembles. Again, it feels like laughter.

I've had enough of this. Enough of Malum and Nevenwolves and mad kings. Rage crackles in my veins, that deep impulse rising up—to do something, fight back. I'm tired of tamping it down. My focus lands on the apple tree, its limbs glistening with ice. Bellowing a cry, I descend upon the tree, clawing at the bark and yanking on low branches. The answering snap of wood is immensely satisfying, and I jump up to try to snag another. It's too high and I miss, promptly falling onto the flagstones. Pain shoots up my hip and I snarl a curse. Even the apple trees in this wretched place are conspiring against me.

"What are you *doing*?"

Heat flames in my cheeks at being caught attempting to hack apart a tree with my bare hands. But it's not the king, or even Marion, who has followed me. Instead, Jacquetta leans against the doorframe, her brow pinched as she observes the scene.

"I was . . . it doesn't matter. Did you see anyone in the halls?" I ask, pushing myself up. "Someone running with a box?"

"A box?" She'd clearly found her way to a wine pitcher, for the words are slurred.

"Yes, a box," I repeat, impatient.

Jacquetta looks back at the palace, bewildered. "I didn't see anyone. What do you care about a box anyway? And what did that tree do to you?"

She must be drunk if she cares enough to ask. I shake my skirts free of the bits of bark and ice. "The Bloodstones might have been inside that box. Now they're gone. Again."

This is too much to be coincidence. Someone *wants* those stones. But who? And why? A crow calls in the night.

Jacquetta sways slightly where she stands. "Stop wasting your time with those *magic rocks.* Just . . ."

"*Don't* call them that!" I shout. Jacquetta doesn't get to pretend to help me one day and then discard me the next. "You've made your feelings about the Bloodstones and the Ancients abundantly clear. Not to mention your feelings about *me.*"

Jacquetta swallows but remains silent.

What could she say that she hasn't already? that voice asks.

"Just leave me alone," I barrel on. "That's what you want, isn't it? You said you were relieved when you walked away that night in the clearing? Good. You were right—it would have been madness for us to run away. There's nothing holding us together. There never was."

The branches of the apple tree creak in the quickening wind. There's a storm coming. I sense its heaviness in the air.

I expect Jacquetta to snap back with some cutting remark, but she just stands there. Perhaps it's the wine, but her expression softens. She almost looks . . . fragile. Vulnerable. The pulse at her throat is rabbit-quick. Her smell of juniper drifts beneath that of the ice and snow. For the briefest instant, her gaze twitches down, to my lips. Much as I try to smother it, that part of my heart that has always been hers *aches*.

Don't, that voice whispers.

But what if I did? What if I *want* to? My blood hums.

A piercing scream rips between us.

I whirl. "What was that?"

Another scream answers, coupled with a stampede of racing footsteps inside the palace. Jacquetta and I rush back through the doors to investigate. The hall is flooded with panicked courtiers fleeing the banquet.

"She has the plague!" a woman shouts, nearly tripping over her hem in her haste.

Plague? Jacquetta and I shove our way into the Great Hall, until we're close enough to spot the source of the commotion—Marion.

The courtier is on her knees, her skirts pooled on the floor and the snow-wolf mask discarded. She's yanking silver and jeweled combs out of her dark hair as if they're burning her. One of them spins toward us and collides with my foot.

"Help me!" Marion wails. "I don't . . . I can't . . ."

By the Spirits, what happened? I bend down to pick up the comb. Had someone poisoned it? I inspect it, careful not to let its teeth pierce my skin. Sapphires and opals sparkle in the candlelight. But it's not poisoned. Instead, etched into the metal of the comb is a marking.

A *rune*.

"Jacquetta," I whisper, nudging her.

She immediately spots the symbol and sucks in a breath. "What does it mean?"

I shake my head. Mother forced me to learn hundreds of runes during our lessons, but I've never seen one exactly like this: Four lines drawn in a box, with three slashes through the center. Where had it come from?

"What's going on?"

The buzzing hive of courtiers parts for the king.

"Keep your distance, Sire." Ignatius pulls him back before he gets too close to Marion. "She may be contagious."

She's not. Marion's condition has nothing to do with mortal illness. I study the rune again, still trying to guess its meaning. What is it doing here? And who put it on the comb?

"Take her away," Ignatius commands the guards. "Isolate her. And burn her clothes, in case . . . Mistress Ayleth."

I'd been so absorbed with the rune that I hadn't noticed the High Priest's attention. Horror flashes in my veins as he approaches.

"What is that?" He beckons for the comb.

My mouth goes dry, instincts warring in my mind. *Run, hide, stab him with the comb.* But panic wins out. I pass him the comb. Maybe he won't notice—

"*Witchcraft*," he sneers.

The word rolls like thunder through the hall. I hardly register the cries of the other courtiers above the pounding of my own heart. Jacquetta's shoulder brushes mine.

"We knew there was a witch lurking near the palace"—Ignatius gestures around him—"but apparently she is much closer than we imagined."

This is it. I was caught with a runed comb. I'll be burned. I brace myself for the guards to descend. To be dragged away and strapped to a pyre. The High Priest's robes ripple like flame. But his amber gaze does not return to me. Instead, he looks to Marion.

"This is your comb, Countess? One that has been in your possession this entire evening?"

"It is," Marion stammers. "But I didn't—"

"You tainted it with your sorcery." The High Priest brandishes the comb. Its silver teeth gleam like knives. "Used it to spell the king."

By the Spirits. Ignatius is accusing *her*?

King Callen blanches. Marion gapes between the two men, her hair falling in inky tendrils around her face, her pupils blown wide.

"No. No, Your Majesty. Your Illuminance. One of my servants must have done it. Or someone, anyone else, but *not* me."

"She couldn't have," the king says, but he does not sound certain. "Why would the comb harm her if she's the one who spelled it?"

A few courtiers murmur their agreement.

"Because this is *Meira's* doing," Ignatius determines.

My mind spins. *What?*

"Our goddess sensed Malum present in this palace, and *she* is shining her Light—and her judgment—upon the culprit," the High Priest continues. "After all, Lady Marion attended the hunt, did she not? On the very occasion that the Nevenwolf appeared? One of her *servants* couldn't possibly have summoned the beast, as none of them was among the party."

"I had nothing to do with that," Marion insists.

This is utter madness. But the courtiers begin to whisper, some nodding.

"She must have been worried about losing favor," one comments.

"Desperate to keep the king," another adds.

Marion pivots left and right, helpless. Moments ago, these people treated her as if she were royalty. Now she's just another dish served to satisfy this gluttonous court. I'm so shocked and repulsed that all I can do is stare.

"Your Majesty, *please.*" Tears streak down Marion's face and stain the pale silk of her gown. "You must believe me."

The king's jaw works, but he remains silent.

"There is but one method to determine her guilt or innocence,"

the High Priest announces. "We shall conduct a trial. Meira herself
will guide us to the truth."

Marion's tears fall faster now. "Your Majesty. *Callen.* You cannot
let them do this."

But the king says nothing. *Does* nothing. At Ignatius's signal,
guards haul Marion away. She thrashes and screams, pleading for the
king to intervene. It should probably be satisfying to watch someone
like Marion fall. It isn't. In Marion, I see what can happen to any one
of us. What *will* happen if we make a single false step.

As if drawn by my thoughts, the High Priest's attention swivels to
me. His amber eyes gleam in the light of the candles.

"Mistress Ayleth." He lifts the comb in salute. "We are yet again
grateful for your service to the Light."

Chapter Thirty-Eight

Following Marion's arrest, the entire court is sequestered in their rooms to await questioning.

Joan is the first of us to be summoned. A guard arrives shortly after breakfast the next morning to escort her to the High Priest's chambers. She returns white-faced and jittery and only shakes her head at our questions.

"Just tell them the truth" is all we pry out of her before she retreats behind her bed curtains.

The *truth* will get Jacquetta and me burned.

I find myself watching the other witch almost as much as I watch the door. Though neither of us has directly said as much, I sense that the current circumstances have forged a truce between us. Even so, we're not brave—or foolish—enough to attempt to discuss a plan. The hours stretch on like years, our room so quiet that I jump at every set of approaching footsteps and every knock carrying from a neighboring door. Meals are delivered to our room, but we only pick at the food. Desperate for an occupation, I spend most of my time folding and refolding my garments or arranging the pillows on my bed. Jacquetta opens a book but never turns a page. In the oppressive silence, my mind keeps returning to Marion.

In the howling wind of the winter storm, I hear the phantom echo of the courtier's screams. Marion isn't a witch, I'm certain of that much, but where did that runed comb come from? And what did the rune mean? I picture its four crossed lines, with three slanted hatch marks striking through the middle. Given that Mother forced me to memorize every rune in existence, I find it odd that I didn't recognize it. Maybe the rune is ancient enough that it wouldn't be included in our texts. That would place the symbol before the Age of the Covens, though. What magic could have survived from that time? And, more important, what is it doing at the palace?

A knock—more of a pounding—yanks me out of my thoughts. Jacquetta and I share a panicked glance, neither of us daring to move. The other maiden answers the door, revealing a gangly servant waiting on the other side. Not the king's guard, then. Not even someone from Ignatius's household. But my relief is instantly extinguished when he says:

"Mistress Ayleth. Please come with me."

The halls of the White Palace are eerily silent.

Never did I imagine that I would miss the watchful courtiers, clustered together and trading their gossip, or the shuffle of their endless rounds of card games. I would give anything for such normalcy now, with the false goddess's Eyes bearing down on me in the deserted maze of corridors. It's as if we're walking through the belly of a sleeping beast, and I roll my shoulders back, doing my best to appear like I'm not a witch in disguise.

"Through here, Mistress." The servant halts at a set of doors that lead out to the gardens.

I blink at him. "Out there?"

Given Joan's experience, I expected to be escorted to Ignatius's chambers.

The boy offers no explanation, just motions me through.

My pulse kicks up, foreboding tapping at the base of my neck. This isn't right. Then again, if I were in any real danger, I wouldn't be allowed outside the palace walls on my own. Clinging to that logic, I swallow down my fear and step into the afternoon sunlight. The day is cold, and I breathe deeply, hoping the sting of winter air will cool my nerves. It doesn't—especially not when I'm met with a too-familiar pair of gray eyes.

"Mistress Ayleth," the king greets me, his expression inscrutable. The awful force behind my left ribs rouses. "Please, join me. We have much to discuss."

After the fury of the storm, the garden is like a place out of one of Willa's stories. Ice glitters on hedges and trees as the king leads me down the paths. Delicate snowdrop flowers poke their heads through the drifts. Fountains are frozen, and winter-blooming roses climb their trellises, appearing as blotches of blood against the white. My heart races.

"Have you visited the maze yet?" the king asks, guiding us in the direction of a tall structure of hedges.

"No," I reply, doing everything in my power to ignore the insistent nudge of the force behind my left ribs. A crow calls, deepening the chill of the day.

"It's my favorite part of the whole of the palace."

Which means it definitely won't be mine. Twin sculpted maidens flank the entrance, their arms outstretched, gleaming red apples clutched in their palms. Their faces are veiled, but I swear that they're looking at me. Perhaps even warning me away.

"I detested the place as a boy," the king goes on, oblivious to my discomfort. "My brothers were constantly challenging me to races to the center. They considered it highly amusing to leave me dizzy amid the twists and turns."

As if to illustrate his story, the king steers us left and then immediately right. Hedges tower above us.

"When I complained about their cruelty, my father, King Reginald, was entirely unsympathetic. If I wanted my brothers to stop, he said, it was up to me to *make* them stop."

The king veers right again. Then left. I attempt to keep track of the turns, but the paths are identical. And far too narrow, closing in like the bars of a cage.

"Eventually, I took my father's advice to heart," the king continues. "Each day before my brothers woke, I snuck out here and memorized every detail, every fork and corner, until the paths of this maze became as familiar to me as the palace halls. Soon enough, my brothers were the ones lost in the hedges."

He deals me a grin, and that place behind my left ribs thrums.

Ignore it, I tell myself, anxiety knotting in my chest. *Don't let it get stronger.*

But I am losing that battle. I feel the sinister force winding between my bones, reaching for the king. Pulling me closer.

"When I was older, I learned that my father's lesson applied to far more than petty childhood squabbles," the king explains. "Court itself is like a maze. One must always be on guard. Always one step ahead, lest you find yourself lost in someone else's trap."

Something snags on my sleeve and I flinch, imagining the Nevenwolf's claw. But it's just an untrimmed hedge branch hooked on the fabric of my gown.

"Allow me." King Callen dislodges the branch, his touch lingering on my arm. That pull between us tightens. "You see how easy it is to become ensnared."

I do—far more than he knows.

The king resumes our walk. He turns the next corner, then gestures to an archway. "After you."

I cross through into a wide, circular area—the center of the maze. Statues are set into the curved hedge walls—former kings posed with horses and swords, their marble limbs glazed with frost. But it's the massive fountain that captures my attention. A life-size apple tree is carved from opalescent stone and a man whom I assume to be Braxos is seated underneath it. He wears clothing fit for royalty and a ruby-crowned apple gleams in his hand. The water at the base of the fountain is frozen over, so smooth that it acts as a mirror. But in the reflection, Braxos doesn't appear as a king. He's dressed in peasant clothes. The apple in his hand is ordinary, so lifelike that he might have just plucked it from a tree.

"Magnificent, isn't it?" King Callen says beside me. "It's Dwarvian. A gift from the Guilds to celebrate Braxos's coronation."

If only the Guilds knew then how the White Kings would repay them for their gift.

"The first time I saw this fountain," the king goes on, circling the base, "I asked my father why there were *two* kings. There aren't, he explained. Not two *kings*, anyway, but two *lives*. The piece represents the alternate paths Braxos's life might have taken. In the first, an apple farmer—a peasant. No one. In the second, a king. Leader of the realm. But we cannot walk two paths, can we? Only one."

Something in his words touches a nerve. What does he mean by any of this? Why has he brought me here?

"I spent a great deal of time learning about Braxos." The king studies his ancestor. "There's not much recorded about his early life, but most records claim he harbored no ambition for greatness. He only entered the contest for the crown because his father begged him to participate. By all accounts, Braxos should have been killed immediately."

Would that he had been—that the line of White had never led to this monster.

"I have a theory, though. I believe that Braxos won his crown *because* he didn't want it. Meira saw his lack of ambition, that Braxos was untouched by the corruption and greed of the world, and she *chose* him." Snow crunches under the king's boots as he crosses back to me. "And I believe our goddess has sent you here, to me, for the same reasons."

The force inside me shivers. "I'm not—"

"I know your secret, Ayleth."

Every muscle in my body goes still. He *cannot* know. I'd be in irons if he did. My mind scrambles for a plan, but we are painfully alone in this maze. Those gray eyes bore into my very soul. In the winter day, they carry a blue tint, like the tempered steel of a blade.

The king extracts something from inside his doublet—the fletching of an arrow. Sunlight shines gold on the trimmed feathers. But there's something smeared over it, black and tarlike.

"This was found inside the remains of the Nevenwolf," the king tells me. "Near its head."

Its *head*. Its *eye*. Comprehension jolts up my spine. The arrow I'd used when I faced down the beast—it had been the *king's*. The one he slipped into my quiver. What a wretched fool I am. Alarm bells clang inside my skull.

"At first, I assumed someone shot the beast after it was dead," the king goes on, spinning the broken arrow between two fingers. "But that's not what happened, is it?"

"I don't know what happened."

"Yes, you do." The king points the arrow at me. "You slayed the Nevenwolf with *my* arrow. And I know how you did it."

He's going to name me a witch. I am going to die. All I can think about is Stonehaven and my sisters. *Jacquetta.* I won't even get the chance to warn her. She needs to—

"*Light,*" the king says.

My racing thoughts screech to a halt. "What?"

"Our goddess drove this arrow, my arrow, into the Nevenwolf with *your* hand," the king says. "She was sending me a message about you—your worthiness. A message about the beast as well. Because it wasn't just a creature. It was Malum itself, lurking right under my very nose."

At the word *Malum,* that invisible tether yanks, as if recognizing its own name.

"In all these years, I forgot my father's lessons." The king steps even nearer. "I let myself become lost in the hedges again, blinded by Darkness. But I'm not lost anymore. *You* saved me. And I will root the remaining Malum out—become the true King of the Light, better even than my father. And you, Ayleth, are going to help me do it."

I'd rather be sent to the pyre. "I cannot."

King Callen merely smiles. "That's what I believed about myself—a third son, never meant to be king. When the throne opened for me, I resisted. But Meira had other plans in store—the same as she does for you."

This is madness. But what do I do? What can I say?

"You were guided to this court for a reason," the king says. "You saved the High Priest's life. You discovered Marion's treachery. You killed the Nevenwolf."

The crow calls again, and it sounds like the courtier's screams. I step back, edging for the exit. The king follows, like we're repeating the sinister dance from the banquet.

"You are running from me." His scent of leather and smoke wraps around me, reeling the tether tighter. "The same as you did on the night of the banquet. You ran from His Illuminance as well, when he requested your help."

They're talking about me. *Watching* me.

"I understand, Ayleth. You're afraid of what Meira wants, like I was. Even Braxos himself was afraid. But we cannot walk two paths at once." He indicates the statue. "We cannot be both an apple farmer and a king. We must choose."

The king reaches for me. His hand cups the side of my face, his thumb grazing the line of my jaw and traveling down the tender column of my throat. The invisible tether *sings.* I cannot breathe—cannot *think*—except about where his skin touches mine.

"Choose me, Ayleth," he says in that oil-smooth voice. "All I ask is for your complete loyalty. Give me that, and I will make the world spin around you."

His thumb settles at the soft place between my collarbones, his fingertips gripping the back of my neck, shortening that ominous connection between us. I know better than to trust him. And yet . . . some part of me is drawn in, like a moth to a flame. The king *is* fire, alluring and sinister. And even though I know I will be burned, I cannot deny that somewhere inside me there is an impulse to reach out and touch the flame.

But is it the king I'm drawn to, or Malum itself?

The invisible tether pulses. It would be so easy to give in to it. I doubt it would even hurt, being dragged beyond the Veil. What if I just . . .

It must be undone. Rhea's words slam into me with a gust of wind, cold enough to snap me out of my spell-like trance.

Pain throbs at my throat where the king's thumb digs into my flesh. In the hungry gray of his eyes, I see the truth—he doesn't want loyalty. He wants to own me. *Devour* me—a Nevenwolf in human form. But I won't give myself away.

"Let go of me!" I wrestle myself out of his grasp.

The connection between us instantly slackens, allowing me to draw a real breath. King Callen's eyes flash, but not in anger. In fact, I think he might be *amused*. My blood runs hotter.

"Rare prizes are never easily won." The king leans in, so that his next words graze the shell of my ear. "But I *will* win, Ayleth. I always do."

And then he walks off, snow crunching under his boots as light flakes begin to fall. Alone, I sink to my knees. The wet chill of the ground seeps through my skirts. My uneven breaths frost in the air, hot tears of frustration and rage stinging my eyes. I hate the king—hate this malevolent force that calls him to me.

I'm close enough to the edge of the fountain that I can glimpse my face within its mirrored surface, reflection cloudy and distorted. What is it about me that lured Malum? What told it that it could settle between my bones? As if in answer, a crow calls. The reflection in the ice *changes*. My dark eyes glitter. Lips curl into a vicious smile. What is happening to me? This isn't who I am.

But it will be, that voice whispers.

No—not if I can help it. Letting out a feral cry, I pound at the image with my fists. The ice cracks, breaking my skin with it, my own blood smearing over the fractured surface. I don't care. I keep pounding and pounding until my arms are spent and shaking and I have nothing left inside me at all.

Chapter Thirty-Nine

WITHOUT THE KING TO GUIDE ME, IT TAKES AT LEAST AN HOUR to navigate out of the hedge maze. By the time I return to our room, I can't stop shivering. My uniform is disheveled and my hands covered in dried blood from where I'd attacked the fountain. It requires every ounce of my persuasive skill to prevent Joan from summoning a physician. Jacquetta, however, is another matter. Regardless of what's between us, I need to warn her about the king. After today, it's clear that he's not going to leave me alone. I don't know what he'll do next. She needs to be ready to run. I slip her a note when the others aren't paying attention. We wait until the room is quiet that night and then sneak out onto the balcony.

"He *touched* you?" Jacquetta all but growls.

My hand goes to the soft place between my collarbones, where the king's thumb bruised my flesh. "It's better than arresting me."

"No, it isn't." Her blue eyes snap to mine, glinting in a way that is both terrifying—and thrilling. "How dare he think he can . . ."

The rest falls away and she faces the garden, her breath clouding in short puffs. I can almost feel the heat of her rage rolling from her

HEATHER WALTER

skin. I've seen Jacquetta angry before, but there's something different about this. Like she . . .

She'd react this way if it had been any witch, that voice supplies.

"It's over now," I say. "But it won't be for long. He's going to send for me again."

"Then you have to leave," Jacquetta says. "As soon as possible."

As tempting as the idea might be, I can't. "He'll follow. He might even go to Stonehaven."

My relationship with Mother is complicated, but I can't serve the coven up to the Hunt.

"What then? You just stay here and wait for him to realize what you are?"

It will be sooner rather than later. A crow calls nearby. I shiver.

"I came for the Bloodstones." I clench my fists against the anchor of Rhea's marks. "I'm not leaving without them. But I'm telling you so that you can go—before it's too late."

Jacquetta mutters something under her breath and runs a hand through her hair.

"This is madness," she says, exasperated. "You saw what happened with Marion. If someone like her is accused, what hope do you think you have?"

She has a point. And Marion isn't even a witch. Again, the mystery of the runed comb needles at me. Where had it come from? "Do you think it was another witch who framed her?"

Jacquetta just looks at me. "I don't know. And I don't see how it matters."

"It might." I start to pace, fumbling with the details. "Someone planted that comb. Someone who knew enough about our craft to draw the rune."

Her brow furrows. "What does the rune have to do with anything?"

"Because if they know about our runes, they might know about the Bloodstones."

Jacquetta absorbs this, her eyes widening. "By the Spirits—you're right."

"And that's not all. Perhaps the comb itself was a distraction. I told you about the person I saw running away with the box at the banquet." A box I'm more certain than ever contained the real Bloodstones. "What if that person was the witch, or someone working with her?"

Jacquetta tugs at the sleeve of her nightdress. "But why target Marion? And, if there *is* another witch at the palace, why waste time with all this nonsense when she could simply poison the king?"

I'm not sure, but a thought begins to form in my mind, vague at first, then sharper. Marion didn't climb as high as she did in this court without cunning, and such social acumen includes being *extremely* observant.

"Marion might have an idea."

"She didn't name anyone at the banquet."

"Maybe she didn't know at the time," I reason. "But she's had plenty of opportunity to think since then."

Jacquetta weighs this, frowning. "Even so, we can't just waltz into the dungeon, or wherever they've locked her up, and ask."

We? The word is like a tiny spark in my chest. "I didn't think there was a *we* after . . ."

The memory of our argument crackles between us.

"As I said before," Jacquetta starts, still fidgeting with her sleeve, "two of us are better than one—especially after what happened with the king today."

Her eyes flash again, and that same thrill runs through me.

It doesn't mean anything, that voice whispers.

"And the Bloodstones?" I ask, raising an eyebrow. "Or *magical rocks,* as you prefer to call them?"

Jacquetta shrugs. "I'm not going to change my mind about them. But I would like to know what's going on here."

Because that's all this is—an investigation. I draw myself up, smothering the ridiculous notion that her willingness to work together has anything to do with me.

"Then we stick to our deal," I say, matter-of-fact. "We finish this, then go our separate ways."

Jacquetta looks at me a long time. Moonlight slides over her olive skin, luminous, and I curse myself for the way my heart beats harder.

"That's right," she says softly. "We stick to our deal. Nothing more."

Another moment passes, a thousand unspoken words swirling in the silence. But what good are they? There's nothing to say.

"What about Marion?" Jacquetta asks, changing the subject. "There's no way to get to her without raising suspicion. Not unless you know of a way to walk through walls."

Through walls. The answer hits me: Roland's ring. He could take us through the tunnels. Then again, if Roland wouldn't help me get into the archives, I doubt he'd make an exception for the dungeon. And calling him means telling Jacquetta about the Dwarf—Roland definitely isn't going to appreciate *that.* But I'll have to figure it out.

"I might know someone who can help."

For all my concern, Jacquetta is surprisingly receptive to meeting Roland. Like me, she'd assumed that—whether the king killed them or they left on their own—the Dwarves were gone from Riven. She's appalled when I explain what really happened—the Guild Marks and the bounty on any Dwarf who escapes. Again, I'm struck by how different Jacquetta is from the witches at Stonehaven. Mother never would have trusted a Dwarf, regardless of the circumstances. I'm not even certain that Eden or Willa would have done so. I spent my whole life with those witches, but I'm starting to wonder if I ever really knew them. It feels like losing them all over again, and fresh cracks carve up my heart.

"You're sure he'll take us?" Jacquetta asks, bringing me back onto the balcony. "And what about Marion? Even if she isn't guarded, she might tell someone we came."

Valid points, but I can't let myself dwell on them. This is the only lead we have. "We'll have to take the risk. As for Roland . . . just let me do the talking."

Not that I've been very good at that. But I slip the ring onto my finger and turn it. A few moments later, the nearest wall rattles, then an outline of a door appears.

Jacquetta gasps. "By the Spirits!"

I motion for her to keep quiet.

"Really, Mistress Witch," Roland grouses as he emerges from the shadows. "It's the middle of the night. What could be so—"

He stops short when he notices Jacquetta. "What's she doing here? And if this is about the archives—"

"It's not," I tell him. "We already found the Dwarvian records, but the pages about the Bloodstones had been ripped out."

Roland tilts his head at me. "If the pages were ripped out, how do you know what was written on them?"

Damn everything. "I just do. It's . . . a witch thing."

Jacquetta casts me a dubious look. But I glare at her and she nods. "Yes. I felt it as well."

Thank the Spirits for that.

Roland crosses his arms. "Even if they are missing, what am I supposed to do about it?"

"You must have heard of the arrest."

"Aye." He nods. "Surprised it wasn't you, honestly. Went to the dungeons to check, but it's some noblewoman."

Leaves rustle in the garden.

"You've seen her, then?" I press. "Could you take us?"

"Take yourselves down there." Roland waves me off. "I already told you—"

"I know," I say. "But you can guess how it will look if we visit her. They might suspect us. We're lucky they haven't already."

He points at me. "And *I'm* lucky to have my head on my shoulders after meeting you."

A crow calls in the night. I can't blame Roland for his surliness. I'd probably feel the same if the situation were reversed. But if he doesn't help us . . .

"Ayleth explained what really happened with the Guilds," Jacquetta attempts. "I'm sorry. The king has no right to treat you like property."

Roland jerks his chin at her. "Aye? And what are you going to do about it?"

"There's nothing I can do," she says simply. "But there *is* something strange happening here at the palace. I think you sense it too. I'd like to know what it is. If we can find out, maybe we can also find a way to help the Guilds."

I blink at her. She's good at this.

Roland rubs his chin, considering. "What does the dungeon woman have to do with it?"

"She was framed," I explain. "With a *runed* comb."

That gets his attention. "Runed? You think it was one of your kind?"

"That's what we're trying to find out. Marion might know who framed her—and that person might lead us to the Bloodstones."

He frowns. "That's a lot of *mights*, Mistress Witch."

An owl hoots in the distance.

"It's the only plan we have. And we're running out of time."

Roland hesitates a moment longer.

"You witches," he grumbles. "It's a wonder the covens lasted as long as they did. Fine. But if you get yourselves caught, you're on your own."

Relief swoops through my belly. At least something went right today.

"Is he always this friendly?" Jacquetta asks under her breath as Roland yanks his ring of keys from his belt and summons another door.

I nod. "You get used to it."

"Somehow, I doubt that."

"This is incredible," Jacquetta says as Roland guides us through the dark of his tunnels. "How do these passages work?"

"Oh, I'm carving them myself as we walk," Roland answers dryly. "Can't you see my pickaxe? It's *magic*. Surely you've heard of it."

Jacquetta looks to me, beleaguered. I just shrug, happy to have someone else bear witness to Roland's prickly temperament.

"But why is *your* magic working and ours isn't?" Jacquetta continues.

Shit.

Roland slows, lantern light swinging in the dark. "What do you mean yours isn't?"

"It hasn't since we got here. Didn't Ayleth tell you?"

The expression Roland deals me could melt stone. "No. You did *not* tell me that bit, Mistress Witch. Descendant of Millicent."

Nor did I tell him that I don't have power at all. "Sorry."

"Sorry?" he echoes. "How are you going to fix the Veil, *change things*, without magic?"

"I'll take the Bloodstones back to—wait . . . Jacquetta is right. Why *does* your power work when hers—ours—doesn't?"

"How am I to know?" Roland snaps back. "You two are the witches, not that it shows. Dwarvian magic comes from the Mines."

And not from the Spirits, that's right. And I feel foolish for forgetting that. For assuming, yet again, that our power is the only kind of magic in the world.

"Maybe that's what it is," Jacquetta guesses. "The thinning of the Veil affects us more because we're witches."

"Soon enough, it will be affecting us all," Roland mutters.

The darkness around us seems to thicken. In the distance, I swear that I can hear the click of claws against stone. That place behind my left ribs shivers.

"No, it won't," I tell Roland, banishing the feeling. "We'll mend the Veil. It will be even stronger than before."

Roland grunts. "Road to ruin is paved with promises."

Jacquetta suppresses what I suspect is a smirk. I ignore them both.

"All right, here we are—the *dungeon*." Roland stops, detaches the ring of keys from his belt, and conjures another door. "I'll wait here but be quick. And if you do get caught, scream loudly, so that I know to leave."

Of all the Dwarves in Riven . . .

"You have my word," I tell Roland, giving him a swift pinch as we step out of the tunnel.

CHAPTER FORTY

THE COLD IS DIFFERENT BELOW THE PALACE, SATURATED WITH damp and rot. Water drips in the distance and the stones are slick beneath my feet. The torchlight casts ghoulish shadows in the corners, resurrecting the memory of the presence that followed me in the crypt—the Nevenwolf. I keep my focus trained on the rows of cells. Cells, I realize, that are strangely empty.

"Does the White King not keep prisoners?" Jacquetta asks quietly.

I shake my head. "At least we don't have to worry about anyone seeing us."

"Yes, but where is *Marion*?"

A faint rustling noise echoes in the silence. I jerk my chin in its direction. It doesn't take long to locate Marion. It's odd, though. Not only does the former courtier appear to be the sole prisoner housed in this area but there aren't even any guards stationed nearby to watch her. Why?

"Who's there?" Marion calls out.

The disgraced countess is huddled in the far corner of her narrow cell. It's painfully sparse—no bench or pot or even a pile of straw.

Such surroundings are a far cry from the lavish apartments the courtier enjoyed mere days ago. Again, the speed with which the White Court turned on her is dizzying.

"It's Ayleth." I step into the light of the torches flanking her cell. "And Jacquetta."

Marion emerges from the gloom like a wraith. The sight of her halts my breath. Her dark, lustrous hair is matted. Dirt smears over her light-brown skin. Her clothes are ripped and ragged. She grips the bars of her cell, knuckles white. And it's then that I know Marion is *never* leaving this place. If there's a trial, it will be a farce. They will burn her.

"Have you brought anything?" Her desperate gaze flits between us. "Food?"

"No." Though I should have thought of it. "I'm sorry."

Her cracked lips twist into a sneer. "Come to gawp at me, have you? See how far the *countess* has fallen?"

"No. We—"

Marion barks a gravelly laugh. "Please. You expect me to believe you came here out of the goodness of your hearts? Did *he* send you?"

I press closer to her cell. "Who?"

"You know who." Marion leers at me. "Do you consider me a fool? I've known what's been going on since the pageant. Even then, I could see him choosing you—his newest *pet.*"

She means the king, then. "Marion, you're wrong. I don't want him to—"

"Do you think that matters?" She laughs again. "You think *I* wanted him? I saw the way he treated the queen and the other women before me."

My brow furrows. Marion seemed to revel in her life as the king's mistress. "Then why did you stay with him?"

The thin fabric of her shift slips down her arm. "He doesn't take *no* for an answer. You'll learn that soon enough. His pursuit is constant. Exhausting. Eventually, I . . ."

She trails away, sounding so tired. So *sad.* A new side of Marion comes into focus beneath the torchlight. Yes, she was cruel and petty, cunning as a fox. But foxes have good reason to be cunning, don't they? The White Court is filled with wolves, and I imagine that Marion was always being chased. It doesn't excuse what she did, or how she treated others, but I do wonder what kind of person the courtier might have been under different circumstances.

"Marion." Jacquetta steps nearer to the cell. "We're here about the comb. Did you—"

"I'm not a *witch*," she snaps. "Is that why they sent you here? Two Order girls come on behalf of the goddess to pry out a confession?"

Torches flicker in the draft.

"We don't think you're a witch," I assure her. "But do you have any clue as to who put that comb in your hair, or where it might have come from?"

Marion studies me, her dark eyes depthless. For a heartbeat, I think she might actually name someone. But then—

"Why are you here, Ayleth?" She tilts her head at me. "Is it because you're afraid of winding up like me? You should be afraid. I thought I could hold the king—or at least make a comfortable life for myself. Look where it got me."

Marion steps back and throws out her arms, as if twirling in the Great Hall. She smiles at me and her dry lips crack. Blood shines scarlet in the dimness.

"Marion, please," I attempt. "I'm not here to—"

"Oh yes, you are," she says, cutting me off. "You want to know what fatal mistake I made, in order to avoid it yourself. Well, here it is: I gave him *everything*."

A chill tingles down my spine.

"Callen uses people up," Marion goes on. "He *consumes* us, like we're dishes at a feast. And then, when he's sucked the marrow from your bones, he tosses you away. He puts you somewhere so that no one—especially not him—can witness the damage he's wrought. As soon as I said yes, I was doomed."

A memory from the hedge maze rises up—the king's hand around my throat.

Choose me, Ayleth, he'd said. Even I had known the price.

"Just tell us who might have planted the comb," Jacquetta says.

"Were you not listening to me? *He* did this. They *all* did. Every single member of that wretched court." She points at me. "And they will do the same to you. Because the higher you rise, the further you have to fall. And no one will catch you. They *revel* in the crunch of bone."

The darkness thickens. My pulse races. I need a name. A clue.

"Please," I beg. "The comb, Marion."

"Poor little Ayleth. Do you want to know who did this to me? The reason for my fall?" Marion's hand slips through the bars of her cell, fingertips brushing my cheek. I flinch. "Look in the *mirror.*"

She sneers, blood staining her teeth. Another draft winds around us, far colder than it was a moment ago. Every hair on my body rises.

No, I think. *Not again.*

Beneath the dripping of water, I hear the tap of claws against stone. That place behind my left ribs shudders.

"We need to go," Jacquetta tugs at me. "Now."

I don't need to be told twice. Forgetting Marion and the comb, I sprint after Jacquetta, my feet slapping against the grimy floor.

"Run, Ayleth!" Marion calls behind me. "*Run!*"

Her cackling laughter follows us until she disappears into the dark.

By the time Roland guides us back to our chamber, it's six bells. Neither of us can think of sleep, though. We huddle together on my bed, the curtains drawn. In the dimness, I can still picture Marion's eyes. The pop of embers in the fire is too much like the click of claws.

"Why did it come back?" Jacquetta asks. "And why there?"

Because of you, that voice slithers through my mind.

It's right. Whatever creature lurks beyond the Veil, it's looking for me. Hunting me. Jacquetta should leave while she still can. But I'm too much of a coward to tell her that.

"I don't know," I lie. "What about Marion? Do you think she knew who framed her?"

"It doesn't make sense for her to keep it back," Jacquetta reasons. "And it didn't seem like she was aware of much anyway. Seeing her like that . . . the way she spoke of the king and the court . . . the woman deserves a lot of things, but even that fate was cruel."

"Says the witch who tried to murder the High Priest and the king," I point out.

She hugs a pillow to her chest. "That was different."

"Or maybe it's like I said before—you're not a murderer."

Another ember pops in the hearth. Jacquetta picks at the fringe on her pillow. Whether it's the low light, or the strain of the last few days, she appears younger. More like the witch I knew in the forest, or the one I saw on the balcony, screaming into her hands. Perhaps Marion isn't the only one at court who's hiding her true self.

"Jacquetta," I say, shifting on the bed. "I've meant to tell you . . . I had no right to listen in on your raven or the . . . scrying."

Shame scalds the back of my neck as I recall how I'd rubbed the other witch's rejection in Jacquetta's face. It's something Mother would have done.

"And I'm sorry things ended between you and whoever it was," I add, shoving down the splinter of jealousy that twinges in my chest.

Jacquetta is quiet for a few moments.

"We never would have lasted long," she admits, a touch of bitterness in the words. And then, "For what it's worth, I probably would have listened in on *your* raven, too."

She smirks at me and I toss a pillow at her.

"I'm sorry, as well," she says, sobering. "I should never have spoken of Rhea that way and I . . ."

The seconds drag out. Will she tell me she didn't mean what she said? That she *wasn't* relieved to have walked away? My feckless heart beats harder.

"I said things I shouldn't have," Jacquetta finishes at last.

My stomach sinks. Things she *shouldn't have said*—not things she *didn't mean*.

"It's over now." I draw the blanket closer, pretending it doesn't matter. "We need to think about our next step. Marion was our only lead."

And they're probably going to kill her. They'll kill us next, if we're not careful.

Wind moans down the chimney. The shadows of the room seem to thicken.

"Ayleth." Jacquetta reaches over, her hand stopping just short of touching mine. "What Marion said about the king and how he uses people . . . no matter what happens, I'm not going to let him do the same to you. I promise you that."

I'm suddenly very aware of how close we are on the bed. The smell of juniper fills the small space. It might be my imagination, but Jacquetta's gaze flicks down to my lips. Her pulse beats in the hollow between her collarbones, a cadence that matches mine.

"We should try to get some sleep," she says abruptly.

And then she vanishes through the slit in the curtains—leaving me tangled in the dangerous webs of my own thoughts.

CHAPTER FORTY-ONE

COURT, OR SOME SEMBLANCE OF IT, RESUMES LATER THAT DAY. Marion's arrest hangs like a cloud over the palace. Tension hums in the halls, the air of suspicion thick enough to cut. Guards are stationed at seemingly every corner, the High Priest's inquest evidently far from over.

"Just when I thought this place couldn't get any worse," Jacquetta mutters.

Judging from the lines around her eyes and mouth, I doubt she was able to get any sleep after she'd left me. I certainly hadn't managed it, and not just because of what's happening with Marion. Whenever I started to drift off, all I could see was the blue of Jacquetta's gaze when she promised to protect me against the king.

She breaks promises, that voice insists.

There was something different about this one, though. Just like there was something different when Jacquetta learned what had happened with the king in the hedge maze. Sparks jolt through my blood at the memory—the ferocity of her expression—but I shake them away.

"What on—"

Jacquetta stops short as soon as we enter the queen's suite. It takes me a moment to understand what has her so confused, but then I see it. The walls, which were previously filled with tapestries and portraits of the warrior queens, are bare. Their absence darkens the chamber. Makes it colder, like the dungeon. Foreboding taps at the base of my skull.

"What happened?" Jacquetta asks, staring at the paneled wood.

I have a guess. The king's presence slinks along the empty walls like a poisonous weed choking a garden. "It was—"

"It was time for a change," a voice interrupts.

The queen emerges from a door on the other side of the room. At first glance, she appears as regal and elegant as ever. But as she approaches, I notice faint circles ringing her lower eyelids. Her white skin is paler than it should be. This is more than the strain of the ongoing investigation.

"Would you grant me a moment alone with Ayleth?" the queen asks Jacquetta.

Jacquetta glances at me, questioning, and I nod. She bobs a swift curtsy and veers off toward the main chamber.

Queen Sybil drifts to the walls, tracing the barely perceptible outlines on the paneling where the tapestries and portrait frames used to hang. "I brought those pieces with me when I married the king. I hoped they would inspire me to become the sort of ruler this realm needed."

She is that queen, though. Her armor is simply invisible. And even though she is a mortal and I'm a witch, it pains me to see her so distraught. I know how it feels to be erased. Removed.

"I'm so sorry" is all I can think to say. It's nowhere near enough.

"So am I."

From her tone, I'm not certain if the queen means that she's sorry about the portraits, or the simple fact that she married the king. Both, probably.

"But don't waste your pity on me," the queen says. "I've lived at court since I was younger than you are now. Long enough to understand the workings of this palace. I'm much more concerned for my daughter."

"Is the princess in danger?"

The queen's slender fingers curl away from the ghosts of the portraits. "Everyone is in danger here, Ayleth. Surely you're aware of that by now."

A draft snakes down the hallway, carrying the phantom echo of Marion's screams. Regardless of how much I despised the former courtier, I still feel sorry for her. Sorrier for the queen and every other woman in this treacherous court.

"Do you know what will happen to her?" I ask quietly.

The queen doesn't ask who I mean. "There won't be a trial. She's to be sent away."

For her part, Queen Sybil doesn't appear particularly sympathetic to Marion's plight. It's no surprise, given their history. But the queen doesn't strike me as vindictive either. She's more ... resigned. As though she expected something like this would happen.

"And the former countess's departure is the reason I needed to speak with you." The queen folds her hands over her bodice, and I notice now that the fabric is embroidered with tiny renderings of Meira's Eye. I've never known the queen to wear the symbol of the false goddess. "Marion's rooms are now vacant. They will soon be reassigned to someone else within my household."

What does this have to do with me? "I don't understand."

"You're a clever woman, Ayleth. Think."

The queen's dark gaze locks with mine. In its depth, an answer forms. Slowly, like a beast rising from the deep.

"You mean ... *me?*" I whisper, praying to every Spirit that I'm wrong.

Queen Sybil nods and it seems that the barren walls edge inward.

"Your belongings are being relocated as we speak," she says. "Officially, the rooms are a gift from me—in gratitude for your service, both yours and Jacquetta's. But as I said, you're a clever woman. You can probably guess who wants you there."

Dread pools in my belly. My mind flashes back to the hedge maze—the king's hand at my throat—and that soft spot between my collarbones throbs. This is his doing. He wants me caged, like one of the pets in the princess's menagerie. He wants to possess me. *Own* me.

"No." I shake my head. "I don't want new rooms. Please, let me remain where I am."

Queen Sybil smiles sadly. "I'm afraid my influence has waned somewhat of late."

My gaze flits to her gown again, at the countless embroidered Eyes. The queen is being caged as well, I realize. Forced to conform.

"Your Majesty, I can't—"

She reaches out, cupping the side of my face in the palm of her hand, a gesture so like what Mother used to do when I was a witchling that my chest aches.

"You will learn, as I did—to be smarter. Harder. To use the resources at your disposal."

"I won't," I insist. "I'm not like you. I don't belong here."

Because I'm a witch. Soon they'll all know. And then I will burn. I'll never see Rhea again. I dig my fingernails into my palms, into our marks, wishing I could reach my sister.

The queen tilts my face to meet her gaze. "And yet you *are* here, Ayleth. And you will find your way. All you have to do is trust this."

She places a gentle fingertip on my chest, directly above my heart.

That, the voice in my mind whispers, *is the last thing you should trust.*

"And I will tell you something more—a lesson it took me years to learn." The queen's attention travels back to the empty walls. "If you ever find yourself with the opportunity to strike, do so. But do *not* miss."

Jacquetta is as horrified as I am to learn of the change in our placement. By some stroke of luck, no one else seems informed, not even Joan. We take advantage of their ignorance, slipping away from the queens' rooms early in order to enter the suite unnoticed. It will be the *last* time we escape such notice, though. The rest of the court will soon discover what's happened—likely by the end of vespers—which will only increase the attention surrounding us.

For now, Jacquetta and I stand like statues just inside the former countess's rooms. If I listen closely, I can almost hear Marion's laughter drifting from deeper in the chambers. A hint of her oleander perfume lingers, like the ghost of the courtier is still drifting around us.

"We should check everything," Jacquetta determines, giving herself a shake. "Make sure there aren't any obvious places where they could be spying on us."

Together, we scour the chamber, peering behind the tapestries and lifting rugs, hunting for hidden doors or holes drilled in the wall. I feel like a thief—or a grave robber—rooting around like this. Like someone will barge in at any moment and arrest us for trespassing. I half wish that they would, for at least then we wouldn't have to stay here.

Eventually, we wind up in one of the two bedchambers. Marion's. The mountainous bed looms like a beast in the dimness. Shadows flicker in the corners. A shape flutters in my peripheral vision and I whirl, but it's only my own reflection in the long mirror, the same one where Marion tried to murder me with the corset.

Look in the mirror, the courtier's words from the dungeon resurface.

Like a spell, I find myself drawn to the glass.

My face is even thinner than it was before, cheekbones more pronounced—a combination of gnawing anxiety and sleepless nights. My dark eyes are stark against the white of my face. There's an almost frenzied light to them, almost like . . .

Marion's.

Under my horrified gaze, my reflection shimmers, replaced with that of the fallen countess. She wears my clothes, but her expression is wild and desperate. Marion's lips move and a single word reverberates in my mind: *RUN!*

I yelp and leap away from the mirror, pulse thrumming.

"What's wrong?" Jacquetta pauses where she's poking through the massive wardrobe.

The vision of Marion vanishes. *It wasn't real,* I tell myself, forcing down one breath and then another. *I'm hallucinating.*

"Nothing," I tell her. "It's just this place. These rooms. We shouldn't be here."

Wood clicks as Jacquetta closes the wardrobe. "You can still leave."

Some reckless part of me wants to ask her to leave with me, but I remember what happened last time.

Close off your heart, that voice warns.

"No." I smooth my dress. "I have to stay."

A long moment of quiet passes.

"All right," Jacquetta finally allows. "But—"

A low growl interrupts her. Jacquetta and I both jump, but the sound was too small to have come from a Nevenwolf or any other creature lurking beyond the Veil. It starts again and I track it to the front of the bed. I kneel to check underneath and am greeted by the white slash of bared teeth. Fitz.

"Is that . . . the *dog*?" Jacquetta asks, joining me.

He barks in answer.

"I suppose no one thought to put him with someone else."

And terror though he is, the poor thing must be confused and afraid. Marion was arrested days ago. When was the last time he'd eaten? There's a pitcher on a table beside the bed. I pour some water into the basin and cart it back.

"What are you doing?" Jacquetta asks as I slide the basin toward Fitz. "He can't stay."

"Where else is he going to go?"

I click my tongue, attempting to coax him out, but Fitz snaps.

"I told you." Jacquetta jerks her chin at him. "He'll wreck everything, including our clothes, and likely bite your fingers off."

"Maybe," I allow. "But he reminds me of when I first found Nettle."

She'd only been a kitten when I rescued her from the forest, but she'd hissed and clawed at me with everything she had. She wriggled her way out of any enclosure I could design, shredding countless pairs of stockings and shattering entire jugs of cream and wreaking general havoc on all of us.

"Is that supposed to be a character reference?" Jacquetta asks.

I laugh. "He might surprise you."

Nettle did, in the end. It took time and patience, but she became mine. Fitz huffs a bark, as if he can read my thoughts and is letting me know in no uncertain terms that such an outcome will *not* be what develops between us.

"He's your problem, then," Jacquetta determines, retreating into the main chamber. "Don't ask me to help."

"You know," I whisper to the dog, "I suspect that the two of you are going to get along just fine."

He snorts.

CHAPTER FORTY-TWO

NEWS DOES, INDEED, TRAVEL QUICKLY. WHISPERS SWELL LIKE waves as soon as we set foot out of our rooms the following day, worse than they ever were, because Jacquetta and I are no longer simply amusing curiosities. We're Order girls who now inhabit the former chambers of a disgraced countess.

They revel in the crunch of bones.

Marion's words chase me like the call of a crow, haunting and sinister.

The worst part is that, with Marion gone, we've lost any lead on who might have planted her comb—and who might be hiding the Bloodstones. Jacquetta and I spent our first night in our new quarters tossing out potential strategies, each more implausible than the last. For her part, Jacquetta is convinced that whoever planted the comb will strike again. I can't decide if I want her to be right. On the one hand, another incident like Marion's might provide the clues we desperately need. On the other, *we* might be the next targets. Even if we aren't, how many more women will be rolled up and tucked away like the tapestries on the queen's walls? In the end, we decide that it's better for us to lie low for the time being. Watch and listen, until the attention around us settles.

Lying low, however, is easier said than done. Conversation ceases as soon as we arrive in the queen's chambers. Judgmental scowls and barely concealed mutterings land like so many darts against my skin. My nerves jitter.

"Well, if it isn't our *guests.*" A woman peels herself from the rest. I recognize her as being part of Marion's former cadre—one of the few who had been in the room when we were being fitted for our costumes. "Enjoy your chambers while you can, *Mistress.*"

She hisses the last word and heat floods my face, of both embarrassment and frustration. I want nothing to do with the king. Then again, I suppose Marion didn't either.

"Marion was right about you," the woman goes on. "You're a snake. Soon enough, everyone will see the truth."

They will see right through you, that voice in my mind supplies.

"This is intolerable," Jacquetta mutters as the woman returns to her group.

That's an understatement. "Let's just—"

"There you two are." Joan hurries up to us. Even her usual bright composure is dampened. "I suppose I don't have to warn you that everyone is talking."

Someone else passes, dealing us a glare like the edge of a blade. We should have stayed in our rooms.

"Come." Joan steers us to a more secluded corner of the chamber. "Is it true? You've been given Marion's chambers?"

"Unfortunately." I rub at my temples, pressure already building in my skull.

"I'm so sorry." Joan shakes her head. "I wish I could promise that things would get easier but . . ."

They won't. Even now, I sense the others watching me. How does the queen live under such scrutiny every day? I look to where

Queen Sybil is sitting with a few other women at the front of the chamber. It was only yesterday that we spoke, but she appears worse. Her skin is almost sallow, and even her hair has lost some of its luster. The white roses threaded into her braid are bright against its dull sheen.

"Is something wrong with the queen?" I ask Joan.

She checks around us and leans closer. "The king was here not an hour ago. It wasn't a pleasant visit."

"What happened?"

"I'm not sure." Joan gestures at the doors to the queen's bedchamber. "He stormed in and took the queen in there. We couldn't hear what they were saying, but it was clear that he was shouting. The queen came back out afterward, but she hasn't been the same."

Indeed, Queen's Sybil's usual grace and patience are noticeably absent. She stabs at her embroidery, her mouth drawn into a tight line. What had been said between the royal couple? Was it something about us? *Me?*

"I want you to know," Joan says, reaching for the two of us, "I'm here for you. We're outsiders together, don't forget."

After the strain of the last days, such support is a welcome balm. Even Jacquetta might appreciate it. She doesn't pull away from Joan's touch.

"Thank you," I tell her. "And—"

The chamber doors open, cutting me off. I steel myself for the pull of the king's presence, but it doesn't come. Instead, a different man strides into the chamber, black robes rippling like smoke. He has a strong, beaklike nose and dark, piercing eyes, made all the more striking by the paleness of his white skin.

"Who is that?" Jacquetta asks.

"Master Parnell," Joan whispers. "The steward of the High Priest."

Foreboding taps at the base of my skull.

"Can I help you?" the queen asks as the steward bows.

"Indeed, Your Majesty. I'm looking for—" His attention scans the room and I hold my breath. But Master Parnell's obsidian gaze mercifully doesn't fall on me. "Lady Compton. If you would accompany me, please."

It's the woman who had baited us when we first arrived.

The color drains from her face. "I've already spoken with His Illuminance."

"Yes, but I'm afraid there are some additional details we need to clarify. Nothing to worry about, so long as the Light shines in your heart."

He smiles, wolfish, suggesting that Lady Compton has everything to worry about. But she pulls herself together and follows the swell of his black robes, her fear so palpable that it lingers as the doors snick shut behind them.

Deep in my bones, I know it won't be long before we're next.

The following week is the longest of my life.

Master Parnell flits about the palace like a crow in human form, collecting courtiers for his endless rounds of interrogation. By some miracle, Jacquetta and I continue to be spared, but that does nothing to ease our own nerves. We barely sleep and hardly eat. Our plan to watch and listen crumbles around us. *We're* the ones being watched. I've not encountered the king again, but I find myself bracing for his gray eyes every time I turn a corner or hear a set of footsteps approaching.

If the atmosphere at the palace weren't bad enough, the queen's illness takes a sharp turn and she shuts herself in her rooms, banishing all but her closest ladies. With nothing else to do, Jacquetta and I wander the halls, listening in on snippets of conversations in hopes of discovering something about who might have framed Marion, but it's useless.

"Maybe we should go back to the archives," Jacquetta suggests after yet another fruitless afternoon spent lurking in corridors.

"Blodwyn or not, I doubt the Keepers would let us set foot in there, given the circumstances," I point out. "Even if they did, they might tell someone we visited."

She lets out a frustrated breath. "We have to do *something* more than eavesdrop on rounds of Castles."

"What do you suggest—burn the palace down?"

She deals me a pointed look. "That's not a bad—"

The rest falls away as we enter our chamber and find *Nettle* perched on top of a table. Fruit is strewn around her, the wide bowl upended. Fitz is growling at her from beneath a chair, his ears back and hackles raised.

"How did *you* get in here?" I ask my cat, dumbfounded.

In answer, Nettle simply licks her paw. Fitz barks what is an unmistakable complaint.

"Wonderful." Jacquetta crosses her arms. "Now there are two of them."

I should probably be annoyed, but I haven't seen my cat since the last time I visited the princess's chambers. That seems like ages ago now—too long. Nettle hops from the table and lopes toward me.

"Hello you." I bend to scratch between her ears, grateful for her company, even if she did make a mess. She starts to purr. "I'm sorry I haven't visited."

She meows and winds her way over to Jacquetta.

"Stop that," the other witch scolds as my cat rubs against her ankles.

"That means she likes you."

"Yes, well, I've received enough *affection* from this cat to last a lifetime."

A smile twitches at my lips, recalling the incident at the Sanctum when Nettle clawed Jacquetta's linens to ribbons.

"No more of this," I tell Nettle, picking up the pieces of fruit and putting them back into the bowl. "And be nice to the dog."

She trills in what is anything but agreement. Fitz growls.

"Can't you train her to do something useful instead of making trouble?" Jacquetta asks, scooping up an apple. "Like, find the Bloodstones?"

That *would* be a good idea. "Nettle does what she wants, I'm afraid."

She's currently lying on her back in a spot of sunlight, swatting at Fitz for her own amusement.

"I thought familiars were supposed to be obedient."

"She's not bound," I explain.

Jacquetta pauses in gathering several strawberries. "Really?"

I dump the last few pieces of fruit back into the bowl. "I didn't want her to stay with me because she was compelled by magic."

Mathilde's words flow back to me: *Choice is a magic in and of itself.*

Jacquetta looks at me, intent, like she's realizing something. She starts to speak, but a knock at the door interrupts her, followed by the whisper of parchment being slipped through the crack. Fitz trots over to inspect it. Dread winds between my ribs when I see the seal— bright-red wax stamped with a crowned apple. My hands tremble slightly as I pick up the message.

Come to the mews tomorrow morning.
—C

"It's from the king," I say softly. "He's summoned me."

Jacquetta presses her lips together, her gaze carrying that same fire it did when I told her about the hedge maze. "Will you go?"

From her tone, I can tell what she thinks my answer should be. I toss the message into the fireplace, watching the parchment blacken and curl. "I don't see that I have much choice. I told you—I'm not leaving here without the Bloodstones."

A log collapses, sending sparks dancing up the chimney.

"And what's the cost of finding them?" Jacquetta asks sharply, gesturing around the room. "Because at this point, you may not leave at all."

"You know what happens if the Veil crumbles," I say, clinging to that old refrain.

"Is it the Veil?" Jacquetta presses. "Or is it because you're a Second? A descendant of Millicent? Are those stones, is your *position*, worth more than your life?"

It has nothing to do with my position, or even the Veil itself. I dig my fingernails into Rhea's marks.

Tell her, my reckless heart urges.

Foolish as it is, I want to. Want to separate myself from the likes of Sindony and Mother, obsessed with power and lineage. But if I explain why I'm really here . . .

She walked away from you once before, that voice reminds me.

She did. We might have established a truce between us, but that doesn't mean Jacquetta would understand about Rhea or what I have to do. The others at Stonehaven certainly didn't.

I lift my chin, looking Jacquetta squarely in the eyes. "Yes. The Bloodstones are worth more than my life. They're worth more than anything."

A long moment passes, Jacquetta's expression unreadable.

"All right, then," she says at last. "Enjoy your visit with the king."

And then she turns on her heel and disappears into the second bedroom, leaving me with the sinking feeling that I've made a horrible mistake.

CHAPTER FORTY-THREE

BRIGHT MORNING SUNLIGHT BURNS AGAINST MY BLEARY EYES. Sleep, as usual, eluded me. What dreams I managed to snatch were riddled with images of Rhea in the coven fire. Each time I reached for her, she melted at the touch of my hands—like the prince's body in the crypt. The nightmares were so visceral that I spent most of my hours pacing, my traitorous thoughts replaying the incident with Jacquetta.

It wasn't an argument—not like our previous battles, both of us seeking to draw blood. But I can't shake the feeling that I've somehow betrayed her. In fact, when I emerged from my bedchamber this morning, part of me was convinced that Jacquetta had gone. She hadn't, though. She didn't say a word to me at breakfast, either—but she's still here.

It means nothing, that voice insists. *You cannot trust her.*

I'm not as certain of that as I used to be.

The rustle of wings breaks me out of my thoughts as I enter the mews. Cages line the walls, housing various species of falcons and other birds of prey. I've heard of witches keeping similar creatures as familiars, but not like this. Even the binding ritual would be less confining than these bars. One bird, in particular, catches my notice. It's massive, with inky black feathers and onyx eyes. Its long talons grip its perch, and it flares its broad wings as I approach. The bird's restlessness reminds me of Marion in her prison cell. A sudden urge to release the creature overwhelms me and I reach for the latch of the cage. The falcon edges closer, expectant and eager. Perhaps I'll let them all go. The king would be furious.

"Can I help you?"

I drop my hand, guilty. A boy about Blodwyn's age sets down a bucket near the other door. I recognize him as being the stable hand who'd helped me with Honeywine on the day of the ill-fated hunt. His kind eyes, the green of the forest, light up.

"I remember you," he says, wiping his hands. "Mistress . . . Anne?"

"Ayleth," I correct.

"Right. Sorry about that. I'm Doran." He ruffles his unruly chestnut curls. "What brings you to the mews today?"

Nothing good. "I'm here at the king's request."

"Ah." Doran gestures out the side door. "His Majesty has already gone out with Sir Weston. They're in the training yard."

Maybe that means the king forgot about his invitation, and I have an excuse to ignore it. "Then I won't disturb them."

"You won't be. They took three birds. I'm sure they're expecting you."

Excellent. I pull my cloak closer, then trudge in the direction Doran indicates. The training yard is a vast expanse of land, blanketed in snow. As Doran promised, the king and Sir Weston stand in the center, their falcons circling overhead.

The Lord of Misrule spots me first. "Here she is, Callen."

The king turns, his gray eyes tinted silver against the snow, and the place behind my left ribs vibrates. I tamp it down.

"Mistress Ayleth." Snow crunches under the king's boots as he leaves Sir Weston to meet me. "You look well. Your new rooms suit you. Are you enjoying them?"

About as much as one enjoys a poisoned sweet. And though I shouldn't be surprised, I recoil at how easily the king asks me about Marion's old rooms. It's like the courtier, his former *mistress*, doesn't even exist in his mind anymore.

He'll use you up. Marion's words float under the screech of a falcon.

I'm half tempted to tell the king I went to see her. To force him to say Marion's name and acknowledge what he did. But that would only put me in the dungeons.

"The chambers are too much for me," I tell the king, meaning it.

"They are only the beginning," he replies easily. "I promised you the world, did I not? I always keep my promises."

Especially those related to murdering witches.

"Here." King Callen gestures to a servant. "Another gift for you."

A boy approaches, a falcon perched on his arm. It's a stunning creature, its stark white feathers speckled with a brown that glimmers gold in the winter sunlight. Its dark eyes watch me as the servant transfers the bird to the king's gloved hand.

"White falcons are quite rare," he says, clearly expecting me to be impressed. "As soon as I saw her, I knew she should be yours. A falcon fit for Meira herself."

The bird flares her broad wings.

"Let's see how you take to each other." The king nods to the servant, who hands me a pair of gloves. "Put those on."

Reluctantly, I pull the thick leather gloves up to my elbows.

"Hold your arm out like mine," he instructs, moving behind me to guide me into position. That force inside me jolts at his touch. "And keep steady."

The falcon steps onto my forearm, the grip of her talons light yet firm. I watch, cautious, as the bird adjusts herself, proud and silent.

"Now then. Remove the jesses." The king tugs at the cord attached to the bird's golden anklets. "And let her go."

The falcon requires no encouragement. At my slightest movement, she pushes off my arm, screaming as she glides over the field. As I watch the bird soar, I wish I could sprout wings of my own and join her. Leave this place behind forever.

"Glorious, is she not?" the king asks. He bends, close enough that his next words brush my ear. "Just like her mistress."

That unnerving connection between us hums.

Ignore it, I tell myself. *Don't give it any more power than it already has.*

King Callen puts himself in front of me, those gray eyes like twin hooks, pulling me closer. I inhale his scent of leather and smoke and *danger.*

"Have you given any thought to our discussion?"

A memory of the hedge maze rises up, and the pulse at my collarbones beats harder. "I've been occupied with serving the queen."

"And yet my wife's rooms are closed."

I fidget with my glove. Why can't he find some other woman to entertain him? One who actually desires him? Then again, perhaps such a woman doesn't exist.

A light touch lands beneath my chin. The king tilts my face up to meet his. That ominous tether vibrates, Malum straining its tentacles toward him.

"What else must I do to prove myself to you?" he asks softly.

"Nothing," I say, meaning it with every fiber of my being. I want *nothing* from him.

The wind picks up, stirring my skirts. The king brushes a lock of hair out of my face, his fingertips lingering along my jawline.

"Meira speaks to you. She moves through you. I would make this realm kneel at your feet, if you'd let me." He steps even closer, so that I'm almost pressed against his chest. "Give yourself to me, Ayleth, and watch the whole world spin around you."

It's already spinning. Just as in the hedge maze, I consider how easy it would be to surrender to the pull of this sinister force between us. As if in answer, the tether rumbles. But I picture the queen, surrounded by empty walls. Marion in her prison cell, desperate and alone.

As soon as I said yes, I was doomed, the courtier said.

The king's world revolves only around himself. He will break me, and then he will scatter the jagged pieces into the wind, like I never existed.

"Your Majesty!" Hurried footsteps crunch in the snow. The king's attention pivots to where a servant is running up from the direction of the palace. "An urgent message from His Illuminance."

The boy hands the king a folded piece of parchment. Has there been another arrest? But the king scans the writing too quickly and I don't glimpse a single word.

"I must tend to this." The king tucks the parchment into his doublet. "But we'll speak again later—soon."

A threat and a promise rolled into one.

Light snow begins to fall as the king strides away, flakes sticking to my skin. Maybe if I just stand here, it will cover me entirely. I'll just disappear into the quiet of the depthless white.

"Has the king gone?" Sir Weston calls.

So much for disappearing. "He was needed at the palace."

"Such is always the case. You know, I think I'd hate being king. It's impossible to enjoy uninterrupted sport." He points at me. "But *your* game is just beginning, isn't it?"

I pause in pulling off my gloves. "Game?"

He swings a rope with something attached to the end. It must be a lure, for one of the falcons screeches and veers in our direction.

"I've known the king since we were boys." Sir Weston extends his arm for the bird to land. "But he's never become quite so enamored with a lady. Especially not so immediately."

Heat prickles up my neck. "I have no interest in—"

"Is this the same lack of *interest* you expressed at our Castles game?" Sir Weston interrupts, arching an eyebrow. "Sport is more than a hobby for me. And I recognize a fellow player when I spot one."

I'm nothing like this man. "Please, excuse me."

"I would caution you," Sir Weston calls. "Callen is nothing if not stubborn. He nearly burned down the forest once simply to smoke out boar. He'll get what he wants. I suggest you start thinking about what *you* want."

His falcon clacks its beak.

"I don't want anything." Not from the king.

Sir Weston only deals me one of his unnerving grins, a slash of white against the rich brown of his skin. "We all want something. This whole court is a game of Castles, Mistress. It's important to understand the stakes. Though, more often than not, the *real* bets are those you don't see on the table. Marion forgot that, I think."

A crow calls overhead, swiftly joined by others. I glance up to see a flock of them—a murder—converging above us, the pattern shifting and reshaping itself, like lungs breathing.

"How strange," Sir Weston comments, noticing the formation as well.

It's more than strange. If seven crows herald a curse, there must be ten times that number in the sky—all of them drawn to me. That place behind my left ribs trembles. Again, it feels like laughter.

"By the Light." Sir Weston points at a splotch of white, which pierces through the cloud of crows like an arrow, scattering them in all directions. "Is that your falcon? And I think it's got something. Hurry—put your glove back on."

With a shriek, the falcon glides lower. I fumble with my glove and lift my arm. Just before the bird lands, she drops whatever was gripped in her talons. A small body splatters with a wet *thunk* at my feet. Blood stains the snow, crimson against white.

"Look at that. Perhaps you require no warning after all," Sir Weston comments, gesturing at the gruesome entrails. "A kill on your first attempt. A rodent today. Tomorrow, who knows?"

If you ever find yourself with the opportunity to strike, the queen's advice resonates beneath the falcon's shriek. *Do* not *miss.*

That deep urge, the one I'd felt with Marion, shivers to life, hungry and urgent.

Chapter Forty-Four

TWELVE BELLS RING OUT OVER THE PALACE WHEN I RETURN FROM the mews, a single thought drumming in my mind: *Find the Bloodstones.* But between the whispers and glances brushing against me like insect wings, the encounter with the king, and the memory of the bloodied entrails, my rattled nerves won't stop humming.

They see right through you, that unceasing voice plagues me.

I have to get away from the palace, even if only for a few hours. Before I fully realize where I'm going, my feet steer me to the princess's chambers, craving the quiet of her menagerie. Like Mathilde, I'm beginning to suspect that even wolves provide better company than people. Especially *these* people.

"Oh, hello," Blodwyn says at my approach. She's settled near the fountain inside the menagerie, sorting through a deck of cards. "I wasn't expecting you."

"Your mother's rooms are closed again."

The princess frowns but doesn't comment on the queen's illness. "Do you want to play?"

"As long as it's not Castles," I groan, joining her as she shuffles the deck.

"It's not. I don't think we can play Castles with these anyway."

"What do you . . ."

Sunlight filters through the glass ceiling, illuminating the images on the cards—a man impaled by swords. A tower struck by lightning. My breath halts. These cards don't belong to the typical decks I've seen among the courtiers. They're *scrying* cards.

"What are you doing with those?" I demand.

Blodwyn looks at me like I've grown horns. "I told you—playing."

Playing. So these cards are no better than the false Bloodstones tossed out in the city, cheap replicas designed for the mortals' amusement. And here I assumed Blodwyn was different. After everything that's happened over the last days, this is too much. I snatch the cards from the princess's hands.

"Wait! Those are—" she yelps, horrified, as I hurl them into the fountain.

"They're dangerous," I snap. "Do you want to be locked away like Lady Marion? Do you want to be burned?"

Blodwyn shades paler. "They're just cards, aren't they?"

No. They're so much more. I want to tell her that. Want to scream that our relics and instruments aren't novelties meant to entertain the same people who hunt us. But the tremble of Blodwyn's chin dampens my rage. She's just a child. She couldn't possibly understand.

"It's just . . ." I force my tone to soften. "You can't be caught with those, Blodwyn. Even if they aren't real."

Her brow creases. "How do you know they're not real?"

"Everything related to the covens was burned."

Surely, even the princess knows about the Great Cleansing, or whatever Roland called it.

"Maybe." Blodwyn fishes a card from the water. "But these seem quite old. Look."

She hands me the card. It *is* old. Its faded blue back is detailed with intricate designs of roses and thorns and vines of midnight flower, a similar pattern to some of the decks I'd watched the Diviners use at Stonehaven. I flip the card over.

"That's odd." Blodwyn points. "It's the same card I always pull."

The illustration depicts a golden wheel, surrounded by clouds and winged creatures. At the top, above the wheel itself, a sun shines brightly, gold foil glinting in the light. At the bottom, swirls of black suggest the forces of Malum. There's even a creature that might be a Nevenwolf emerging from the darkness. I know this card. It's the Wheel of Fortune. And it's difficult to explain, but I sense that it's *genuine.* Somehow, this deck survived the burning. Or it was brought here—just like Marion's comb. My pulse kicks up.

"Where did you get these?" I ask Blodwyn.

She presses her lips together. "I can't tell you."

"Please." I reach for her. "It might be important."

"Why?" She shakes me off. "So someone else can be burned?"

A warbler sings in the distance.

"Do you really think I would do something like that?"

Blodwyn frowns. A rabbit hops over and she scoops it up. "You promise not to tell?"

I press a hand to my chest. "You have my word."

The princess hesitates a moment longer. But then—

"I found them in Mother's room."

I hurry back to our suite, hardly able to hear the chatter of the halls above the two words looping in my mind: *The queen.*

Fortune—it's like a wheel, is it not? she'd said at the card game. *One never knows when the next turn will occur.*

No wonder she'd made that reference. She'd been hiding a deck of scrying cards. What else has she been hiding?

A dozen other details smash together in my mind. Marion was arrested shortly after that card game. And when the queen informed me about our new rooms, she didn't seem surprised at the courtier's fate. Is that because *she* was the one to frame Marion? Queen Sybil harbored plenty of motive to do so. Marion controlled the king. She was pushing for Blodwyn to leave court. How had I not made these connections sooner? And where had the queen found the comb? Or the cards? She's not a witch, of that much I'm certain. Even with glamour magic, she wouldn't be able to pull off such a disguise for so long and under such scrutiny. Still . . .

I recall the tapestries in Queen Sybil's rooms, women charging into battle. Women like *us,* I'd thought the first time I saw them. And the queen didn't always reside in Riven. She might have been raised to be sympathetic to witches. After all, now that I think of it, I've never once heard the queen speak ill of a witch, or even praise Meira.

The real bets are the ones you don't see on the table, Sir Weston had said.

He was right. The queen might not be a witch herself, but I suspect she knows one. I fling open the door to our chamber. Fitz growls and barks at me from where Nettle has him cornered. I ignore them, hurrying from one room to the next.

"Jacquetta?" I call. "Are you here?"

Steam billows around me as I open the door on the far side of the main chamber. I freeze, instantly registering my mistake. Marion's suite contains a private bathing chamber, a luxury so rare that I'd completely forgotten about it. And it's not empty.

Jacquetta is half-submerged in the water of the copper tub. A mix of shock, horror, and something *else* floods through me at the sight of her, rendering me utterly incapable of doing anything but stare. Jacquetta yelps in surprise and flails, water sloshing over the rim of the tub.

"What are you *doing*?" She snatches up a drying cloth and flings it over herself.

"I'm sorry!" I cry, summoning enough sense to slap my hands over my eyes. "I was looking for you and—"

"For Spirits' sake, get your cat!"

I peek through my fingers to discover that Nettle has entered the room and is currently standing on her back feet at the edge of the tub, pawing at the bubbles.

"*Nettle!*" I rush to scoop her up—and afford myself a much closer view of Jacquetta.

Fresh heat blazes through my veins at how her wet skin glistens in the late-afternoon light. The delicate ledge of her collarbones. The swell of her chest.

"I'm so sorry," I splutter, hardly knowing where to look. "It's just—I went to see Blodwyn and I think the queen has something to do with Marion and—"

"Slow down." Jacquetta shifts in the tub.

Nettle yowls, struggling enough that I release her, shooing her away with my feet.

"Blodwyn had scrying cards," I begin again when my cat is safely out of the room. "Real ones. She says she found them in the queen's rooms."

"The queen?" Jacquetta repeats. "She isn't a witch."

"No," I agree. "But what if she's working with one?"

"It . . . would explain the comb," Jacquetta allows. "But why would she take such a risk? She has so much to lose."

"But perhaps more to lose if she did nothing," I point out. "The queen made no secret of the fact that she wants Blodwyn to rule in her own right. Marion was pushing for Blodwyn to be sent away. You remember what Joan said about her naming the dog Fitz."

Jacquetta frowns, considering. "Even so, why would one of us care enough to help a mortal queen?"

She has a point. With the war waging, a witch would need a very good reason to—

A thought lands in my mind, swift and sudden as a lightning strike.

"The Bloodstones. She might have them."

Jacquetta stares at me. "Do you really think so?"

"The queen would have access to the crypt—and the archives, for that matter," I reason, ticking the items off on my fingers. "She could have been the one to tear the pages out of the Dwarvian records. Maybe she even sent someone to steal the crown at the banquet. With the promise of the Bloodstones, *any* witch would have helped her."

The wheels behind Jacquetta's eyes work. "But all that is coincidental."

"Maybe," I allow. "But I suspect that it's more than just *illness* keeping the queen locked inside her rooms. You remember what Joan said about the argument when the king visited. Perhaps he or the High Priest suspects her involvement. The last time I saw her, the queen was wearing a gown patterned with Meira's Eyes. She'd never done so before. Don't you find that odd?"

Jacquetta hesitates. "If you're right, we don't have time to waste. Let me just—"

She must be so absorbed in the plan that she doesn't think before she pushes herself up out of the water. The soaked cloth clings to her skin, revealing the outline of her body, backlit against the row of windows on the other side of the room. The swell of her breasts. The dip of her waist. The curve of her hip. Every nerve in my body comes alive.

Jacquetta catches me staring and flushes. "Could you—"

She gestures at a pile of drying cloths. My clumsy hands fumble to fetch one, our fingers brushing as I pass it to her. Lightning jolts up my arm. This is not like with the king, revulsion mixed with the sinister pull of Malum. This is warm. Real. *Wanted.*

You do not want her, that voice whispers.

But that is not how I feel as we stand there, staring at each other. A thin line of water trickles down the column of Jacquetta's throat and disappears beneath the cloth. A wild desire wings in my belly. What does that place feel like? The pulse at Jacquetta's throat quickens.

"I'll change," she says, shattering the moment. "Then we'll go."

I give myself a swift shake. "Yes."

And then, before I do something I regret, I walk to the door, ignoring that aching part of myself that wants her to ask me to stay.

CHAPTER FORTY-FIVE

THE QUEEN'S CHAMBERS ARE TOMBLIKE AND SILENT.
Gone is the usual chatter, rustle of skirts, or crackle of the
hearth. The curtains are drawn, throwing the room into a
dimness that makes shadows slide like oil over the furnishings. The
apple boughs sculpted into the ceiling appear like reaching tentacles
and the dull gleam of crystal like the sheen of a hundred eyes. Wind
groans outside, raising the hairs on the back of my neck.

"This feels . . ." Jacquetta starts.

"Wrong," I finish for her. More than simply illness, though I can't
pinpoint what.

A door opens on the other side of the chamber, flooding us in
light.

"What are you two doing here?"

Limned in the glow from the other room, Duchess Poole appears
more shadow than woman, like she's crossed through the Veil itself.

"We came to visit the queen," I explain, which was all it had taken
for the guards to let us through the doors. The duchess, however, is
another matter.

She steps nearer, the gold embellishment on her gown glinting. "Did she send for you?"

"No, but—"

"She did not," the duchess snaps. "She *would* not, brazen climber that you are."

I bristle, though I'm unsurprised by her vitriol. The duchess is only saying what the rest of the court is thinking. They all want a villain to blame. I don't even bother arguing.

"Enjoy your position." The duchess shifts the basin she's carrying. "Though, you should know by now that swift rises give way to equally swift falls."

Wind howls down the chimney, sounding so close to Marion's screams that I shiver. Even the duchess reminds me of the former courtier. She might not be locked in a dungeon, but Duchess Poole's usual impeccable appearance is frayed around the edges. Wisps of her hair escape from beneath her headdress and a corner of her shift peeks above the neckline of her bodice. This is not the same woman who trained us on court etiquette. None of us are the same.

"Is that Mistress Ayleth?"

It takes me a moment to register that the voice, so soft and weak, belongs to the queen.

"Yes, Majesty," Duchess Poole replies. "I was just telling her to—"

"Send her in."

The duchess's jaw tightens. "Majesty, you need your rest."

"Let her come," the queen repeats, firmer this time. "Then go."

"Your Majesty—"

"*Go.*"

For a moment, the duchess just stands there, her lips pressed together.

"Well," she says at last, jerking her chin toward the other chamber. "You heard the queen. Go and take a good look at what you've done."

Look in the mirror, Marion had said, blaming me for her plight.

But I haven't done anything. Not to Marion and not to the queen. This is the king's doing—the workings of this entire rotting court. Even so, guilt prickles against my conscience. Had I set something into motion by coming here? Like how I lured the Nevenwolf? The place behind my left ribs shivers.

"By the Spirits," Jacquetta whispers as we stand at the threshold to the queen's chamber.

Queen Sybil is pacing in front of the hearth, her body bathed in gold from the light of the flames. She's become so thin. Her night-dress hangs from her frame, like she's been ill for months, not days.

"There was a raven," the queen mutters to herself, evidently having forgotten that she summoned us. "And blood. And snow."

What is she talking about? What's wrong with her? There's an array of small bottles on a tray beside the queen's bed. I motion for Jacquetta to follow me and edge toward them.

"Anything?" Jacquetta whispers as I sniff the contents of a slender green vial.

"Willowroot, maybe. And elderberry," I say, inhaling again. "But it's laced with something else."

Sharp and bitter and earthy. I've smelled it before, but where . . .

The dinner, my mind supplies. *In the wine.*

"Thornapple," I breathe.

Jacquetta's eyes widen. "She's being poisoned."

"It makes sense. Look at her."

The queen continues her pacing, plucking at the long, loose tendrils of her hair. Perhaps this isn't the first time someone has attempted to harm her. Was my glass at the dinner meant for the queen? But why?

"Find Joan," I tell Jacquetta. "She knows where the medicines are kept."

"What do I look for? What's the antidote for thornapple?"

Time, I recall from my lessons. And time we might not have. I swallow.

"There isn't one—she either survives this or she doesn't. But we can try to help."

Jacquetta hesitates, like perhaps she wants to argue. Maybe she believes a mortal queen isn't worth saving. A month ago, I would have agreed. But eventually, Jacquetta nods and slips out of the room. The crackle of the fire fills the silence.

"Ravens," the queen mutters to the flames. "The raven."

Has the poison already reached her mind?

"Your Majesty," I say softly, trying not to startle her as I approach. Her head jerks up. "*Ayleth.*"

By the Spirits. The queen appears even worse up close. Her eyes are glassy, the whites yellowish. The veins showing through her sallow skin are dark. I don't need to be a Blessed to know that she doesn't have long. Much as I want to help the queen, I have to help myself as well.

"Your Majesty, I must ask you—"

"Has she gone?" The queen's attention whips back toward the door.

"Jacquetta? She went—"

"Not her." The queen waves me off. "The other one."

My brow rumples. "Duchess Poole?"

A piece clicks into place. Had the *duchess* been dosing the queen? Was that the reason for her harried appearance—guilt and fear of being caught?

"Has she served you anything?" I ask. "Food or wine or . . ."

The queen snatches my arm, her skin unnaturally cold through the sleeve of my dress. "They will kill her."

A log collapses in the hearth.

"Kill who? The duchess?"

"I cannot say," she whispers, shaking her head. "They will hear. They hear *everything.*"

Darkness thickens around us. Shadows lengthen and swell in the corners of the room. I sense a faint twinge behind my left ribs.

"Is it a witch?" I ask, abandoning caution. "Have you been working with a witch? Is that what happened with Marion's comb? Is that where you got the scrying cards?"

Her eyes snap to mine, pupils blown wide, like twin mirrors. I can see the outline of my face inside them. "Marion. I tried to warn her. I *tried.*"

"Warn her about what?" I beg. "The comb? Were you the one who framed her?"

Her lips move, but no words come out.

"Please, Your Majesty." I grasp the queen's shoulders. "Do you remember when I told you about my sister? I'm trying to get her back. And I want to help you too. But you have to tell me what's going on."

"Sister," she echoes, plucking at the neckline of her nightdress. "I had a sister. The raven saved her. Blood in the snow."

An image of the falcon's kill resurfaces in my mind, its innards splattered on the white ground. "I don't understand."

The queen jolts, like she was struck. She abruptly lets go of me and rushes off to another part of the room, then starts frantically rooting through drawers.

"I will show you. Then you will know," she says. "They will not find it."

"Find what, Your Majesty?" I follow her. "Is it the Bloodstones? Do you have them?"

The fire snaps. Curtains sway and billow in a fresh draft, like wraiths. The queen freezes, her terrified gaze fixed on something I can't see.

"It has come for me," she rasps. "Just as I always knew it would."

"What . . ."

The rest of the question is swallowed by a low growl. An instant later, the slow tap of approaching claws fills the chamber. Every hair on my body rises. *No. Not here.*

"Not again," I whisper.

The queen creeps nearer, her shoulders hunched. "You hear it too?"

I nod, mouth dry. That force inside me thrums as the growling starts again, closer now.

"Come." I snatch the queen's wrist. "We need to leave. Now."

I start pulling the queen toward the door, but she resists me.

"I must stay. It is the price."

"Price?" I repeat, frustrated. "The price of what?"

She doesn't answer. Instead, the queen begins to cough. Blood stains the sleeve of her nightdress and drips down the front—crimson against white.

"Please, Your Majesty. Sybil." I tug desperately at her arm. She won't budge.

"You will stay." She smiles at me, her lips glistening red. "For my daughter. Keep her safe."

Another draft shudders through the chamber. That force strengthens, reaching outward, its invisible tether tightening as the claws click nearer, slow and ominous.

"We need to *go*," I urge the queen.

But she doubles over, seized by another coughing fit. It worsens, until her whole body is wracked with convulsions. Beneath it all, that low, sinister growl rumbles between us. And somehow, deep in my bones, I know that it's here for the queen.

"Go away!" I shout at whatever this *thing* is. "Leave her alone!"

The fire dims in the grate and the temperature drops. I have to *do* something. But what could I possibly . . .

A frantic thought swoops into my mind. Rhea helped me kill the Nevenwolf in the forest. Perhaps she can keep this creature back. I stare down at my hands, at Rhea's marks. If they protected me, can they protect the queen?

"Please, Rhea," I whisper, grasping Queen Sybil's shoulders.

Another growl fills the chamber, angrier now. The queen's breathing is fast and shallow. Her eyes roll back in her head.

"Not yet," I beg, reaching for my sister in my mind. Picturing her amid the flames at my Ascension. "Please, Rhea. *Help!*"

By some miracle, warmth prickles in my hands, just as it did in the forest when I gripped the arrow. I hold the queen tighter, willing her to fight. Urging Rhea's magic to intervene. The triangles on my palms pulse in time to my frantic heartbeat.

"Just hold on," I tell the queen. "It will be—"

The invisible tether *yanks.*

Malum surges inside me, as if it's taking a breath of its own. Shadows descend from every corner of the chamber. And then, to my utter horror, they *dive* into the queen's mouth. Her eyes fly wide, solid black.

"*Stop!*" I scream.

It's too late. The queen's entire body lifts, suspended by the shadows, which wrap tighter and tighter around her like a hideous cocoon, spun from darkness itself. There's a *roar* and a blast of air, and then an invisible force slams into the queen. She shudders with the impact, her body going limp as she sinks to the ground. Her head lolls to one side. A line of black trickles from her bloodstained lips.

The eerie silence of death settles over us.

Tears prick in my eyes. I don't understand. Rhea's magic protected me in the forest. It killed the Nevenwolf. Why couldn't it help the queen?

The answer forms slowly, like frost crackling over a windowpane: Because this had nothing to do with the queen. I was wrong. The creature hadn't come here for *her.* It came for *me.* The shadows didn't claim her until I touched her. I guided Malum to Queen Sybil. Threw her in front of the beast.

That force behind my left ribs trembles, as if . . . satisfied.

CHAPTER FORTY-SIX

THE QUEEN IS DEAD.

I race back to our rooms, jumping at every shadow, haunted by the memory of the darkness pouring into her mouth. The blood leaking from her lips, her eyes like black marbles. All because I touched her. I *killed* her.

Mother and everyone else was right. I can't pull Rhea out from beyond the Veil. I'll only attract something worse. Something . . . *wrong.* Soon enough, whatever killed the queen will be back for me. I fling open the door to our suite, run into my bedchamber, and start stuffing my things into my satchel. Nettle appears from wherever she'd been hiding and trills in concern.

"We're leaving," I tell her.

I was a fool to come here in the first place. Not even the Blood-stones can help me now. I'm lost. Cursed, just like those wretched crows warned me.

"Ayleth?" Jacquetta's voice carries from the main chamber. "I couldn't find Joan and then the guards said you left. What—"

She stops short in the doorway, registering my half-stuffed satchel.

Fitz noses his way in beside her. He lays his ears flat and halfheartedly growls.

"What's going on?"

"The queen," I tell her, the truth tumbling out of me before I can stop it. "She's dead. And it's because of me. I killed her."

Jacquetta gapes at me. "*What?*"

I drop the shift and start pacing. Images crash together in my mind—the queen lifting into the air. The shadows wrapping around her, squeezing the life from her body.

"Ayleth, talk to me," Jacquetta presses.

Don't, a voice in my mind warns. *If you tell her, she will leave.*

But she was always going to leave, wasn't she? All we had was this insane quest holding us together—nothing else. In fact, it's better if she goes. It's not safe for her here, with me. I need to *make* her go.

"I lied to you," I say, my voice trembling with adrenaline. "I came here for the Bloodstones, but not because I'm a Second. I came for Rhea."

Jacquetta pauses. "I don't understand. Rhea is . . ."

"Rhea is dead, yes. But on the night of my Ascension, I saw her in the flames. I *touched* her. I tried to pull her out. See?" I thrust out my hands, showing her the triangles. "My sister gave me these marks. They're *our* marks. Our runes, connecting us—even through death. That's why I need the Bloodstones. They're the only things with enough magic to bring her back."

For a moment, Jacquetta just stares at my hands.

"You . . ." she starts, her brows knitted together. "You . . . touched Rhea? You reached beyond the Veil?"

The fear in her voice threatens to break my heart. Because it's *exactly* what I expected.

"I just wanted my sister." Tears track down my face and sting on my lips. "I thought that if I could just pull her back, everything would be fine. I was never meant to be Second. I'm not even gifted."

"Not *gifted*?" Jacquetta shakes her head. "You killed the Nevenwolf. You said—"

"I lied." The admission sears in my throat. "I'm not a Second. I never even made a vow. I have no power. Not like Rhea did. She's the one who killed the Nevenwolf. Through me."

"Ayleth, that's not—"

"It's true," I all but shout. Nettle meows, concerned. "Rhea's magic killed the Nevenwolf. But *I'm* the one who brought the beast out in the first place. When I reached for my sister, something reached back. Malum. It's been *living* in me this whole time."

As if in answer, that force behind my left ribs shudders. I claw at myself, as though I could dig it out with my bare hands. I would, if I could. I would tear myself apart just to pry it out from between my bones.

"That's why the *thing* in the archives has been following us," I barrel on. "It's why the Nevenwolf stalked me in the forest. It's probably even why your power doesn't work here. *I'm* drawing Malum from beyond the Veil—smothering your magic. And tonight, with the queen . . ."

I dig the heels of my palms into my eyes to block the surge of swirling images. Wind pushes against the glass panes of the windows, and I can almost hear the click of claws against stone, like whatever killed the queen is out there, trying to get in.

"I should never have come here," I whisper. "I can't get Rhea. I ruin everything I touch. I'm . . . broken."

Quiet hums between us. I brace myself for the sound of Jacquetta's footsteps walking—no, *running*—away. I would run if the situation were reversed. But she doesn't move.

"You're not broken."

"Did you not hear me? I meddled with the Veil. Something marked me or it—"

"I knew," Jacquetta interrupts.

I blink at her. "About . . . what I did?"

She shakes her head. Swallows. Just like on the night of the banquet, in the courtyard, there's something fragile about her. Vulnerable.

"In the forest . . . when we were supposed to run away together"—she pauses—"I knew it wasn't you who came to the clearing."

An ember in the fire pops.

"You . . . *knew*?"

But she can't have. Because that would mean—

"I wasn't completely certain," Jacquetta continues, the words rough. "But yes. Deep down, I sensed it, like I do other magic. I *knew.*"

Thoughts collide together in my mind, trying to make sense of what she's saying. But there are too many contradictions. "But at the hunt, you were so angry with me . . . and then when we fought you said you were—"

Relief. The word plunges into me again.

"I know what I said." Jacquetta tugs at her sleeve. "I lied. I didn't know it was your mother who met me in the clearing, but I sensed that it wasn't you. I left anyway."

Nettle hisses at her, tail twitching.

All I can do is stare at the other witch. What does Jacquetta want me to do with this information? Why is she confessing it now? Sudden anger spikes in my chest.

You were right all along, that voice whispers. *She left you on purpose.*

"Why didn't you just tell me?" I demand. "It would have been simple enough. You could have said that you knew all along. That you didn't want me and—"

"I *did* want you." Those cobalt-blue eyes blaze and my heart knocks against my chest. "You were all I wanted. And that terrified me. That's why I walked away. I'm a coward."

Thunder rumbles outside. I wait for the rage to fill me up—for betrayal to twist between my ribs. But the wound is small. Nothing compared to the pain etched on Jacquetta's face. In this moment, all

I see is the scared young witch alone in the forest, frozen in fear as she faced the path that lay before her. It's a scar that exactly matches my own.

"We were sixteen," I say. "You weren't a coward."

"Yes, I was." She laughs, bitter. "You said yourself—I could have admitted the truth every day since we met at the Sanctum, and I . . ."

She trails off, folding her arms around her body, like she's trying to hold herself together.

"Why didn't you?" I ask.

"Because . . ." She hesitates. Inhales. "Because over the years I'd convinced myself that I was wrong. It had been you that night. When I saw you at the Sanctum—the things you said—I was even more certain. You were a Second, exactly like you—or your mother—told me you wanted."

Damn my own stubborn pride. "I was pretending. Trying to hurt you."

She nods. "Well, you did a good job of it. It wasn't until the hunt, when you pieced everything together, that I knew I'd been right."

I hold her gaze. "And you still never said?"

"I almost did," she admits. "But . . . I told myself that it didn't matter who met me in the forest. All that was too long ago. We're different witches now. Whatever I felt for you was just a remnant of before. It would pass."

The same words I'd repeated to myself, like a spell. Say it enough times and it becomes true.

Because it is true, that voice insists.

For the first time, I lock it away.

"Did it pass for you?" I ask, daring a step closer. "Because I still feel it."

Love. It trembles between us, fragile and brittle-edged. Because this love wasn't the sort from Willa's stories—not for us. Ours was hard-won and easily lost.

But I will not lose it again.

The space between us is achingly narrow. Jacquetta's juniper scent wafts around me and blood pounds through my veins. Our faces tip toward each other and I hold my breath as our lips brush, slow at first and then deeper. The taste of roses fills my mouth, along with something else, so familiar that it's painful.

Home.

A lock unclicks in my heart, opening a door I believed was sealed forever. I bound through it now, returning Jacquetta's kiss with the hunger of all the wasted years we've spent apart. This is not slow and sensual, but urgent, like we're both worried the other person might slip away. Our hands fumble with our clothes as we topple onto the bed, still wrapped around each other. Jacquetta straddles me on the mattress, pulling her shift over her head. Firelight gleams against the perfection of her body, all soft curves and sculpted angles.

"You're so beautiful," I whisper.

Jacquetta keeps her eyes on mine, a thousand unspoken words swirling within them. She picks up my hand, deliberately kissing each fingertip. Waves of heat course through my limbs as her mouth travels down, pressing against the triangles at the base of each ring finger.

"You're not broken, Ayleth," she murmurs against my skin.

My entire body *melts.* Gently, Jacquetta guides my hand so that it rests on the curve of her waist. A sigh shudders through me at her softness. I let my hands explore the plane of her back. The ridges of her shoulder blades. The dip of her spine where it meets her hips. It's like another language, one I want to understand in the very core of my being.

Jacquetta lets out a tiny gasp as I find the place between her thighs. She catches my wrists and pins my hands above my head, her mouth crashing into mine. But she doesn't stay there long. A groan escapes me as her lips move down the curve of my neck and over the ledge of my collarbone. With agonizing slowness, she pauses at each of my breasts, teasing the nipples until a delicious ache blooms between my legs. This is more than simply desire. It's need, pure and simple and so all-consuming that it will burn me up. But I don't care. I want to burn.

Jacquetta nudges my knees apart, her teeth nipping at the inside of my thighs. Groaning, I lift my hips toward her, until her tongue at last moves against me.

"*Jacquetta,*" I gasp, gripping the bedpost.

She pushes harder, faster. My hips rock in time to her rhythm, sparks dancing through my blood.

"There," I manage, back arching. "Like that."

Jacquetta moans, the vibration traveling from her mouth and through my entire body. Release explodes inside me and I cry out, sinking into the bed, breathless and damp and still craving more of her.

She climbs up to meet me and I push her onto the pillows, our gazes locked together. I want to explore her. To watch as she loses herself and know that her pleasure came from me. I take my time in finding her tender places. My mouth lingers on the thin skin of her wrist. Her earlobe. The curve where her neck meets her shoulder.

"Ayleth." Jacquetta's hips push against me. "Please."

That one word will be my undoing.

I lower myself between her legs, finding the velvet softness between her thighs. Her hands tangle in my hair, fresh heat igniting in my limbs at her sounds of pleasure. Her hips move in time with my quickening tempo, her muscles tensing beneath my hands. My name spills from her lips and it will be the absolute end of me. With a last cry, Jacquetta relaxes, her hands still buried in my hair.

She pulls me up to lie beside her. And for once, curled here with Jacquetta, I let myself drift away, feeling safe and wanted in a way I never believed possible.

Sometime later, I wake to the sound of rain pattering against the window. Gradually, I register the shape in the bed beside me.

Jacquetta.

The last hours crash back into my mind—the warm silk of her skin and her taste, like roses and juniper and *home.* The word fizzes in my blood and I skim my fingertip along her shoulder, just to make sure she's real.

Jacquetta stirs. Her eyes flutter open, their cobalt blue glimmering in the dimness. A hidden, fragile part of me worries that she might not feel the way she did before—that she might regret what we did—and I shrink slightly into the bedclothes.

"Hello," she says, her lips curling into a lazy smile.

Wings flutter in my stomach. "Hello."

In that single word, all the history between us is washed away. It's like there was a string attached to our hearts, one that held no matter how many times we tried to cut it.

Jacquetta catches my wrist and turns my palm up, her fingertip tracing the lines of my skin before pausing at the triangle etched under my ring finger. Somehow, this slight contact feels more intimate than what we just shared, and my heart beats harder.

"I wish you'd told me."

There's no accusation in her tone, no judgment. In fact, she sounds sad—like she blames herself for my secrecy.

"I didn't know how. At my Ascension, the others were . . ." The memory of Selene and her suspicion resurfaces, along with the sting of Mother's slap. "They didn't believe me."

Jacquetta tangles our fingers, pressing our palms together. "I'm sorry."

"It doesn't matter. And they were right, in the end. I might have been reaching for Rhea, but now . . ." I pull my hand away, the room suddenly colder.

"That wasn't your fault." Jacquetta props her head up on her hand. "You reached for your sister because that's who you are, Ayleth. You're brave."

A short laugh escapes me. "I'm not brave."

"You came here alone," she says simply. "The only one of the Ancients' descendants who dared to reclaim the Bloodstones. You were ready to pull your sister from death itself."

I roll onto my back, staring up at the bed's canopy. "And look what happened. Something else reached for *me*. It's only a matter of time before . . ."

Thunder rattles the windowpanes.

"Do you really think it's Malum?" Jacquetta asks.

On instinct, I press my hand to my left ribs.

"Yes. You saw the Nevenwolf in the forest—sensed whatever was following us in the archives. And then, earlier, with the queen . . ." I picture her solid black eyes and the shadows diving into her mouth. "It took her, but it wanted me. I won't escape it again."

Jacquetta pauses for a long moment. "Then we fix the Veil."

She says it like it's a simple errand to be run. "How? The queen is dead. Whatever she knew about the Bloodstones is gone with her."

"What if we didn't need the Bloodstones?"

My brow furrows. "Of course we need them."

"We *did*," she allows. "Just like the covens needed Heirs and Seconds. But it's as I said before—that hierarchy isn't helping any of us. We could change it."

This again. I push myself up, gathering the bedclothes around me. "Jacquetta, I can't—"

"Just, hear me." She raises a hand. "The Veil is failing. For all we know, the Bloodstones were never enough to hold it. Nevenwolves?

Shadow creatures? It's only going to get worse. If we don't do something, we'll be fighting a different battle."

I won't be fighting a battle at all. Wind groans against the palace.

"What do you have in mind?"

Jacquetta never takes her gaze from mine. "We go to Stonehaven."

To . . . *Stonehaven*? She must be joking. But there's not a hint of a
smile on her lips, only fierce determination—an expression that
sends fire racing through my limbs.

"I can't go back. I explained what happened."

"But you won't be alone this time," she says. "We'll bring your
coven and mine together. The other Heirs as well, if we can manage
it. *All* of us will devise a new method to hold the Veil, one that
doesn't rely on the Bloodstones. Just magic."

Just magic. The words strike a chord and I lean toward the idea
that magic can simply exist. That *I* can simply exist. But I turn my
hand over, tracing Rhea's marks. Two lines drifting apart, yet always
coming back together. If I walk away from the palace, abandon the
Bloodstones, I'll never see my sister again.

It must be undone, Rhea's words float back to me beneath the
storm.

"If I leave, I'll have failed her," I say, the old wound of my guilt
opening. "Again."

Jacquetta's brow furrows. "What are you talking about?"

There's no point in keeping it back. "The night of the raid. I was
supposed to be on patrol with her. Supposed to be watching for the
Hunt, but I was . . ."

With you, I don't say, because I don't want it to sound like I'm
blaming her. I'm not. It was my fault. My choice.

"Oh, Ayleth," Jacquetta breathes. "Have you been carrying this
around all these years?"

I pick at the fringe on a pillow. "It's true."

"No," she says firmly, snatching up my hand. "It's not. Rhea wouldn't have blamed you for what happened."

"Then why did she appear to me?"

"I don't know," Jacquetta admits. "But I know that your sister loved you more than anything else. She would want you to have your own life—not live in the shadow of hers."

Live in shadow. That's all I seem to be doing of late, running from Nevenwolves and kings and—*myself.*

I have been blaming myself—hating myself—for what happened with Rhea. I thought that if I brought her back, everything would be fixed. I'd be forgiven. But what if there was never anything to forgive? As if in answer, the triangles on my palms twinge. I don't realize that I'm crying until I taste salt on my lips. Jacquetta wipes the tears away with her thumb.

"You asked me to choose you once." She cups the side of my face with her hand. "I was too afraid, then. But I'm not afraid anymore."

"You were smart," I tell her. "This plan is madness. It will never work."

She lifts a shoulder. "Then at least we'll have tried."

"And if we fail? If the Veil breaks and Malum swallows me whole?"

Jacquetta presses her forehead against mine. "Then it will have to take both of us."

Us. My chest aches, like my heart is growing and breaking at the same time. Instead of shying away from the feeling, I let myself trust it—trust *us.* And for the first time since Rhea died, I do not feel alone.

CHAPTER FORTY-SEVEN

B Y MORNING, THE PALACE IS ROCKED BY THE NEWS OF THE QUEEN'S death.

In one fell swoop, the court sinks into mourning. Longest Night activities are suspended. There is to be no feasting or merriment in the Great Hall. Sport such as hunting or hawking are forbidden, as are dancing and gambling. Delicacies from the kitchens are abandoned in favor of bland soups and plain bread. Black gauze is draped over Queen Sibyl's portraits. Mirrors are covered and windows shuttered in accordance with the Order's protocol. A wardrobe of black crepe arrives at our door, simple gowns and veils for the late queen's household.

Given the condition of Queen's Sybil's body, which evidently melted like those of the prince and the Nevenwolf, the whispers of *witchcraft* intensify. Unless we're praying in the palace chantry, we're expected to remain in our rooms as the High Priest and his steward stoke the flames of their investigation. The world Jacquetta and I created together is clouded by the constant hum of dread. It's only a matter of time before they call for us, or before the king sends for me. We need to leave, but we have to prepare our covens first. We decide to wait until the night of the funeral to escape, using the days in between to plan.

"And so that's it? You're just running off?"

Roland's gemstone-colored eyes glitter with fury in the moonlight.

"We have to go," I tell him. "They'll come for us otherwise."

"What about the Veil?" He points at me. "What about *changing* things?"

I twist his silver ring, the questions pricking at my conscience. "We will. We just can't rely on the Bloodstones to hold the Veil. Not anymore."

"And what will you rely on?"

"I'm not sure yet," I admit, shifting on my feet. "But we'll find a way. Then I'll be back."

"Oh, that makes me feel much better." He snatches the ring out of my grasp. "Good luck, Mistress Witch. Enjoy the rest of your life. I'll certainly enjoy mine."

"Roland—" I call. But he's already jamming a key into the wall of my bedchamber. A door appears and Roland yanks it open, then stalks through it. I feel the slam in my bones.

Nettle trills, her golden eyes bright and perhaps reproachful.

"What? I couldn't take him with us. And I *am* coming back."

She licks her paw, which does nothing to assuage my needling guilt. When Jacquetta and I devised this plan, it seemed so right. But the details are proving much more complicated. I roll my shoulders against the tension I've carried for weeks. This is the way things have to be. It's madness to remain here, searching for the Bloodstones while the High Priest hunts witches. We'll find a new way to seal the Veil, and then everything will change.

My cat follows me as I pull on a dressing gown and go out into the main chamber. Jacquetta is sitting at the table, a book propped open in front of her. And I must be hallucinating, because *Fitz* is dozing contentedly in her lap.

"Are you *petting* him?"

Jacquetta's hand freezes on the dog's back.

"No," she says at once, then flushes because she very obviously is. "He wouldn't stop pawing at me. It's the only way I could get some peace."

A smile twitches at my lips. "Nettle does the same thing."

Nettle meows, as if to deny the accusation. And Fitz, to my surprise, only sniffs as I approach. Progress.

"How did it go?" Jacquetta asks.

"About as well as I expected," I say, plucking a piece of cheese from her plate. "He thinks I'm abandoning him."

And I am. The fire crackles.

"You're not," she says. "You did what you could."

It doesn't feel like enough. "It's not just about the Dwarves, though. What about Blodwyn? You've seen what this court does to its women. What's going to happen to her now that the queen is dead?"

You must help her. Queen Sybil's words rise from her grave, laced with the howl of the wind down the chimney.

"We didn't start this war, Ayleth," Jacquetta reasons. "And two witches alone cannot stop it. We can't save everyone."

I can't argue with her logic, but I feel like I should be doing *something*. I watch the flames chew away the logs.

"When will you contact your mother?" I ask, changing the subject.

"Soon."

But I note the way she pauses in petting Fitz. "You're not having second thoughts?"

"No. It's just . . . things have been complicated between us since we left Stonehaven."

Jacquetta hasn't shared much about our lost years, and I find that I'm hungry for every detail I missed. "What do you mean?"

Fitz nudges her hand so that she scratches between his ears again. "Mother feels pressure to prove that she was right in breaking with Stonehaven and the traditional covens."

"Is that why she sent you here?"

"She didn't send me," she corrects. "I chose to come. But yes. We wanted to end the war without the Heirs—prove that the hierarchy of the Ancients wasn't necessary. Which is why . . ."

Jacquetta trails off, her cheeks flushing slightly.

"What?"

"Well. Mother won't exactly be pleased to find out that I've literally wound up in bed with one of their descendants."

Heat prickles up my own neck. "Do you regret that?"

She looks at me, the blue of her gaze so bright that it steals my breath. "No. Never."

My heart kicks. "Neither do I."

Jacquetta grants me a small smile, but then her attention tracks to the windows. Worry carves a line on her forehead, and I remember that night when I heard her muffled scream on the balcony after Nerissa's raven.

"Are you sure your mother will agree to work with the others?" I ask carefully. "Because if you're not—"

"She will." Fitz complains as Jacquetta shoos him off her lap and joins me at the fireplace. "We'll make them see. The two of us."

The two of us. I cling to those words. With Jacquetta, I don't have to be a Second or an Heir. She just wants *me.*

Choice is a magic in and of itself. Mathilde's words resurface in my mind.

I think I finally understand their true meaning.

The night air is cold and misty in the garden. My breath frosts as I hurry down the deserted gravel paths, as far away from the palace as I can venture without leaving the gates. It's been two days since the queen died. There are another two remaining before the queen's funeral, which means we need to alert our covens to our plan. Jacquetta and I decided to conduct our scrying separately, which is probably for the best. Nerissa won't be the only unhappy witch when it comes to our pairing. In fact, if Mother saw Jacquetta, she might refuse to speak to me at all. It *would* be highly satisfying, though, to see Mother's face as she realized Jacquetta and I found our way back to each other after her meddling. But I let that temptation go. For now, I have to convince Millicent's Heir to agree to work with a coven that actively despises the Ancients.

Nettle trills as she lopes along beside me.

"I don't suppose you have any ideas?"

She swishes her tail, helpful as always.

Eventually, we come upon a fountain surrounded by hedges. We're deep in the garden and the night is cloudy, so this is about as safe as I can get. Exhaling a jittery breath, I pull out the small knife I'd carried with me. Nettle perches on the lip of the fountain and watches, her golden eyes glowing in the night.

"Let's get this over with," I mutter, wincing as I slice the skin of my palm.

Blood wells in a thin line. I hold my hand over the fountain. Crimson drops bloom and swirl in the water.

"*Departed Sisters, hear my plea,*" I whisper the words of the spell. "*Let this stream a vessel be. Water churn and water flow, the words of my Mother I would know.*"

For several moments, nothing happens. Doubt creeps into my mind. What if the strangeness of the palace—or even Malum itself—has smothered even my most basic gifts? What if Mother is deliberately ignoring me? But then the wind gusts, sending leaves skittering over the walking path. Tendrils of crimson smoke curl up from the surface of the water, which swirls and undulates. When it stills, a face begins to emerge. Mother.

"Ayleth," she says.

My heart punches in my chest. I wasn't fully prepared to see her. Even through the distortion of the water, I notice the dark circles under her eyes and the tight lines bracketing her mouth. The last time she appeared so haggard was immediately after Rhea died.

"Has something happened?" I ask, imagining the worst.

"You mean, aside from the fact that my soon-to-be Second vanished in the night, betraying her coven, yet *again*?"

My hackles rise. She wasted no time in pressing on *that* particular spot. But Mother is not the only one with a blade—not anymore.

"And what of your own betrayal?" I throw back. "I know what you did that night in the forest, with your glamour. You pretended to be me and sent Jacquetta away."

I add another tally mark to the number of occasions I've witnessed genuine shock on Mother's expression. It feels good to be the one causing it.

"Who told you that?"

"*She* did. She's here with me."

"She . . ?" Mother pauses. Inhales sharply. "Did you . . . *join* with them?"

Part of me wants to tell her yes, just to watch her bleed. Because breaking with the Ancients would be the gravest betrayal I could commit, perhaps even worse than if I'd killed a witch in our coven. It's so ridiculous that I almost laugh.

"We met by chance," I say instead. "At the White Palace. That's where I am. I came here to find the Bloodstones."

For a moment, Mother stares at me. "And . . . did you?"

That's her first question. Not if I'm all right or if I need help.

Doesn't she care? Perhaps she doesn't. "No. Sorry to disappoint you. And that's not why I've called you."

Mother flinches, but instantly recovers. "May I deign to ask *why*, then?"

I pull myself up straighter. "As I said, I'm here with Jacquetta. The Veil is crumbling. We've come up with a plan to fix it."

"A plan with Nerissa's brat?" she snaps back. "I think not. They abandoned us. They rejected our ways. How could you forget that? I was protecting you when I got rid of her."

This is too much. "You *robbed* me. You stole my choices. My freedom."

Mother scoffs. "I see your journey hasn't cured you of your flair for dramatics. I saved you, not that you'll thank me."

"Saved me from what?" I throw up my hands. "And why? For the precious bloodline? *Our ways?*"

"Those ways protect us."

"Not anymore. We're losing this war because we're clinging to the past—to a system of power that's driving us apart. I saw it with my own eyes at Stonehaven. There's too much infighting among the Heirs—no loyalty."

A crow calls in the night.

"Do you mean the sort of loyalty Jacquetta and her mother displayed by walking away from us?" Mother raises an eyebrow. "It didn't take much to get her to leave you, Ayleth. She practically bolted out of the forest."

The jab lands as intended. Pain lances through my heart.

You see, that voice whispers. *You cannot trust her.*

I clench my fists against it.

"Things are different now," I say, as much to myself as to Mother. "And at least Jacquetta is willing to talk instead of worsening the divisions between us. The Veil isn't just thinning, Mother. It's *failing*. There was a Nevenwolf here."

That gets her attention. "A Nevenwolf?"

I neglect to tell her that I'm the one who drew it out. If she suspects, she doesn't say. And it doesn't matter. Once we seal the Veil, it will all be set right.

"We have to do something," I go on. "Jacquetta is speaking with her coven as well. I want to bring them to Stonehaven. If you can gather the other Heirs again, we can devise a way to mend the Veil without the Bloodstones."

"There isn't such a way," Mother says, but it sounds practiced, like the old rhyme about the crows.

One for sorrow.

"There must be. If the Ancients could forge the Veil on their own, other witches should be able to do the same thing. Together."

Mother is quiet for a long time.

"And if they come," she starts slowly, "what exactly am I agreeing to do?"

"Only to talk. And listen."

She frowns. We both know that *listening* isn't among her talents. But then: "Your sister made a similar request before she died."

Her admission is so unexpected, and so unguarded, that I blink. "Rhea did?"

Mother nods. "She was always telling me that the covens were splintering. She didn't trust that the Heirs and Seconds—or even the Ancients—were enough to hold them together."

It must be undone. Rhea's words come back to me beneath the rustle of leaves.

All this time, I assumed my sister was begging me to bring her home so that she could be Second and Heir. So that things could go back to the way they were before. But what if I've been wrong? What if, like Jacquetta suggested, Rhea hated being Second? What if she didn't want me to share that fate? That's why she stopped me from joining the coven. Because, like Jacquetta and the others, Rhea believed that the whole hierarchy was broken. It *all* needed to be un-done, the very structure of the covens remade.

I press my thumbs into our marks. And I might be imagining it, but I think I feel a slight answering pulse beneath the triangles.

"Your sister had so many ideas," Mother goes on, almost to herself. "But I was always fixated on how things were before. How things *should* be."

The lines around her mouth deepen. I'm torn between vindication that Mother might finally understand how wrong she's been and the urge to comfort her—take her pain, even though she's the one who inflicted it. It's as uncomfortable as it is awkward.

"There's still time to change things," I tell her instead.

Mother doesn't reply right away. An owl hoots nearby.

"Very well," she says at last. "Let Nerissa and the others come. To *talk*. I make no promises about anything else, nor can I speak for the other Heirs."

A weight lifts in my chest, one I didn't fully realize I'd been carrying. I have no idea how this meeting between the covens is going to end, but at least it's happening. It's a step.

"Thank you," I say to Mother, meaning it. "And you should prepare as well. Jacquetta and I are leaving in two nights' time. I don't know when the palace will realize we're gone, or if they'll follow. You should strengthen the wards and plan for the possibility of the Hunt."

I expect Mother to be angry about the Hunt or ask questions about why anyone at the White Palace would be following me. But she just smiles softly.

"You remind me so much of—"

"Rhea?" I ask tightly.

"No." She tilts her head. "You remind me of myself when I was your age. You always have."

Wind rattles the branches. "You've never told me that."

"I suppose I haven't." She pauses. "Though I should have. You're my heart, Ayleth. You've always been my heart."

Bittersweet pain expands in my chest.

"I'll see you soon" is all I manage in reply.

Mother nods. "I look forward to it."

And then her image swirls away, leaving nothing but my own reflection staring back at me in the water. For the first time, I do not see my sister.

That night, I lie in bed, waiting for Jacquetta to return from her own scrying. As I listen to the fire crackle, I replay the conversation with Mother, still not quite believing any of it was real.

You remind me of myself. You're my heart.

Words I thought I'd never hear again.

Wind groans against the windows. I trace the three crossed lines of the triangles on my palms. Perhaps they're not just a reminder of my relationship with my sister but with Mother as well. After all, there are three points on a triangle. It's time we all came together, even if Rhea won't be with us on this side of the Veil.

The door to our chamber eases open, breaking me out of my imaginings.

"Are you all right?" I ask, sitting up as Jacquetta slips into the room. "How did it go?"

"Not well, at first," she admits. Her hands tremble slightly as she unfastens her cloak. "But she agreed. And you?"

"Same," I tell her. "Mother will let your coven through the wards. And she said she would invite the other Heirs."

"Then it's settled."

It is—impossible as that seems. Jacquetta quickly undresses, her movements a touch jerky and her eyes ringed faintly in pink. Perhaps she and her mother fought. "Are you sure you're all right?"

She climbs into bed. "I'm cold and tired and ready to leave this place behind."

That makes two of us. And I decide not to press further about what happened with her scrying. Jacquetta burrows under the coverlet and pulls me to her, my back against her front. It's not long before I drift into sleep, the deepest since coming to the White Palace, without a single shadow or nightmare to disturb me. Sometimes, though, I wake just long enough to feel a body shuddering against mine. But it's probably just a dream.

CHAPTER FORTY-EIGHT

THE MORNING OF THE QUEEN'S FUNERAL IS GRAY AND SNOWY.
Jacquetta and I spend our final hours in the suite combing over every detail of our plan, repeating it back to each other as we eat and dress and stuff our satchels.

"We go to the funeral as expected," I say, balling up a skirt. "And then the feast, but only long enough to be seen. Then we slip out one at a time."

"And meet back here," Jacquetta finishes.

But the lines around her mouth are tight. In the two days since we scried with our mothers, her anxiousness has only seemed to worsen. I've watched her fold the same shift three times now. And she only picked at her breakfast.

"Are you sure you're all right?" I ask, cautious.

"Of course," she replies, too quickly. "Why wouldn't I be?"

I huff a short laugh. "Because we're about to attempt the most insane plan two witches ever dreamed up. Between your mother and mine, we might come to regret this meeting."

I'd meant the comment as a joke, but Jacquetta doesn't laugh. She fidgets with a pair of stockings. There's something more she wants to say—I know there is. Why doesn't she tell me?

She keeps things from you, that voice whispers.

I shove it down. I'm done listening to its poison. Jacquetta isn't the witch I thought she was, and neither am I.

Bells begin to toll, signaling the funeral.

"Time to go." Jacquetta shoves the stockings into her satchel and fastens the clasps.

A pathetic whine leaks from under the bed—Fitz. The poor thing hasn't stopped whimpering since sunrise, likely aware that we're about to leave.

"We can bring him," I tell Jacquetta.

Whether she wants to admit it or not, I know she cares about the dog. But she only shakes her head. "It will be hard enough traveling with your demon of a cat."

Nettle trills. I try to scratch between her ears, but she swats me away. She's been agitated all morning. "Don't go wandering. When I come back, we're leaving."

She swishes her tail, golden eyes fixed on Jacquetta as the other witch stashes our satchels in the wardrobe for later.

"That's it, then," she says, shutting the cabinet. "Are you ready?"

No. But there's nothing more I can do to prepare. Giving my bodice a last tug, I head for the door. Jacquetta pulls me abruptly back.

"What's—" I start.

The rest is lost in the pressure of her lips against mine. My bones soften as the taste of roses fills my mouth, so intoxicating I'm almost dizzy with it.

"I love you," she whispers.

It steals my breath. I've felt those words in her touch and in the way she looks at me, but hearing them . . .

"I love you too."

She kisses me again, soft and slow and not nearly long enough before she breaks away, my blood still humming with that word—*love*.

But as we leave the suite and enter the hall, instinct prickles between my shoulder blades. It reminds me of the feeling I experienced before my Ascension, like the fabric of my world is splitting apart.

No, I tell myself firmly. That's just nerves. The only thing that matters now is Jacquetta and the future we will build together.

Hundreds of candles blaze in the throne room, their light lapping against the queen's glass coffin. Within it, her remains are covered by a gold cloth—which I find surprising. Given the decimated state of her body, I assumed that Queen Sybil would be laid to rest in stone, as was done with the prince. A sea of lilies surrounds the casket, likely intended to mask the scent of rot, but their heady perfume only mixes with that of decay. The sweet and fetid smell, coupled with the closeness of their air, aggravates my already knotted stomach.

Each minute seems to stretch an hour as Ignatius preaches about the perils of Malum and the threat of witchcraft. Courtiers slide each other suspicious glances and whisper behind their hands, the sound hissing against the high ceiling. I'm convinced they're talking about me—us. Jacquetta must feel the same way, for she discreetly hooks her pinky around mine.

I love you.

The words bloom like midnight flowers behind my sternum. I hold them close, each one a jewel far more precious than any Bloodstone. Love. That's all that matters now. We just have to reach for it, like Mother's mirror said. Is this what it had meant? Had it seen the two of us together? Known that, if Jacquetta and I learned to trust each other again, we could forge a new world? If it did, I owe the mirror an apology for all the years I spent despising it.

At long last, Ignatius's eulogy ends, and the court rises for Blodwyn, who approaches the queen's coffin with a single winter rose. Tears stream down her face as she lays the white petals on the glass. My heart clenches. Grief has aged the princess. She looks nothing like the carefree girl who chased hedgehogs around her chamber.

Help her, the queen had begged. Guilt needles my conscience, but I can't do anything for the princess—not here.

When the ceremony concludes, Ignatius himself leads the procession out of the throne room. The king is second in line. Unlike every other instance in which he's been near, I hardly feel that place behind my left ribs. In fact, all manifestations of Malum—the shadows and nightmares and the creature that's been stalking me—have calmed since the night the queen died. Is that a coincidence? Or was I right when I sensed that the ominous force was sated? Had it fed off the queen's soul? If so, how long until it returns for mine?

I shove the thorny questions down. Jacquetta and I join the other courtiers as they file toward the Great Hall. The rules of mourning have been somewhat suspended for the occasion. Music is absent, but there's plenty of food—and wine, which is good. Jacquetta and I are counting on the nobles being too drunk to notice we've gone.

"I'll slip out first," she says.

"I won't wait long after that."

She nods and I brush my hand against hers, earning a tight smile before Jacquetta melts into the crowd. I smooth my skirts and keep to the edges of the room, attempting to attract as little notice as possible until I can leave.

"Ayleth." An arm loops through mine—Joan's. "What an awful day. Did you see the princess? I can't imagine what she's going through."

Neither can I. Guilt twists again at my leaving the princess alone in a court that will swallow her up. But I'll be strapped to a pyre if I remain here. What help would I be to Blodwyn then? Unless . . . an idea feathers in my mind. I might be leaving, but Joan isn't.

"Will you promise me something?" I ask her, steering us away from the tables.

"Of course. Anything."

"Would you . . .?" I struggle for the words to phrase the request so that it doesn't sound suspicious. "Could you look after the princess? Make sure she's all right?"

"Can't *you* look after her?" Joan asks, puzzled. "I know she's fond of you."

Joan isn't trying to make me feel worse, but I do.

"After I leave," I say. Then realize how it sounded and amend, "After Longest Night."

"Oh." Disappointment tugs at the corners of Joan's mouth. "Right. Of course, I'll do what I can for her, Ayleth. But do you really think you'll have to leave after the season? I was rather hoping you would stay. We've become such good friends."

We have. Joan is one of the best people in this wretched palace—probably one of the best I've known my whole life, witch or otherwise. A fresh pang of guilt knocks in my chest. Here is yet another person I'm abandoning to the whims of this gluttonous court.

"I think I'll have to," I tell Joan. "But I want you to know that I appreciate your friendship much more than I can express. You're kinder and cleverer than all of these vultures."

I gesture around the room and Joan's eyes shine.

"Well, there's no need to say our goodbyes now." She blinks, waving me off. "There's still a few weeks left of Longest Night."

Not for me. I scan the crowd, searching for Jacquetta. Has she already left?

My attention grazes the High Table, and the force behind my left ribs *kicks*. After days without feeling it, the sensation is a thousand times worse than it ever was. I gasp, my hand going to the spot as if I might feel it straining beneath my skin.

Joan grips my elbow. "Are you all right, Ayleth?"

No. Not when I discover King Callen's gray gaze fixed on mine. It's not hungry or desirous, as it was in the hedge maze, but harder. *Dangerous*. The king holds what looks to be a piece of parchment in one hand. As he stares at me, he crumples it in his fist.

That ominous force rumbles.

"Ayleth." Joan gives me a shake. "What's wrong? You look like you've seen a ghost."

I think I have—mine.

Mumbling an excuse, I fight my way through the clusters of courtiers and out of the Great Hall, dodging servants as I race back to our chambers. I don't know what was written on that parchment, but I know it's time to leave.

"Jacquetta!" I call, flinging open the door to our suite.

Fitz barks from where he'd been curled by the fire. Other than that, there's no answer. Had she not left the hall yet? I rush into our bedchamber, but it's empty except for Nettle, who trills a question from her place on the coverlet.

"Have you seen . . ."

My cat meows, insistent, and paws at something beside her. A scrap of parchment. I snatch it up. Two words stare back at me.

I'm sorry.

Sorry? The word stretches, long and thick in my mind. Sorry for what? Unless—

"No," I whisper, comprehension winnowing through my skull. "She wouldn't."

I drop the note and throw open the wardrobe. My satchel is still there, but Jacquetta's is gone. *She* is gone. Shock rolls over me in waves. This must be a mistake.

I love you, she'd said. And she meant it. I know she did.

Not enough, that menacing voice supplies. *You could never be enough.*

It's wrong. This is all just—

Hinges rattle as the door to the main chamber bursts open. Relief floods my veins.

"Jacquetta?" I call, racing to meet her. "Where—"

It's not Jacquetta. Fitz growls and flattens his ears as guards trample into the suite. Without a word to me, they fan out through the rooms.

"Wait!" I call. "What are you—"

The rest dies in my throat as a set of flame-colored robes sweeps through the doors. Ignatius. A high note of panic rings in my ears.

"Ah. Here she is, Sire."

Instinct urges me to run, but I'm frozen. Trapped. The king strides into the chamber, every thud of his boots matching the pulse of the horrible tether as it unfurls from behind my left ribs. For a long moment, King Callen only looks at me. The gray of his eyes is like steel, twin blades that will carve me up.

"This was left for me," he says at last, extracting a piece of parchment from his doublet. It's the one from the Great Hall. The king smooths it so that I can read the words.

The witch you seek is already in the palace. Search Mistress Ayleth's rooms.

My blood turns to ice. Not because of what is written, but because it's the exact same handwriting as the note that was left on the bed. It's from *Jacquetta.*

No! my mind screams, the word looping over and over. *No, no, no.* What has she done?

The same thing she did last time, that voice hisses.

"It's not—"

"Here, Your Illuminance." A guard tromps in and passes a book to the High Priest.

Ignatius thumbs through the pages and sighs. "I had hoped this was an empty accusation, Your Majesty. But I fear she's deceived us all."

The king snatches up the book. I catch a glimpse of diagrams and drawings. Is that a *grimoire*? Had Jacquetta left that? By the Spirits, I'm an utter fool. No wonder she'd been so preoccupied the last two days. She'd been planning to frame me. Despair settles in my stomach. Even with the evidence right in front of me, I try to convince myself it isn't true.

You know it is, that voice again. *You knew what she was.*

"The rise of Malum." King Callen throws the book at my feet. "The comb, the *Nevenwolf*. It was all you."

It wasn't. But I wish that it were, for that would mean I had power. I might be able to save myself. But I can't. I'm helpless. And Jacquetta saw that. She knew. That's why she did this. Because it would be easy. Because I'm *nothing*.

"Take her," Ignatius orders, tracing the sign of the Eye between us.

And I'm too shocked and stunned to resist as the guards drag me off. In fact, I don't feel anything at all, save for the scalding shame of my own stupidity. I trusted Jacquetta. I listened to my wretched heart.

And now I will burn for my mistake.

CHAPTER FORTY-NINE

TIME IN THE DUNGEON IS SWALLOWED BY DARKNESS. THE ONLY indication that the hours are passing at all is the few instances in which a portion of dry bread is tossed through the bars of my cell. I don't eat. I don't sleep, either. Sooner or later, they're going to come for me. I probably won't even get a trial—just a pair of hot iron shoes. But I don't even care about that. All I can do is huddle against the gritty stone walls of my cell, breathing in the scent of dampness and rot.

Jacquetta.

Her name alone is like a spell, sparking both fire and ice in my veins. Flashes of our nights together emerge at random, each one like a knife digging into my flesh.

I love you.

Lies. Exactly like her promise that she wouldn't let me share the same fate as Marion. Here I am, perhaps even in the same cell as the fallen courtier. I pace from one side of the narrow space to the other, combing over the last weeks and spinning tangled webs of theories.

How long had Jacquetta been plotting this? Did it stretch back to when we met at the Sanctum? Before? But that doesn't make any sense. I watched Jacquetta attempt to kill the High Priest, and then the king. Why would she take such risks if that wasn't what she came here to do?

Unless she wanted you to see her try, that voice whispers.

Could that be right? Had those incidents merely been distractions? Revenge would have been the perfect cover for Jacquetta's presence in the White Palace, believable enough that I wouldn't ask questions. And I hadn't, not even obvious ones. Like, if Jacquetta actually intended to murder the king, why hadn't she done it? She summoned the lightning strike in the forest easily enough. She didn't need to waste an arrow on the king. Had she been crouching in the bush, wanting me to see her? But I still don't understand *why*. Why pretend? And why go along with my plan to find the Bloodstones? Why agree to the meeting with the Heirs at—

"Stonehaven." The word rattles between my bones.

Jacquetta left right after I persuaded my mother to summon the Heirs and meet with Nerissa. *That's* what she wanted—access. And to gain such access she needed to earn my trust. Feed me enough lies that I would convince my mother to summon the Heirs and allow Nerissa through our gates. But there's not going to be a meeting, I realize dully. Because the one thing I *know* Jacquetta never lied about is her disdain for the Ancients and their Heirs. What better way to dismantle the hierarchy than to destroy those at the top?

I slump against the damp wall, rage and despair coursing through my veins. The more I put the pieces together, the more I'm certain that I'm right. Nerissa and her coven aren't going to Stonehaven to talk. They're going to kill Mother and the Heirs, just like the Hunt did at the start of the war. Only this time, I'm the one who let them in.

The chill of the dungeon seeps into the marrow of my bones.

I was protecting you, Mother claimed.

She was right all along. Fresh shame burns in my lungs as I think of how easily I'd played into Jacquetta's hand. Of how little it took for her to gain my trust—a few kind words. A kiss. What a stupid wretch I am. I slept with the witch who will murder what's left of my family—opened the damn door for her to do so. I might as well have handed her the knife. How many other witches will die because of me?

Rage pounds in my wrists and that deep urge rises up, hungry for vengeance. For *blood.* This time, I do not tamp it down. I don't care if it's connected to Malum. If I get out of this, I vow, I *will* find her. I will hurt her the way she's hurt me.

That place behind my left ribs twinges, as if in anticipation.

Blinding light cuts through the cell. I wince, shielding my eyes. Is it the guards? Am I to be taken to the pyre? Fitted for a pair of iron shoes? My panicked mind summons images of Eden and Willa and even Mother. I won't get the chance to warn them about Jacquetta.

I failed you, I tell my sister, digging my fingernails into our marks. *I'm sorry.*

"Well, well." A familiar voice resonates against the stone. "If it isn't Mistress Witch."

I blink, squinting against the brightness. Gemstone-colored eyes gleam at me from the other side of the cell.

"Roland?" His name croaks from my dry lips. But I must be hallucinating.

"Guess you decided to extend your stay at the palace after all. Wouldn't be my choice of accommodations, but to each their own."

He's real. I scramble to my feet. "How did you find me?"

"Thank this one." He nods to where another shape lopes through Roland's door—one that meows in what is unmistakable reproach.

"*Nettle.*" I gather her up. She struggles, but I don't let her go, burying my face in the comfort of her fur. "I never thought I'd see you again."

Roland grunts. "Aye, I expect your beast shared that opinion. Heard it yowling from your rooms and went to investigate. I could guess what happened from there."

My tired mind travels back to when Jacquetta and I were packing. Nettle had been so agitated.

"You knew, didn't you? You were warning me." Nettle trills her confirmation. "I should have listened. I'm sorry."

She swishes her tail.

"I'd say you're a fair bit more than *sorry*." Roland indicates the cell. "How'd you get yourself down here? Thought you were leaving."

The rage, exhaustion, and fear that's been building since I found Jacquetta's note finally works its way up my chest. "I'm here because I'm an idiot. Stupid and useless and I shouldn't have—"

But the rest is strangled by a sob. I gulp for air, shoulders shaking. Roland pats frantically at his jacket, then fishes something out of his pocket.

"There now." He edges closer, holding his handkerchief as far away from his body as possible. "No need for that. Dungeon's wet enough as it is."

I accept the handkerchief and swipe at my face. Tears won't do me any good now.

"What happened?" Roland asks, gentler.

A vision of a pair of cobalt-blue eyes sears in my mind. Would that I could smash it into a hundred pieces. "*Jacquetta.*"

Nettle lays her ears flat and hisses.

"The other witch?" Roland asks. "She's the reason you're down here?"

"She gave the king a note that accused me. And then she left." I fist the damp fabric of the handkerchief. "She's been using me the whole time to get to my mother. I think her coven is probably headed to my Sanctum. She's going to murder them."

And it will be my fault. All those crows were right—I'm cursed.

"By the Mines," Roland mutters. "I will never understand you witches."

Neither will I, and I feel even smaller.

"Right then," he says. "Let's go. I can't take you the whole way to the stables, but I can help get you out of the palace, at least. After that, you're on your own."

I blink at him. "You're helping me?"

"Seems that way."

"But why? You don't owe me anything. And I have no idea how I'll fix the Veil after this—if it's even possible."

I'm not even sure how I'll fix myself.

He heaves a sigh. "Aye. But I seem to remember a witch telling me we were kindred. We Dwarves don't leave each other behind."

Not like witches, apparently.

"Thank you, Roland."

"Keep your thanks." He waves me off. "This is as much for me as for you. Like I told you—can't risk you giving me away when they torture you."

Despite everything, a smile twitches at my lips. I'm going to miss this Dwarf. Roland walks through his door and I follow, Nettle padding beside me into the dark.

The enchanted tunnels unspool through the palace as Roland takes me first to fetch my satchel—which miraculously hadn't been confiscated during the three days I was locked in the dungeon—and then as close to the stables as we can get. Fitz trots alongside our unlikely party, much to Roland's disapproval.

"Are you packing him as a meal?" he'd asked wryly when I insisted on bringing the dog.

Maybe it is a bad idea, but when we'd returned to the chamber, I'd discovered Fitz snuffling around Jacquetta's side of the bed—looking for her, I think.

Please don't leave me, his baleful eyes pleaded.

I couldn't. Not when I understood so well how it felt to be used and discarded.

"Here we are." Roland halts us, then jams one of his keys into the wall. Another door appears, leading outside. "Stable's that way."

He points to a building in the distance. Moonlight glimmers against its stone walls.

"You think you can make it back to your people in time?" Roland asks.

I honestly have no idea. Three whole days are already wasted, and Jacquetta most certainly stole a horse when she escaped. Was her coven already poised to attack when I was arrested? And those witches aren't the only threat.

"Have you heard of the Hunt being dispatched?" I ask.

Roland shakes his head. "Not yet."

But that doesn't mean they won't be, especially now that the king believes a Sanctum housed a witch. I picture a storm of flaming arrows sailing over Stonehaven's walls, and fear crackles along my spine.

I need to get to the coven—even if it's the last thing I do.

PART IV

I am with child again.

Given the tragedies of my previous pregnancies, Callen is cautious and distant. My physicians swarm my chambers, inspecting the food I eat and hardly allowing me out of bed for more than an hour at a time. I must be careful, they urge. The king must have his son.

But what these supposedly *learned* men do not know—what only I know—is that this pregnancy will be different. I have made sure of it. I have paid the price of blood and snow.

My child will be born. Not a son, but a daughter. The king will hate me for her. Let him. This realm has enough of greedy, grasping kings. What it needs now is a queen to forge a new age.

In my bones, I can already sense the dawn coming.

—*From the secret writings of Queen Sybil,*
Age of the Light 33

CHAPTER FIFTY

SMOKE RENDS A GAPING, BLACK GASH IN THE SKY—VISIBLE FOR miles before I reach Stonehaven.

No! my mind screams. *I'm too late.*

I urge my horse faster through the trees. Dread pools in my belly when we finally sail over the silver ribbon of the stream, because there's no warmth or hum of magic to indicate that the wards are intact. They've broken again. But was it Jacquetta's coven or the Hunt?

Either way, it's your fault, that malevolent voice needles.

Guilt pounds alongside my fear as I at last spot the portcullis—not closed, as it should be, but yawning wide. The guard towers are painfully vacant as well. So, I discover, is the courtyard. The stable is empty. Even the chickens have vanished.

Ears pricked for intruders, I slip from the saddle and enter the Sanctum, Fitz and Nettle at my heels. Broken glass and ripped parchment litter the halls. But there are no pools of blood or scraps of flesh as I would expect from a battle—and my sisters would have fought. They defeated the Hunt once before.

But perhaps not again.

My heart in my throat, I follow the crackle of flame to the cloister. The smell of woodsmoke and ash sears my lungs. Are my sisters out there, reduced to charred bones? I force myself to look. Bits of glass and metal shine amid the still-burning patches of flame, along with curled and blackened shells that might have been books. But none of it, I realize, is flesh or bone. None of it is *them*.

Relief rushes through me so quickly that I grip the ledge of the stone railing. But if my coven survived whatever happened here, where are they?

Something pops behind me, and Nettle yowls a warning. Fumbling in my panic, I snatch up the nearest object—a chair leg—and scramble to hide behind an upturned bench. Footsteps approach. I grip my makeshift weapon tighter, bracing myself to swing.

Before I get the chance, a crow calls, its feathered body swooping close enough that I feel the wind stirred by its wings. I flinch away from it and the damn thing squawks again, as if in laughter. There's something vaguely familiar about that call. I've heard it before.

Still clutching my chair leg, I peer around my bench and through the archway. The crow lands on the shoulder of a white-haired figure standing in the middle of the hall, her gnarled knuckles toying with a string of teeth hanging from her waist. Recognition slams into me. That's not just a crow. It's Cornelius. Which means the figure is . . .

Mathilde.

"Who's there?" she calls.

After everything that's happened, my heart aches at the sight of the other witch.

"You're here." I drop the chair leg and hurry over, crushing Mathilde in an embrace. "You're all right."

"By the Spirits, what—" Her hands travel over my back, and she inhales deeply. "*Ayleth.* Is it really you?"

I'm honestly not sure. "Where is everyone else? I didn't see . . ."

See their broken bodies in the fire, I almost say, but the words snag.

Nettle meows, winding herself around Mathilde's ankles in greeting.

"They've gone." She bends to scratch between my cat's ears, her white eyes gleaming in the afternoon sunlight. "Left over a week ago."

Over a week? My mind scrambles with the calculation. Hard as I pushed the horse, it still took me five days to get here from the palace. And I was in the dungeon for three—which means Mother left *after* our scrying. When she knew I would be coming. Why?

"Did anyone else show up here?" I ask Mathilde, trying to piece together an answer. "The Hunt or another coven?"

"Haven't seen the Hunt. But another coven, yes. They came and went a few days back."

So I was right. Jacquetta was planning to attack Stonehaven. The satisfaction of guessing her scheme mixes with the shame of my own part in it. But at least she didn't succeed. "They did this? Wrecked the Sanctum?"

"Not them." Mathilde gestures around us. "All this was on your mother's orders. Coven was to destroy everything they couldn't carry, and then they were off."

My brow furrows. "*They* did this?"

Wind pushes in, carrying the ash from the fire. But why would Mother order . . .

Slow comprehension creeps over me. I'd asked Mother to gather the other Heirs for the meeting with Nerissa. They must have refused to come to Stonehaven. More than that, they must have told Mother to leave—drawn a line, with themselves on one side and me on the other. I suppose it shouldn't be a surprise which one Mother chose.

You're my heart, Ayleth.

But Mother locked her heart away years ago. The knife of her betrayal slices through my chest. Just like with Jacquetta, it's my own fault. I should have known that I'd never be enough—that no one would ever choose *me* when presented with a better option.

"Why didn't you go with them?" I ask Mathilde, smothering my emotion.

"I wasn't exactly invited."

Of course she wasn't. Selene and the other Heirs would never allow a Wayward witch among them. "I'm sorry."

"Made no difference to me." Mathilde waves me off. "Besides, I knew you'd be back."

And she'd waited for me. In this moment, with the wound of Mother's rejection bleeding, Mathilde's loyalty means more to me than anything else.

Fitz emerges from wherever he'd been hiding and snuffles around Mathilde's shoes. The older witch steps back. "What is that?"

"A dog," I tell her. Fitz growls. "He's not very friendly."

"Neither am I." Mathilde reaches down and lets Fitz sniff her hand. He sneezes. "Nice to meet you as well. Come on. You all must be hungry. And I expect there's a story to be told."

A long one. With one last glance at the smoldering fire, I follow Mathilde down the wrecked hallway, passing the ghosts of the witch I used to be along the way.

The kitchen is mostly stripped bare, yielding only a forgotten sack of flour and some yeast, along with lentils and enough herbs in the pots by the window to brew a calming tea. The lentils simmer in the kettle as Mathilde and I sit together at the table, the scent of mint and lavender wafting around us.

She listens as I recount the weeks since I left the Sanctum for the White Palace—the haunting shadows and that ominous pull I felt toward the king. The Nevenwolf and how Rhea helped me kill it. Marion's comb and the queen's death. Mother's broken promise and Jacquetta's note.

I'm sorry.

I'm the one who should be sorry. I'm the one who believed in her—in *us*—again.

"Well," Mathilde says when I finally finish. Nettle has curled herself on the elder witch's lap and fallen asleep. Fitz is nearby, gnawing on a sweet potato I discovered in the root cellar. "That is . . . interesting."

"Interesting," I repeat, gripping my mug. "That's all?"

"You cannot expect me to have *wise words* at the ready after that odyssey."

Maybe not, but I had hoped she'd be able to offer *something*. I sip my tea, but it's gone cold. "I can't believe I fell for her tricks again. And not only Jacquetta's. Mother's too. I should have guessed she'd side with the Heirs. Her position is all she's ever cared about."

"Families are complicated," Mathilde says, as if that explains everything. "And her position is all your Mother has ever been *taught* to care about. If my memory serves, your grandmother was one of the witches executed at the start of the war. It can't have been easy for Cassandra to lose her own mother, and then to become Heir, under such circumstances."

I suppose Mathilde has a point. My mind summons the tapestry in the palace, those five witches forced to dance in the barbaric hot iron shoes. Even though I know my grandmother was among them, she's always seemed like a character in our history rather than a real witch. Mother spoke of what happened to Grandmother, but never who she was. Maybe it was too difficult. Maybe, like me, Mother just wanted her own mother to be proud of her.

But I'm not in the mood for empathy. "I don't forgive her."

"No one said you had to." Mathilde sips her tea. "And as for Jacquetta—you're not the first witch who's followed her heart in perilous directions. Love is complicated too."

Love. It spears through me. But that's not what I feel. Not anymore.

"Easy for you to say. You're not the one who was locked in a dungeon cell."

She tilts her head at me. "Perhaps not. But I've faced my own consequences where love is concerned. Or did you assume that I passed the last centuries in solitude?"

I frown. Honestly, Mathilde seems like a witch who has *always* existed, never needing anyone else. "Did you?"

"No." Mathilde scratches under my cat's chin. "I loved someone—dearly. In fact, that love is the reason I'm Wayward."

What does love have to do with being Wayward? "I don't understand."

"Like you," Mathilde continues, "I'd been training my whole life to face the flames. But then I met a man in a nearby village. We fell in love—enough so that we wanted to spend our lives together. Mortals, however, are not permitted to reside within the walls of a Sanctum."

No. They used to visit before the war, bearing gifts of appreciation, or seeking our help. But they were never allowed to stay. Not even for the night.

"But you *could* have been together, even if he lived elsewhere," I point out. "Witch and mortal couplings are commonplace."

Or they used to be. Necessary, even, as male witches are so rare.

"True," she allows. "But I was young and stubborn. I told my sisters that if he couldn't stay, then I would go."

Even for Mathilde, this surprises me. "And you ... left?"

"I did. The other witches warned me against it." She strokes Nettle's back. "Passion, they promised, was fleeting. He would grow old, they said. He would die ages before me. I didn't care. I eschewed my vow, left my home, and started a new life in another part of the realm with the person I chose."

There's no regret in her words. No bitterness. "What happened between you?"

"We lived," she says with a soft smile. "He was a good man. A kind man. We never had any children. It was always just the two of us. I used my gift where I could—tending our crops or helping those who didn't mind a Wayward over a coven witch. We were happy."

Happy. The word trembles through me. I thought I knew what that meant, especially during those nights wrapped up with Jacquetta. But now . . .

"And then he grew old." Mathilde's white eyes shine. "And he died. Just like my coven swore that he would. I hadn't even reached my hundredth year when he passed. Most people thought I was his daughter, or granddaughter, near the end."

"You never searched for a way to keep him with you?"

She arches an eyebrow. "You know that's not what we do, Ayleth. A life is a life, regardless of how far the years stretch. We were lucky to walk the earth at all. I take it you've realized that about your sister?"

I press my thumb against one of the marks stamped into my palm. During the long days of my journey, all I could think about was bringing Rhea back. After all, the only reason I'd abandoned the idea was because of Jacquetta. But the urge to return to the White Palace, find the Bloodstones, isn't there. Deep down, I've always known that Mathilde is right. I don't understand why Rhea appeared to me in the fire, but it wasn't to bring her home.

"Yes. I have," I tell Mathilde. And then, "You really don't regret leaving your coven?"

She taps her mug, considering. "Choosing *love* could never be a regret. Not for me."

So that's her story. Mathilde is Wayward simply because she followed her heart. Shame prickles between my shoulder blades when I recall how the other witches treated Mathilde when she arrived here, their suspicion and judgment. All Mathilde did was spend her life with the person she loved.

"What about after he died?" I ask. "You could have returned—Ascended?"

Ascensions typically occur during the first blood moon of a witch's twenty-third year, to honor the Ancients. But a witch can bind herself anytime after that, so long as it's during a blood moon.

She pauses.

"I entertained the idea, especially when the grief of his loss was fresh and I was facing the world alone. Like love, grief is its own spell. A dark one." She reaches for the string of teeth hanging from her waist. "But in the end, I decided that if my coven didn't want me as I was, we were better off apart. And I had no inclination to join another."

A breeze pushes through the open window, carrying the call of a crow. Cornelius.

"I know you're worried about what's next for you," Mathilde says gently. "And I'm sorry about what happened. Whatever her reasons, your mother made a terrible choice."

Again, that knife of betrayal twists.

"There is no *next* for me," I reply, bitter. "Mother was right about one thing. When I reached for Rhea, something reached back. Sooner or later, Malum will consume me."

That place behind my left ribs trembles—faint, but present.

"You seem well enough to me."

"For now. But at the palace, it was so strong. I told you about the Nevenwolf and the king. It's only a matter of time before all that starts again."

"Or maybe you'll find a way to stop it. You're a clever witch."

Intelligence has nothing to do with it. "You don't understand."

"No, of course not." Mathilde flicks her hand, dismissive. "You know everything, young witch that you are. What wisdom could I possibly offer?"

I grumble into my mug.

"You have to stop punishing yourself," Mathilde says, pointing at me. "Why did you reach for your sister? Because you wanted to upset the balance of magic? Meddle with the Veil?"

"Of course not. I just wanted Rhea. She's the only one who . . ."

"Saw you?" Mathilde finishes for me. "There's nothing wrong with that, Ayleth. Think of what it meant that you were surrounded by so many other witches, and yet you were still compelled to reach for the one beyond the Veil."

My eyes sting. "It doesn't matter now."

"It does," Mathilde insists. "Intent is key in magic. Even we Way-wards understand that."

Dark intents reap dark rewards—the old lesson resurfaces.

"But what does that have to do with Malum?"

"As you said, all you wanted was your sister," Mathilde explains. "You reached beyond the Veil for *love*. Should you have done it? No. But you didn't mean harm by it. That matters. Don't assume that there's a price to pay."

I watch the leaves float in my tea. What Mathilde says makes sense, but there are still too many questions about the White Palace. "Then why were the shadows following me? Why was I being hunted?"

The other witch merely lifts one shoulder. "I suspect those are questions only you can answer. If you—"

The rest is cut short as she starts to cough. Nettle meows, concerned, as Mathilde presses her sleeve to her mouth. It comes away spotted with scarlet. Alarm shoots through me.

"You're ill." I hurry to the cupboards. "I'll find something for you. I'm sure I missed—"

"I'm *dying*, Ayleth."

I freeze but refuse to turn around. If I do, then what she says is real.

"I'm an old witch. I've lived my time."

"How much longer?" I whisper.

"Weeks—days, I'm not sure. But I can hear the Spirits calling to me. And there's someone else I'd like to see beyond the Veil. You understand that."

All I understand is that I cannot lose her after everything else.

"It's all right, Ayleth. I'm not gone yet."

"But you will be," I say, swallowing the lump in my throat. "And then what?"

Cornelius calls outside again.

"We Wayward witches sew up our wounds and keep moving," Mathilde replies. "That's precisely what I expect you to do."

CHAPTER FIFTY-ONE

FOR A FEW DAYS, WE SETTLE INTO A SEMBLANCE OF NORMALCY. Mathilde helps with cleaning and cooking, offering droves of her cryptic, unsolicited advice when I least expect it. No matter what I'm doing, I keep one eye trained on the gate, expecting the Hunt to descend, looking for witches. They don't, though, which is odd. Both the High Priest and the king know what I am. Why haven't they come to investigate Stonehaven?

But I suppose it doesn't really matter, especially not when Mathilde's coughing fits increase. Any attempt to convince the other witch to remain in bed is blatantly ignored. And I stubbornly refuse to believe that there's nothing to be done to help her. I scavenge the Sanctum, searching for something—anything—that can keep her with me just a little longer.

It's strange to roam the empty halls. I keep imagining that I hear a round of laughter or the shuffle of footsteps. Once, I even follow what I'm sure is the flash of white-gold curls. It's nothing, of course. And I might prefer when the shadows were haunting me to these

hallucinations. But the force inside me is oddly quiet now. Sometimes, in the night, the darkness seems to thicken, but it's nothing
like it was at the White Palace. Even so, I can still feel that faint nudging behind my left ribs, as if Malum is reminding me that it's still
there—waiting.

Like calls to like.

How long until the Veil is thin enough for a Nevenwolf to tear
through it and swallow me whole? Let it come. There's nothing here
for me anymore.

Eventually, my wanderings lead me to Mother's rooms. She'd
been thorough when she left. The shelves are empty. Broken jars and
splintered wood are scattered over the floor. The table where she
convened with the other Heirs is on its side. Her mirror is here, but
it's shattered, nothing but jagged shards still clinging to the frame.
I'm surprised—that mirror is the last thing I'd expect her to leave
behind. And what happened to the silver-eyed raven? Is it dead, used
up and discarded—just like me?

I give myself a shake, banishing my self-pity. There's a chest on the
other side of the room and I pick my way across the debris, hoping
it might contain a useful tincture or balm for Mathilde. But when I
lift the lid, the jeweled handle of a knife glimmers in the afternoon
light. Several markings are etched into its blade—runes. This is the
knife Mother gifted me on the day of my Ascension. The one I'd rejected. And not just that. Beneath the knife itself is a swath of red
material. No, not red—*crimson*. Black and green embroidery glimmers on the fabric, the careful stitches picking out runes for protection and strength.

This is *my* cloak.

Or it would have been. There's no note attached to the fabric, but
Mother's message is clear. These items were meant for her daughter—
her Second. That's not who I am anymore.

I'm not one of them. I never will be.

Fighting the ache in my chest, I drag the cloak out and pull its heavy weight around my shoulders. I turn toward the mirror, glimpsing pieces of my reflection in the fragmented glass.

You remind me of myself, Mother said.

Another lie. Or maybe it wasn't. Perhaps Mother left *because* I remind her of herself. She didn't want to be reminded. Didn't want *me.* Anger rushes up, hot and swift. There's a bottle nearby and I snatch it up, hurling it at the mirror. Glass shatters against the center, the brittle smash immensely satisfying. I throw a jar next, then a pestle. Object after object—even the runed knife—crashes into that vile mirror. Still, it is not enough.

"I hate you!" I shout at the wasted frame, hoping Mother somehow hears me. "I hate what you made me."

Wind rattles the shutters. A crow wings past, its cry echoing in the quiet.

One for sorrow.

Enough of this. I rip the cloak from my shoulders. It pools on the floor like a puddle of blood. Let it stay there forever. I never wanted it anyway. I never wanted any of this. But just before I leave Mother's room for the last time, I look back at the mirror, what's left of my own reflection carved up by ragged glass.

Ayleth, I swear I hear. *Ayleth.*

Before the week is out, Mathilde does not rise from her bed. The heaviness of yet another impending loss weighs me down. I sit beside her with Nettle, who, along with Fitz, has refused to leave the older witch's side since we returned. So much for being unfriendly.

"Do not put me on the coven fire," Mathilde says as I press a cool cloth to her forehead.

"No," I agree. The fire in the cloister finally died, but smoke still streams into the air. "It's desecrated, I'll have to—"

"That's not what I mean," she interrupts. "I'm a Wayward witch. I don't belong there."

"But your bones," I insist. It's bad enough to think of Mathilde dying. I cannot bear to believe that she won't be among the Spirits. "Without a Ceremony of—"

"Ceremonies are for the living. Do you really believe a witch is trapped in her skin for all eternity if she is not wrapped a certain way, or lying beneath a special pile of ash?"

Just a few months ago, I would have said yes. After everything that's happened, I don't know what I believe. "Where do you want to be buried?"

She considers for a moment. "Somewhere nice, where the sun will shine down on me."

Nettle meows and swishes her tail in approval.

"Then that's where you'll be." I wring out the rag in the shallow basin beside the bed, struggling against the fresh twinge of sadness in my throat.

"And what about you?" the elder witch asks. "Have you decided what you will do when I'm gone? You can't keep moping around here."

Even near death, Mathilde has lost none of her charm.

"I'm not moping."

"My mistake. What shall we call it—brooding?"

By the Spirits. "I call it taking care of you."

"You won't be taking care of me for much longer. And the others aren't returning."

A crow calls outside. Cornelius, probably. He's been flitting to the window and back all morning, checking on Mathilde.

"I don't know what I'm going to do," I admit. "Without power—"

"Just because you haven't made a vow doesn't mean you don't have power. Such wasn't the case for me, was it?"

I can't argue with that. Mathilde is just as gifted as any of our Diviners, if not more so. Yet another lie I was taught about Waywards, that they're not as strong as the coven witches.

You're not Wayward or coven, that voice whispers. The ridges of my ears burn.

"Vow or not, I've never showed any sign of talent," I admit, bracing myself for Mathilde's questions. Worse, her judgment. She only laughs.

"No talent? From what you described of your time at the White Palace, you enlisted the help of a Dwarf—no easy feat, if I recall some of their temperaments. You went toe-to-toe with the White King himself and lived to tell the tale. You killed a *Nevenwolf.* You may not have made a vow to an Ancient, but don't discount the gifts you possess all on your own."

Her words resonate in a place deep inside me. But as much as I might want them to be true, they're not. "Rhea killed the Nevenwolf. I killed the queen. And a gifted witch would have been able to spot Jacquetta's treachery before she had me arrested."

I hate myself for the way her name still sends shivers through my blood. Even my dreams betray me. I see us together almost every night. Sometimes I even wake with the smell of juniper clinging to my bedclothes.

Have you learned nothing? that voice scolds.

"Do you really believe you caused the queen's death?" Mathilde asks.

"What else could it have been?" I ask, picturing the shadows diving into the queen's mouth. "I touched her and then Malum claimed her."

"But you think it wanted you?"

"I *know* it wanted me," I correct. "I told you about how the shadows followed me. The dreams. Even the king's attention—all of it was Malum."

"Yes, the king," Mathilde says, more to herself than to me. She worries at her strand of teeth. "You said you felt drawn to him. Like a . . ."

"Pull," I finish for her, cringing against the memory of the tether.

Talons clack as Cornelius settles on the windowsill, flaring his wings. Nettle watches him, her tail flicking.

"May I see your hand?" Mathilde beckons.

I wring out the rag again. "You know I don't like readings."

"This isn't a reading," Mathilde says. "And I'm dying. You have to do what I say, or I'll haunt you."

Cornelius chuffs, as if to second her threat. The two of them, honestly. But what harm could it do? Heaving a sigh, I nudge Mathilde's hand with mine. She accepts it, her thumb kneading between tendon and bone.

"This is interesting," she says after a few moments. "I didn't sense it before."

"What?"

"I assume you're familiar with your Fate line?" She presses down on the center of my palm, where a faint crease runs from my middle finger down to my wrist. "It's believed that these lines can be linked, intertwined with another witch's or, in rare cases, with a mortal's. Some witches report being able to sense the link physically. A pull, as you described."

Or a tether? "And is that what's there? A link?"

"Perhaps," Mathilde says. "There's definitely *something*. It could be a second line."

"But why would my Fate line be connected to the king's?"

Mathilde raises an eyebrow. "That's a better question for you."

Even if it is, I don't want to know the answer. King Callen is far away at the palace, and that's where he'll stay. I want nothing to do with him. Besides, Mathilde's theory doesn't explain the other instances I felt the pull—like in the forest with the Nevenwolf.

"It was Malum," I insist. "Like calls to like—it attracted the king because he's a murderer. He *is* Malum."

"The king may be vicious, but he's *mortal*," Mathilde points out. "And surely there were others at court with hearts as dark as his. Did you ever feel the same sensation around anyone else?"

No. Not even with Sir Weston or the High Priest, two men as wicked as the king. Mathilde releases my hand and I study my Fate line. Could she be right? Am I linked to the king? If I am—why?

"*Like calls to like*," Mathilde repeats, scratching between Nettle's ears. "Haven't heard that in a while. It's a Wayward saying, did you know? From before the covens."

"Is it?"

She nods. "Funny how that's been forgotten. But then, such is the way of things. Elementals, Diviners—those distinctions didn't exist until witches created them. That's another reason I never bound myself. I didn't want to be held captive by the flames of a coven fire—to lose sight of my unique strengths. You possess the same freedom now."

"It doesn't feel like freedom."

"Maybe that's because you're so accustomed to being caged."

Cornelius chuffs, as if to agree. I look past him, at the smoke still curling from the scar of the coven fire. None of my sisters appeared *caged* when they faced the flames. But I think of what Jacquetta said about Rhea and how miserable my sister might have been.

It must be undone. Those words swirl inside my skull.

"Remember, Ayleth." Mathilde grips my wrist. "Not even an Ancient can grant you a power that isn't already there."

Mathilde does not survive the night. I sit beside her as she releases her last rattling breath, tears streaming down my face and staining her blanket. I might have been raised in the Sanctum, surrounded by my sisters, but Mathilde is the only witch who really accepted me. And I worry that no one else will, ever again.

I spend a long time with her, unwilling to let her go. Mathilde was right. Grief is like a spell. Its inky tendrils reach for me, dragging me down to a bottomless oily sea. I nearly drowned there after Rhea died. In fact, I wanted to drown. Now that sea is waiting for me again. But Mathilde would be furious if I surrendered to it.

Eventually, I force myself to move. Even Fitz is sad, lurking in the room and whimpering as I clean Mathilde's body with lavender-scented water. Wrap her, even though she claimed it was a useless gesture, and whisper the rites of the dead. If these ceremonies exist for the living, that means they're mine to conduct. But I respect Mathilde's wishes regarding the coven fire.

Cornelius follows us through the forest as Nettle helps me choose a resting place for the fallen witch, a bright clearing with vines of midnight flower winding up the trees. Mathilde would approve. In the day, it will be sunlit and airy. In the night, illuminated by the glowing jewels of the flowers' petals. It takes half the day to dig her grave. A storm trudges in from the east, but I don't hurry as I lower Mathilde's body into the earth, singing the Song of the Dead as the wind quickens around us. As the final note trembles from my lips, Cornelius emits a single mournful cry and then disappears into the thickening clouds. I doubt I'll see him again.

Thunder growls in the distance by the time I return to the Sanctum. Fitz barks as we near the gates, zooming ahead. Instinct taps at the base of my neck. Someone is there. I toss the shovel away and reach for the knife at my belt. There's a horse in the courtyard—not the one I stole from the palace. Its rider is standing just inside the Sanctum's open doors. I realize immediately that it's not a Huntsman. This shape I'd know anywhere, one I have traced and held and explored. One I never thought to glimpse again.

It's Jacquetta.

Chapter Fifty-Two

F OR A HEART-STOPPING MOMENT, ALL I CAN SEE IS JACQUETTA. *My* Jacquetta—our heads bent together as we pored over books in the library, or the way she looked in her gown for the banquet. I can almost taste her lips. Feel her hands on my body. But that sparkling, exquisite happiness is instantly burned up by hard truth— none of those memories are real. It was all a fabrication. *My* Jacquetta never existed. The vow I made in the dungeon comes crashing back to me. Now is my chance to make good on it.

Whipping my knife from its sheath, I stalk toward the other witch. Horror flashes across Jacquetta's expression, but she doesn't run. Perhaps she doesn't believe I'll actually harm her. She's wrong.

"Ayleth." She puts her hands up as I approach. "I came here to talk."

"You've said all you need to say." I press the blade to her throat. "What was it again—*I'm sorry?*"

She blanches. "I *am* sorry."

I dig the knife into her skin. A thin line of blood blooms on her neck. The pulse at her throat beats harder. Good. Let her be afraid.

"Sorry for what? Having me arrested? Leaving me to burn? Or are you sorry for using me so that you could come here and kill my mother and the Heirs?"

Storm-charged wind whistles around us.

"We were never going to harm them."

But she was going to do *something*. I can see it in her expression. By the Spirits, I was right. I hadn't realized that there was still some small, broken part of me that wanted to be wrong until this moment, as it shrivels and dies.

"You're as bad as the Hunt," I seethe. "How can you even call yourself a witch?"

Her eyes flash, sapphires beneath the heavy clouds of the coming storm. "Me? What about the Heirs? Why do they get to decide who holds power and who doesn't?"

"*I'm* holding the power now," I snarl.

Hurt her, that deep urge screams. *Hurt her the way she hurt you.*

My heart slams against my sternum. I want to hurt her. I want to *destroy* her. Carve out her heart and grind it to dust, exactly like she did to mine. But this close, I smell the tang of the forest mixed with juniper. The phantom taste of roses fills my mouth and I hate myself for the desire that ignites in my veins.

"Please, Ayleth." Hesitant, Jacquetta's hand covers my own around the knife's hilt. The rhythm of her pulse hums beneath her skin, furious and terrified—just like mine.

More, the dark instinct thrums. *Push harder.*

Blood trickles down her neck, a slick garnet against the white of her skin. She deserves this. Worse, even. And yet . . . my hand trembles.

I can't do it. Curse my feckless heart, I can't.

A cry of rage and frustration bursts out of me, and I wheel away from Jacquetta, despising my own weakness. Have I learned *nothing*?

"What are you *doing* here?" I shout at her, throwing my arms wide. "They're gone. What's left? Have you come to finish me off because you failed with the others?"

Nettle hisses, her muscles coiled and ready to spring.

"I came to talk." Jacquetta touches the cut at her neck. Red smears her fingers. I'm not sorry. "You deserve to know what happened."

"Oh, do I?" I laugh, bitter. "And when were you planning on telling me? After I was made to dance in a pair of hot iron shoes?"

A crow calls overhead. Cornelius? Maybe he'll come back and peck out Jacquetta's eyes.

"I knew you'd make it out of the palace," she says, as if it weren't sheer luck and Roland's kindness that saved me from her trap.

"I see." I tilt my head at her. "And how would you have known that?"

"Because you're smart. And . . ." Jacquetta flushes. "I've been . . . keeping up with you."

Keeping up. The same way Mother did? I imagine Jacquetta watching me wallow in the dungeon while she was safe with her own coven. My anger burns hotter.

"I was entertainment, then? Is that why you left me there? So you could all gather around your mirror to—"

"No," she says, cutting me off. "It wasn't like that. I didn't use a mirror. I sensed you, like I do with other magic. It's difficult to explain, but I could tell you were safe—even pinpoint where you were on a map if I felt the connection strongly enough. It happens with those I . . ."

Love. The word shimmers between us. But I will not be fooled by it again.

"Enough with your pretty speeches. What do you want? I can smell Nerissa's bidding on you, Second that you are."

"I'm not—" But she stops. Inhales a visible breath. "Are you going to let me explain?"

Thunder rolls, closer now.

There's nothing she can possibly say that will make a difference at this point. I should tell her to leave and never come back. But I no-

tice that her cloak is streaked with mud. She looks hungry—like she
hasn't seen a decent meal in days. How long has she been traveling?
And why *is* she here alone? That's not my problem. *She* isn't my
problem—not anymore. Still, I want to know just how far this plan
stretched, if only to understand the depth of my own stupidity.

"Fine," I say, crossing my arms. "Start talking."

Jacquetta settles herself on an upturned bucket and Fitz trots up
to her, snuffling around her skirts. *He,* apparently, harbors no recollection of being abandoned. Traitor.

"The Heirs were never part of any plan," Jacquetta begins, absently
petting the dog's head. "Neither were you. Not at first anyway. When
we met at the Sanctum, I was as surprised as you were. And I *was*
there to kill the king."

More lies. "No, you weren't."

"Yes, Ayleth," she insists, holding my gaze. "I was. It's as I said—
Mother wanted to end the war without the Heirs. My coven made a
deal with Rycinthia. If they sent their army, we'd help them secure
Riven's throne. Recognize their leadership."

That gives me pause. Similar arrangements had been bandied
about at Stonehaven, but Mother never acted on them, unwilling to
rely on the loyalty of mortal rulers. After what I'd witnessed at the
White Palace, I don't blame her.

"But Rycinthia didn't attack," I point out.

"No," Jacquetta agrees. "They wouldn't. Not unless we struck
first—and hard."

If you ever find yourself with the opportunity to strike . . . do not *miss.*
The queen's words float back to me beneath the biting wind. I shiver.

"We would kill the king," Jacquetta goes on. "Pave the way for
Rycinthia to invade."

There's no trace of deceit in the hard lines of her expression. And
what she says makes sense, save for one detail. "Then what were you

doing at the Sanctum? Praying to the false goddess that the White King would visit so that you could flatten him with a statue?"

She ignores my sarcasm. "I tried to go to the palace first, but I couldn't even secure a position as a scullery maid. The Sanctum was my only option if I wanted to remain in the city. I decided I'd figure things out from there."

It's the same reasoning that led *me* to the Sanctum. But that doesn't mean I believe her.

"You were there for weeks, though," I press. "What took you so long?"

"Now you sound like my mother," she comments, bitter. I don't take it back. "But you're right. Once I was inside the Sanctum, I realized how difficult it was to leave. And I had no idea how to find my way to the king. When the High Priest came, I thought *his* death might be enough for Rycinthia, but . . ."

But I'd ruined that. I cross my arms. "If you want an apology, you'll be disappointed."

"I don't," she says tightly. "And it didn't matter. I finally got the opportunity I needed at the pageant. When you were offered the position with the queen."

Her blue eyes lock with mine and my pulse jumps.

"So that's when it started?" I ask. "You used me to get into the White Palace."

She doesn't deny it. "I expected that to be the end of our interaction. I thought I'd be gone in a matter of days, helping with the Rycinthian invasion."

"What stopped you?"

"I told you—my power wasn't working properly."

Because of you, that voice whispers.

I shake it away, thinking back to our early days serving the queen. Jacquetta was always skulking around on her secret errands—always returning frustrated and sullen. She could have been trying to kill the king, as she claims. But I'm still not sure.

"Even if that's true, I watched you stalk the king in the forest. He'd be dead if you'd loosed that arrow. But you didn't."

"I didn't because . . ." she pauses. Her jaw works. "I couldn't."

I stare at her. "You expect me to believe that? You nearly crushed Ignatius."

"But I *didn't,* did I? And if I'm telling the truth . . . I was relieved when you interfered."

"*Relieved?*" I echo, arching an eyebrow. "That's not how it seemed when you pulled me aside and threatened to gut me for meddling."

"Because I was angry at myself. I shouldn't have been relieved. And you . . ." Twin spots of pink bloom on her cheeks. "You *saw* me. Even then, you knew who I was underneath everything. I didn't want to be seen. I didn't want to be *weak.*"

She spits the word, and I know exactly where it came from—Nerissa. How often had my own mother made me feel precisely the same way? Useless. Nothing. As Jacquetta sits there, the storm rolling in above us, I'm reminded of the witch I saw on the balcony, screaming into her hands. A scream that resonated in the marrow of my bones.

"You weren't weak."

Jacquetta swallows. "Then why didn't I walk away? I could have. *Should* have. Especially when Mother . . ."

Leaves skitter over the ground.

"When she what?"

"After I failed to kill the king at the Hunt, Mother was furious," Jacquetta continues, halting. Fitz whines at her feet. "We argued, worse than we ever have before, and I wound up telling her about you—that you were at the palace."

My brow furrows. "You hadn't before?"

She shakes her head. "I wanted . . . I don't know. And it doesn't matter. I told Mother what I tried to believe myself—that what happened in the forest with the king was your fault. I said that I was helping you find the Bloodstones so that you would leave. Then I could finish things. But Mother was fixated on you. She decided that if I couldn't get close enough to kill the king, then I should get close to *you*. Earn your trust—so that we could learn more about what the Heirs were planning. She wanted to be one step ahead of them."

Numbness bleeds over me, even though I'd guessed the truth. There's absolutely no satisfaction at hearing her confirm my suspicions, only shame. My traitorous mind dredges up our nights together—our promises. It was nothing. Meant *nothing*. I blink back the infernal tears stinging in my eyes, refusing to let Jacquetta see how deeply she's wounded me.

"What a good Second you are," I grind out. "Did your mother give instruction as to *how* to earn that trust? Or were you just having fun with the assignment? Toying with your food?"

Nettle growls, her tail twitching.

Jacquetta's fists clench. "You know I wasn't."

"Oh, I don't know anything." I jab the knife at her. "You've made sure of that."

"What I felt was real, Ayleth," Jacquetta insists, her voice rough. "The more time I spent with you, the more I—"

Love. There it is again, fragile as spider's silk.

Ignore it, that voice whispers, *it's just another lie.*

"Regardless of how you felt, you left," I throw back. "What changed?"

Jacquetta stares off into the distance, at the line of clouds building, a thick swell of black. The wind whips around us, our cloaks flapping in the storm-scented air.

"Without the king's death, we couldn't rely on Rycinthia. We needed a new plan. *Our* plan." She looks at me. "I didn't lie about that. I persuaded Mother to go along with it—convene with the Heirs and develop a way to mend the Veil. Restructure the covens."

My brow furrows. "Then why was I arrested?"

Jacquetta hesitates. "Because Mother didn't trust that the Heirs could be so easily convinced. She decided to put . . . assurances in place."

Another peal of thunder rolls over us. "What *assurances*?"

She tugs at her sleeve. "An Heir's Second—the last of an Ancient's line—in a dungeon."

Cold comprehension oozes down my spine. If I died, Mother would be the last remaining witch with a link to Millicent's Blood-stone. Once she was gone, its power would sputter out. Probably the Veil itself would collapse, releasing Malum back into the realm.

"I was leverage," I whisper.

Of course I was—that's all I've ever been, a pawn to be pushed around by Mother and the king and now Jacquetta. A mirror that reflects everyone's face but my own.

"I didn't know until the night of our scrying," Jacquetta says, as if that's of any consequence. "I begged Mother to reconsider—to let you come back with me. But she insisted."

"And you listened," I say quietly. "You *left* me there."

Jacquetta's eyes shine. "I stayed close, making sure you were safe. As soon as the Heirs agreed to Mother's plan, I was to get you out."

But they wouldn't have agreed. I look back at the Sanctum, cast in shadow from the coming storm. Bloodline or not, Mother would have let me die. I was dead to her already. I'm not sure how she plans to continue Millicent's lineage, but it's not through me.

And I suppose that's one bright spot to this situation. Mother didn't just leave me—she left everything. A smile twists my lips as I picture the shock on Nerissa's face when she discovered that all her careful plans were thwarted. Perhaps *this* is why Mother broke her mirror, in case anyone was using the connection to follow her.

"But there was no agreement, was there?" I ask, smirking. "There wasn't even a meeting. Is that why you're here? Are you running from your failure? Or have you come to fetch me back like a prize?"

"I came for *you*," she says, the words quickening my blood.

They don't mean anything, that voice warns. *Don't let her close.*

"Then why did I walk out of the White Palace alone?"

She flinches. "You weren't alone. I hid nearby until I knew you'd escaped. And I didn't find out that your coven had gone until Mother sent a raven. I was on my way back to my own coven by then, but I could have gone after you. I could have told Mother you were free—but I didn't."

"And do you expect my gratitude for that? You abandoned me." I brandish the knife at the Sanctum. "Just like *they* did."

"That's not fair."

"No, what isn't fair is that you kept me in the dark." I step closer. "You could have told me about your mother's plans. We could have found a solution together. But you betrayed me. Worse, you went back to Nerissa after—"

"And where are you?" She rises swiftly enough that Fitz barks. "You could have gone anywhere after you left the White Palace, but you came here—again."

"Because of you! Because I thought you were going to murder my coven. My family."

"If they're your family, then why aren't they here? Mother says they must have left right before the queen's funeral. Just after we scried. After Cassandra promised to welcome you home."

Shame scalds my chest. I've had enough of this. Enough of *her*.

"Leave," I tell her. "You shouldn't have come here at all."

She doesn't move. "I broke every promise I ever made to you. I know that. And whether you believe it or not, I am sorry."

It's empty currency, no more valuable than the coins tossed around at the White Palace. "What do you want me to do with that?"

"I want you to live." She throws her arm toward the gates. "It took every ounce of strength not to ride after you when I learned what happened here. But I didn't because I wanted you to get away. I kept checking on you, waiting for you to move on—*do* something. But you just stayed here."

My knife glints as I point the blade at her. "Don't you *dare* judge me."

"No one knows where you are," Jacquetta goes on, heedless of the threat. "No one is looking for you. Go—make a life somewhere else."

Despite my rage, my attention travels to the gates and the forest beyond. Leaving is exactly what Mathilde encouraged me to do. But where would I go? That place behind my left ribs twinges. "What kind of life would that be? Have you forgotten the war? Malum?"

Thunder rumbles between us.

"There's nothing like that inside of you." Jacquetta's hand twitches, like she wants to reach for me, but she stops herself. "You're not broken, Ayleth. You never have been."

She's wrong. I'm shattered inside—nothing but shards of glass.

"And you?"

Cold raindrops begin to fall.

She hesitates. Her scent of juniper tangles with the charge of the storm. Jacquetta's gaze flits to my lips and, even though I know it would be the worst mistake I could make, I want her to kiss me. *Choose* me.

"I have to go back."

The words land like a blow. Jacquetta turns, the space between us like a widening chasm.

Let her leave, that voice inside me urges. Fool that I am, I can't.

"You said you loved me," I call after her. "What's more important than that?"

She pauses, her shoulders stiff.

Say it back, I scream in my mind. If she would just say it back . . .

"I told you who I am, Ayleth," she replies instead. "A coward."

How many times can a heart break before it kills you? As I stand there, rain stinging my face as I watch her mount her horse, I think I might discover the answer.

Fitz whines as Jacquetta gallops away through the portcullis. She doesn't look back. Not even once—like I'm nothing more than a discarded cloak stuffed into a chest.

The storm hits not long after that. Rain pummels the Sanctum, pooling on the floor inside. I listen to it howl, all my old wounds bleeding afresh. What is it about me that makes people leave? Is it that same dark place Malum found in me—tender and easy to sink its hooks into? As if in answer, that force shivers. It won't be long until the Veil breaks. I wish it would happen now. Let a Nevenwolf or some other sinister force swallow me up. At least then I would be free of this fury and hatred. And I *do* hate—Jacquetta and Mother. Nerissa and the covens and the Ancients themselves. I even hate the Bloodstones. *They're* what led me to the White Palace. To Jacquetta. In fact, if I held those stones now, I would . . .

Destroy them, that deep urge whispers.

The words bloom in my mind, like drops of blood in water. What if I *did* destroy the Bloodstones? Instinct rebels against the idea. Those stones are what hold the Veil—keep Malum contained. Without them, we lose our tie to the Spirits, our very power.

But what do I care about that? I have no power, and Malum was always going to take me.

It will have to take us both, Jacquetta had promised.

Well—a delicious thought swoops into my mind—perhaps this is one promise I can force her to keep.

Lightning flares and that place behind my left ribs trembles. This time, I lean into its malevolent pull. The threads of a plan weave together in my mind, dangerous and reckless, but *perfect*. I'm going back to the White Palace. I don't know how, but I'm going to find the Bloodstones. And then I will crush them to dust. Thousands of years of our history ripped apart by my own hands. And I will *revel* in the destruction.

Let Mother and Jacquetta and every other witch understand what it means to have their world yanked out from underneath them. To lose everything they hold dear. I am done with covens and *feelings* and witches who don't matter.

A crow calls, its cry piercing through the storm. I think of the seven birds who watched me in the south tower.

A secret, mystery, or curse.

For so long, I assumed those ominous creatures were warning me of Malum. But Malum was never my curse. No. My curse is *love.*

And the time has come to break it.

PART V

Daughter of glass, worth yet unseen,
From the darkness will rise a queen.
But every throne carries a cost,
A price to pay, a heavy loss.
A beating heart must she drown,
If she is to wear the crimson crown.

—*Final prophecy of Aphelia, First Diviner,*
Age of the Covens 300

CHAPTER FIFTY-THREE

T HE WHITE CITY GLOWS BLOOD RED IN THE DUSK.

It seems like a lifetime has passed since I first walked its cobbled streets, filled with merchants and shops and more people than I had ever encountered. I recall the witch I was then, determined to bring my sister back. But there's no going back—not for Rhea and not for me. Nettle meows, agreeing.

I adjust my satchel on my shoulder, gaze fixed to the turrets of the White Palace, like spears stabbing into the clouds. Memories of my last days in that place flash through my mind—the dungeon and the queen's horrific death and the night Jacquetta and I . . .

No. All that is done.

What matters now is finding the Bloodstones. For the whole of the journey here, I combed over the details of my previous search. My last lead regarding the stones' location came on the day Queen Sybil died. She'd wanted to show me something before the shadows claimed her. Had it been the Bloodstones? There's only one way to find out.

The windows of the White Palace gleam in the dying light, like so many eyes watching. Escaped witch that I am, I'll have to make every second within those walls count. My fingers drift to my waist, brushing the jewel-handled knife Mother left alongside my crimson cloak. The cloak, I left to rot. But the knife . . .

Much as I despised the blade when Mother gifted it to me, she had promised that it would strike true. Given the dangers waiting in the White Palace, that's a promise I might need, whether for someone else . . . or for myself.

But I don't dwell on that possibility. Throwing a last look over my shoulder, at the path I've traveled and the witch I once was, I start down the road toward the city. This time, however, I don't sense that the fabric of my world is splitting apart.

Instead, I feel like something is beginning.

"Come on, Joan," I whisper from the shadows of the main courtyard.

By some miracle, I'd managed to slip through the gates of the White City and into a wagon headed for the palace. So far, no one has recognized me—not even the gangly servant I'd bribed to deliver a message. But my luck may be running out. Without Roland's ring, I need assistance in sneaking into the palace. Joan was the only other person I could think to ask. But it's been nearly half an hour since the servant disappeared into the palace with my coin and parchment. I pull my hood lower.

Fitz whines at a nearby wagon filled with food. Hunger gnaws at my own stomach. Given how hard I pushed our horse to return, it's been days since I ate anything decent. But I can't think about that right now. My fingers tap out an impatient, nervous rhythm as I watch the door.

At long last, a figure steps out into the courtyard. Torchlight glimmers on an embellishment on her dress, and I recognize the queen's crowned pomegranate. Finally.

"Joan," I whisper from my hiding place. She edges nearer, rightly suspicious of a stranger. I pull back my hood. "It's me."

"*Ayleth?*"

I hold my breath and brace myself for her to call the guards. I'd known this would be a gamble. Instead, Joan hurries over, eyes wide with concern.

"Are you all right?" She snatches my hands in hers. "What are you doing out here? And where have you been? They're all saying that you're . . ."

"That I'm a witch," I finish for her.

A nearby horse whickers.

"Is it," Joan glances around us, "*true?*"

I should deny it. Insist that I've been falsely accused. Joan would likely believe me. But after everything that's happened I just . . . can't. And it doesn't matter. Joan reads my expression.

"I thought as much," she says quietly. "I've suspected for a while."

A *while?* Nettle trills, as if even she is surprised.

"How long?"

"I'm not sure." Joan shrugs. "There was just . . . something different about you and Jacquetta. When I heard the rumors, they felt right. I never said anything, though. I promise you that. Remember what I told you about the Dwarves in my family?"

That's right. I'd nearly forgotten about Joan's lineage. No wonder she's sympathetic to witches. "Does that mean you . . ."

"No, I'm not gifted." She dismisses the idea. "But those of us who were . . . well, I don't have to explain how it went for them. The king's edict—the war itself—is the most horrible thing to happen in this realm. I'd never give you away."

I believe her. Joan is a better friend than I ever realized.

"Why are you back, Ayleth?" she presses. "And where's Jacquetta?"

Much as I try to fight it, the memory of cobalt eyes sears in my mind.

"Gone," I say tightly. "And I need your help."

"Of course—anything."

I'm not sure she'll be so quick to agree when she learns the details. On the way here, I'd considered lying to her. But now . . . I know how it feels to be deceived. Used. I won't do that to someone like Joan.

"What do you know of Malum?"

She blinks at me. "*Malum?* What everyone else knows, I suppose."

"You mean what the Order teaches about Meira and her Light?" I ask. She nods and I huff a laugh. "Lies. It's always been the witches keeping Malum locked behind the Veil—the Bloodstones."

Joan's brow furrows. "Bloodstones? I didn't think those were real. And anything related to the covens would have been burned, wouldn't it?"

"They're here. I've come back to find them." I pause. A cart trundles past, wheels rattling. "To destroy them—and the Veil itself. I've come to release Malum into the realm."

"*What?*" Joan gapes at me, horrified. "Ayleth, that's—"

I raise my hand against her objections.

"There's nothing you can say that I haven't already told myself. But I have to do it. The covens have become as corrupt as this court." I gesture at the palace. "They treat their own like outsiders, all because of the Bloodstones and who controls them. It's time for that to end."

Joan weighs this, pressing her lips together. "But . . . Malum. I've read of the time before the covens—the blights and plagues. Monsters, like the Nevenwolf. You want all that to return?"

The place behind my left ribs shivers.

"I do. Because then the people of this realm will finally see that Meira isn't holding Malum back. They'll know that the Order lied."

And Mother will have everything she's ever cared about ripped away from her—the same way she ripped it all away from me. And Jacquetta ...

"But you don't have to help me," I say to Joan. "I'll understand if you can't."

She considers this for a few moments.

"If you do this," Joan says at last, her green gaze fixed on the palace, "the king and the others won't get to hide behind those walls anymore."

"No. They won't. And they'll pay for their crimes."

I hope that the shadows take the king—that a Nevenwolf rips out his heart. That force inside me trembles.

Joan exhales a shuddering breath. "All right. I'll help."

"Are you sure?"

She nods, though her expression suggests otherwise. "What next?"

"Can you get me into the queen's rooms?"

She hesitates, considering. "I think so. But you must do exactly as I say."

"Deal," I promise.

With that, Joan motions for me to follow her out of the shadows and toward the looming doors of the White Palace and whatever fate waits for me within.

With a deftness that would put any witch's spell to shame, Joan explains my way past the guards, claiming that I'm a guest of her family. Fitz and Nettle in tow, she guides us to the nearest servants' quarters, where we switch out my travel-worn dress for a uniform of the palace maids. Properly disguised, we sneak into a deserted hall. Joan pauses at a tapestry, pulling back the fabric to reveal a narrow door. She promptly slips a pin out of her hair to pick the lock.

"Where did you learn to do that?" I ask, torn between shock and awe.

"You can learn a lot of things when no one pays attention to you."

She grins as the lock unclicks and the door swings wide. Joan ushers me through it, letting the tapestry fall behind us. As my eyes adjust to the darkness of the space beyond, I realize that I've been here before, or close enough.

"Are these the old servants' passages?" I ask.

Joan fumbles to light a candle. "You know about them?"

"The princess showed me."

"Clever girl." She laughs. "I might have guessed she'd find them."

A smile twitches at my lips as I recall my excursions with Blodwyn. But then I remember the last time I'd seen her—placing a rose on the queen's coffin. She'd looked so lost.

"Is she well?" I ask Joan. "The princess?"

"As well as any of us are these days," Joan answers with a frown. "From what I've heard, she's barricaded herself inside her menagerie since the funeral."

I don't blame her. That same guilt from the ceremony churns in my stomach. Mother, Jacquetta, and all the rest might deserve to have their worlds upended. But Blodwyn . . .

"You'll look after her, though?" I ask Joan. "I'm not sure what will happen, once . . ."

"Of course I will." The light from Joan's candle flickers. "But you could help, now that you're back."

I'm not back, though. And whether I succeed in destroying the Bloodstones or not, soon I won't be doing much of anything. The thought isn't as frightening as it probably should be, perhaps because I've already resigned myself to my fate. That place behind my left ribs shivers, as if in anticipation.

Fitz whines, drawing Joan's attention.

"Poor thing. Are you hungry?"

The dog does his best to imply that he has never eaten a day in his life.

"We've relied on dried meat for the last few days," I explain.

Fitz huffs, as if to emphasize his ill treatment. Nettle watches him with a self-satisfied expression, likely insinuating that his hunger is his own fault. With all her hunts, I think my cat might have *gained* weight on the journey back to the palace.

"I can take care of him," Joan offers. "That is, if you don't mind."

"Mind?" I laugh. "Good luck with him."

Nettle meows, agreeing. Joan smiles and passes me the candle as she scoops Fitz into her arms. He growls, but only barely.

"So," Joan says, sliding me a look, "are you going to tell me what happened with Jacquetta?"

That searing pain from our encounter at Stonehaven plunges into my chest. I can still see Jacquetta walking away. Choosing another life over me—again.

Let her go, that voice urges.

My grip tightens on the candle. "She's the reason I was arrested."

Joan pauses in turning us down another passage. "That can't be right."

"She admitted it."

A tense moment of quiet passes.

"I'm so sorry, Ayleth," Joan says at last, wisely deciding not to press. "I don't mean to defend what she did, but . . . I saw you two together. She cares for you."

That traitorous chamber of my heart swells. I smother the emotion, hating myself for feeling anything. "Not enough."

Joan squeezes my elbow. "I meant what I said at the banquet. You deserve to be happy."

And what is that? the voice in my mind whispers. I'm not sure I'll ever know.

"How much farther?" I ask, distracting myself.

"Just here." Joan stops us at a door set into a wooden panel. "This leads to the queen's sitting room. But you should know—they searched Her Majesty's chambers not long after you were taken. I don't know what they were looking for, but His Illuminance was involved, along with several other Order priests."

Foreboding taps at the base of my neck. What did they want?

"Thank you," I say to Joan. And it occurs to me that this will probably be the last time I see her. "You're a true friend. I'm glad I met you."

Her green eyes shine, and she crushes me in an embrace, pinning Fitz unhappily between us. With a last squeeze of Joan's hand, I gather my remaining courage and slip into the gloom of the queen's chamber, the light of Joan's candle disappearing behind me.

It takes a moment for my eyes to adjust to the darkness. Outlines of chaises and chairs begin to emerge, stuffing spilling from their ripped cushions. Broken pottery crunches under my feet. Whatever Ignatius was looking for, he was thorough. But worse than the physical destruction is the sensation of *wrongness,* that same feeling from the archives and the crypt. It spiders over me, raising every hair on my body. Nettle meows, her golden eyes glowing.

"I feel it too," I tell her, reaching instinctively for the knife at my waist.

Moonlight floods through the tall windows as I pad into the queen's bedchamber. In the ethereal light, I can almost see Queen Sybil on the floor, her lips black and eyes sunken. Every few seconds, a strange thudding sound, like a faint heartbeat, knocks in the quiet. Drawers have been opened and dumped out, contents strewn over the rugs. Jewels glitter, the queen's necklaces and brooches and rings tossed about like dry leaves. What had Ignatius been searching for? Did he know what the queen had been hiding?

Wind moans down the chimney and a chill sweeps through the chamber. That strange thudding noise sounds again. Nettle meows and trots toward a far wall. She starts sniffing at a pair of curtains. But that couldn't be a window, I realize. It isn't an outside wall. I pick through the debris and pull back the embroidered brocade fabric, revealing a tapestry behind it—a queen charging into battle with her sword raised. I thought all these tapestries had been removed. How had the queen saved this one? The thumping starts again. Nettle trills.

"What is it?"

She paws at the corner of the fabric, insistent. I kneel to investigate and discover that the tapestry's holdings have loosened. That's what was causing the sound—the wooden frame at the bottom is knocking against the wall in the draft. And something else about the piece strikes me as odd. There's a rough seam on the left edge, one that doesn't match the rest of the stitching, like it had been patched. Brow creasing, I feel the fabric. It *crinkles*. There's something inside it.

Quickly, I pull my knife from my belt and slit the seam. I reach my hand into the open pocket. My fingertips brush against something soft, yet brittle. Like . . . book pages. Gingerly, I slide out the stack. It *is* parchment. Why would the queen have hidden these? The first few sheets are filled with what I assume is the queen's looping script. But the writing doesn't make sense.

Black as the raven's wing

Red as blood

White as snow

The queen had repeated similar words just before she died. But what do they mean? I flip the page over, discovering a list of unfamiliar names, but no hint as to why the queen recorded them. I sift to the next, then immediately pull up short. *This* page I recognize. My eyes widen as they skim over the neat, meticulous lines of a ledger. It's part of the Dwarvian records, one of the pages that had been ripped out of the books in the archives. A few of the entries are underlined.

Royal sword set with Bloodstone, it reads. *Age of the Light 2.*

My pulse kicks up. The king's commission *had* been recorded. But where had the Bloodstones gone after they'd been pried from the swords? The rest of the page offers no clues, and I hurriedly move to the next, but it's not part of the ledger. Instead, I find a map of the palace, with various areas circled, including the crypt and the archives.

"By the Spirits," I mutter.

It appears as though the queen really *was* searching for the stones. Had she found them, as I suspected? Was she working with a witch? I scour the map, desperate for answers. The queen indicated only one other chamber. It takes me a moment to place it—the High Priest's rooms. My brow furrows. Ignatius? Written within the circle is one word: *Underground?*

The hair on the back of my neck prickles. What does this mean? I rifle through the remaining pages, but they don't contain notes or anything else that might explain the queen's reasoning. Instead, the sheets of parchment are inked with illustrations. The first is very similar to one I saw in the library's history text—Braxos is in the center, a witch on one side of him and an Order priest on the other. In fact, this might be a copy of the same drawing, for the priest appears strikingly similar to Ignatius. The queen circled his face. Why?

The next illustration details a different king with a priest, one whose face is also circled—and who also resembles Ignatius. The similarity isn't as noticeable as the first, but it's close, especially in the eyes—that unsettling amber. Questions tangle in my mind. Why was the queen collecting these drawings? Did she want evidence of the High Priest's vanity? I pause at the final page, yet another illustration, one noticeably older than the rest. Its edges are crumbling and the ink fading, but I can still discern the gathering of men wearing Order robes. One face is marked. It's a small drawing, but there's no mistaking those eyes. It's *Ignatius.*

And there, scribbled in the bottom corner, I discover something even more horrifying.

Age of the Covens 2300.

"By the Spirits," I whisper, the roots of my hair prickling.

This isn't possible. If the date is accurate, this drawing is centuries old. I'm not sure that any *witches* are alive today who can claim to have seen this year. How could Ignatius . . .

Nettle yowls a warning, and I wheel around, one hand flying to my knife. I'm too slow.

"Mistress Ayleth," a voice in the shadows says. "It appears I am once again in your debt."

I'm just able to catch the sheen of flame-colored robes before I hear a low growl and a rush of cold wind slams into me, plunging me into the dark.

CHAPTER FIFTY-FOUR

DULL PAIN THROBS IN MY HEAD.

My leaden eyelids struggle to open, hazy surroundings sharpening slowly into focus. I'm lying on stone. And it's too bright. What must be a hundred torches flicker around me. But no. I blink. Not torches. *Mirrors.* Dozens of them hang on the walls or are propped on the floor, reflecting the light. What is this place? How did I get here?

Ignatius.

The name fights through the sludge in my skull, and the last hours come careening back—Joan and the queen's rooms and the hidden papers in the tapestry. Ignatius's face in the drawing from hundreds of years ago. His voice in the shadows, followed by that ominous growl, exactly like what I'd heard in the crypt and the archives.

Had he brought me here? Where is Nettle? My stiff muscles complain as I stagger to my feet. Tall shelves stretch along the walls, stuffed with vials and bottles and books. Dried herbs hang from the ceiling. There's a long table in the center, its wooden surface strewn with various instruments. My brow furrows. If I didn't know better, I'd say this looked like our workroom at Stonehaven. But that can't be right.

I shuffle closer to the shelves. Colorful powders and liquids fill the jars. In some, animal feet, or even the head of a raven, float in a yellowish substance. My skin crawls, recalling Mother's silver-eyed creature. I pull down one of the books. The Eye of Meira stares back at me from the first page, surrounded by a series of meticulously recorded notes:

Connect the magic?

How much power required?

Magic? I flip through the rest of the book, discovering lists of ingredients and diagrams. These are ... *spells.* Not the sort I learned at Stonehaven, though. These call for carrion flowers and grave dirt and fresh, still-beating hearts.

Like calls to like.

Footsteps echo and I slam the book closed, wheeling around. A staircase curves down the wall on the other side of the room.

Underground? the queen had written on the map.

Is that where I am? Some secret lair below the palace? Panic drums in my chest and I reach for my knife, relieved to discover that it hasn't been lost. The blade glints as I point it at the figure descending the stairs. It's a woman, I think, humming a strange, tuneless melody. Torchlight slides across her face.

It's ... *Marion.*

I blink, certain that I'm hallucinating. Marion was sent away. But there's no mistaking the former courtier. Her light-brown skin is cleaned of the dirt and grime from the dungeon cell. Her raven-black hair is combed and neatly braided. And her dress is far simpler than anything I'd seen her wear at court—more like a servant's.

"Marion?" I ask, my voice trembling.

She doesn't even look at me as she crosses the room and sets her basket on the other end of the table. We're only a few feet apart. She must know I'm here. But Marion only continues to hum, pulling empty bottles from her basket and standing them up in an eerily precise row. I put myself directly in front of her.

"Marion! What—"

The rest disappears in a gasp. Because her eyes are no longer dark brown but solid silver, with no irises or pupils. I can see myself reflected within the unnatural color, almost like . . .

"*Mirrors,*" I whisper.

Recognition tingles down my spine. These are the same sort of eyes that belonged to Mother's raven, the one she'd bound to her mirror. But it *can't* be. That would mean . . .

"Unsettling, isn't it?"

Time itself seems to slow at that voice. My entire body freezes, like a rabbit caught in a snare, as Ignatius enters the chamber. The ruby Eye of Meira glimmers on its golden chain.

"Typically, I disguise the color with a bit of glamour magic, but I didn't see the point," he says, as casually as if we were discussing the weather. "After all, our dear Marion couldn't possibly return to court after the . . . *incident.*"

He laughs, like Marion's arrest was a joke, one of his own design. Instinct taps at the base of my neck and my attention flits around the room again, at the instruments and books and *mirrors.* The silver of Marion's eyes flashes in the torchlight.

I can disguise the color with a bit of glamour magic.

Sudden comprehension slams into me. Marion wasn't sent away—she was brought here. To *him.* "You're . . ."

"A witch," Ignatius replies, slow and patient. "Just like you, Ayleth."

Revulsion knots in my belly. *No.* Not like me. He's something *else.* I need to get out of here—away from him. Ignatius has moved so that there's a clear path to the staircase and I hurl myself toward it, my feet tripping over themselves in desperation. But I don't get five steps before a blast of cold knocks me back, just like it did in the queen's rooms. My knife flies out of my grasp and I land hard on the floor, breath whooshing out of me.

"I suspected we might experience initial difficulties." Ignatius clicks his tongue, disappointed. "But don't mind Nox. He's just here to make sure we can speak without any further interruptions."

Nox? Shadows thicken in the far side of the room, coupled with a too-familiar growl. My heart rate kicks up as a shape solidifies in the darkness, black fur and claws as long as my fingers. One of its eyes is red, but the other is hollow, as if it had been shot out—or stabbed.

The king's arrow.

Memories of the forest rush back to me—the arrow shaft smoking as it pierced the Nevenwolf's crimson eye—and that force behind my left ribs *jolts,* as if in recognition. This is the same beast. It didn't die. Or, if it did, it came back. Panic ratchets up my spine and I crawl backward on all fours, until my shoulders collide with a wall and there's nowhere else to go.

A witch.

The word stretches and distorts in my mind. It's the only explanation for Marion and the Nevenwolf and even this room, but I still can't comprehend it. Male witches are rare. I haven't heard of one living since before the war. And this isn't our magic. Those weren't our spells in the books. We don't summon Nevenwolves.

Dark intents reap dark rewards.

"You're a priest," I splutter, unable to formulate anything more coherent.

"It is the perfect disguise, is it not?" Ignatius adjusts his ruby Eye pendant with unmistakable pride. "Burn enough witches and no one suspects you of being one."

Rage roils in my veins, snapping me out of my stupor. "You're *murdering* us! Razing the covens to the ground!"

"The covens mean *nothing* to me," Ignatius barks, his expression twisting in a way that makes my heart race impossibly faster. "And I nothing to them. The Spirits made that fact abundantly clear when I faced the flames. But then, we have that in common, don't we, Ayleth? Daughter of Millicent—or you would have been, had the coven fire accepted your sacrifice."

My skin prickles. The mirrors gleam, like so many eyes in the torchlight. He's been watching me. For how long? Does he have an army of crows circling the realm, reporting back? And how many more of his minions are in the palace, like Marion, their hearts bound behind glass? Is this why I glimpsed the countess in the mirror when Jacquetta and I were exploring her chambers? It wasn't a hallucination—it was Marion herself, reaching out from her prison and urging me to run. I should have listened.

"But we're starting off on the wrong foot." Ignatius rolls his shoulders back, his expression smoothing. "This isn't how I want our relationship to begin."

Relationship? He's lost his mind. In the corner of my vision, the jeweled handle of my knife glints where it fell. I start to edge toward it, but the shadows thicken and the Nevenwolf growls. I press myself closer against the wall, that force inside me humming. It's everything I can do to keep it contained.

"First, I owe you my thanks," Ignatius goes on. "As you likely surmised, my own search of the queen's rooms proved somewhat frustrating. And I might have run into considerable difficulty if anyone else had discovered my little secret."

He holds up the illustrations I'd dug out of the tapestry. His *secret.* So it was Ignatius in that ancient drawing. He's immortal, or near enough. I don't even want to know the sort of magic that would allow such a thing.

"Like you, Queen Sybil was a clever woman. Determined." He lights a candle and then feeds the parchment to the flame. "Once, I thought we might work well together. But she, evidently, disagreed. It's a shame when our strengths prove to be our downfall."

I watch the edges of the illustrations blacken and curl. Are those drawings what Queen Sybil had been trying to show me before the shadows claimed her?

They always hear, she'd whispered, frantic.

The Nevenwolf rumbles a growl, as if in confirmation. Shadows waft from its body, curling toward me—exactly as they had in the queen's room. And that's when I realize—they *are* the shadows from that day. All this time, I believed *I* was responsible for the queen's death. But it wasn't me luring the Nevenwolf. It was Ignatius. He must have been watching us through his stolen mirrors. He knew what the queen was about to tell me and silenced her.

"You killed her," I say, numb.

Ignatius doesn't deny it. Instead, he smiles, all teeth.

"You see? That's the sort of intelligence I knew you possessed. It's a pity you've only just started using it. I expected you to piece all this together long ago—as soon as you tasted the thornapple in your wine, in fact. After all, I *was* sitting right next to you at that dinner. But I didn't even cross your mind as a suspect, did I?"

The wine. By the Spirits, of course. It would have been simple for him to switch our glasses. The ridges of my ears burn at my own carelessness.

"And I left so many other clues. The thornapple in the queen's rooms, Nox in the forest, Marion's comb." He counts them off on his fingers. "I practically begged you to come to me after the hunt. But I suppose my disguise worked too well."

My mind spins with all these details—moving pieces I'd been too naïve and oblivious to see. Rhea would have guessed it, though. She'd have known better.

"Why?" I manage. "Why bother with the mystery?"

"Daughter of Millicent or not, you can't expect everything to be handed to you, Ayleth," he reasons. "Besides, I wanted you to prove yourself worthy of our partnership."

"I want nothing to do—"

He holds up his hand. "Don't be so quick to reject me. You haven't yet seen what I'm offering. I did promise you a reward, did I not?"

He's even more of a lunatic than I realized if he believes I would accept anything from his duplicitous hand. But Ignatius steps closer. He unclasps the chain draped around his shoulders. As soon as he does so, the ruby Eye *shifts*. Its color darkens to a deep red, flecked with green and black. The shape of what I assumed was a single, huge jewel splits into several—*five*. Roughhewn ovals that gleam in the torchlight, exactly like the one in Millicent's portrait.

"The Bloodstones," I whisper, hardly feeling the words leave my lips.

They're real—not the dyed pieces of glass tossed out in the White City. I can sense them, a deep, undulating power that resonates in my very bones. How had I not felt it before? Not known that they'd been *here* the whole time, close enough to touch?

"They speak to you, don't they?" Ignatius asks. "I knew they would, given your lineage."

But there's something else beneath the low hum of the Bloodstones' power, like cutting open a piece of fruit to find it rotten and worm-ridden. Every nerve in my body rebels.

"What have you done to them?"

"Improved them," Ignatius replies smoothly. "Made them my own. And together, we can make them ours. *Yours.*"

That deep urge rises up, hungry and insistent. "That's not possible."

He tilts his head at me. "Just like it isn't *possible* for me to command a Nevenwolf?"

The beast prowls nearer. That invisible tether pulls taut, like calling like. I fight against it.

"Or for me to do this?" Ignatius snaps his fingers. "Marion, get on your knees and beg Ayleth's forgiveness."

The former courtier, who has been drifting, wraithlike, along the shelves, instantly sinks to the floor. "Forgive me. I'm so very sorry. Please, forgive me."

"Tell her you are nothing," Ignatius prompts.

"I am nothing," Marion parrots, her mirrored eyes fixed on me. "Nothing at all. I—"

"Stop!" I shout, clapping my hands over my ears.

"Why?" Ignatius's robes whisper on the stone floor as he approaches. "Doesn't it feel good to see her like this? Does she not deserve such a fate?"

That dark part of myself whispers that yes, she does, especially after every unkindness and cruelty she'd bestowed upon me. But I shove that down.

"It's not right."

"Says who?" Ignatius lifts an eyebrow. "The covens? The Ancients? What good did those witches ever do for you? You're here alone, Ayleth."

The wound of my coven's—of *Jacquetta's*—rejection opens and bleeds.

"If you're going to kill me, just do it," I say through clenched teeth.

"Kill you?" He laughs. "You mistake me. I've been waiting for you for a long time. We're going to accomplish great things together."

"And what *great things* could I have accomplished in the dungeon? You were quick enough to send me there. Let me rot for days."

"You have my apologies for that." He presses a hand to his chest. "And it was only a temporary arrangement. After all, I had little choice in the matter, seeing as the king received that note. I take it your *companion* wrote it?"

She betrayed you, that voice whispers.

I dig my fingernails into the skin of my palms, fighting the sting of tears.

"As I said before," the High Priest continues gently, "you and I have more in common than you might care to admit—both of us shunned by the flames. Cast out by our covens. Deserted by those we allowed into our hearts."

If he thinks to gain my trust with such a speech, he's sorely mistaken. "You don't know anything about me."

"No?" A corner of Ignatius's mouth lifts. "I know what it means to have a door slammed in my face. To be convinced of my own worthlessness. That is, until I discovered my true purpose."

"Butchery?" I throw at him, ignoring my own good sense.

His amber eyes glitter. "*Justice.*"

The word crackles through my blood, stirring that deep impulse.

"I see I've captured your interest." Ignatius returns to his worktable. "When the flames rejected me, I was desperate to prove myself—convince the Spirits to change their minds. But then I met others like me. Like *us.* Those who could instruct me in the true nature of our craft."

Does he mean Wayward witches, like Mathilde? But no. Mathilde may not have bound herself to a coven, but she wasn't like . . . whatever Ignatius is.

"Soon," the High Priest continues, "I came to understand that the teachings of the covens were nothing more than a method of control. And I *refused* to be controlled. I would bend magic to my will— show the covens what power truly entailed. And on the day I crossed paths with an Order priest, I knew precisely how I would accomplish it."

The torches burn hotter.

"At that time, the covens were at the height of their power, the Order all but forgotten. I realized that I could use the faith's obscurity to my advantage. And so I hid among those doddering priests, deciding how best to strike. Eventually, the answer came." Ignatius holds up the Eye. "I realized that these five stones were all that bound the covens together. If I had them, I had everything. It would take time, of course. Patience and strategy. But by then, time was something I'd learned to harness. All I needed to do was wait for the right moment. It was simple, in the end. An entire age undone in a single night. The covens, for all their power, never even saw it coming."

The Night of Flames. A horrible vision of the tapestry looms, the five Heirs dancing in hot iron shoes.

"You killed them," I whisper. "You murdered the Heirs. You *stole* the Bloodstones."

He rounds the worktable. "I took the power they claimed I was too weak to hold, and I shoved it in their faces."

"It's not your power! It never was."

"And whose was it? The covens'? If that's true, then why can't the Heirs storm the city and squash us under the force of their so-called magic?"

The Bloodstones glimmer in the torchlight. Much as I despise Ignatius, I can't deny that I'd asked myself the same questions.

"Because these stones hold no loyalty," he goes on. "Power, Ayleth, is for the taking. Your precious Ancients took it, hoarding it among the covens. Letting everyone believe the world would be lost without the witches. Well—who's losing now? I hold the stones, which means I control their power. I control the Veil itself."

No. He can't. But the Nevenwolf prowls closer.

"Yes, Ayleth." Ignatius's eyes blaze, slightly manic. "The Veil is a fragile thing. It can hold Malum back, if I wish it, but it can also tear. I can pull Malum out of it. Command the darkness itself."

I think of the eyes in the forest at Stonehaven, and fear prickles down my spine. Is that what he's been doing? Using Malum to slink and spy? Is that why I've been plagued by shadows and crows? As if in answer, the Nevenwolf growls, its claws clicking against stone. That force behind my left ribs shivers.

"But I'll admit that my plan wasn't perfect," Ignatius goes on, examining the Bloodstones. "The more I funneled the Bloodstones' power for my own uses, the faster the latent magic of the Ancients began to fade."

Yet another reason why the Veil is failing. "Serves you right, thief that you are."

Ignatius only smiles at me. "I prefer *resourceful*. And I devised a different method to feed the stones, one much more efficient than a yearly ritual. If power was what the Bloodstones required, the covens possessed a *sea* of such magic. I merely needed a way to draw from it. In the end, I discovered that the answer was right in front of me."

Ignatius taps the Eye.

At first, I have no idea what he's talking about, but then torchlight glints against the Bloodstones, trapped in the gold casing of the Eye. I recall the book I'd seen earlier, the pages scrawled with illustrations of the Order's symbol.

Connect the magic? Ignatius had written.

"What have you done?" I whisper.

"I'm gifted in many areas of the craft," he goes on. "But my specialty is rune-making. I've invented several of my own, like the one you discovered on Marion's comb."

An image of the marking comes back to me—four lines drawn in a box, with three slashes through the center. By the Spirits, no wonder I hadn't recognized it. It came from *him*.

"And like this one." Ignatius traces the sign of the Eye in the air with his fingertips, as if blessing me. "Fitting, isn't it? That the Eye itself should be a rune. And it's a very special one. It absorbs power and funnels it back to the source."

The source—he means the Bloodstones. But what power could those stones be—

Horrible truth oozes over me.

Ours. Ignatius has made it so that the symbol of the Order—the Eye itself—is siphoning our magic. I think of the countless Eyes scattered throughout the realm, molded into Sanctums and drawn on houses and dangling from necklaces. For Spirits' sake, Stonehaven was riddled with them. No wonder my power never manifested. The Eyes, the runes, were bleeding my gift dry. And not only mine. At Mother's meeting with the Heirs, they'd all expressed that their gifts were waning. Because the false goddess's Eyes are *everywhere.* This is why Jacquetta's power didn't work properly when she was here—near *him.* It's a horrible web of magic with Ignatius squatting at the center like a spider.

"You're a *monster,*" I gasp.

His unnerving grin widens. "Are we not *all* monsters, somewhere inside?"

That deep part of myself rises up.

"And what are you going to do when there are no more witches to feed off of?" I demand. "You can't kill us all *and* continue to drain our power."

The Nevenwolf growls, low and ominous.

"And now we've come to it." Ignatius picks up a knife. "Time to call Castles, as Sir Weston would say. Allow me to show my hand."

The High Priest crosses the room to where a full-length oval mirror is propped against the wall. Rather than slicing his palm, as I'd seen Mother do, he opens the skin of his finger, then draws something on the mirror's glass, probably another of his twisted runes. The surface ripples. I brace myself for whatever horrible event is coming next.

"Come," Ignatius beckons, but not to me.

As I stare in shock, a *hand* reaches through the glass. Then a foot steps out of it, and then an entire person.

"By the Spirits," I mutter, my heartbeat thudding in my veins. "What is—"

The rest falls away as the person turns. She's wearing my face, but it's not mine.

It's Rhea.

CHAPTER FIFTY-FIVE

RHEA IS HERE. RHEA IS *HERE.*

Ignoring the Nevenwolf and the insane priest and everything else, I rush toward my sister. My frantic hands press against her face and her hair, greedy after so long without being able to touch her. Her scent of honeysuckle fills my nose. This cannot possibly be real. But I lift her hand and find the three crossed lines etched beneath her ring finger, identical to the marks on my own palms.

"You're here," I whisper. "You're—"

It's then that I realize Rhea isn't responding. Her white skin is cold and her eyes unfocused. They're not silver-colored, like Marion's, which is a relief, but they're vacant. Hollow.

"What's wrong with her?" I demand. "Why is she like this?"

"You already know," Ignatius replies. "It's why you journeyed to the White Palace."

My gaze snaps to his.

"Did you think I wouldn't find out?" He raises an eyebrow. "I admit, I wasn't convinced that you were after the Bloodstones until you chased down my servant at the banquet—the one who ran off with that ridiculous crown. I had it made it especially for you."

So it wasn't the queen's servant. It was him. I shiver, picturing the High Priest turning the wheels of this palace.

"At first, I assumed you were a typical coven witch, here to reclaim the stones for your own benefit." He wrinkles his nose. "But you only wanted your sister. Touching, really. Even more so to see you reunited."

He brushes a finger down the side of Rhea's face, and I slap him away. "*Don't.*"

"Such a fierce heart," Ignatius comments, amused. "But your sister doesn't have a heart anymore, does she? She needs an anchor. Like this."

He passes me the Eye. My breath catches as my fingers close around its golden casing. The power I sensed before is amplified by a hundred times, the Bloodstones like five tiny hearts pulsing against my hands, thrilling and addictive. I'd come here to destroy these stones and all they represent. But now, with Rhea standing in front of me . . .

Nothing is without cost, that voice in my mind whispers.

"What do you want?"

Ignatius adjusts his robes. "As I mentioned before, the Bloodstones require considerable magic. In the past, with my runes spread throughout the realm, gathering that magic wasn't a problem. Now, however, those runes aren't enough."

"Because you're killing all the witches," I snap back.

He shrugs. "I'm not here to argue the details. I want what you want—a source of magic powerful enough to last forever. One that could keep your sister here, exactly as she was before."

My focus returns to Rhea and the emptiness of her gaze. Mathilde's warning resounds in my mind: *She would not be the same.* But what if she could be?

"And what do I have to do?"

Shadows dance on the walls.

"The two of you will bind your magic to the stones, like the Ancients did."

I stare at him. He really has lost his mind. "That spell *killed* the Ancients."

"True enough," he replies, as if the point is a mere inconvenience. "But I devised a new method for the binding. A stronger spell—one that will draw even more power."

More power? It shouldn't be possible. But then, *none* of this should be possible.

"The spell doesn't matter," I say. "Rhea doesn't possess magic anymore. Even if she did, the two of us could never be—"

"But you *are* enough," Ignatius cuts me off. "Who in your coven has ever told you that?"

No one, that voice whispers.

Fresh pain sears in my chest and I curse myself for feeling it, hating Ignatius even more.

"As I said," Ignatius continues, "I've been waiting for you a long time. Both of you."

I glance at him. "Why us?"

He smiles. "Because of those marks on your hands, Ayleth. The *rune* you created, one that forged a bond that not even death could sever."

Torches snap. I grip the Bloodstones harder, pulse pounding beneath the triangles etched into my skin. "It's just a marking."

"Do you think a few scribbled lines can carry magic all on their own?" Ignatius asks, stepping closer. "That *marking* works because of the power that lies inside you. Your connection to your sister. A bond that rivals even the magic of the Ancients. One that could last forever."

"Not even the Ancients lived forever," I argue.

"Because they *lived*," Ignatius says, gesturing to Rhea. "Your sister is a Spirit. She may not carry the sort of latent magic that you do, but she holds enormous power. *That* is the difference between the Ancients' spell and mine. If Rhea binds herself to the stones with *my* ritual, she brings the full power of the Realm of the Spirits with her. It's a force that can fuel the stones for eternity, keeping you together, always."

I stare down at the jewels, five beating hearts in the palm of my hand. Questions swarm in my mind. What if Ignatius is wrong? What if the spell kills me? What if it harms Rhea? But one tantalizing thought rises above the rest: What if this *works*?

There's still one glaring problem.

"She can't bind herself to anything," I say, watching Rhea's vacant expression. "She can't even speak."

"You would have to assist her," Ignatius allows. "That's part of why I need you. But after that, she would be fully restored."

Assist. I step closer to my sister, protective. "You mean force her. *Steal* from her. Take—that's what you do, isn't it? It's what you'll do with this spell. Rhea and I will give our magic, and you'll keep feeding off of it, glutton that you are."

The High Priest doesn't even flinch. "Yes, Ayleth. I would benefit. I consider it a fair bargain. After all, you can't complete the spell without me."

Fury burns in my chest, mostly because I know he's right.

"But *I* also cannot complete the spell without you," Ignatius goes on. "If all I wanted was Rhea, I could have called her myself. But she would not have come—not for me. It was your connection, your power, that brought her here. She crossed into this realm for *you.*"

Like she did on the night of my Ascension, protecting me—like she always has.

I swallow, the Bloodstones pulsing against my hands—against

Rhea's marks. *Our* marks, two lines drifting apart and then back to-gether. We're together now, despite everything. What if we were al-ways supposed to wind up here? If, when Rhea drew our runes all those years ago, she began a spell that is finally culminating?

"I've made this realm mine," Ignatius continues. "Let's make it *ours*. We'll find whoever wronged you and drag them back here. Make them *bleed*."

That dark part of myself rises up. Hadn't I come here for exactly that purpose—to show the others how it felt to lose everything? If Rhea and I bound ourselves to the stones with Ignatius's spell, it would likely achieve the same end as breaking them. It would sever the covens' connection to the Spirits. If I agree to this, I could have the best of both worlds. Rhea could stand beside me, alive and whole again, while Mother and Jacquetta . . .

Destroy her, that voice whispers.

Ignatius, damn him, sees my desire. "Yes, Ayleth. Don't be afraid to *take*."

Perhaps he's right. After all, what could I have done on my own? But together—

So quickly that I gasp, Rhea's hand snatches my wrist. The trian-gles on my palms blaze.

Her eyes dart to mine, suddenly alert. *It must be undone.*

"What's happening?" Ignatius asks.

It must be undone.

Rhea's voice echoes, long and resonating, in my skull. Her fever-bright gaze twitches down to the Bloodstones and back.

Undone.

She looks at the Bloodstones again, and understanding begins to dawn.

"Do you mean the stones?" I whisper. "You want me to . . ."

Break them. The pressure of her grip increases.

"No." I shake my head. That was my plan before, when I thought Rhea was beyond my reach. Now she's here and I can't lose her again. "Please, Rhea."

"Ayleth," the High Priest repeats. "What's happening?"

I don't answer, my breath catching at the smell of honeysuckle, so strong that I might be back in Rhea's rooms again, tucked beneath her quilt.

Always be with you, Rhea's voice floats through my mind, gentle as a breeze. The marks on my hands burn hotter. *Let go, Ayleth.*

And that's when I know. Rhea can't stay here. She never could, no matter what spell I attempted. Salt stings my lips and I suddenly comprehend the gravity of the error I was about to make. I'd come to the White Palace for my sister—because I love her, yes. But also because I believed I needed to hide behind her. That I wasn't enough on my own. Here I am again, about to give myself away—bind myself to a monster—because I thought there was no other choice. But there is *always* a choice, I've discovered. Choice, like Mathilde said, is magic.

Rhea intertwines her fingers with mine. Our rune marks pulse together. My tears flow faster. I don't want to let her go. But I have to live.

"I love you," I whisper, lifting my sister's hand to my lips. I might glimpse the faint twitch of a smile on her lips before her fingers go limp and her eyes glaze over. She's gone—and I know it's for the last time.

All I want to do is curl up in a ball, follow Rhea beyond the Veil, but I shift my focus to the Bloodstones. Their power throbs against my palm. How many have died for this magic? How many have killed? How many lives have been ruined—my own among them?

No more.

"Ayleth, what—" the High Priest starts. But something must warn him as to what I'm about to do, for his amber gaze narrows. He edges toward me. "Give that—"

Turning on my heel, I clutch the Eye to my chest and run.

The High Priest lunges for me, catching my arm in his viselike grip. I try to shake him off, but he's too strong. "Enough! Give me—"

A yowl splits the chamber, and then a blotch of dark calico soars out of nowhere.

Nettle.

That wonderful, glorious creature. My cat lands on Ignatius's head, spitting and clawing. Ignatius releases me and I sprint to the worktable, where Marion is methodically cleaning the instruments. Panic beats against my eardrums. What next? My frantic gaze scans my options—tongs, pliers, a mortar and pestle. Is any of this capable of shattering the *Bloodstones*—the magic that has held the Veil for centuries? Surely not. Ignatius is still grappling with Nettle, but I don't have long. How could I—

The place behind my left ribs *jolts.*

Malum. It strains inside me, desperate to be released.

Let go, Rhea said.

What if I did? For so long, I've tried to keep that sinister force contained. What if I simply let it free?

My mind screams against the idea. Malum will consume me. Destroy me.

But it was going to destroy me anyway. My fate has been sealed ever since I reached for Rhea and let it in. What if *this* is the reason that Malum wheedled between my bones that night? Not because there's some broken part of me but because the Veil was always supposed to fall. And I'm the only witch who would do what's necessary to break it.

"All right," I say, arms trembling as I lift the heavy pestle over my head. "If you want me, have me!"

That dark force rushes up and I do nothing to tamp it down. In fact, I lean into it, driving the pestle into the stones with every ounce of my strength. A crack rattles up my arms, followed by a thunderous boom and a blaze of crimson light. Blinding pain explodes beneath my skin as that ominous force expands, surging through me in all directions. I cry out, sure that my whole chest is being wrenched open. Glass pops as one of the mirrors splits down the center. Another follows. Then another, shards exploding outward in a glittering storm. Wildfire courses through my veins. I'm going to die. This is how it feels to be dragged beyond the Veil. Except there is no Veil anymore, only Malum swirling in a cyclone around me. Faster and faster, until—

It stops.

I slump against the worktable, chest heaving as I stare around at the room. Broken glass litters the floor. Marion is crumpled like a rag doll a short distance away. Rhea is gone, her body transported back into the realm of the Spirits. How am *I* still here? Why am I not dead? Or am I dead?

Nettle emerges from her hiding place and trills, winding herself around my ankles. I'm alive, then. But what—

A rattling wheeze catches my attention.

It's . . . *Ignatius*. Or I assume it is. The High Priest is doubled over, his withered frame swallowed by his robes. I watch in horror as he straightens. Now that his hold on the Bloodstones is severed, the years have piled onto him. He is *ancient*. Tufts of wispy hair cling to his scalp. His shriveled, nearly translucent skin hangs from his bones.

"You *fool*," he rasps. "You could have had everything. And you've ruined it. Well—I have just enough left to ruin you. *Nox!*"

The shadows thicken and the Nevenwolf materializes in the darkness. Nettle hisses, her ears flattening. I stumble over debris, backing up until my shoulder blades collide with the far wall. The Nevenwolf's single red eye glimmers. Claws snap against stone as the crea-

ture bounds toward me. This time, Rhea can't protect me. A scream
climbs up my throat and I throw my arms over my face, bracing
myself for the rip of my own flesh.

It doesn't come.

Heart slamming against my sternum, I open my eyes to find a
wall of shimmering darkness in front of me. The Nevenwolf is on
the other side of it, perched on its haunches, its tail curled around
itself. Confusion tangles my thoughts. A moment ago, the beast had
been ready to strike. Now it's not attacking at all. In fact, if I didn't
know better, I'd say the Nevenwolf was behaving more like *Nettle*.

"What have you done?" Ignatius shuffles closer.

I have no idea.

Darkness bleeds from the corners of the room like spilled ink
and creeps toward me. Smoke swells from the torches and drifts in
my direction. Shadows begin to wind around my body like vines
of midnight flower climbing a tree. I should be afraid—repulsed.
Instead, I feel . . . alive. The force that once dwelled behind my left
ribs is . . . everywhere, like sparks in my veins. Everything is brighter—
louder.

But in a good way. Eden's words from the night of my Ascension
come back to me.

Is this what she'd meant? But I didn't face the flames. I didn't
make a vow. Unless . . .

Have me, I'd shouted at the force inside me—Malum itself.

Those weren't the words I was taught to utter, our sacred vows to
the Ancients, but had it been enough? Like Jacquetta's vow to the
stars?

As if in answer, ethereal music rings in my ears. But it's not stars
that are singing, not for me. It's . . . *darkness.* I sense the presence of
the shadows like the tang of a breeze in the forest. The wild heart of
the Nevenwolf beats alongside mine. It's not natural. Not our way.
But what good has *our way* ever done for me? I'm tired of following

the same paths, expecting them to lead me where I'm supposed to be. It's time to start forging my own.

At my mere thought, the wall of shadow dissipates, leaving nothing between me and the High Priest. I step toward him, head held high and shoulders back.

"Ayleth," Ignatius attempts. "There's still time to fix this."

Fix this. That's exactly what Mother told me to do. Because I wasn't good enough unless I was her Second. Unless I fit into the mold she made for me. Well. I may not have faced the flames, but I *have* Ascended. And I am bound to no one but myself.

"Oh, I fully intend to fix it," I tell the High Priest. And then, "Nox—go."

The creature—*my* creature—roars and leaps. Ignatius lifts his spindly arms in a vain attempt to shield himself as the Nevenwolf knocks him backward. I do not look away. Not as the sickening sound of tearing flesh and cracking bone fills the chamber. Not as the Nevenwolf claws open the High Priest's chest as easily as if it were made of parchment, his insides spilling onto the floor in wet, fleshy pools.

Ignatius's screams ring against the stone walls, louder and louder, until the beast rips out his heart and swallows it whole.

CHAPTER FIFTY-SIX

FOR A LONG TIME, I SIT IN THE QUIET, STARING AT IGNATIUS'S MANgled body. His entrails should be red, but they're greenish and tarlike and *wrong*. So much about the High Priest was as disgusting and rotten as his corpse. But even though he was drunk off his own ambition and arrogance, he was right about the covens. We decided what was *good* magic—our magic—and what wasn't, a decision based on nothing but fear. It dragged us down. Divided and poisoned us. No longer.

A shadow slinks toward me. This time, it doesn't seem foreboding, but curious. Playful, even. Nettle pounces on it and it winds around her paws like smoke. I extend my hand and allow the inky tendril to wrap around my wrist. My skin prickles at its featherlike sensation. I sense something else as well—affection? But why?

Perhaps because, unlike Ignatius, I didn't wrench Malum from beyond the Veil. I didn't compel or force it to do my bidding. I merely opened the door. And now the darkness is coming to me on its own, like Nettle did all those years ago. It's *choosing* me.

Choice is a magic in and of itself. Mathilde's long-ago words resurface again.

Maybe that's why the crows were always following me. The birds were never a sign of a curse but of a gift. I just had to be brave enough to accept it. Surrender myself, as I did when I shattered the Bloodstones and set Malum free.

She must reach, Mother's mirror said.

I finally did. And Malum reached back.

Something scrapes against the wall behind me. Nettle hisses a warning, her hackles raised. My pulse speeds up. There's nowhere to hide, but I spot the jeweled handle of my knife nearby and snatch it up, bracing myself to strike as a portion of the wall opens. Gemstone-colored eyes glimmer on the other side. Roland.

"Mistress *Witch?*" His mouth drops open as he gapes at the damage. "Was that . . . did *you* do this?"

My power—*Malum*—hums inside me.

"It's a long story. How did you know I was here?"

"You shook the whole palace," he says. "Everyone is looking for what did it."

The whole palace? I suppose I'm not too surprised, given that the barrier between worlds was just broken. Did they feel it in the rest of the realm? Did Mother? I hope she did. I hope she knows what I've done—that they all know.

Jacquetta, my stubborn heart whispers. I shove it down.

"By the Mines." Roland's face shades green. "Is that . . . *a heart?*"

He points at something on the ground, festering and fleshy. It is a heart, or it was—Marion's.

The former courtier's body is splayed out among the wreckage. Several more hearts are scattered among the jagged shards of glass. How many others are in the palace, struck down now that the High Priest's spell is ended?

"It was Ignatius," I tell Roland. "He bound Marion, and who knows how many others, to a mirror."

Roland recoils. "The High Priest . . . a *witch*?"

No. I will not use that word to describe him.

"Whatever he became was something unnatural. He had the Bloodstones." I gesture to the table, where the Eye is in pieces.

Roland approaches the pile of shards and picks one up, horrified. "They're ruined! Might be able to fix them if we—"

"No."

He stares at me. "*No?* These stones—"

"Divided the covens," I say. "And look what happened when they fell into the wrong hands. It's time to do things differently."

"Aye, *differently.*" He brandishes the shard at me. "And how's that?"

I don't know. Out of habit, I clench my fists against the triangles on my palms. But I don't sense Rhea's presence anymore. Instead, nearby shadows shimmer. My pulse kicks up, my power quickening in my veins—power I need to learn to trust.

"I'll figure it out."

"Yes, that makes me feel *loads* better." Roland huffs. "There's no need to—"

Hinges whine. Nettle hisses, her attention fixed to the top of the staircase.

"Come," Roland says, motioning to the wall behind us. "Follow me."

It's probably the smart thing to do. But my power trembles inside me and I sense that there's a reason I need to stay here. "Go ahead."

"I rescued you from a dungeon cell once already." Roland points at me. "I make no promises to do it again."

"I'll be fine." I shoo him off, though I have no idea if that's true.

Footsteps clip on the stairs and Roland casts me one final beleaguered look before conjuring another door and hurrying through it.

I motion to Nettle and she makes herself scarce. Then, knife in hand, I tuck myself in a far corner of the room. Shadows creep toward me and I somehow understand that they're offering protection. I accept it, letting them wrap around me, hiding me.

"This is where we heard it coming from," someone says.

A pair of guards come into view and then—my breath halts.

It is the White King.

Silence hums. King Callen halts halfway down the staircase, that gray gaze widening as he absorbs the scene. It must be late in the night, for he's dressed in only his simple breeches and a plain linen shirt, the sleeves pushed up to his elbows. His chin-length hair is loose and falls down around his face. And he's not alone. Master Parnell, along with several guards, accompanies the king, the steward's dark robes billowing like smoke.

"By the Light," one of the guards splutters, swiftly drawing the sign of the Eye in front of him. "What's all this?"

The king continues down the staircase. My heart pounds in my chest. Did he know about this place? I can't read his expression as he pauses at the High Priest's mangled corpse, kneeling to inspect the gaping wound left by the Nevenwolf's claws.

"Careful, Sire," a guard cautions. "This isn't right. It's witchcraft. Malum."

The shadows pull tighter around me.

"Master Parnell, what do you know of this?" the king asks, his voice low and even.

"Nothing, Your Majesty," the steward insists. "I admit that I harbored suspicions regarding His Illuminance's . . . indiscretions. But nothing to this scale. I don't think anyone was aware."

Glass pops under King Callen's boots as he rises. "And it will stay that way. There are only four people who have witnessed this . . .

abomination. If any of you utter a word of this chamber, it will be your last. Do I make myself clear?"

The guards immediately clap their fists to their chests.

Master Parnell bows low. "Of course, Your Majesty. His Illuminance merely returned to the Light. Leave the rest to me."

"Go, then." The king waves them off. "All of you."

"But, Sire," one of the guards starts.

"I said *all* of you."

Trading uncertain glances, the guards tromp up the stairs and out of sight, Master Parnell trailing like a shadow behind them. I remain where I am, watching the king drift around the room. Every so often, he snatches up a stray vial or jar and flings it down again. And then he discovers Marion's corpse. I expect some show of emotion, or at least recognition, for the woman who shared his bed for so many years. But King Callen doesn't even touch the former courtier, save to toe her body with his boot, grimacing, like she's one of the rotting hearts.

Fresh hatred broils in my veins. Marion was right about the king. He *consumes* people. Perhaps it's time someone did the same to him. That deep urge rises up, my power beating in my blood. The Nevenwolf vanished after the High Priest's death, but I sense that it's there in the shadows, waiting for my call—that it *wants* me to call. I'm about to do it, let the creature rip out the king's heart like it did the High Priest's, when another idea strikes.

If I can call a Nevenwolf, what else can I summon?

So much of my power remains a mystery, but I think back to what Jacquetta said about how she'd snapped the tree in half. She hadn't used a spell—not like a Caster would. Instead, she'd asked the storm to lend its strength. Perhaps I could accomplish something similar.

Go to her, I say to the shadows, my attention fixed on Marion's corpse. *Become her.*

To my sheer astonishment, the darkness answers. Shadows slink toward the dead courtier's body. The wisps of black and gray climb over her flesh and congeal together, then peel themselves from Marion's corpse. It's uncanny how much they resemble the fallen courtier.

"By the Light!" Callen cries when he spots her.

Shadow Marion extends her arm to the king as a lover might. He stumbles out of her reach, tripping over a toppled chair. That deep urge thrums at his fear. And I am only just beginning.

"S-Sybil?" The king stammers as the dead queen also materializes from the darkness. "What are you ... *How* are you ...?"

She drifts around him, wraithlike and silent. But she doesn't need to speak; neither does Shadow Marion. The king knows what he's done to them.

"Go away," he pleads as they circle him. "Just go!"

They do not go. In fact, I summon more women from the shadows. It doesn't matter who they are. Plenty of ghosts haunt the king's past. They dart and dive around him, a macabre version of the dance at the banquet. Except, this time, it is the *king* who is being pursued. Controlled. Possessed.

More. That dark place whispers, no longer terrifying but utterly intoxicating. *More.*

Yes. And I realize then that I don't want the Nevenwolf to kill the king. *I* want to do it. I want to watch the life drain out of Callen's gray eyes, my hands soaked red with his blood. I want him to see my face as he exhales his final breath. I grip my knife harder, jewels biting into my palm—a blade runed to strike true. That's what the queen had told me to do, wasn't it?

Strike, her words echo from beyond the grave. *And do not miss.*

I let the shadows fall away from me and step into the light. King Callen wheels around at my footsteps, his eyes red-rimmed and hair tousled from where he'd been pulling at it. He looks more like a little boy than a man who sits on a throne. But he is *not* a boy. And it's time for him to answer for his crimes.

"*You*," Callen snarls. "I might have known. First my wife and now the High Priest."

"Your wife?" I laugh. "Funny, I don't recall that you treated her with such respect when she was alive. What about Marion? Or every other person you used up and flung away?"

The shadow women press closer. Somewhere in the chamber, the Nevenwolf growls. Glass crunches under the king's boots as he retreats, his white skin shading paler.

"What's wrong?" I ask him. "Are you running? But this is Meira's plan for you."

He swallows. "I didn't. I never—"

Even now, he will deny it.

"You're a child, Callen. You've spent your whole life believing in fairy stories. Hunting imaginary monsters. The real monster has always been staring out at you from your mirror."

Torches flicker and the shadow women loom larger, feeding off my energy.

"What do you want?" he asks, the question tinged with panic.

"How easily you fold." I click my tongue. "This isn't a game of Castles, *Your Majesty*. I want my sisters back. I want the past to be undone. Can you do that?"

"Not for them," the king admits. "But for you. *Think*, Ayleth. Whatever else has happened, I meant what I said before. There's a reason you and I were brought together. I've felt it since the moment we met."

At those words, I sense a tug behind my left ribs. I pause, half reaching for the invisible tether I once thought was dragging me toward the Veil. But the Veil is dissolved. Why do I feel the pull again?

Fate lines can be intertwined. Mathilde's words drift back to me, as if carried by the shadows themselves.

Was she right? Was this connection between me and the king never Malum but fate itself—always reeling us toward this moment? And, if it is fate, what am I meant to do?

The figures weave around us. Callen pivots one direction and then another, vainly trying to evade them. He trips again, falling to his knees in front of me.

"Ayleth, please," he begs, shielding himself. "Make them stop. I'll do anything."

Anything. That tether rumbles. And a shadow wreathes around me, brushing my cheek before slinking across the room, toward— a mirror. It's the same one Ignatius used to summon Rhea. The only one that didn't break when I shattered the Bloodstones. I see myself reflected in its glass, no longer tired and weak and afraid. My skin glows with power. Shadows swirl around me, almost like a garment. A mantle. In fact, with the king kneeling in front of me, this could be a scene from one of the tapestries. Like I'm a . . .

Queen.

The word blooms in my mind, rapidly spreading its roots.

No, I think, shying away from it. A crown is the last thing I want. But the tether tugs again, insistent. Torchlight flashes on my knife's blade, illuminating the delicate lines of Mother's runes.

You'll use it to make your first offering, she'd said.

At the time, I'd been repulsed, imagining that I'd have to dig the heart out of a raven or some other innocent creature. But what if my sacrifice *wasn't* innocent? What if they deserved to have their heart locked away?

And it's not just the king who would suffer if I sat on the throne. There's Mother and the coven and the Heirs. *Jacquetta.* My blood runs hotter. They're out there, somewhere, hopefully reeling from the loss of the Veil. But I could make them hurt even worse. Make them cower before me as the king is now. Make them *beg.*

Yes, I imagine the shadow women whispering, *Yes.*

A new path unfurls before me. The tether binding me to the king, the line of our connected fates, sings. Because this isn't merely a plan. It's a destiny—one that has been waiting for far longer than I ever knew.

"There is something I desire," I say to the king, inhaling his scent of leather and smoke.

"Anything." He tilts his face to mine. "Name it and it's yours."

I bend so that my next words brush his lips. "Your heart."

And then I sink my knife into his side.

Runed as it is, the blade doesn't make a sound as it tears into his flesh. The king bellows, crumpling into himself. His hand flies to the wound and he scrambles away from me, stumbling toward the stairs, but it will do no good. The blade struck true—the single promise Mother kept.

The king reaches the staircase and staggers up the first few steps, blood pouring from his side and staining the stones. His boot slips on the slick red and he falls, crying out as he tumbles to the ground. I take my time approaching him, darkness following me like the train of a gown. The shadow women glide after me, eager to deliver their justice.

"Wait," the king begs, lifting his scarlet-stained hands. Blood drenches his shirt and is streaked across his face. "Please."

But the time for pleading is over. The shadow women surround the king, pinning him down.

"Ayleth," he manages, flailing against them. "Don't. This isn't who you are."

Not that long ago, he might have been right. I was weak then. Afraid of what lay inside me, as Mathilde accused at her reading. But I am done being afraid. Done with letting others dictate who I am. From now on, *my* voice is the only one that matters.

Fueled by the memory of Marion and the queen and every other woman who's had the misfortune of crossing this man's path, I plunge the blade again into Callen's chest. Warm blood spatters my face, tasting of copper. A final scream rips from the king's lungs, and then his gray eyes—those that have haunted me since the day I set foot in this palace—roll back into his head.

I don't have time to waste. My enchanted knife carves easily through Callen's tendon and bone. Still, it is gruesome, horrible work as I wrench open the king's chest and reach inside the cavity. My stomach rises at the sensation of hot, slick flesh against my fingers as I feel my way through the web of veins and muscle. But I swallow the bile in my throat, refusing to let myself stop until I locate the king's still-beating heart. The shadows writhe around me, urging me on, as I sever the cords of its arteries, grimacing at the sucking sound the organ makes as I extract it.

Blood dripping from my arms, I carry the king's unmoored heart to the mirror. Its glass ripples as I approach. The shadow women look on, still and silent witnesses as my hand slips beneath the surface and, an instant later, the weight of Callen's heart is lifted. When I pull my hand free, all the blood and gore and bits of his flesh have been washed clean. Behind me, the shell of Callen rises. His flesh has knitted back together. There's not even a hole in his shirt, or a drop of blood on the floor. And his eyes are a glassy silver—just like Marion's. I'm not sure how I'll hide the unsettling change from the court, but that's a problem for later.

For now, I return to the mirror.

As I'd watched Mother do a hundred times, I slit the skin of my palm, then press my hand to the glass. But I don't utter the words of the waking spell—I don't need to. The mirror chooses to obey me, its surface swirling as a face appears. Callen. The *real* Callen. I'd always wondered if Mother's raven knew it was trapped behind glass. Now I get my answer. The White King pounds the inside of the mirror with his fists, gray eyes blazing. This time, however, I do not sense the tether. It's snapped—our fates at last fulfilled.

A smile curls my lips and I run my fingertip down the line of the king's face in the glass. "Tell me, Your Majesty, how do you like your menagerie?"

He rages back at me. But that's all he can do—watch and bellow—as I bleed his realm dry.

Shadows dance through the chamber, stirring a draft. At first, I think it's the wraithlike women, celebrating the king's fall. But then I catch the reflection of tiny bits of red flying through the room. They gather above my head like a swarm of bees and start to spin. One flits close enough that I recognize it—the shard of a Bloodstone. Dozens of them swirl around me, the shadows knitting them together until they form—

A crown.

Ayleth, I hear. *Ayleth.*

As I stare into the mirror, a drop of red rolls from one of the jagged bits of Bloodstone and down my forehead. Another. Faster and faster, until my face is coated in a mask of glistening crimson. A mask—a crown—of blood. Of vengeance, against everyone who has wronged me, mortals and witches alike. Even *her.* They will see the witch they rejected, and they will *kneel* at my feet.

Because the time for covens—or for kings—is over.

Let the reign of the Witch Queen begin.

"Mirror, mirror on the wall," I say, the words pulled from my lips like a spell. "Who is *fairest* of them all?"

The story of
The Crimson Crown
will conclude in book two,
The Witch Queen.

ACKNOWLEDGMENTS

Some books are easy to write. This was not one of them. I've honestly lost track of the number of drafts, let alone words, I've written for this story. The first iteration came to me way back in 2018, but I didn't fully find its heart until 2023—*two years* after it sold. I have, very literally, cried, sweated, and bled over this book. For so long, I was sure that it would never be finished. But despite my perpetual doubt, the book exists. I survived it (for now). But I certainly wouldn't have done so without the help of an extraordinary team of people.

First, to my incredible agent, Laura Crockett. Laura, you snatched the earliest version of this story from your slush pile and have never wavered in your certainty that it would find its way to shelves. Thank you for believing in Ayleth—and in me.

To my sorceress of an editor, Tricia Narwani. No matter how many times I turned in a tangled mess of a manuscript, you never doubted that we'd reach the end (the real one). Your patience, encouragement, and impeccable insight have been my north star throughout this process.

I also owe a huge debt of gratitude to the whole team at Del Rey—

there are too many of you to name, but thank you to every person who helped make this book the gorgeous, gothic wonder that it is. Thank you also to my friends at Barnes & Noble (especially the real Blodwyn, who knows who she is). Books like mine—LGBTQ, in particular—have historically been suppressed, ignored, and erased. But these teams have championed my work in ways I never dreamed possible.

And I never would have found my way to the end of this book without the support of my friends and family. To my mom, dad, and brothers, thank you for proudly bragging about your author daughter/sister to literally everyone. Thank you to Ashley, Bentley (coolest kid ever), Kristin, Tom, Liam, and (most especially) the real Fitz, for always being there to celebrate or commiserate, depending on how the writing was going. Thank you to my author friends, including Saara, Tasha, and Chloe, for cheering me on even when I was ready to burn this book. And thank you to Andrew (aka Nettle), who was always ready to listen to me complain about my plot holes with an air of profound boredom.

Most important, thank you to readers. New books are never guaranteed in an author's career. The support I receive is directly because of your enthusiasm. *Thank you* for championing my books, buying them, checking them out from your libraries, and raving about them to your friends. Thank you to every librarian, bookseller, and blogger who has put my books in the hands of readers. Your influence on my career cannot be understated. It has been the highlight of my life to share stories with you. I hope to keep doing it for a long time.

And thank you, with my whole entire heart, to Lindsey. I'm not always a nice person when I write books. You love me anyway.

ABOUT THE AUTHOR

Heather Walter is the award-winning author of
The Crimson Crown and the Malice duology. She holds
degrees in both English and library science.

ABOUT THE TYPE

This book was set in Sabon, a typeface designed by the well-known German typographer Jan Tschichold (1902–74). Sabon's design is based upon the original letterforms of sixteenth-century French type designer Claude Garamond and was created specifically to be used for three sources: foundry type for hand composition, Linotype, and Monotype. Tschichold named his typeface for the famous Frankfurt typefounder Jacques Sabon (c. 1520–80).